THE
SEVENTH
POWER

Anna opened the door. Dark thunderclouds filled the room, with long, sharp bolts of lightning shooting out in all directions.

"He's inside the cloud," Kevin said.

Anna could see the little boy's clothing and toys and the room's small furniture scattered all about as though there'd been an explosion. Panic took over. She charged into the room, feeling the hallucinated lightning flicker like gnats attacking her arms, face and legs.

Suddenly she was on a mountain peak, miles high, surrounded by clouds. Anna could see entire ranges of other mountains in the distance, with deep valleys and rivers winding through them. A few feet away, a tiny black cloud floated above the crest.

The little black cloud churned and parted. And there was Matty. He was sitting about five feet above the ground. Floating.

"Mamma!" he exclaimed gleefully. "Look what *I* can do!"

TO THE SEVENTH POWER

FELICE PICANO

AVON BOOKS  NEW YORK

AVON BOOKS
A division of
The Hearst Corporation
105 Madison Avenue
New York, New York 10016

Copyright © 1989 by Felice Picano
Published by arrangement with the author
Library of Congress Catalog Card Number: 88-26669
ISBN: 0-380-70276-2

Published in hardcover by William Morrow and Company, Inc.; for
information address Permissions Department, William Morrow and
Company, Inc., 105 Madison Avenue, New York, New York 10016.

First Avon Books Printing: April 1990

AVON TRADEMARK REG. U.S. PAT. OFF. AND IN OTHER COUNTRIES, MARCA
REGISTRADA, HECHO EN U.S.A.

Printed in the U.S.A.

RA   10   9   8   7   6   5   4   3   2   1

"Wolfgangerl wrote this Minuet & Trio on January 26th, in half an hour, at half past nine in the evening, one day before his fifth birthday. . . ."

—Leopold Mozart, in a family exercise book

BOOK ONE

BARRY

CHAPTER ONE

"I know what *you're* thinking!"

Barry Allen Brescia didn't have to turn to know who it was. The voice, steel-wire sheathed in dripped honey, could belong only to Martina Kalb, who had somehow or other snuck up on him while he was poring over the shop's checkbook entries.

"Hi, Marty," he said, closing the large rectangular folio and attempting to smile. She was wearing one of her more outlandish outfits today: white leather boots reaching almost up to the fat knees of her stubby legs, a deerskin skirt wrapped around what she proudly if coyly called her child-bearing hips, a Tibetan sweater in sky-blue wool covered with an overlarge embroidered shawl, alive with multicolored thread tassles. Her broad face was, as usual, cosmetized in broad strokes and defended on either side by enormous silver slabs of earrings. Not an outrageous getup among the Back Bay's affluent amateur mystics and witches: the bane of his existence since he'd taken over the management of Ephemeris, Newbury Street's glitzy boutique of the supernatural.

"Well?" She pursed her lips in a half-sneer meant as a moue. "Aren't you going to ask?"

Barry reminded himself that Marty Kalb was a good customer, dropping a hundred, two hundred dollars per visit at the store—and her visits were frequent. This encouraged him to try to forget the sinus headache he'd awakened with that morning, still not gone despite three Tylenol tablets and two mugs of black coffee; forget his hemorrhoid flare-up and the fact that his taxes were late and still unpayable; and forget that he would probably have to "sleep" with Marty again sometime in the near future, which meant toothmarks on his genitals for days afterward.

"Shoot!" he said, as she neared the desk. He half wished she would put him out of his misery.

"Well," she began, coming closer, fudging, "I believe you were thinking about how much money I owe the shop. You know, my bill? I've been off in Barbados the past week, and just got back. So I brought you a check." She made an elaborate show of dropping her large purse onto the desk and riffling through it for her checkbook, then of sitting on the desk and leaning over him as she wrote out the amount.

In fact, her bill had been unpaid longer than usual, which he'd forgotten. The money would help tomorrow when he had to face Tom Jarmin, his accountant. Sweet of her to come by with it. He smiled at her as pleasantly as his throbbing sinuses would allow, despite the overwhelming musk of her perfume.

"I was wondering how to make ends meet this month," he said.

"So I *was* right." She held up the check, then stuffed it down into his shirt pocket, brushing a nipple.

"As always," he admitted.

It was at that moment that Barry noticed the young girl in the shop. He hadn't heard her enter—where was Elaine today? She was an hour late already. Dark-haired, a teenager, the girl seemed to be a student—Harvard or MIT—over among the more expensive astrology texts. He'd lost three of those big books last week. Maybe she was the one . . . So quiet, almost motionless; that was the type who got coffee tables into backpacks without your noticing.

" . . . and of course *you* must come, not only because of your position at the shop, here, but because we'll *have* to have a mediator. You know how that Marblehead crowd

10

gets!" Marty was going on and on, and slithering even further around on the desktop toward him so that her skirt was rising a half-inch at a time over her meaty white thighs. The advantage of this was that Barry could hide behind her and still watch the girl. Now she was perusing Hans Witte's *Treatise on Solar-Arc Timing of Exact Predictions*, heavy reading, not to mention the $29.95 price tag for a soft-cover.

"So you *will* come, promise me?" Marty begged in a girlish whine, "I'll do something *nice* for you if you do," she added, her pointed tongue circling her near-ebony lipstick.

"If the others don't mind."

"They won't," she declared, then stood up, straightened her skirt, and smiled. "God, you are good. Jill was a fool, if you ask me. If I weren't bound to Chas by karmic links going back to the time of Akhenaten . . . " She stopped, her threat hanging. "I'll pick you up. All right?"

"Sure. All right," he said. "Day after tom—"

"Six-thirty. Wear that lovely Harris-tweed jacket and leather tie. You're positively edible." She smacked her lips in his direction, flounced away, stopping a second at a low table to idly flip open a book on Mayan temples; then she continued her way out the door, a hand raised back in a wave.

Silence. The girl was still reading. Outside, it looked as though it would rain. He hated Boston when it rained. The city was made for clear skies, summer-hot or winter-frigid. Whenever it rained, the building colors looked wrong.

Barry wondered whether he should go up to the girl. Whether he should call Elaine. Whether he should . . .

"It's going to come back."

The girl had turned, barely lifting her head and slightly angling it; she had spoken quietly.

"What?"

"The check she gave you. The one she put in your pocket. It's going to come back from your bank marked 'insufficient funds.' It won't be her fault."

"Really?" he said. "That will be quite surprising. Her husband practically owns downtown Boston."

11

She was in profile to him now, and the profile was somehow familiar. "Are you planning to buy that book, miss?"

"Yes."

"You know it costs thirty dollars."

"I know." Her voice had gotten even smaller than before.

"Just bring it up to the counter here, when you're ready."

She turned to face him, and she wasn't mousy at all, but actually quite pretty in a European way, all angles and sharpness with lovely lips, large brown eyes. Angry eyes.

"I'm *not* going to steal it, you know."

"Who said you were?"

Determination in her now. She marched up to the counter and slapped the book down on it, pulling out two twenties.

The girl nodded left. That familiar profile again for a second. Whose profile?

"Sorry, I'm not normally suspicious. I've got a splitting headache, and I'm worried about a meeting with my accountant.

"I told you. Her check is going to bounce."

That stopped him.

"Are you telling me you're the real thing? We get so many phonies in here I almost can't tell."

"I don't know about that. . . ." she said, the little voice again, the blush spreading, her eyes cast down.

"You're very pretty," he said.

"Really?" The determination back in her.

Even that was familiar, so he went on.

"What else do you know about my future?"

"Nothing. I shouldn't have . . ."

"I can take it."

"You'll get more money in less than a week. From a completely unexpected source. More than enough for what you need. And I'll bet she'll be so embarrassed about the check bouncing she'll pay you in cash."

"And that's all?"

She was silent.

"How about if you did my chart for me? That's how you

12

know all this, isn't it? Through that Uranian system of astrology? The few customers I know who use it claim they can get to the day, hour, and minute, if they bother calculating enough."

"Yes. That's how I do it."

"I'll pay."

"I don't . . . won't . . . not for money."

"Whatever then. For trade. Books, I meant." He smiled.

"What else could you mean?" He had evoked a tiny smile from her.

The phone rang before he could answer—saving him from formulating an answer to her question. Barry started for it, then stopped. "Wait, I'll predict something. It's my assistant, Elaine. She's calling to say she'll be another hour late."

"She won't be in at all today."

He stared at the girl, picked up the phone, identified himself, and listened to Elaine, who sounded like hell. Before she could get six sentences out, Barry said, "Don't worry about the shop. Is there anyone to take care of you? Do you want me to come over?"

Through her tears, Elaine said she was okay. Just a little shaken up. Complications with her D and C. She'd be fine tomorrow. No, she had everything she needed. Her friend Steph was there with her. Barry was good to be so understanding, etcetera, until he hung up.

"Nice work," Barry said to the girl. "You hit it right on the head."

"It scares some people. But not you—why not?"

"It's been a long time since I scared easily."

"You mean you aren't apprehensive about the future?"

"Not really. Not anymore." Barry felt the sadness gather within him, and his jaw was set as he said, "Maybe there's nothing left for me to lose."

Then he laughed. "You spray truth serum in here, or what?"

"I'm sorry."

He brushed that aside, leaned over the counter, took out

13

one of the shop's finely printed bookmarks, and began writing on it.

"Here. My birthdate, year, time to the minute, and place. You'll do it, won't you?"

"Why, if you don't care about the future . . . ?"

The shop door buzzed, and two middle-aged women Barry recognized came in. He nodded hello, slipped the bookmark into her book, put it into a plastic bag, and handed her the two twenties back. "A deal?"

"Look, I sort of promised someone . . . you know, that I wouldn't do it." She handed him back the money, began gathering her things. "I'm sorry."

"Wait. Don't go yet," he said. "Were you looking for anything in particular, Mrs. Fayette? Or just browsing?" he asked.

It turned out that the two women were looking for a particular translation of Lao-Tse that Barry had in stock in the Oriental Philosophy section.

"You go to school here?" Barry asked the girl, who was still at the counter, now leafing through the astrology text.

"Harvard. Don't say it: Aren't I a little bit too young?"

"Not if you're a genius. But you're not from the East Coast, are you? Where, then? California."

"Is my accent so obvious?"

"Not at all. But I've been around the country, you know. Lived all around the U.S. of A. There's a slight peculiar accent from the middle of the state, some people often take it for upper Midwest, but I know better. Say around the Monterey Peninsula. Santa Cruz . . ." Barry was pleased at her surprise.

"Not bad. Listen, I really am sorry about not being able to do your horoscope. . . ."

"Hey, no problem. How did you get involved in it? When I was a kid, no one ever was. All that pretty girls were interested in were boys and dates and cars and rock stars. Unless . . ."

"Go on, say it."

"Unless they were unattractive or . . ."

"Or?"

"Or weird. But you're neither," he quickly added. "Just a little bit mysterious. Now tell me, if you won't do my horoscope, how will I see you again to find out about my finances?"

"I'll drop by," she said casually.

"You feel it, too, don't you?" Barry asked, suddenly serious. "The . . . what should I call it? . . . Rapport? Communication? If I were Marty, I would say we'd shared past lives together, or something like that."

She smiled again. "Tell you what, there is a way." She paused just long enough for Barry to lean forward a few inches, then she opened the back of the astrology text where there was a listing of other books by the same author. "See this title?—*Weekly Transits of Trans-Plutonian Points and Midpoints*—I'd like to get it. I didn't see it on the shelf. Could you order it? The publisher is right here in Cambridge, and when I called, someone in their office said they didn't sell direct to customers."

Barry was already writing down the title and publisher. "How do I contact you when it comes in?"

"I'll come in every once in a while. . . ."

"I'm not going to make obscene phone calls to you at three A.M., you know."

"All right. But the phone belongs to my landlady. She lives in the building. My apartment doesn't have one." She wrote the phone number. "Yes, it's local. And, please, don't give the number to anyone. Not *anyone*," she stressed.

"You can count on that, sweetheart." He gave her his best Bogart imitation.

She had packed the text into her shoulder bag and slung it over her shoulder. She was at the door when Barry realized something else was missing.

"Do I get a name with this number? Or do I ask for Miss X?"

She turned. "Kyra. With a y."

15

"And I'm Barry. With a y, too. But of course you already knew that, didn't you?"

"Bye," she said simply, and was gone.

At first, Barry didn't get around the counter and follow her figure down the street. Marty had knocked awry some books on his desk so they fell in a clutter as he moved past them. By the time he arrived at the window, the girl was already a block away, her small, slender figure in the long plum coat receding quickly before she rounded the corner. He was about to turn back when he noticed a man in a trench coat reach the same corner and turn sharply, too. Why shouldn't he? Both streets were trafficked by pedestrians. Still, it seemed strange, rehearsed or . . . And she had said he shouldn't give her phone number to anyone. Insisted on it. Even though it wasn't even in her apartment but in her landlady's.

Were his suspicions due to her mysteriousness, her indefinably familiar profile, the real kinship he had felt with her—or was he just fooling himself?

Still, it had been a pleasant encounter. It almost wiped out Marty's visit and his headache. Almost erased the fact that Elaine wouldn't be in today, and possibly tomorrow. Barry felt better. Immeasurably better.

The restaurant Kyra had chosen for them to meet in was on a corner of Charles Street: Rebecca's, a busy, modern "bruncheteria," as Barry thought of it, with lots of glass on the streets, yet withal quite cozy. At three o'clock on a Tuesday afternoon it was almost empty—the late Beacon Hill lunch crowd gone, the dinner mob not due for some time yet. Two young men in jeans and leather jackets were quietly, intensely having something out at one table; two waitresses and a managerial-looking young man sat at another, taking advantage of the lull to have a bite. Barry had left Elaine in the shop and wouldn't answer her questions as to when he'd be back. Today was her first day back, and he needed a rest. This morning he'd sent her across the Charles

River to the office of the publisher of the book Kyra had ordered. It now sat in a manila envelope upon the seat of one of the four chairs around the bleached wood table. Barry was already sipping his second cup of coffee.

Waiting for another woman. Barry wondered how many minutes becoming hours becoming days in his life he'd waited for one woman or another in a restaurant, or in a movie theater or concert-hall lobby, at an airport lounge or in an outer office, in the front seat of a car in some parking lot, its engine running or finally turned off. Figure what, an hour a month, that would make two days a year for say twenty years . . . damn! Forty days! Could that be right? More than a month of his life? It was possible. Who was the worst? Cherie? Kono? No, Jill had definitely been the worst. Going out at night was her specialty. She'd come into the living room of their Brattle Street loft, where the huge, ornately framed full-sized mirror leaned against a wall, look at herself, moan, then disappear back into the bedroom, while he called out, "You look great," to no avail. A half hour later, she'd emerge, having gone through twelve different changes of dress. In the meanwhile, Barry would have read every magazine in the room, and begun some novel he'd been meaning to get to for weeks, not to mention killing a good portion of a fifth of scotch.

Forty days of waiting out of his life. Where had it gotten him? Well, on some sort of tour throughout the country for one thing: Key West, Los Angeles, all over the Bay Area with Kono, finally here in Boston, settled, first with Jill, then, through her, alone and stuck with a business. He still didn't know whether buying out Jill's share of the Ephemeris and becoming full owner himself hadn't been a mistake. Scarcely a year had passed since then; too early for him to decide. But when she'd left, he had wanted the security, the responsibility. To his surprise, he'd wanted them desperately.

"Don't tell me. You couldn't get the book? It's out of print?"

Kyra: white wool sweater with cable-knit patterns and tan slacks under her purple overcoat. She didn't have the backpack today, but instead a largish leather purse, the kind hippies used to drag all their possessions around in, twenty years ago.

"You're late."

"I know. Forgive me. It's my fault. The subway was so slow." She sat down and pulled off her coat. "I'm starved." She evidently knew the menu. As the waitress slouched over, Kyra ordered, adding, "And a coffee now, please!"

"I was at the Gardiner Museum," she exhaled. "Have you ever been there? It's all wonderful, of course, but there's one little Rembrandt, downstairs, a small oil of Christ calming a storm on the Sea of Galilee that is so . . . all blue and white and fresh, even with the storm. He must have been so young when he painted it. The world he looked at must have been so much younger, too. It's so different from his other . . . Oh, good. The coffee. I'm in sort of a daze from looking so hard."

Barry put his hand over his mug to keep the waitress from filling it: He was wired enough already. But this girl was marvelous. She made him remember how much his eyes had once reeled with colors and shapes. Nowadays he'd walk into the Museum of Fine Arts almost without looking at what was on the walls in those rooms he had to pass through to get to whatever new exhibit was up. As though he had on blinders.

"Your book," he announced, and lifted it onto the table.

"That was fast."

Kyra didn't look through the book, but satisfied herself with tapping its cover.

"I glanced through it, through Witte's *Solar Arcs,* too. I concluded you must be a math major."

"Psychology."

"You mean to say you know all the math to do those calculations and you're studying psychology? You must be pretty smart. Not to mention how shrewd you must be to keep me waiting here a half hour."

Her hand came out and touched his, then quickly withdrew. Another apology.

"Well? *Are* you that bright? A genius? Is that it?"

"It's a symbolic language. Once you learn it, it doesn't go away. And the math isn't that complicated, really. But I usually test high, if that's what you're asking, although I've never been fussed over."

Over the course of the lunch, Barry kept probing. She answered him openly. Kyra was sixteen years old and was accustomed to living away from home. She'd been in a private school in New Hampshire. She liked living by herself. Once she got to Boston, she refused to consider dorms or sharing a place in Cambridge, since "I got used to my privacy." She came from California, as Barry had guessed. Pacific Grove, outside of Carmel. Barry had seen the area once: big houses, a few big enough to be considered estates. Her father had been in the military, and he still had ties to various bases in the area. Both of her parents had inherited money, and the family lived quite well. Kyra had one sibling, a younger brother named Skip. He was nine years old and "one of those distressfully normal peanut-butter and baseball-card types." The woman she lodged with on Louisburg Square was a maternal cousin: Mrs. Bryan. Kyra had tea with her twice, and the older woman had shown her some very old letters from sea captains. She was very prim and proper, and Kyra knew that she slept with a married, slightly pot-bellied man whose family owned a popular Italian restaurant in the North End, and who visited three times a week. "He's her one human touch," Kyra concluded.

"You're changing the subject," Barry said. "The subject is you. Kyra . . . Bryan? See? I don't even know your last name."

"My mother's a Bryan. Kyra Nilsson." She opened the book to browse through it, and Barry knew she was lying, although Nilsson probably was the name she was using here in Boston. Who was she trying to hide from? Her parents? She'd carefully weighed each fact she'd released to him. It was difficult to tell where truth ended and fiction began in any of it. Why should a sixteen-year-old girl do that? She couldn't be a criminal, a terrorist or something, could she?

"Do you know anything about Witte?" he suddenly asked.

"He was a German. Posited a half-dozen planets beyond Neptune, sometime during the First World War. Used them to predict battles and executions. Supported Lowell in predicting the existence of Pluto. Worked for Hitler for a while. Left Germany in the thirties, disillusioned with the Reich. Invented the Uranian school of astrology."

"Of which you are an adept. That's pretty good, but I know that much about Witte," Barry said, "and most of that came from hanging around middle-aged women and reading book-jacket copy."

She looked at him as though wondering why he was bothering to challenge her. "How did that meeting with your accountant turn out?"

"I'm still waiting for Marty's check to bounce."

"It will."

"I told him to wait a week more for my check." Barry smiled. "You did say a week, didn't you, before my windfall arrives?"

"Something like that."

"You calculated my horoscope. You found out my birth date. That's how you know all that?"

"Tricks of the trade. Surely you know I'm not going to tell you how."

"You know the one thing I never could buy with astrology—with any of the so-called occult arts—is the factor of predestination, the idea that something will occur no matter what we do. Do you really find that easy to believe? Something that . . . cynical?"

"It's not, 'no matter what we do.' It's just that so many people are unaware of what's actually happening around them that they never sense what's *about* to happen to them.

That's why it's accurate so often. Those who are more, shall we say intuitive, usually can get around some of the worst things. Unless, of course, they don't want to."

"You know why I want you to read my horoscope?"

"Money, travel, change of job, romance . . ." She stopped. "I'm being a brat, I know. But that's what interests most people. I did sort of peek at yours. I mean, nothing formally calculated; just a glance."

"So. What can you tell me?" he asked.

"I can tell you some important past dates in your life," she said. "I wrote them down. She pulled out a little address book, thumbed through it—mostly blank, Barry couldn't help but notice. "Here we are. April 12, 1985."

The date that Jill and he split up. The date, actually, that he signed the final papers taking over the Ephemeris. "Pretty good," he said. "Do you know what it was?"

"Disintegration of a partnership. A new business venture. Want another?" He nodded.

"December 9, 1974."

Barry remembered it instantly. "The phone call from my sister telling me our parents had gone down in a DC-11 over Roanoke. Don't you have any good dates there? These are both bummers."

"It's your life. How about July 14, 1978?"

It had to be Kono, but they'd met two years before, hadn't they? What could that date be?"

"You got me," Barry admitted.

"On that date you were made an heir."

"I hope it's true. It's a lovely idea."

"One more: August 28, 1969."

"That's really going back. You probably weren't even born yet. And I . . . hell, I must have still been in college. "

Suddenly he remembered: not the date precisely, but the summer, *that* summer, all of it. Any date would have been an important one for that particular summer.

"Well?" she questioned. "Do you remember? That's the day you betrayed someone you loved," Kyra said.

He almost didn't hear her words. He could still see the newspaper scrawled with lipstick on the little deal bureau in Anna's room on the top floor of the pension at rue du Champignon, "I'll be home at midnight!" And her violin and the red silk kerchief he'd bought for her at Deauville.

"Yes, I remember. And you're right, partly. I was intensely in love. And there was a great betrayal. But *I* was the one betrayed. I was the one who tried to commit suicide."

Anna. Anna's scarf. Anna's violin. Her room bathed in the azure light of evening—*l'heure bleue* Anna had always called it. He moaned, put his hands over his face.

Kyra was talking rapidly now, and he looked up and saw she was very nervous, very frightened, as if she'd struck him and miscalculated the force of her blow: ". . . I guess I was overdramatizing it or something. I didn't mean to . . ."

"Just a little flash from the past." He smiled. "You couldn't know. . . ." Or could she?

"You didn't get all that through my horoscope, did you? You have a gift, don't you? You're a psychic, aren't you? An honest-to-God psychic."

"You don't really believe . . ." she began.

"You don't need to calculate horoscopes, do you? All this"—tapping the book—"is just to throw me off." He went on, knowing from her embarrassment that he was right. "You just pull it out of the air or something, don't you?"

"You're crazy!" she said, trying to make it a joke.

"Then you must also know that someone is following you," Barry said. She'd been smiling. The smile dropped off her face.

"So you do know." He hadn't meant to scare her. "I'll help you. If you let me."

Kyra half snorted a laugh, then caught herself. "That's chivalrous of you. But I'm afraid you'll have to find some other damsel in distress."

"Why should you trust a stranger?" Barry finished her thought for them both aloud. "Although I hope you will.

No kidding. Though I guess with your psychic ability, you don't need my help, do you?"

"Why are you insisting . . . ?"

"Because it's true. And there's something else funny about you, too."

Kyra called the waitress over. "Can I write you out a check for the book?"

"Don't worry, Kyra, you secret is safe with me. I guess it can't be easy, hiding it from everyone in the world. Is that why you ran away? Come on, I know you ran away. And your parents probably sent some detective after you. Something like that, right?"

"Something," she admitted. She'd filled out a check for the book and slid it under his fingers.

"But think of all the good you could do if you went public with it."

"It doesn't always work that way, Barry. A few years ago, a little boy from Denver revealed his psychic gift, and the media were all over him. Television, newspapers. *People* magazine wanted to put him on its cover. 'Lost and Found Jefferson,' they called him. Because he located the local high-school football team lost in a Rockies' blizzard for two days. Suddenly people were calling asking him to find missing papers, lost dogs, buried treasure, every stupidity you can think of. His family was besieged! They had to move, get a new phone number. And poor Lost and Found! He was just a sweet, retarded seven-year-old, with this weird gift!"

"Did you know him personally?"

"Maybe."

"You do know him," Barry declared. "And maybe you're right to keep it a secret. But still, think of the good you might—"

"My friend Kevin says no possible good is worth the hassle."

"Kevin who?" Barry asked.

"Vosburgh."

"Is Kevin also psychic?" Barry asked.

"Kevin and Lost and Found and I and a few others formed this group in L.A. with—"

She stopped and looked at him, appalled.

"Look I won't tell anyone," Barry said. "Cross my heart."

She jumped up from the table and grabbed her coat and purse and book and was out the door before Barry could do anything to halt her. He hoped his prying hadn't chased her away for good. Well, he had her phone number. Maybe he'd call her. And maybe she'd understand he was just trying to be friendly.

When he arrived at the Ephemeris, Marty Kalb was at his desk, contrite. "I hope you didn't pay any bills with that check I gave you a few days ago," she said out of the corner of her substantial, overly lipsticked mouth.

"Rubber?"

"It wasn't my fault, Barry, believe me. I had the guy responsible fired from my husband's office, and brought *cash* to clear it up, and I promise I'll make it up to you personally tonight after those bitches have all gone home."

Marty Kalb might be vulgar, transparent, oversexed, and completely full of shit about 90 percent of the time, but at least she was honest, Barry thought. Honest and predictable.

"What is it?" Marty asked groggily.

"Can't sleep," Barry said. He was wide awake. Suddenly awake, as though an alarm had gone off inside his brain.

"Want a Valium?" Marty rolled over onto her back, moaned a little.

"No. I'm going to go back to my place. No sense the two of us being awake." He leaned over and bussed her bare shoulder. "Don't get up. I can find my way out."

"You sure? It's awfully late."

He dressed quickly, feeling somehow that he had to get moving, now.

"Bye," he whispered. "I enjoyed tonight."

Outside, Beacon Street was absolutely still in the yellow glow of the streetlights. Barry hunched his jacket collar up

24

against the dampness and walked fast, wondering if he should call a cab or whether he should forget it and just make the longish walk to his loft.

Good thing Marty was so easygoing—or simply too sleepy to bother with him. Barry didn't know how he would explain what he was doing. All he knew was that he'd been awakened out of a deep and dreamless sleep by the premonition of trouble, and he had to get home. No hint of what kind of trouble—fire? burglary?—just trouble.

On the way, Barry walked past the Ephemeris. The shop sat closed and quiet among its row of boutiques and speciality-food shops. The new window display Elaine had put up for the vernal equinox looked good. He peered into the window, checking to see if anything was out of place. Anything, a single book, a single paper. No. Nothing.

Fifteen minutes later, he arrived, chilled, at the loft entrance. The more garish street lights of the business district were off. Still, nothing seemed wrong. No fire engines outside, at least.

He let himself into the elevator with his key, turned the key to his floor, and began to ascend. What if Jill had come back? He dismissed the thought instantly, as the elevator arrived at four. The foyer light was on, all seemed fine. Moving cautiously, he went into the kitchen area and toward the huge living space, with its dozen high windows. Nothing wrong. Outside, the sky was beginning to pale. Five A.M. Nothing wrong in the sleeping area, either. He tried the bathrooms, the closets, still nothing. Not a thing. What the hell!

"The subconscious is a funny thing, Barry," he said out loud, in Kono's lilting accent. "It tells you things you don't want to hear." Meaning what? he asked himself. That he'd awakened himself to get out of Marty Kalb's town house because he hadn't wanted to be there? Because he suspected her husband might suddenly arrive? Because . . . ? He'd run out of reasons; and he liked his sleep too much to cater to vague anxieties. Five hours until he had to be at work.

25

He pulled down the bedroom shades and began to undress . . . and noticed the telephone answering machine's little yellow light blinking. He'd gotten calls while he was away. Not too surprising. He'd been away all evening, first at the society's meeting in Jenny Greenham's big place in Quincy, then at the fancy French restaurant in the South End with Marty and Bob and Blancheur Rolfe, then at Marty's place for a "nightcap."

Still not fully undressed, he went over to the machine. One call had come in. He tapped the time button. The call had come at four-fifteen. About the same time he'd suddenly awakened.

He flipped the machine to replay. It took him a few seconds to recognize her voice.

"Barry, it's Kyra. Sorry to call at this hour, but since you're not home . . . About what happened this afternoon at Rebecca's. I shouldn't have said what I did. We kids promised to keep it a secret. You understand what trouble we could all get into . . . if people knew. . . . Please don't tell anyone what we talked about. Okay? Thanks. I'll see you soon."

He played the message again. It was a damn good thing he wasn't here tonight, he concluded: He would have been pulled out of bed at 4:15 A.M. only to hear this nonsense.

"Weird kid," he said to himself. Now he would need a Valium to get to sleep. Maybe a little reading to tire his eyes . . .

"Barry, are you *ever* coming in?"

It was Elaine on the phone.

"It's almost noon. Don't I get lunch today?"

"I'll be right over," Barry groaned. Damn! Even half a Valium had been too much. He'd sacked out a full seven hours on top of his previous three.

He dressed quickly, hoping there would be coffee left in the shop when he arrived.

There was. Sipping his second cupful, he finally felt able

to step out of the small office onto the shop floor, where something like a rush was going on: a half-dozen customers. Elaine imputed this success to her window dressing, and was so pleased she stayed on till one. Then he was alone, with the morning mail.

He'd torn open a score of envelopes—bills, orders, flyers for local events—when he came to what was unmistakably a check. He tore open the envelope, read the letter with difficulty—Cherie's scrawl was almost as bad as his own. The check was his half of the rent on the Key West house for the past year. She had promised him, remember?

Garble, garble, garble, now that she was married and settled in Galveston with garble Frank—was it Tim? Jim? Slim Frank? She didn't need the money, but she was keeping the place on Whitehead Street as security. The check was for just over nine thousand dollars. Barry would be able to pay off the taxes, get a start on this year's, even get that portable computer he'd been eyeing for the past few weeks. Maybe even take a vacation. Close the shop for a few weeks. Give Elaine time off.

"She said I'd get money I wasn't expecting," he said out loud. "More than enough."

The next letter had a résumé attached and was from a guy—photo included as though he were a model or actor—who'd managed a large occult bookstore in Manhattan Beach. He was looking to relocate to the Northeast. Did Barry have an opening for him? Phone number and address right here, in Dorchester. Maybe Barry wouldn't have to close up to take that vacation.

He called Marty and was sweet but vague to her answering machine. A customer came in, then another, then Elaine came back from lunch, and Barry decided to step out.

On impulse he called the number Kyra had given him. He wouldn't berate her for last night. But he would tell her about his windfall.

An older woman answered and said Kyra wasn't home. She'd take his message, yes. No, she hadn't seen the girl.

Kyra must have gone out early, before she was up. She sometimes did that.

Elaine left the shop at seven, and because he'd gotten in late and had nothing better to do and it was a Friday evening and balmy out, Barry decided to keep the store open until nine o'clock. A few customers came in, more browsers than buyers, but perhaps that might pay off later on. All the other shops on the block stayed open late weekends, why shouldn't he? Besides, he had to admit he didn't really want to go back to the loft tonight, to watch *Miami Vice* and eat a burger with a bottle of beer. A phrase went through Barry's mind: "married to that business!" His mother had accused his father of that for years. And now it could be applied to him, too. Only now that he was almost his father's age then, Barry understood why he gave the Ephemeris so much of his time, and why his father had given his larger and far more lucrative business so much of his time—he preferred it to boredom. And now Barry preferred it to the nothing that awaited him when he would get home, open the loft's locked elevator door, and walk into nothing. To think, he, Barry Brescia, kid on the move for twenty years, was in a rut. Maybe he did need a vacation.

He called Kyra's number again and was a bit more frostily told by the same female voice that she wasn't home.

"Well, didn't she come in yet? Didn't you give her my message?"

"I left your message on the phone table. This isn't an answering service. Nor is it a boarding house. Miss Nilsson's my guest. I don't keep tabs on her."

"Same to you," Barry said, after he hung up.

He dialed the guy in Dorchester who'd sent in the résumé and said he'd like to meet him, maybe try him out for nights, weekends. The guy's name was Albert Prints—"I know! I know! But it's real"—and he seemed eager to come look at the place, even with all of Barry's qualifications about the job. It sounded like Al Prints had fallen on hard times. He might even take part-time work.

Later, at home, a bottle of beer in one hand, next week's *Falcon Crest* teaser shut off, he called Cherie in Galveston, thinking he'd use the excuse of the rent check to talk to her a bit. She was out. Then he called Elaine and told her he'd be in the shop late tomorrow morning and would stay open at night. The eleven o'clock news was over, and Barry wasn't in the least bit tired. Might as well go with the flow. Hang around, listen to some records, read a bit, drink some of that Armangnac.

Twice during the evening, Barry found himself thinking about the girl. Each time, he ended up shaking his head.

CHAPTER TWO

"**W**ho?" Barry asked.

"Mrs. Bryan. Kyra Nilsson stayed with me."

"Oh, right. Excuse me a second. Uh, Albert we have a computer terminal. You have to check any charge over fifty dollars." Into the receiver, he said, "Mrs. Bryan?"

"This is Mr. Brescia?"

"Yes."

"You called a few days ago looking for Kyra?"

"That's right.

"I have something for you from Kyra."

"A note?" Barry asked.

"It looks more substantial than a note. A rather thick envelope."

"Is she there? Can I speak to her?"

"She left Boston the day before yesterday. I was cleaning out her room, and I found this addressed to you."

Prints had gotten an okay on the Visa card and was now talking to another customer. A good salesman. He knew the books, he knew all the key chatter. Unlike Elaine, who moped around the shop.

"Go? Where did she go?"

"She didn't say. I suppose she went back to California. She didn't say. Naturally, I didn't pry."

"Naturally."

A long silence. "If you'll give me your address, I'll mail it to you. I don't see why Kyra didn't herself."

It was as close to irritation as a Brahmin lady of sixty-five would show. Barry said she shouldn't bother, he wasn't far away. He would send someone to pick it up.

A half hour later, Barry slid a thick wad of folded-over papers from the envelope and began to read:

Dear Barry,

I'm sorry I couldn't tell you all this in person. I do like you. Which is a good thing, I suppose, since even in a letter, it's hard to say. Imagine how impossible and embarrassing it would have been with you sitting right there. I seem totally unable to hide anything from you. Which is odd. But I guess it's part of . . . I'd better just come right out and say it. Barry, I have *very* good reason to believe that you are my natural father. I've always known I was adopted and didn't really ever belong to my family. Once I found out about you, though, I came to Boston and went out of my way to meet you.

At first, I wasn't going to say anything, just look you over. Then you pulled me into a conversation, and I guess I wanted to know you better. I don't know who my mother is. I wanted to ask you so badly, but I just couldn't bring myself to do it.

I know this must be a big shock to you. You probably don't even want to have a daughter. When you found out about my abilities, I knew it had all gotten too complicated. So, I'm going away and I won't *ever* contact you again. But I wanted to write this letter, to tell you about my "gift"—because you were so interested in it.

My friend Kevin is fond of quoting Oscar Wilde, among five hundred other authors he's read. "Getting what you most desire," he once quoted Wilde at me, "is sometimes worse than not getting it at all." They're right: both Wilde and Kevin. Who should know that better than they?

I do. Ever since I was a little girl, I always wanted to be special. Longed for it, really. Growing up, I seemed so ordinary, with my ordinary dark hair, and ordinary somewhat pretty face, and ordinary body, which was fine except that it wasn't coordinated enough to make me a ballerina or swim star. Yet I was certain that someday a special talent would suddenly descend upon me or emerge from out of me and show everyone—my parents, my friends, myself most importantly!—what I'd known all along: I was unique, absolutely unique.

Some girls dream of being actresses or models, talk-show hosts or investigative reporters or pop singers. But I always knew that whatever I would accomplish would be with my mind. My, everyone would say, she *seems* ordinary. Imagine her being so gifted, so special.

By the time I was eleven years old, I was sort of special. Put into a class for gifted students at the private day school I attended, given extra lessons—high-school reading and math and science, three foreign languages.

Now, of course, I have to laugh at that intense little girl I can still make out in photographs, with her scowling countenance and blazing eyes. After all that's happened, I wish I *could* be normal, just another sixteen-year-old girl intrigued by Sting and worried about how far to go in petting sessions. God, how I wish it!

I see I'll just go around in circles unless I start at the beginning.

It began at home late one afternoon when I was thirteen years old. It was a Friday afternoon, and I had no homework. No one else was there but Sandy, she's the "girl" from Monterey who cooked and cleaned and usually spent time with Mother, and she was in the laundry room and kitchen. I had nothing much to do, and passing by my father's study, I was struck by how neat and unused the room was, yet how dark and cool on this very warm June afternoon. The shades were pulled all the way down over the two tall windows, and the dark wood paneling and ice-blue and white material covering the furniture looked so inviting that I decided to lie down a minute on Father's leather chaise.

I closed the door, and it was so pleasant and silent I

could barely make out the distant chugging of the clothes dryer, the sounds of the cooking utensils Sandy was using, the passing of cars out past our curved driveway on Loma Rioja Drive. I would be lying if I said I was thinking about anything in particular. I wasn't. Just sort of emptying my mind, as Sandy always insisted Mother must do when they practiced meditation together. Refreshing myself, I suppose you might say, after a hectic week of school.

Then, quite suddenly and out of nowhere, with my eyes half-shut in that dim, quiet room, I found myself seeing something: some kind of pattern, a thick rectangle attached at the lower end to another rectangle. I remember thinking, What's this? And suddenly I seemed closer to the two rectangles, as though I were a bird looking down at them. I could see a slight curvature of the surroundings, and what I'd at first thought to be merely a design suddenly took on the characteristics of land—the same winding ribbons of roads, with an occasional crossroad and patches of lighter color I was certain were parking lots.

I was so surprised, I opened my eyes. But the minute I shut them, I saw the rectangles again. Even closer, though of course still far far away, and I thought the rectangles might be walls, thick walls surrounding smaller buildings, or perhaps buildings themselves in an odd, open-court design. Wasn't that the glare of sunlight off one side of the building's window panes? And weren't the rest in shadow behind it?

I opened my eyes, closed them again, and saw the whole design from a slightly different angle, as though I were slowly turning, wheeling above. I continued to look at this until I began to feel strange, as though I were some sort of camera lens that could see but that had no idea what it was seeing. The feeling that I was doing something very odd, the strangeness of the buildings and of the land, the weirdness of that particular design of buildings, all became so oppressive I couldn't stand it.

I opened my eyes and sat up. I threw open the shades

and let sunlight flood in. The image was gone. But something lingered whenever I blinked, a ghost of that same design, still slowly revolving. By then I was upset. I ran out of the study into the kitchen. Sandy was at the sink, chopping vegetables for a stew, happily singing along with Crosby, Stills, and Nash on the radio. "Kenny proposed to me with that song," she said. "And I liked the song so much I accepted."

I had always liked to hear Sandy talk about herself, so I stayed in the kitchen, sitting on a stool, eating chunks of celery and carrot she handed me. I stayed there a half hour, until my brother Skip arrived home from Little League practice and began to fix himself a snack, and we got to taunting each other and I completely forgot what had happened in the study.

Of course, I hadn't really forgotten. I'd merely pushed it out of my mind because I didn't understand it. Kevin says no one knows how a spatial eidism begins anyway, despite thousands of hours of study of the subject, nor what subject it will first select to bring to awareness. He thinks that perhaps 2 percent of all children between the ages of nine and fourteen have a precog-eidetic. Some children never understand what it is and keep it hidden. Others confess its existence only to close friends, making it a "play image." Others revere it as a guardian angel, a ghost, even a friend, like E.T. When I met Lost and Found, he told me his P-E began when he was yawning—a little speck of star just at the edge of his visual perception range. That little blue-white star appeared one day, and it never went away.

Lost's is a particular kind of sign, what's called "mutual eidism control," and of the children who have P-E's, an infinitesimally small percentage possess MECs, myself among them. What makes a MEC so special, of course, is that when the imaging begins, not only can it communicate to you, but you can also manipulate it, utilize it.

Another week went by before it happened to me again. I was lying on a plastic lounge chair at the side of the pool, listening to a Duran Duran cassette. Father and Skip were in the pool splashing about and making a great deal of noise. Mother was on another lounge in the shade under the eaves of the house, talking to her friend Linda on the telephone. I closed my eyes, and the sun still shone through, making red and blue explosions, so I grabbed Dad's eyeshade and put it on, which helped. A minute later, it was as if I'd suddenly gone very far away: All the sounds from the pool, from my mother, from the radio, seemed very distant. And there was the image again, this time from much higher up, so high up I wasn't certain it was the same.

Until I seemed to swoop down upon it, and it was the same exact two rectangles, but in slightly different light, as though it were early evening, the shadows very long. I must have blinked in disbelief, because suddenly I was much closer than before, as though swooping down into it, almost as though I were flying—a flying camera looking down. And I could see bumps and cylinders and boxes on the long roofs, which I was certain were air-conditioning units and water tanks and who knows what else. Every time I was unsure of what I was seeing, I got closer, or got a slightly different angle. I could make out more landscape—what seemed to be a striated field or desert—it was so barren—and was that water sparkling on top? Yes, water, the edge of a lake or something.

It was fascinating, but really so odd that I willed my eyes open and jumped out of my chair and leaped into the pool. This time the image followed me longer than before. By the time I had broken the surface of the water again, Skip was crying and my father was yelling at me, and all I could do was to hang onto the pool ladder and hope the image would go away. I was so unhappy and frightened I was shaking and didn't know what to do, and finally I ran into the house, crying, which at least cleared the image out of my eyes.

The third time it happened was a week later in the

35

parking lot of our local mall. I'd gone grocery shopping with my mother, which had taken forever, and we'd emptied the bags from the shopping cart into the BMW's trunk and backseat, and then she said she had to go to the pharmacy. Even though I knew she would take a long time in there, it was such a pleasant afternoon, I decided to wait in the car. This time the appearance was sudden and total: I was sitting there crying when my mother returned to the car, and I didn't even hear or see her until she began to shake me and ask what was wrong. I was so afraid, I clung to her all the way home in the car.

Once inside the house, she put drops into my eyes, which did nothing—the images were gone by then, anyway—and telephoned my father to tell him I was having trouble with my eyes and could he arrange to have me see an optometrist on the base. That night everyone was solicitous. My father kept on giving me these compassionate glances, saying that after the next day everything would be all right.

Well, he drove me to the optometrist, and my eyes were checked out and nothing was wrong. Nothing at all! The man tested me more than an hour, and shrugged his shoulders at my father. Then he asked me to tell him again about the visions—as he called them. I did. Afterward, while I waited in his outer office, I could hear them talking about having me get a CAT scan. Since nothing was wrong with my eyes, something might be wrong with my brain. My father was very pale when he came out of that office, very tight-lipped. My mother was pretty upset, too, when she heard. Father arranged a CAT scan through his own Air Force doctor.

That was just the beginning of a month of tests. The CAT scan showed nothing unusual. So my next stop was with a psychiatrist—a woman barely out of college who asked me all sorts of questions about my physical health and how I got along with my parents and my friends in school. She even asked whether or not menstruation bothered me. I told her Mother had explained it all.

36

During all this time I had the images again, but not as clearly. Probably because I was so afraid of them—whenever they began, I would immediately get up and do something to distract myself: play the radio loud, dance around, run outside and make trouble with Skip, go to my mother and just hold her hand and make her talk to me about when she was a girl in New England. She could tell I was frightened, and she was, too.

Oh, I should mention that I already knew that I'd been adopted by Dunstan and Nicole Anthony. Knew it from the age of about six, I think. I'd discussed it with my psychiatrist. I told her I didn't mind being adopted. After all, as Nicole had always said, it didn't mean that someone hadn't wanted me, but that someone couldn't keep me, and someone else—them!—had wanted me very much. I also didn't mind that Skip was natural born. I knew that often happened after a childless couple adopted. Besides, I was my father's princess and absolutely my mother's best friend. If anything, I felt better treated than Skip. By then, too, I'd had enough experience with my friends' parents to see how totally terrific Nicole and Dun were, by comparison.

The next time I had the P-E image was in school, in study period, which was outdoors because the weather was so great. I was sunbathing, thinking about what I'd been reading in our earth-science text. Did you know that millions of years ago North America was separate from South America, and was much lower, over the equator, and there weren't any of the mountains and rivers we know? Especially back in Pre-Cambrian times, when the earth was mostly ocean and tidal pools and low-lying land, no animals, hardly any fish, either, just mollusks and jellyfish. Imagine! At any rate, I was imagining that, wondering if the skies and ocean and all were the colors we know them to be, and I became aware of the silence. I opened my eyes, and of course everything was as it should be, and then I knew I was going to have the P-E image again. I just held my fists, and closed my eyes tight, and mentally said, "No, No, No! NO, NO!!, *NO!!!!*" as hard as I could.

Guess what? Nothing happened.

Nothing! And that was the last of it—for a while. Except for one thing. At the same moment I realized I wasn't going to have to experience those plans, designs, buildings, that place again, I suddenly experienced something else: Next Tuesday, at four in the afternoon, I'd see Nicole's friend Janice, who'd tell me something very important.

I was so relieved that I'd avoided the other business, I didn't think anything about it. Everyone thinks stuff like that, no? What was important was that I'd stopped whatever had tried to take over my mind and eyes. You can imagine how that pleased me.

What I didn't suspect was that it wasn't over, but just beginning. My apprenticeship in being a MEC was over.

The following Tuesday, at four o'clock in the afternoon, not ten minutes after I'd returned from our science-club meeting at my friend Larraine's house, I heard a car come up the driveway: Janice.

Janice wasn't a usual visitor. She was a friend of Nicole's from college. She'd married before Nicole and had moved out West. They didn't see each other for years, not until my father's work for the Air Force brought him here. When I was smaller, I'd seen a great deal of Janice. She was my godmother and always brought me great gifts that no one else would think to get, Russian dolls and a unicorn stuffed animal. She always treated me as though I were very special. Then she and her husband moved up to Fairchild, and her visits became much less frequent.

Anyway, that afternoon Janice said she had been in the area looking at property—she "dabbles" in real estate—and thought she'd pay a surprise visit. Nicole and Sandy were there, all of us out on the side lawn, and I said, "Oh, I knew you were coming, Janice. I knew it last week!" She was surprised. I'd never seen her so surprised, not even when she was kidding around with me. "But how could you, Kyra, when I didn't know myself that I was coming to this area until yesterday evening? And to tell the truth, I thought I might have to drive back to Fairchild immediately. It was only at Mr. Ellis's house that I decided to cancel a date in Carmel. You know I'd never come without a gift for you. All I brought was this!"—a bottle of brandy, for my folks.

I didn't want to seem too weird, so I changed the subject. Janice said she'd stay to dinner, and I hung around her more than I usually did. You see, since the first part of that thought had come true, I was certain the second part would, too. Even though I walked her out to her car afterward, and she kissed me and asked me all kinds of questions, Janice didn't tell me a single important thing.

Now, of course, I know what the important thing was: Janice's surprise when she arrived, and how she hadn't even known she'd be there—and of course the fact that I had known, for a week!

Two nights later, Chet Diebold, a friend of my father's, came for dinner. Skip was young enough to sneak out of that, but I had to be there. Chet was also in the military, a doctor, my father said, and right away I was sure he was there to observe me, if in a casual manner, which sort of unnerved me. But the subject of my P-E never came up during the meal, so I relaxed and began to enjoy some of their stories; they'd been together in some famous places—as young men in Southeast Asia, in Cuba before Castro took over there. We "retired" to the terrace for coffee and "nightcaps," and Nicole brought out the brandy Janice had brought by. "Funny thing," she told Dun. "Kyra knew Janice would be there. Knew it last week, even though Janice did it on the spur of the moment."

Chet was very interested. Had it ever happened before? When, how often, etc. Dun told Chet Diebold about my "vision problems," and Chet wanted to see the design I'd seen. So I got paper and pencil and drew it, explaining, "This is the angle it's on when I first see it. But sometimes it turns around so I can see all around it."

"May I have this?" Chet asked.

And that was the end of the subject. For three days.

Diebold and another, younger man named Peter Roy came by the house after dinner and talked to Dun, who called me into his study.

"Now don't be afraid," Dun said. They were all sitting around drinking. I could smell the scotch. Dr. Roy asked me exactly what had happened, and I sort of acted it out and ended up lying down on the sofa.

"Do you think you could visualize it again?" Diebold asked.

"I haven't in a while. And anyway . . . I don't like doing it."

"Dr. Roy will help you if you have the least bit of discomfort," Dun said, which I thought was stupid—how could he know how it felt? But I could see they wanted me to try. So I got comfortable on the chaise.

Of course, nothing happened, and I sat up and explained that I had to be totally relaxed, and Dr. Roy asked Dun, "May I?," and Dun nodded yes, and Dr. Roy shut my eyes, then laid me back slowly and did something to the left side of my neck that I later found out was an instant hypnotic technique, and I completely relaxed.

The image appeared a few seconds later, this time colored very palely. They shut off the lights in the room, and it was bright again. The shadows were different on it, and it was getting brighter as I looked.

"Sunrise," Dr. Roy said. "Tell us everything you see," he told me. And he held up the drawing and I compared it, and pointed out everything.

"Can you get closer?" he asked.

I could.

"Even closer? I want you to read what it says on the rectangle you think is a parking lot."

I saw the following: K P e H H e K O B

"Can you get closer?"

I tried and couldn't.

"Can you turn left, so you're at the top of the upper rectangle?"

Easily. I wheeled around to where he asked.

"Read what it says there!"

"CCCP."

"One more question, Kyra. When will you be at this place again?"

"Nine days from now," I said without any hesitation.

"What time?"

"At one-thirty in the afternoon."

He sat me up and he asked how I felt and thanked me and said he'd like to meet with me at the time I'd mentioned. He'd sign me out of class for the rest of the day. I left the study and didn't feel oppressed and sad as I had before, I suppose because they hadn't said I was crazy or anything, and because it was clear that Dr. Roy knew what was going on.

He picked me up at school nine days later, and we drove over to some offices in Carmel where we met two other men, neither of whom were dressed in military clothing. They looked at the diagram and showed me two photos. "That's the place!" I said. "Exactly." Dr. Roy relaxed me on a sofa there as he had the first time, and the image came again, and they asked me more questions, none of which made much sense to me. When I got up, I asked Dr. Roy what I was seeing.

"It's an installation of some sort. A pumping station, we think."

"In Russia?" I asked. "Those are Cyrillic letters."

"Do you know Russian?"

"I've seen a Russian newspaper in class. *Pravda*."

Dr. Roy said, "Kyra, we don't know how exactly, but we think you've been hooked up to a Soviet surveillance satellite. A sort of sky camera."

41

"That kind of imaging won't last very long," the second man said. I'd looked at him before because he was rugged and dreamy-looking, with lots of blond-silver curly hair, like a TV actor. "We think you may be an advanced case of precognition with specific attributes. Do you know what I'm talking about?"

"ESP?"

"Well, like that. But quite a bit more advanced. While this visual business is fascinating, I'm more interested in your times and dates. How long have you been having them?"

I told him when it began and the five instances following, excluding Dr. Roy's. It all sounded so dumb, I mean that Sandy's husband would buy a car on Tuesday the twelfth and Nicole's bridge partner would be having an operation. I was almost embarrassed by it, and told him so.

"It's not dumb to me," he said. "By the way, call me Burr. We're going to be friends and colleagues. I hope you'll join us?"

When he smiled, I was just blown away. "Us? Who else?"

"We're an informal group with special abilities. It's funded by the government, but it's my group. All of us are P-E's, that is precognitive-eidetic. And some are MECs, that means we have more special skills. We meet after school, drink soda, and talk. Oh, and a colleague tapes our sessions from outside the room."

Burr told me when and where they would meet again, and said he could have me picked up in a car, and I guess I was flattered and wanted to see Burr again, so I agreed to try it out.

Nothing much happened during those first meetings. We fooled around with Rhine cards for ESP (named after J. B. Rhine, a professor at Duke University who developed them), and with alpha-wave machines and stuff like that. It was a bit of a gas. What took me a while to figure out was that most of the people in the group were not P-E's but p-e's—lowercase—which you can almost hear when it's spoken aloud. That means they had some receiving power, or some transmitting power, but not much, or not worked out.

I'd been attending Burr's Carmel meetings about a month when he phoned one day to say the group wasn't going to meet anymore. I was disappointed, and couldn't hide it. Burr said he was going to Los Angeles, where he had his main offices.

Come with us, Kyra! I suddenly felt someone say; not Burr. Someone else. Yet only one phone line sounded open. I'd like to, very much, I thought.

"Don't you have off from school next week?" Burr asked me. "Easter vacation? Come to L.A. There's plenty of room."

"I promised I'd visit my godmother, and . . ."

In the middle of that I felt that other voice say, *You know you can get out of that. We know you'd rather come to L.A. We'll have fun. You'll meet me.*

"Is someone else on the phone with us?" I asked Burr.

"It doesn't have any extension," he replied.

"That's not what I was asking," I said, but I wasn't sure what I was asking.

I'm Kevin.

"There it is again!"

"That's Kevin. He's a MEC," Burr said.

Come to Los Angeles and you'll meet me. You can postpone your trip.

I remember asking, "What's going on here?" and Burr answering, "Well, that's the way MECs are."

I was intrigued. "Oh? How?"

"Like you and Kevin. Using me and my telephone line to talk to each other. Kevin does it because he knows it irritates me."

I thought about what he'd said: a lot to absorb. "You mean I'm a MEC, too?"

"The only one from the Carmel group."

"Okay," I told Burr—and Kevin, "I'll postpone the trip north."

Kevin was glad. Burr said it would be the easiest thing in the world to fly me down. It would take less than an hour from the Santa Cruz airport.

Without much persuasion, Dun and Nicole let me go to L.A. to be with Burr. Although my mother said she understood how important it was for me, she looked worried.

I was the only passenger on a small jet, which seated ten people, even though a woman was on board, a sort of chaperon. And two pilots. After we landed, one of them, Bernie, drove me to the outskirts of the University of California at Irvine. The building was on a tree-shaded boulevard and had been part of a Spanish mission in the seventeenth and eighteenth centuries, and it was super. Wisteria hanging down off the old tile roofs, a madhouse of scarlet canna and birds of paradise. Inside, big, dark rooms with wooden rafters and alabaster fireplace mantels and really old, age-stained wood sculpture. Marble floors in all sorts of colors, wrought iron everywhere. The floor-boards had been worn away and a new parquet laid down. Aside from that and electricity and new plumbing, the place was just as it had been when it was built as some bishop's palace. Downstairs, the huge receiving room, a big old kitchen, offices, and "work rooms," as Burr called them. Up a double stairway, bedrooms and living quarters. Outside were gardens on two levels, and a big pool.

Burr said, "Kevin's waiting for you. You'll have to look past the obvious, with Kevin."

"Okay," I said, and somehow I knew what he meant: Kevin looked odd.

Burr led me to a work room, one wall of which was dominated by a bank of computer monitors—seven or eight of them—and all sorts of electronic equipment—keyboards, tape recorders with huge reels: I later found out it was called a mainframe.

In the middle of it all, was Kevin. Burr introduced us.

"I'm weird-looking, huh?" was Kevin's first comment. "You're beautiful! Don't worry, everyone has the same first reaction. I don't mind."

My second reaction was better. What deep, knowing, mature eyes he had. And my third was even better: I was so awed by the array of computers, which were beyond any setup I'd ever seen, and which he obviously controlled.

"You compute?" Kevin asked.

"I'm not sure."

"Are you a savant? Like those twin boys who used to call up calendars for the next ten thousand years and who mentally masturbated each other with nine-digit prime numbers?"

I had to laugh. "God, no! I'm not like that! I don't think!"

"I am. Like those boys, I mean."

"A savant? Or an idiot?"

"Ha, ha! It's true, though, I compute faster than a computer. Want to test me?"

I didn't think I was smart enough to test him, and, anyway, why be impolite? "I believe you."

"I use this rod, in my pocket." Kevin showed me and took out this thin metal rod from his pocket and slipped it between his lips. *For really complex mathematical problems.*

I guess I was surprised that I was still hearing him, even though he had it between his teeth. I thought he was throwing his voice.

That is, when I'm not in alpha, Kevin explained. *It's easier to keep track of things this way. And to convey them to the "house"* (by which Kevin meant his giant computer). *But when I'm in alpha, I sit back and—whammo!—think math.*

Instantly I felt what he must mean. Not exactly, I guess I would need Kevin's knowledge of formulas and all for that, but I got a real, an almost three-dimensional sense of something I'd only vaguely known before.

"I don't understand," I said. "How did you do that?"

He looked at me. With the rod still in his mouth, he said, *I'm a MEC. Boy! Are you going to be surprised when you find out what MECs can do!*

Of course, you noticed, Barry, that I've left out my own MEC skills. At first, they were simple, a feeling—certain knowledge of some future event, like Janice's unexpected visit. During the Carmel sessions, Burr put me on the alpha-wave machine and asked me to think about past events: He chose dates in his own life for me to experience. I got to see Burr when he was twenty years old, fifteen, thirty. I attended his wedding (his wife later died). It was fascinating. I did a little of it with other people in the group. It was always exhausting.

You see now, Barry, that all that business about my using the Uranian system of astrology wasn't completely on the level. It wasn't completely lying, because I am studying it, especially for long-term trends. Burr never told me I could operate that way—but I believe I can. In fact, I need to know long-term trends to make sense of some future dates that come to me. The other thing is, I have blind spots. Including dates that concern me. I can sense which dates will affect me, but I don't always know how. Maybe my emotions get in the way.

In Los Angeles with Burr and Kevin, I first began doing controlled futures. The week I was there, once again hooked up to the alpha-wave machine and relaxed under autosuggestion, I produced seventy-five futures, not one of them more than four hours in the future, or concerning anyone but people I knew. Needless to say, these "future" incidents were of astonishing banality. Burr was pleased; I wasn't.

For the next month after I'd returned home to Pacific Grove, anytime I wanted to go to sleep, I'd begin to receive futures spontaneously. Totally boring ones, concerning people I knew, and usually less than a day ahead. When I called up Burr to tell him about it, he was very pleased.

"You don't need biofeedback!" he said. He asked me to do it during the day.

I was hesitant because of those baffling "visions" that introduced me to P-E, but I said I'd try. And I did, lying by the pool, or inside on Dad's chaise, and I succeeded a few times, but I always felt exhausted afterward.

While I was back in Pacific Grove, Burr telephoned every week. I talked to Kevin for the longest time and to Burr only a few minutes. From Kevin I found out about other MECs, like ourselves, whom Burr had located. He wanted to bring us all together. Kevin thought it was a great idea. I guess so did I.

Burr flew up to visit several times the remainder of that school term. He talked to Dun and Nicole, asking whether they would mind if I came with Burr and Kevin that summer. I was thrilled. I wanted to meet other MECs. By then I'd also developed what is known as a "schoolgirl crush" on Burr.

I was with them all summer. We started off in the Spanish mission-style house in Irvine, moved to a large, very modern group of buildings in the mountains where we wouldn't be bothered by interference from jet-pilot radios, television, or microwaves. I learned to sharpen and concentrate my MEC skills. I met several others with P-E skills. Lost and Found, for one.

When I returned to Pacific Grove to begin my sophomore year at our local high school, I got a few rude shocks. I consciously future-dated on a limited basis. But when I tried to stop doing it, I found I couldn't. As it kept happening, I became unclear of what had already happened and what was going to happen. I'd be sitting in the cafeteria with my friends Sarah and Jody and I'd say, "Wasn't that stupid, what Ken Allister did with the erasers!," and they wouldn't know what I was talking about. And two days later, while Mrs. Chin had her back turned, Ken would stand behind her and stop cleaning the blackboard to balance the erasers at the very

47

end of her desk, distracting us all—no one more than Jody and Sarah.

It got hairier. I began to future-date so often, so spontaneously, that I was exhausted by it. I began monitoring whatever I said, hoping to turn my friends off what was really going on, which would be "too weirdo, Kyra, uuggh!" if they knew. Phone calls were the worst: Where we used to talk an hour at a time, I cut conversations short, preferring to talk where I could gauge how "off" I was getting by watching facial expressions.

My parents noticed how much more I stayed at home alone, and how quiet I'd become. Lonely, too. My life became more difficult every day. I guess it all broke open when Dun and Nicole had our annual New Year's Day party. This was a sort of open house, with people coming over all day, drinking, eating, dancing, playing games, watching football games on TV. In the midst of them, I became so thoroughly inundated with past and future dates I couldn't take it anymore. I ran out of the house, ran mindlessly awhile, hitched a ride in a neighbor's car to the beach cliffs. I stayed there till after midnight; calm for the first time in weeks. When I got back to the house, I dialed Burr's number in Los Angeles and told him what was happening. "Please come get me or I'll go crazy."

He was there the following afternoon, explaining something or other to Dun and Nicole while I packed clothing, books, records, even dolls. Aside from one or two holidays, I haven't been back to Pacific Grove. I write and call my parents, and I *think* they understand. . . . At least I'm not pregnant or doing drugs!

I've used up a lot of paper already, Barry, and I'm still not sure I've told you all I wanted to or convinced you that I . . . Oh, well, maybe it's better like this. *Please* don't try to locate me. I'll be okay. Really, I will. I hope despite all this that you still like me. God, that sounds so stupid!

Love,
Kyra

CHAPTER THREE

It was here somewhere! The phone number had to be here! Inside a wallet he hadn't used in more than a decade. A wallet he'd kept pretty much only because of the phone number. From apartment to apartment, city to city, coast to coast, the wallet had followed him, packed open between his passport—now out of date—his college diploma, his birth certificate, and a mass card. He'd put it all right here, in the back of the top drawer: his past wrapped with an inch-thick red rubber band. Now that he needed it, where in hell was it?

There! The wallet, not flat between the other two objects as he'd recalled but doubled up under them, closed, as he'd carried it in his back pocket throughout law school, throughout Europe. And yes, there, behind his several student I.D.'s, his Eurail pass, stubs of airline tickets, receipts, a Kennedy half-dollar, even an old condom still wrapped—"Elite, for comfort and security!"—was the paper: the phone number: the code.

Barry sat down. Suddenly the room telescoped out hugely, enlarging the length and width and height of the loft, walls so white, so undiluted by art or decoration . . . . He who hesitates is lost.

Barry dialed the prefix, the area code, the seven digits. What if it's out of date? All of it? What if no one answers?

"What number did you want, sir?" The operator. He gave her the number.

"That number has been changed." She didn't offer it.

"I have a prefix," Barry told her.

"Go ahead, sir."

He rattled it off.

"The *new* phone number is . . ." And he scrambled to copy it. "I'll connect you directly, sir."

"Is it still located in Langley?" But she was gone, ringing.

"Central Intelligence Agency!" answered a cheerful female voice with a southern accent.

God, how open they were about it!

"I have a code prefix," he offered, and gave it.

"Yes, sir. Can I help you?"

"I need some information. I'm trying to contact someone. I'm not sure if he's still . . . at your number." When he got no help, Barry said, "Alex Land. That's L-A-N-D. Alexander."

"Checking," she said, and he was listening to a Mozart wind serenade: plaintive oboes trilling over grumbling bassoons.

"I'm sorry, sir. I don't show that name as current."

Which meant nothing.

"It's been a while," Barry said. "I wasn't sure if . . ."

"Might Personnel be of help? I could transfer you."

She did, and this time the southern accent was sharp and precise, and belonged to a man.

"I was field. Europe. Sixty-nine/seventy. I'm looking for a colleague. It seems that neither of us is still active. It's for personal reasons."

"Any case name over twelve years old is deep six in Records," the sharp voice responded.

"What if I gave you the operation and code names?"

"I'm not really supposed to. But . . . I was in Archives for two years. I might know. If not, you'll have to write us, using forms . . ."

"It was called Little Broom. Europe. Sixty-nine. I was Golden Straw. I'm trying to locate Rumpelstiltskin."

"Hold on, sir." More Mozart; the adagio of the same piece

ending, then a bright, perky march and it was over. The radio announcer went on to say that weather in the Capitol tristate area was cloudy and unseasonably cool, with sun expected tomorrow. "I don't even know who my mother is," Kyra had written. "I've always known I was adopted." Well, *she* might not know. But he did. He was sure of it. Her profile, her nose, lips, the way her hair hung so straight, how she'd walked. No wonder she'd seemed so damn familiar!

"Sir? Are you still there? I found that operation, sir, but it was coded up the kazoo. It must have been quite—"

"Unsuccessful," Barry finished the sentence for him.

"Yes, sir."

"How do I find my friend?"

Friend? Alex Land, friend? God, he'd acted like it. Until . . . and then . . . Yet who else but a friend could betray like that? "I don't know who my mother is." But Barry knew. It couldn't be anyone else but Anna. And if Barry knew, then Alex Land *had* to know.

"Sorry, sir. As I said before, this file is so coded I can't break in anywhere."

"Look," Barry tried, "he's obviously retired. So am I. However, I don't plan on looking him up in every phone book in the Washington area. And I'll only be in your area a day or so. Let's do it this way: His family used to live somewhere near Monticello. He always said he was going to retire there. Now why don't you give me that phone number?"

Hesitation, then: "Sir, I'm not supposed to give out *any* information."

"Please!"

"I'll try."

What had thrown Barry off about Kyra was her eyes. Those large, brown Mediterranean eyes. Anna's had been blue, cobalt blue. But of course! They were Barry's eyes Kyra had. His eyes, his mother's eyes, his grandfather's eyes, going back, back . . .

"Sir, did you say it was near Mount Vernon?"

"I said Monti . . . That's right! I used to have it, but I must have lost—"

"I do have an address for your friend. No telephone number."

Barry copied it, thanked the man.

Knowing that to stop now would be the worst possible move, Barry called the Ephemeris. Elaine answered.

"I'm not coming back. You're going to have to close up tonight."

He waited to hear her say, "Damn!" She didn't.

"Cancel the date," he suggested before she could speak. "It's only this once. Is Albert Prints there?"

"He's with a customer. Moira Callahan." Elaine made it sound like something was going on between them. From what Barry knew of Moira, one of Marty Kalb's "dearest friends" and a prominent member of her close-knit group, Albert was exactly to her taste: slight, bookish, bright-eyed.

"Tell Albert to sell Moira that set of Aleister Crowley that's been sitting around for years," Barry suggested. "No matter what it takes."

That cheered up Elaine. "I'll pass it on, boss."

"I've got to leave town," Barry began. "Family business: can't be helped."

"You'll be back tomorrow?"

"Don't know. Possibly."

"You know, of course, that all the other shops on the street are closing at eight. We're the only one open till nine."

"You can use the overtime," Barry said. "Tell Albert that I'll look over what he gave me. Oh, and if anyone calls, repeat what I told you."

"Barry?"

"What?"

"Nothing. It's just that . . . Forget it."

"Make some money there," he said, all business now.

The call to Marty Kalb was more disturbing.

52

"Bullshit!" was her response. "It has something to do with a girl."

"Is that ESP or jealousy?"

"Fuck you, Barry. The minute you left the other night, I got out of bed and did a Tarot reading. You *know* I know exactly what you're up to every minute. But wait a min, I'm working on another reading for you and it *is* family business, after all. Although I'm not clear exactly how. Oh, and Barry? You'll be away longer than you think. *If* you take the other path."

"What are you babbling about? What other path?"

"Take it, Barry. Tarot says it's filled with danger. I mean all sorts of dangers—mental, physical, emotional, but, oh, Barry, it's so seldom anyone has an honest-to-God adventure anymore, and that's what all this looks like to me. I'll miss you, but go ahead and—"

"I'm *not* going on any adventure. I'll be back in a day or two. And do *not* read my cards anymore!"

"You going to stop me?" she challenged.

The hour-and-a-half jet ride to National Airport seemed over almost before it began. He just had time enough to settle into his seat—on the aisle, to accommodate his long legs—to sip his "complimentary" coffee, and to look over Albert Prints's carefully written scheme on how to remodel the shop—a plan that included diagrams with such labels as "high point-of-purchase area" and "dead space/suggest graphics on wall here."

Short as the trip was, and as involving as Prints's scheme was, Barry relaxed for the first time that day. He remembered the room on the top floor of the little pension on the rue du Champignon at evening, and the violin case on the floor and the red scarf fluttering.

Actually that had been at the very end. The beginning was in 1969, at a student demonstration on the steps of the Low Library at Columbia University on a late April afternoon. . . .

"A love that should have lasted years," crooned Paul Mc-Cartney bitterly against a twanging guitar.

"Hey!" Barry knocked on the dorm door a second time, until Simon glanced up.

"Whaa! I heard you." Simon was stoned, stretched across his bed, his head against the wall—frayed pale blue Oxford shirt, filthy chinos and scuffed boots, long blond hair and granny glasses. "So come in, already."

McCartney ended his short, sour song, and a Ragalike drone of guitars began as intro to the next cut of the album.

"Could you turn that down, or even off, for a minute?" He was aware that he was being a drag, but what the hell. "I really have to talk with you."

Simon frowned but did turn down the reel-to-reel. Then he sat staring at Barry. To think, in a few years Simon would actually be out in the world practicing law. God help his clients!

"Look at this." Barry held up the letter with its subway token affixed to the top.

"When?" Simon asked.

"I report for the physical in two weeks. There's no way I'm going to fail it."

Barry knew that. He had quit the football team that past January so he could buckle down to study. The Lions would miss him badly. Barry had possessed an almost instinctive knowledge of where Danzel would throw. He'd weave around defensive backs, being shoved here, slammed there, unable to look back, heading toward the ten-yard line, the five-yard line, and then actually *feel* Danzel throw the ball at him. He'd just reach up and snatch the pigskin out of the air and step into the end zone for a touchdown!

"I could fix it so that in two weeks you'd be a physical wreck," Simon said.

"I'm not shooting heroin, thanks. And," Barry added, "you didn't, either. Yet you're still here. How did you do it?"

Simon smiled. "Told 'em I was gay."

"Bullshit! Your old man would have killed you."

"Actually, Bar, lad, I did better than that. I already served my country."

"Double bullshit!"

"Not in the way you might think. But then your rabid anti-Americanism makes you, how shall I put it? A bit narrower than I am."

"You think Johnson's a crock of shit, too."

"What I mean is, there's more on heaven and earth, Horatio . . . etcetera."

"Yeah? Like what?"

Simon seemed to come down from his high for a second or two, to look as serious as his dad, old Skinner Costain, millionaire financier.

"You've got to promise to keep this quiet. I mean from *everyone*."

"You want a blood oath or something?" Barry held out his arm.

Simon tapped Barry's wrist with a roach clip. "Consider it done."

"What is all this, Simon?"

"Serious business, Bar, lad. National Security. You know I don't give half a fuck for the government . . ."

"Simon Costain, boy patriot."

"But, when I was approached with an offer I couldn't refuse," Simon went on, "to keep me out of Nam, I agreed"—Simon hesitated for emphasis—"to become a spook."

"The CIA? You work for the CIA?" Barry's voice rose to a tenor of disbelief. "I don't believe it."

Barry had to sit back against Simon's roommate's bed.

"You're shitting me, aren't you?"

"Not a bit, Bar, lad. And in so doing, I fulfill all military obligations and will receive an honorable discharge. *And* a special commendation."

"What do you have to do?"

"Why, not much at all! I hang around various demonstrations, getting high, sunning myself, having a great time. Every once in a while, my contact comes to see me, shows me a photo of someone he wants.

"I'll admit I didn't think at first I could do it. Especially since I'd be skinned alive if Rudd or Kellogg or any of the others found out about it. But I'm not doing the movement any real harm. They're basically interested in foreign agents—Commie infiltrators and all that."

"Jesus, how can you live with yourself, Simon?"

"Listen, I may even get a free summer in Europe. Interested?" Simon asked. "I could connect you to my contact. He's always looking for people. You'd be a primo candidate, Bar, what with your jockability and school letter and all . . . primo!"

"I don't think so. Simon, have you considered the ethics involved in this kind of thing?"

"Bar, lad, you asked, I told you. I considered *everything* involved, the ethics versus the politics versus the amorality versus hacking through the jungle in the DMZ versus . . . If you ever repeat this, I'll make sure you regret it."

"I won't say anything, Simon. Blood oath, remember?"

Stunned, Barry got up to leave. A freak like Simon working for the CIA.

"Consider it, Bar. My contact is right here on campus. And you wouldn't have to work on campus or even in the old U.S. of A. You could play in Europe this summer, all expenses paid."

Barry shook his head. "Not for me."

A week later, after two nights of insomnia and nightmares about dying in the jungle, Barry went to Simon's room and said, "How do I contact your friend?"

"Smartest move you'll ever make, Bar, lad. I'll have him contact you."

Which he did, on the steps of the Low Library during a demonstration against the latest bombing announced by

Robert McNamara. It all happened so casually that Barry was astonished—not the last time he'd be astonished in his dealing with the CIA.

"Hey, man, would you hold this sign, while I light a J?"

Some undergrads were astride the sundial burning their draft cards—one was using a gold Cartier cigarette lighter. Everyone was watching, cheering. Barry took the sign—OUT NOW! NO MORE LIES!—and looked at the slender guy who popped a tightly rolled stick of grass between his lips, smiled through a honey-gold moustache and unclipped, full beard, and inhaled deeply. Barry had seen him before on campus, but didn't know him. When the guy offered him a hit off the joint, Barry frowned. Barry figured he was a major head. He handed the sign back and moved away through the crowd.

The guy ditched the sign and followed. "You and me got something in common," he said. Despite his toking, his eyes were sharply blue, alert. A slight rash of acne pitted his lower cheeks. He wasn't in any way distinctive from the other few hundred male students yelling.

"You got a dick, too?" Barry asked. "Congratulations."

"I've got a dick and a buddy named Simon Costain."

Barry looked again. "You trying to tell me you're the guy who's getting him a trip to Europe?"

"Call me the travel agent! Let's go. I'm all demo'ed out."

Barry followed him off campus across and down Broadway to a Hungarian restaurant. The guy introduced himself as Alex Land and said hello to a half-dozen Maoists eating chicken paprikash.

"What if any of these folks knew you were heat?" Barry asked.

"I'm not heat on them," Land made it clear. "I have one job. I'm after foreign agents. Period."

"Sure."

"Believe it or not. You interested?"

"I'm probably going to split to Canada anyway," Barry finished.

"Then Mr. Alex has a magic solution expressly for you.

57

Mind you, all this *can* be dangerous. They're getting wise to us being over there."

"Simon didn't say anything about danger."

"Company policy, always have to warn volunteers."

"What kind of danger?"

"Well, for a sensitive football jock like yourself . . ." Alex pondered, as Barry thought what a joke Land was. For all the others in the restaurant knew, they were closing a deal for window-pane acid or something. "But seriously, we do sometimes like to see our men work for it."

"Meaning?"

"You'll see." Bushy eyebrows fluttered behind taffy-colored hair falling across his forehead. "You see, we've decided this summer we're going into them really *deep*. Round up some big ones. Maybe close their shop. You want in, you get to share the glory."

"What's happened to make you decide that?"

"Let's just say some of our guys got themselves dead. *Not* pickers, like you'll be though."

"I can handle myself," Barry declared.

"Great! Tomorrow night come to this address and bring enough cash to buy half a lid of grass off me."

"Why?"

"Some other folks have to look you over."

"I'll be there."

Two months later, Barry was checking out the pushcart vendors along the *rive gauche,* riffling through old postcards, when Land slid into his peripheral vision. It was a fresh, sunny early afternoon, a gorgeous day in late June. Barry had just lifted out two splendid illustrations in profile of a Bugatti Royale and a Mercedes SK drophead coupé, circa 1933.

"Like 'em? Buy 'em!"

"I don't know," Barry said. "They'll probably get crushed before I can get them home."

"Get 'em framed first."

Barry weighed them in his hand. Maybe. They were light. Cheap enough, superbly drafted. His two absolute favorite cars. They'd never made handsomer models. "I guess I could mail them home."

"Better yet," Land suggested, "hang them up right here. You're settling down for a while."

"Yeah?"

"You're going to be auditing courses in medieval law at the Sorbonne. Think how great that'll look on your school record. How's your French?"

"Not bad."

Barry did buy the two illustrations, and had them rolled up. Land treated Barry to lunch at a local bistro.

"So where is it that I'm settling down?" Barry finally asked.

"Rue du Champignon. Not far from school. It's a pension. You'll have a studio under the dormers, top floor. Nice view. Your own toilet, but you share the bath with another tenant."

"And I do what?"

"You study medieval law at the Sorbonne."

"Stop jerking my chain, Land."

Alex's blue eyes were those of a six-year-old. "Hey! That's all I've been told."

"All right, so I just lay low?"

"Check. Mrs. K. G. and B. are now aware that we've got us some wonderful pickers, and we're walking all over them. So they'll be out looking for us. But we've still got some big apples to pick. Operation Clean Sweep has just changed name, codes, and directives. It's now called Little Broom, and we're going after one particular person, code-named Rapunzel. You're Golden Straw. And me, I'm . . . Rumpelstiltskin!"

"Come on, Alex, what is all this shit?"

"I don't know how you fit in yet."

"Obviously you do. Refresh my memory, what exactly did Rumpelstiltskin do?"

"He spun straw into gold." Land's eyebrows were dancing à la Groucho.

"And I'm your straw?"

"You could be fools' gold. But"—and here Alex laughed—"We don't really know if we can move yet. So you're laying low. Low, lower, and lowest. Got it?"

"That's beautiful country around there, sir. Horse country," the woman at the car-rental booth at National Airport said when Barry asked for a road map to find the address he'd been given by the man in Archives at the CIA. Perfect description: The hills rolled green as a billiard table, with white-fir fences and, here and there, primrose ha-has for a beauty of a roan to sail over.

No sign announced Little Raphank Farm, but this next gate had to be it. Sure enough, there were red brick stables in double rows and, of course, an orchard in the background—white with pear blossoms—then the inevitable riding ring, and, behind that, the house: large, Jeffersonian, white columns, fan-light windows, the works!

A tall whiplash of a woman in ebony leather slacks and a gray chamois shirt was turning a skittish chestnut colt in a wide circle on a long lead; she was talking to the young animal all the while. She half turned as he drove by, and Barry thought, Yes, that would be Alex's type. He drove on along the high hedges and walls that half hid the house from the road and out the other side; kept driving till he reached a small, abandoned-looking building. He parked close to its wall and slowly walked back toward the house, keeping near the wall as much as possible; old habits died hard, and one always approached potential trouble with only one side open.

"Hold it there, sir!" The voice was behind him, young and unfrightened. Barry turned. The boy was about fifteen, the gun a sawed-off rifle. "You are trespassing, sir, on private property!"

"You're the fifth person today to call me sir," Barry said. "Have I aged suddenly, or what?"

"Please turn around and I'll escort you back to your vehicle."

"The hell you will! Tell your father, or whatever relation Alex Land is to you, that I'm here. Pointing that thing is rude. Put it down."

There was a moment in which the boy might have done anything—burst into tears, shot him. Then Barry heard a voice over a walkie-talkie attached to the boy's belt: "Bring him here, Dean. Barry? Is that really you?"

The change in Alex Land wasn't so enormous, really. In spite of a slight gut, he still had basically the same slender, longish body. His "beetle brows" were more unruly, threaded with gray hair. The beard was gone, the moustache a western cut that reminded Barry of TV Texans. His florid complexion was a bit less mottled, but his smile was as photogenic as ever, and his blue eyes just as sharp as they'd been when he was twenty.

"This Land is still your Land," Alex said, hand out, big grin.

"You bastard!" Barry pretended delight, hugged Alex, pulled back. "All you fucking sixties hippies struck it rich! Those cutthroat Monopoly games we played should have warned me."

"Okay, Dean," Alex tried not to dismiss the boy. "Nice job. But this fucker could talk himself into the pope's *pissoir*."

Off the hook, Dean stepped back.

"Surprised, eh?" Land asked, sitting them down poolside. Barry took off his shoes, dangled his feet in the cool water.

"Great spread you have. I'm not even going to ask how."

"My last operation. That's when I met Win. You must have seen her out back at the ring. She thought that I was far too good-looking to have to work for a living, so she brought me here. She knows the horses. I'm just the business end, sort of a glorified accountant. It's easy living. Dean," he went on, anticipating questions, "is Win's by a very shiny gentleman lately of Bar Harbor and Nob Hill. There's another boy, too."

"Also on guard duty?"

"These high-bred boys need lots of discipline." Pause. "I'm not going to ask how you found me. But what the hell brings you here? Last time we saw each other, you tried to strangle me."

"Garrote you, to be precise."

"I was in big trouble for a minute or so. I trust you're all over that?"

"*Agua* under the *ponte*. Except . . ." —waiting to see how Land would react—"except, that lately I've been wondering about . . . our mutual friend, and thought I'd look her up."

Land could not hide his surprise. "*Anna*? You're kidding!"

"Not at all, Alex. I'm sure she's forgiven me. It's a long time, God knows."

Land seemed really uncomfortable. "Come on, Barry. The past . . . well, it's something else, you know?"

"I know. I just want to see Anna again. What harm is there in that?"

"You know that's not possible."

"I'm sure she's all clear by now."

"Barry! The operation was a failure! Anna was killed by the KGB! You saw it yourself!"

"I didn't see it. I always assumed it was a cover."

"Look, Barry. It's real good seeing you and everything, but facts are facts."

"Anna didn't die, Alex. No matter what you said then. No matter what you say now. I've met her daughter. Our daughter."

"Shit, Barry! This is like . . . I don't know, fantasy time or something! It's really weird." Taking him by the shoulder, Alex walked him away from the pool. "You're moving into uncharted waters here. Let me be your friend, okay? Even though I'm not closely connected anymore, I could work it out so the government pays for you to see someone."

Barry had half expected this. He shrugged away from Land.

"Hey!" Alex went on. "If you don't believe me, ask . . . well, who the hell's still there?"

Then, quietly, Alex the psychiatrist: "Anna bought it, Barry. Seventeen years ago. I know you believed it then. Hell, I still have scars on my neck from that hawser chain. That's how much you believed it, and how much you blamed me, rightly or wrongly."

Five little red marks where the hawser screws had bitten in deeply. Yes, Barry could see them. He'd meant to kill Land then, had pulled back only in the last second when he'd realized he himself was to blame for Anna's death.

"I'm never going to apologize," Barry said.

"Hey! Understood! But I thought you were over it?"

"Maybe I just wanted to hear you say it, Alex. Maybe after all this time I wanted to hear from your lips that Anna was killed."

"You got it, Barry."

"Fine! How about a vodka tonic and a change of subject?"

"You always were a sly fucker, Barry! I never did know what to make of you."

It took over an hour, a rather extensive tour of the farm, and more patience than Barry thought he possessed to get Alex to forget the subject. The wife was visited. She was even taller and sexier up close than Barry had figured; older, too. She sized Barry up fast, didn't really like any of Alex's old friends, but might make an exception in his case. By then Alex was relaxed, his old self again, until he asked:

"By the way, what's this about a daughter?"

"Pretty kid I thought looked like Anna."

"Golden boy becomes old lecher. Don't laugh. If the shoe fits . . . and it could happen."

"She disappeared anyway."

A horse and its rider dashed up the gravel toward them, in a mad scramble to stop. A boy in a riding cap dismounted. Taller than Dean, different features than his brother's or mother's—all sharpness subsumed in an almost feminine beauty. Angelic features. The boy pulled off his cap to reveal, not the expected military crew cut, but a tumble of pale blond curls.

"When I passed the old field barn, I saw"—he had to get his breath—"dozens of them! This big!" He spread his hands two feet apart. "Just like Pete said. There must be nests of them!"

"Calm down," Alex ordered. "Get Dean, and a few more guns."

Turning to Barry: "Looks like you're in time for a rat hunt."

They started off, and the boys caught up with them as they were crossing a dried mud road. Across a weedy unused pasture were two large, decrepit-looking barns with a silo.

Just outside the big barn, all four stopped to load their rifles.

The years-old hay was alive with motion the minute they entered. The blond boy was sent upstairs to lift the loft gate for better light. Meanwhile, Alex and Dean found some old, half-filled cans of gasoline.

All in a line once again, they cocked their rifles, released their safeties. Barry couldn't help but think, Look at these kids! Scared, excited. What bullshit!

"Ready?" Alex asked.

"I am," Barry replied.

"You bet!" the blond teen enthused.

Alex tossed one can of gasoline into the midst of the hay. It landed hard, and immediately sank out of sight. A hundred brown objects dashed out.

Ba-boom! Ba-boom!

For five minutes, they shot and reloaded and shot again. One rat came out directly at them, and the blond boy casually stomped it with a bootheel, then jammed its head with the rifle butt just to make sure. The air was blue and acrid with smoke.

The rats weren't easy targets: They were terrified and fast

and unpredictable; they were also survivors. The two men and two boys moved forward slowly, methodically, prodding the hay with their feet and shooting at whatever moved, and after a while, nothing jumped out.

"Got 'em!" the blond boy said.

"Get those rakes," Alex commanded, and the boys put down their rifles and obeyed. "Keep stirring," Alex said, as he loped up next to the area of old hay they were clearing with pitchforks. The first nests were only a few feet deep. Barry almost gagged on the odor and the sight of a dozen blind, pink, slimy, squiggling creatures. Dean had pulled back from the distasteful work, but the other kid was really going at it, using his boots and pitchfork to kill any creatures old enough to try to escape.

Alex applied the gasoline, then dropped a match. The squeaking was terrific, the stench even worse.

"Keep raking!" Alex shouted at the boys. "There're dozens of nests here."

The sport was done for Barry. He put down his rifle and backed off, watching another flame shoot up from another nest. Then he turned and went outside for fresh air. He'd just lit a cigarette when he noticed a good-sized rat out on a tuft of weeds not twenty feet away, looking on: Mamma got away, but she couldn't stay away. Barry threw a rock, and the rat slinked off.

After a minute or so, Dean stumbled out of the barn, green-faced, dazed. Barry grabbed the boy and sat him down fast against the side of the barn, leaning his head over his knees. Dean began to retch, but nothing came up. Barry continued to hold him until the boy looked up, pleading.

"I don't know how you stood the stink that long," Barry said.

"I hate it."

The boy retched again, and a little bit of brown liquid came up. The boy stood up and squashed it into the dirt.

"He ever tell you I almost killed him?" Barry asked.

"I don't hate him or anything. . . ."

Barry sat Dean down again and squatted next to him. "I hated him."

"But you were friends!" Dean protested. "He told me how you two bagged the KGB's biggest operator."

Go on, a voice inside Barry urged, tell the kid his step-daddy is a scumbag.

"And made the world safe for democracy," Barry said, "or whatever the hell it was that we did." He grabbed the kid by his shoulder. "Get out of here! You're not right here, you understand? You're not like your brother. What's his name?"

"Brother?" Dean asked weakly, as though unable to understand. Then: "You mean Tim in there?"

"Right! You're not like Tim. Go be a poet or something, okay? But get away from here as soon as you can. Look me up when you get to Boston."

"There they are!" Alex came out of the barn, the other teen behind him, flushed with effort, doubtless puffed up with Land's compliments for not finking out. "I guess I should have warned you guys about that part of the hunt."

Above them, a cloud of dark smoke rose through the barn-loft door, continuing to fritter away the remains of a thousand infant rats.

"How about a nip of scotch guys? Dean?"

Both boys were given a full glass at the house but drank only a quarter-inch or so before thanking Alex again and stepping out of the study. The way that Dean looked in Barry's direction as he left made him certain the kid had gotten his message, or at least *a* message: something to make him consider.

"Got to live on a farm sometime, Barry."

"Spare me the eclogue, Alex. Anyway, it's time I got back to D.C."

"Word of advice? Forget Anna. And don't fuck with the past, Barry. It's nothing but heartache."

As Barry left the house, he saw Dean standing near his

66

rented car. He didn't speak, indeed seemed to have forgotten the incident at the barn.

". . . a poet, a beach bum. Anything but what he wants you to be! You hear?" Barry shouted as he started up the engine. Before he could take off though, Dean stepped over to the window. He looked behind himself, then said:

"That woman you were talking about? Anna? She's still alive."

Barry's eyes met the boy's own: He'd made a friend. Better than that, they both had the same enemy.

"You sure about this? This is important."

"I'm sure! I heard him talking about her with some other guys a while back. She runs some sort of boutique in Big Sur, California. I don't know what it's called."

Barry offered a hand to shake. "If you're right, I owe you a big one!"

Dean backed away from the car.

"You shouldn't have let him live," he said. "Not when you had the chance!"

"Next time, I won't," Barry said. "That's a promise."

There was chatter on the walkie-talkie, and Dean waved Barry on.

Anna was still alive, alive and living in California!

CHAPTER FOUR

"You're going to hate me," Barry said into the telephone, waiting for his employee to throw a fit. "I've got to stay away a little longer." Nothing from Elaine immediately, so he asked how things were at the store.

"Okay," Elaine had answered. She'd seemed distracted, not at all upset. "It's okay, I guess. You needed a break." Then, in a slightly less indifferent tone of voice: "Have you used your new toy yet?"

"Not yet." Barry had the portable computer and its modem attachment in a slim attaché case by his side. "Why don't we try it? Hang up. I'll set it up and ring again."

The computer fit on the telephone-booth shelf, and the phone receiver fit right into place. He punched in the commands, and watched the computer screen.

EPHEMERIS SHOP!
Is that you, Barry?

Barry typed back, "Sure is."

"Look, about Prints. Is it true he wants to move things around here?"

"He showed me some plans. And I like some of his ideas. Why, he say anything?"

"What he told me seemed okay." Then, a bit more enthusiastically: "He told me about the last place he worked at and how he fixed that up."

"You think he just changes shops around and moves on?"

"He seems to like it here in Boston."

"Do I sense romance? I always thought your type was two-hundred-pound defensive tackles."

"Barry! That's not true."

"Well, while you're busy being seduced, make sure he doesn't walk off with the cash register, okay? I'll check in again tomorrow."

"Do you want to leave a number where we can reach you?" was Elaine's last message.

"I'm sure that between the two of you, you can handle whatever comes up," Barry typed. The truth was, he didn't know exactly where he'd be. He was making this call from a public phone in a rampway at San Francisco International Airport's arrivals building. A few minutes later, he walked up into the glass-enclosed sunlight, rented his second car in two days, began his second car trip into the past. What had Marty Kalb said? Take the path? As though Kyra had stepped in the door of his shop and thrown open other doors he'd closed years ago.

"So you're laying low. Low, lower, and lowest. Got it?" Alex had said that long-ago day in Paris.

"Low" turned out to mean the top floor, which meant under the roof, which in the summer, even with an electric fan, was too hot for clothing. An old woman in the facing building saw Barry in his BVDs, harrumphed quite loudly, and slammed her shutters on him.

Ten days of living as an American student picking up extra credits at the Sorbonne passed. The lectures were three times a week, late in the afternoon, located in what he thought was a former medical amphitheater (until he was told all the lecture halls looked like that) attended by close to a hundred students. The crowd managed to turn the huge room into a hot box despite the high, open casement windows. The warm weather, the lecturer's monotone, the limited interest Barry had in the subject of early French law (exactly how did *droit de seigneur* begin? The Roman's didn't have it), and his limited abilities to comprehend French legal jargon induced a stupor (some dozen students had already succumbed). He finally roused himself enough to list the places he would visit the next day—the Jeu de Paumes, a bookshop on the rue de Rivoli, the barge docks. He was a tourist and loving it. He sent home postcards and inexpensive little presents every other day. He lounged with his Sorbonne classmates at cafés on the Boul' Mich looking at girls. Twice a day some Parisian made an outrageous offer to buy his Levi 501's. When, finally, a handsome, well-dressed woman asked to buy them, Barry had replied in his best French that his pants weren't for sale, although what they contained could be hers for free. She'd trilled a laugh. "You think I don't pay for that, too?" She walked off laughing at her own witticism.

It was almost as hot at night as it was during the day; Barry would lie in bed, directly in front of the electric fan, and read Proust's endless sentences.

A timid knocking on his door. Then louder. A young woman's voice: *"Au secours!"*

When Barry leaped out of bed and unlocked the door, he saw it was the mysterious tenant who shared his bathroom and whom he'd seen but once before going down the stairs, a day after he'd moved in. Now, she was barefoot, wearing a pink slip, and terrified.

She pulled him toward her apartment, and he dashed in looking for the intruder. The studio—identical to his own—was empty.

"Voilà!" she pointed, and Barry saw the tail of a mouse flash around the corner of a cabinet.

"But it's only a—"

She shoved a coal scuttle into his hands and pushed him forward, then she cowered behind the studio door.

Poor mouse! Barry had seen it a few days ago picking at

the rind of a piece of Emmenthal he'd left on a plate near his bed. The mouse had scampered away; then, when Barry had kept still, it had come back and nibbled long enough for Barry to see how tiny and ill fed it was.

Still, for her sake, he pretended to hunt it down from one corner of the room to the other.

"Elle est là-bas!" she yelled, pointing to a spot three yards away, and Barry lunged after it. He actually did glimpse the mouse again, and he raised hell trying to scare it out of the room. He charged into another corner knocking off wall plaster with the coal scuttle. The mouse finally escaped, as Barry slipped on a small throw rug and came down on his butt with a thud.

"Oh! You're hurt!" She spoke English.

"It's gone." He tried to catch his breath.

The girl—she couldn't have been more than eighteen— warily looked around the room. She *knew* it was foolish to be afraid of mice, but she couldn't help herself. Her chest was heaving with excitement, her slip had dropped a strap off her shoulder. The pink silk slid to the very nipple of one perfectly formed breast.

She noticed, lifted the strap and said: "You're the American law student."

"Yes, ma'am," he replied. He then introduced himself, adding, "I don't think our little friend will bother you for a while."

"Anna Grigorievna Kuragin," she said, taking his hand. "Anna what?"

"Grigorievna Kuragin. I am a music student."

He repeated all her names. It came out garbled. She corrected him slowly, and he followed her pronunciation, staring into the largest pair of deep blue eyes he'd even seen, ringed with dark lashes, set in . . .

"You see, Gregori is the name of my father. The patronymic," she explained. "In Russia we call a person by the first name and the patronymic. Kuragin is my family name."

It was at that moment that he realized that he was standing

in front of her wearing only his underwear, and he had an erection and she . . . she was completely unperturbed. "I'd better go now," he said.

"Wait!" she called as he reached the door. "Thank you. You will soon have—" she searched for the words,—"a surprising experience! A musical experience."

Before he could ask what she meant, the door was closed on him.

A full two days went by before he saw her again. This time it was because of a poster in French and Cyrillic on a kiosk outside the Luxembourg Gardens announcing a concert by an emigré chamber orchestra playing that night. The oboist, Dimitri Semyonovich Tikhov—a recent defector from the Soviet Union—was to be featured in a benefit performance, playing concerti by Telemann. Joining Tikhov in J. S. Bach's Duo Concerto in C minor was a violinist listed as A. G. Kuragin.

Could it be her? Barry bought a ticket ten minutes before the performance. He was one of the few people in the audience not part of the large Russian emigré community in Paris. He walked around during the intermission wondering whether he'd wasted his money.

"You know Tikhov?"

Barry turned and saw Sergey Ravlev, who suffered two seats away in medieval law.

"I *think* I know Kuragin."

"Anna Grigorievna?"

So it was her. "She's my neighbor. We share a bath."

"Aaaah!" Sergey said.

"Don't say 'ah' like that, Sergey. I just met her. God knows I've heard her playing, but I didn't know she was good enough for, you know, this."

"If she had remained in Moscow," Sergey said with a sigh, "she would be world famous today. Instead, she chose freedom—and this—obscurity!"

"She defected?"

"She was fifteen. Her parents managed to get her out. They had 'pull.' They were party members in high standing—intelligentsia—but since Anna Grigorievna came here, it has not been easy. One might almost say that her life is a tragedy."

Chimes were ringing in the lobby, and Sergey excused himself and dashed away toward an overdressed dowager with whom he'd come.

Anna appeared onstage in a mannish blue suit and a crisp, frilly white blouse. Her hair was plaited almost peasant fashion in back of her head, a few wisps of hair over her brow softened the otherwise stark effect. Next to the squat, slovenly, red-headed Tikhov, who swayed and hopped and played with his heart on his sleeve, Anna seemed restrained, almost wooden. Until the second movement, when her violin playing wove in and out of the oboe line so tenderly, so sensuously, that Barry was reminded of how she'd looked when they'd met in her room, and perspiration had broken out on his forehead. The finale was light and delicious. An ovation followed.

"You're not leaving?" Sergey asked. He was standing with an ancient man of military bearing who looked as though he'd once led a cavalry charge at Sebastopol. "We must congratulate the artists. And you must also meet Dimitri Semyonovich."

Barry let Sergey and his elderly friend drag him into the green room, filled with people and noise. He was rather hastily introduced to the star oboist.

"American!" Tikhov said in English. "You know jazz?"

"Afraid not. But I love the Bach concerto."

"Aaah, Bach!" And Tikhov sailed into Russian.

Sergey translated, and Barry tried to concentrate and not look around too obviously through the crush for Anna.

She found him still in Tikhov's clutches a few minutes later, as Barry attempted to fend off another vodka.

"So, you didn't tell me you like music!" she said far less shy than before, evidently relaxed among her own people, in

73

her own element. Before Barry could answer, Anna was pulled away by admirers. She shrugged at him as though saying, "What am I to do?"

"Dimitri Semyonovich says that not since Oistrakh and Kogan has he heard such a violinist as Anna Grigorievna" said a middle-aged lady who had materialized at Barry's side.

"Yes, of course," Barry agreed, trying to find Anna among all those heads. He remembered that she'd told him he'd have a surprise musical experience. How had Anna known that?

That night he tried to remain awake till she arrived home, but he fell asleep. The next morning when he knocked on her door, she had gone out already. At least that was what the concierge told him.

So it wasn't until that evening that he heard Anna step into the bath between the two small studios, heard the running water, and decided he had to see her. He waited until she had been there some fifteen minutes, then emerged from his room with a towel over one shoulder, his soap and wash-cloth in one hand, and went to try the bath door handle. He knew it was a transparent move, but how else . . . ?

The door opened and Anna was standing there, a puce towel wrapped around her body, another around her head in a turban.

"Oh, God. Sorry. I . . ." he stammered; that absolutely direct gaze of hers stopped him. "I'll come back."

"I'm finished. I only hope there is hot water."

A joke, since there was seldom enough hot water for one bath.

"I'll go." She began gathering her things.

Barry stopped her, a hand on her hand. "I already bathed."

"Really?"

"You make me feel so clumsy. When all I want is . . ."

Unable to explain, he simply began kissing her.

To his amazement, Anna didn't stop him, but when he

74

was on his knees in front of her, she held his head up by the chin and said, "Yes."

They went into his room and made love. At first it was all heat and perspiration. She was strong, lithe as an athlete, and she moved quickly, so that at times she appeared to be wrestling for the best position. When he finally managed to hold her steady enough to enter her, Barry felt both of them go utterly still. Anna had already begun to climax, and she arched higher and higher and it seemed as though he weighed less than she did, instead of more than half again her weight.

He didn't know how she would react afterward, and he was pleased when she held his hand and remained close, despite the heat, despite the perspiration that soaked their bodies and the sheets. "You are so strong," she said. "You are an athlete?" she asked.

"Football. Wide receiver."

"It's been such a long time since . . ." she began, didn't complete the sentence.

"*You* were pretty tight," he said. He wondered if he could ask her about her previous experience.

"Now perhaps, we take a bath," she said, "together?"

"A little later. I'd like to . . . you know, again."

A half hour later, she said, "So this is American decadence we hear so much about, growing up in Moscow. And you must be an American degenerate."

"You haven't seen anything degenerate yet, ma'am." Barry laughed, then suddenly grew serious. "Anna, remember when you told me I'd have a musical experience a few days ago—and then I ended up at your concert? How did you know I would?"

Anna laughed, and her eyes sparkled. "Sometimes I know things like that."

Barry looked at her quizzically.

"Really," Anna said. "Ever since I was a little girl, I sometimes get 'feelings' that things will sometimes happen. I believe in English you call it ESP. It's very silly, really. I

75

think it's woman's intuition. But I was even tested for it back in Russia. The doctors were very interested."

"What did they find out?"

"Nothing, really. Nothing at all." Anna looked a little embarrassed, as if she'd revealed too much about herself. She refused to discuss it any further.

They bathed together, finally. She played her violin for him—Faure's *Elegie*. He used pillows and chairs to show her what a "post play" and "nickel defense" meant in football. They made love again and then remembered they hadn't had dinner yet. It was close to 3:00 A.M. but they managed to find a small Lebanese café still open and stuffed themselves on tabouleh and falafel. They walked along the Île de la Cité as the birds began to wake up and sing. They returned back up to the top floor, and without a word of protest, she followed him into his room, where they pulled the shutters against the dawn light and slept.

"Sounds great," Alex said. He and Barry had met, as usual, once during the week on the steps of the Opera.

"So what's this new girlfriend like? What do you two talk about?"

"I'm crazy about her. And Anna feels the same about me." Barry paused. "But what about, you know, work?"

"Far as I know, you're still on your own, Barry."

"Do you think it will still happen? Operation Little Broom, I mean?"

"Can't say. I'm just hanging around myself. Met me a good hash connection down in the Vietnamese section of town, not to mention a great chick named Cao Han. I'm doing all I can to personally make up to her for our national bad behavior in her homeland."

"What I mean is," Barry tried to find the words, "what if I skipped this coming term at school and stayed here in Paris? I'd pay rent in the pension, if I had to . . . and . . ."

"You mean you'd be willing to wait around for the

76

operation? Sounds great, Barry. Shows stick-to-itiveness, gumption, all those other good old American Eagle Scout virtues."

"If Little Broom is still on."

"You really want to catch Rapunzel, don't you?" Land said. "Or do you want to stay here because of your new girl?"

"Sure I want to stay because of Anna. But didn't you say that Rapunzel was the top man in the KGB's European network? The meanest, orneriest . . . ?"

"Nah. All *I* said was that Rapunzel was the KGB's linchpin. We're not sure exactly *how* he or she works. We don't even know if Rapunzel *does* anything. Rapunzel is a real smoothie, and the KGB knows well enough not to dirty up their centerpiece with all sorts of activity. Am I getting it across?"

Not really, Barry admitted. It was all rather vague, and he was only half listening, because as Land described their quarry, he might be anyone, and probably someone it would be difficult to get near: some French minister's wife or important industrialist. He'd probably be surrounded at all times by bodyguards, or at least by protective servants. Maybe the Company was beginning to rethink the operation—and Barry's part in it. He hoped he could string them along a while longer.

"So, I'll certainly put in your request," Land was saying. "Whether it's accepted or not, it will be a further sign of your interest." He stopped. "When do your classes begin at Columbia?"

"I have to be there the twenty-second to register."

"We've still got a month. So tell me more," Alex changed the subject again. "Is it true what they say about Russian women? It isn't true about Asians."

"What do they say . . . ? Jerk!" Barry realized he was being had. "And she isn't really Russian. She's White Russian. It's a separate nationality. Her grandfather was a prominent physicist so he didn't end up a victim of Stalin's purges.

Her mother was a scientist, too, so she grew up privileged. You'll meet her, of course."

"Sure. Let's double date." He laughed. "If Colby only knew exactly *how* we were screwing the enemy!"

"I told you before, Alex, she's . . . Oh, what the hell!"

"You really like her, don't you." Alex said.

"But what will you do?"

"I'll stay here. My visa's good for years if I leave the country every few months. I'll hop over to London or Amsterdam for a day."

"And how will you live?" Anna asked.

"I have some money put away back in the States," Barry said. "I'll have my folks wire it."

"But what if they won't? What if they want you?"

"It seems to me that you're throwing up obstacles that don't yet exist. Maybe you don't want me to stay. Maybe you've got another lover."

"What lover? Who?"

"I don't know. Sergey!"

"Sergey! How ridiculous! Sergey has hair growing out of his nose."

"Don't you want me to stay in Paris?"

"You won't! You'll leave Paris soon," she said, sadly.

"If you're here, I'll stay forever. Really."

"Forever?"

" . . . "

And later on:

"You know we're double-dating tomorrow with my friend Alex and his girl. He's not really a friend. I just met him over here. I knew him a bit at school, where I believe—now don't be scandalized, Anna—where he dealt drugs. See, I knew you'd be surprised. Come back here. That's better. Just grass—marijuana to you. But he's latched onto this Vietnamese girl. He's a radical at Columbia, more than me. Very antiwar. Always at demonstrations. And before you ask, yes, we *have to*. Okay? For my sake. It *won't* be a long night tomorrow with them. We'll make up some reason to leave early.

"..."

A week later, it was still, "No. Not yet," though it was Labor Day weekend back in the States and Paris was filling up again with the millions who'd abandoned it in August. Anna wouldn't explain why he should wait to tell his parents he wasn't returning to Columbia. She brought up all the usual arguments, then some irrational ones, and Barry would stare at her speechless wondering why, why, why? Was he interfering in her life? No, she said. Then, yes. She hadn't played with her string quartet in weeks, not since they'd . . . And she never practiced enough anymore. She didn't seem to have enough time for Barry *and* the music.

So Barry said he'd go to a movie and she could play with her three friends the next day. That worked, and the following afternoon, Anna went off to meet with a pianist. He did not like her absence, but he did agree to it.

It was that day that Barry's first suspicion about Anna arose. He was just coming in the door when he saw a familiar older man leaving the little lobby of the pension. Barry was certain the man had been at Anna's benefit concert with Tikhov, and that Sergey Ravlev had introduced them. But when Barry said hello, the older man turned his head away and stalked off. Later that evening, Barry mentioned the visitor to Anna, and she denied knowing who he was talking about.

"Sure you remember him. He was at the green room. Wearing some kind of uniform. He talked to you."

"Oh, Barry, everyone talked to me that night."

So he dropped it.

Barry sought out Sergey in his usual café, and point-blank asked him about the old, military-looking gentleman he'd been with at the concert.

Yes, Sergey said, he was a pianist, a teacher, too. But Sergey didn't know much about that aspect of General Detloff's life. Anna would know more. After all, they'd given a recital together at the Salle Pleyel the previous year. Didn't they still play together?

Barry had never experienced jealousy before. He was astonished by how quick and insidious it was, how relentlessly it constructed a second, secret life in his mind for Anna. Of course, old man Detloff was her accompanist. But she hadn't been practicing with Detloff when she said she'd been. She'd been off that afternoon meeting her lover, the man whom she'd hidden from Barry; someone she'd probably met and known long before; someone even less acceptable to her emigré set than he, and the reason why she kept saying, "No. Not yet," whenever he wanted to make definite plans to remain in Paris for the autumn.

Oddly, the jealousy struck him only when Anna was out or about to go out. Whenever she returned, he kissed her with relief and never thought of her betrayal—Anna so filled up his life when she was there.

Sometimes he insisted upon going along with her to her rehearsals with the string players, and he'd remain outside the building for three-quarters of an hour, before he'd stalk home, feeling like a fool.

He never knew what exactly it was that made him follow her secretly one afternoon. Perhaps the manner in which Anna had taken up her violin case, then hesitated, put it down, and finally picked it up again. Or perhaps it was that she had put on not his favorite red silk scarf, but instead a pale, almost transparent purple one. Something set off all sorts of alarms in him, though, and the minute she was out the door, Barry was dressed and following her.

She descended into a metro station, and he did, too. He hid behind a pillar while waiting for the train to arrive, and leaped into another car where he could keep her in sight. It was a long subway ride through the northern industrial suburbs, and he almost missed her getting off, but managed to hold open the door and wiggle through at the last second. She was walking ahead, oblivious to him.

Outside, the glare of the afternoon sun was reflected a

thousand times by tall glass buildings, an apartment complex of some sort under construction. Construction machines idled and sat empty for the day. The signs around him gave a bucolic name to what was in effect a housing project, which perhaps had replaced orchards and farms.

Barry hid behind an earth-moving vehicle and looked at concrete benches, footpaths, and reflecting pools, awaiting a final lacquering or truckload of gravel. The place was huge, yet in no way grand.

She entered a building, one of four towers of future residences that faced the central courtyards. So it *was* true, what he'd suspected, what he'd feared, and her lover must be what? A construction worker? A site foreman? How had Anna met him? Where did they keep their trysts? Which of those hundreds of unfinished apartments in that huge building?

He felt suddenly drained. Then so angry, he started forward. He would follow her inside. Follow her and knock on every door on every floor of that building until . . .

"Don't!"

Barry turned to the voice. Alex Land!

"You're making a mistake."

"What? Why are you . . . ? You followed me, didn't you?"

"Not *you*," Alex said, it seemed sadly.

It took him a minute. "You followed Anna? Why?"

Before Alex could answer, Barry spun out of the other man's grip, suddenly chilled.

"C'mon, man! Get yourself together. Let's go over there," Alex said. "To get out of sight."

When they'd reached a spot behind a huge abstract sculpture of poured concrete, Alex pulled a small silver flask out of the pocket of his worn chamois jacket and offered it to Barry. Barry took it, sipped, sputtered most of the liquor out again. The premonition again, icy within him.

"She's KGB."

"Please, God," Barry moaned, "don't let this happen to—"

"Shut up a minute and listen." Alex grabbed him. "More than just KGB. She's our Rapunzel."

Barry looked up at the stony blue sky. "Why?"

"We planted something a while ago. It was supposed to arrive at this very spot at this very moment by an extremely circuitous route."

"You're wrong, Alex. She's . . . !"

"It was foolproof."

"It can't . . . I don't believe . . ."

"It's unimportant *what* you believe, Barry. We've been setting this up for five months. It's true, period. You were our extra set of eyes and ears. Now listen carefully. We can take her in one of two ways. Smooth or rough. It's up to you. If you really care for her, then help us, and Anna will not be hurt. There is *no* reason for us to hurt her. Quite the opposite. But if there's a hint that we're onto her, she's dead. They'll kill her."

"You told me Rapunzel is the linchpin without whom the entire network will fall apart. Anna can't be . . ."

"Believe me, Barry, we have ways of knowing these things."

He grabbed Barry. "We're going back to your place and we're getting all your stuff and you're leaving. Right now. You'll write a note for her saying you were called back—family illness or some shit like that. Then you're on the first plane out of Orly, no matter *where* it's heading for. If you won't help us, I won't have you in the way. Don't try anything, Barry. I have a gun here and I'll use it on you."

Barry remained quiet. Then: "How will you do it?"

"I don't know. We'll take her. We'll protect her. But you saw how nasty the Sovs are. When someone is deemed no longer useful, they're garbage, thrown away."

"You're one-hundred-percent certain it's her?"

"Yes."

"And if I agree to help you? What then?"

"It's too late for that, Barry."

"No! It can't be, Alex. Trust me. I can't see her get killed.

I can't. I'll do anything you want. Just tell me. Tell me, Alex," he pleaded.

"Will she go wherever you take her?" Alex asked.

"Yes, I'm certain. When?"

"As soon as possible. Tomorrow is Saturday. That's best."

"She has a concert at two P.M. tomorrow. Right afterward, I can get her to come."

Now Barry grabbed Alex by his lapels, gun be damned. "I'll bring her. But you have to promise, no, you have to *swear*, that you won't hurt her. If I find out that you've hurt her in any way, I'll kill you."

"I swear it."

"I mean it, Alex. I'll follow you to the ends of the earth and . . ."

"I said, I swear it."

"Then it's on," Barry declared. "I'll bring her, after the concert."

"I thought I might see you here." Sergey sidled up to where Barry thought he'd pretty well hidden himself for the intermission outside the small lobby of the Théâtre de la Musique. To their right, the Beaux Arts Institute loomed, blocking out anything else along the rue de Caire. Straight ahead, in the distance, one might see the very top of the back of the steeple of Sacré Coeur. Lovely as it was, Barry was no longer sure how he felt about Paris.

"Let me have one of those, will you?" Barry pointed to Sergey's cigarettes.

Sergey slid one of the ecru cylinders out of the squat orange packet and lit it for Barry, who inhaled the perfumy taste and used the business of exhaling to cover the nervousness he was certain must be evident in his voice. "What made you think you'd see me here?"

"Anna Grigorievna has developed quite a following of admirers. Especially now that she's no longer dressing like a major domo on stage. You like it?"

"The concert? Sure. Oh, the cigarette? Don't know yet."

"Egyptian." Sergey showed him the packet with its Sphinx and camel drivers. "I didn't think you smoked." And when Barry didn't answer that: "Her tone is wonderful! So clear, yet so rich-hued."

"You're practicing your English on me again," Barry said.

"Why not? I'm not going to stay with this group of do-nothings in Paris all my life." Sergey gestured at the crowd out on the steps, and Barry thought they were probably exactly the same people who'd attended the Tikhov concert weeks ago, the same people who'd been at last week's Mayakovsky play, the same people who'd filled up the Bunin memorial reading two days ago. "America is where I'll end up," Sergey declared.

"Really."

In gesturing, Sergey had made eye contact with the old dowager he'd escorted before, and he now half bowed a greeting. No sense in riling her until he was ready to leave.

"Yes, really. You saw Detloff?" Sergey asked.

"I saw him."

Barry hadn't been able to help seeing the old military-looking man who'd snubbed him so recently. Detloff was onstage throughout the first half of the program—leading the orchestra from the harpsichord, embroidering the Mozart violin concerto Anna had played, then joining her and Tikhov in a Handel trio sonata. Doubtless he would be onstage again during the second half, too. Thankfully, that would be shorter, only one piece: a Haydn symphony.

Barry didn't know how much more he could take. Despite the soothing effect of the music, he was badly keyed up waiting for it to end, waiting for Alex to escort Anna away. Where was Alex, anyway? He hadn't been in the audience. Had he gotten here yet? Or would he arrive at the last minute?

It was a good thing Anna knew nothing; nothing but that

Alex and Cao Han were going to meet them. Imagine playing under that kind of stress.

"I told you he and Anna Grigorievna played together," Sergey said, and he looked mischievous.

"This is awful!" Barry threw down the cigarette and stamped it out on the step.

"An acquired taste." Sergey shrugged. "By the way, I have a note for you."

He handed Barry a closed American matchbook. Outside, it read, "Draw Me and You Too Can Be an Artist," with a profile of a snub-nosed girl and a Streisand bouffant hairdo. Inside was handwriting: "Trouble. Mrs. K's here. We leave as soon as A. leaves stage. Keep your eyes on the stage."

"Who gave you this?" Barry had turned around, looking for Alex.

"A Vietnamese girl. A pretty one. A billet-doux?"

"Something like that," Barry said, but even to him it sounded as though all tone had drained from his voice.

"People are beginning to go in," Sergey excused himself. "I should go say words to my last duchess."

Barry watched him slide through the crowd. The note was definitely from Alex—he always carried American matchbooks in this land of tiny little boxes of waxy *allumettes*—but what did it mean? That the KGB had gotten wind of a possible snatch? That the abduction was canceled? And how would Barry's role be affected? "Keep your eyes on the stage." He would have anyway. What was he supposed to be looking for?

Barry returned to his seat in the small theater, and as other concertgoers settled around him, he attempted to read the program notes. He suddenly felt conspicuous: too large, too casually dressed, too un-Russian, above all too anxious. Which made him try to concentrate all the more on what he was reading.

This symphony was appropriately enough called *Les Adieux*—the Farewell Symphony. It was one of fifty symphonies written when Haydn was composer and orchestra leader for the immensely wealthy prince of Esterhazy. The prince and his orchestra had been at the summer palace most of the summer of 1772, and the prince had extended his stay week by week until the musicians, missing their wives and families, who'd been left behind at Eisenstadt, begged Haydn's help. His solution had been an eloquent and witty joke. He wrote a symphony, the finale of which suddenly turned into a lilting adagio. During this, parts for the members of the orchestra dropped out, one by one. As their playing was done, the musicians would blow out the candles at their music stands and leave in twos and threes with instruments in hand, until only two, then only one, then no musicians were left on the stage. The prince got the idea that everybody wanted to leave. Anna had talked about the final movement a few days ago, and told Barry that she—as concertmaster—would be the last one on stage, playing all alone before she, too, left. The stage lights would dim, then go up again as the orchestra returned for applause. The original plan had been to spirit Anna away after the concert. Now, evidently they would not even wait for the curtain call. When the orchestra came back onstage, Anna would already be on her way to the airport.

The musicians were arriving now—Barry counted sixteen chairs—sitting down, chatting while leafing through their scores. Anna came onstage, looking lovely, and she remained standing while she tuned the violins and violas, then, satisfied, found her seat. There was scattered applause for her, and even more for Tikhov, who was first oboe, the great soloist humbling himself. The stage lights dimmed slightly, and Barry tried to make out the wings. Perhaps he should leave his seat during one of the earlier movements. No, Alex hadn't said to do that. Only: "Keep your eyes on the stage."

Detloff took his place at the harpsichord to more applause. It was then that Barry thought he saw the back left curtains part for an instant and, briefly, Alex's face. The symphony began.

Barry found his attention split between the music and

what he knew was about to happen. The first movement had an almost military clamor to it, and the old general at the harpsichord seemed to be watching over his troop of players and exhorting them with an occasional imperious gesture. The second movement was languid, beautiful, the violins muted against strange syncopations from the winds. Detloff didn't have much to do during the adagio, and Barry could have sworn the old man was looking around—had he seen Alex in the wings?—then toward the rear of the hall. Barry was too far forward to see if anyone was standing in the back.

The next movement was a trio, which, unlike the peasant dances Haydn usually favored, was somber, almost liturgical. It was barely over when the finale began, nervous strings and wheedling oboes charging along. "Keep your eyes on the stage," the note had said, and Barry kept his eyes on the stage, especially on Detloff, whom he didn't like to begin with, and whom he now suspected was the Mrs. K. referred to in Alex's message. Was Barry expected to leap onstage when the lights dimmed and somehow keep Detloff occupied while they spirited Anna away?

The finale seemed just about to end with a flourish when it stopped and the strings began what would become the real finale. At that moment, Barry thought he saw two figures move toward the stage along the right wall of the concert hall. They scurried up the five or six steps onto the stage and slipped behind the curtain. No one but Barry seemed to notice them. Except for Detloff, who'd looked right at the men, although without any sign of recognition.

Onstage one oboist and one French hornist stood up and began an interpolated little section while the rest of the players were silent. Once finished, the oboe player and hornist left the stage. The original theme returned and was developed a bit before the bassoonist also stood up, played a little solo, then left. Tikhov and the other hornist now stood up, repeated the theme their colleagues had played before, and left the stage. Barry noticed that Tikhov stopped and looked at the spot in the opposite wing where the two men must now be. He vanished into the left wing. Could he have recognized them?

Imperceptibly the stage darkened as lights went out more or less above the chairs of the players who left. Which was why the bass player—a slender red-haired young woman—now seemed spotlighted among several empty chairs. She played a complicated solo, her huge instrument harrumphing through acrobatic triplets. After she finished, she tried to tug along the instrument, and finally left it as snickers filled the audience. The light above her spot went out. The strings alone were left to play.

The original adagio theme was brought back as first the two cellists, then the violists, departed. Even with the stage becoming dimmer, Barry could make out figures in the wings on the left side of the stage whenever someone went through the curtain. Tikhov for certain was there, gesturing and miming something at someone Barry couldn't see.

Two violinists left. Anna and a paunchy near-retirement-aged man among the many empty chairs, playing the theme that had become almost desolate in its tenderness. Would Detloff at the harpsichord leave before they did? Barry tried to calculate how he might get out of his seat and around to the steps onstage as quickly as possible. Anna would leave, like the others, at the left. If Barry could get to the right and do something, even just tackle the men in the wings, Anna could get away.

The second violinist left the stage, and Anna stood up and played on alone, spotlighted. Then her light went off, and the stage was completely dark.

As the audience rustled preparatory to the lights coming on again, Barry ran up to the right. He pushed his way past the two people sitting on the aisle and dashed for the steps he'd seen the two men head for. Behind him, he heard scattered clapping. It was dark backstage. And worse, empty.

Barry felt the wall and located the edge of a door. He opened it and found himself in what looked to be a dimly lighted storeroom with stacks of folding chairs and music stands. A storage space. No other doors out. He headed back, trying to cross the stage toward the other wing, which must lead to the dressing rooms, green room, and exit. The lights came on when he was inches from the left wing. He dashed into the curtain, directly into a crowd of musicians ambling back onstage.

Getting past them in the narrow corridor and then finding the exit seemed impossible. Finally he spotted the exit sign. He cracked open the door.

Directly in front of him, the two men were kneeling in the middle of the puddled Boulevard de Sebastopol shooting, while to one side Detloff and Tikhov were pummeling each other against a poster-covered wall.

Barry saw Alex's mustard-colored Deux Chevaux some thirty yards away, saw the glow of gunfire from behind its cab. One of the kneeling men fell over, clutching at his shoulder.

At the same time, the back door of the little car was flung open, and Cao Han tried to get a body in. It had to be Anna. That was her dress. But why was Cao Han lifting her? Why was someone in the driver's seat turning around to help her?

Barry rushed forward as though tackling a wide receiver and threw himself onto the second shooter. The man fell over with a grunt as his forehead hit a cobblestone. The gun flew out of his hand and into a sewer grating.

Barry got up and ran for Alex's car. The doors slammed shut and the little Citroen's tires squealed as it took off down the Boulevard de Sebastopol. He ran, shouting for them to stop, it was him, it was him! He ran faster than he had to score any touchdown. He ran and didn't stop running until he'd crossed the bridge onto the Île de la Cité when a blowtorch of a stitch in his side sent him crashing into a wall. The mustard-colored car was nowhere in sight.

*　　*　　*

"Why *can't* I see her?"

It was two days since, and Barry hadn't been able to find Land or raise him by telephone. Only when he'd driven down to Interpol headquarters at St. Quentin and physically threatened people had this phone connection been put through to Alex.

"Barry, you did a great job, a superb job! But it's over!"

"Where's Anna?" Barry demanded. "I want to see her."

"It's o-ver. Don't you understand," Land said. "O-ver! All done!"

"I want to see Anna."

"You *saw*, Barry. You were there! We couldn't get her into the car in time. They opened fire and . . . You were supposed to help us."

"I helped. How the hell do you think you got away?" Barry asked.

"You weren't fast enough."

"You said Anna would be safe. That's the only reason I agreed to help."

"You knew the risks involved."

"Why didn't you cancel the snatch?"

"*They* would have gotten her if we hadn't."

"I want to see Anna."

"I told you, Barry. She was hit. Anna's . . . dead!"

"If Anna's dead, so are you, Land."

"Come on, you know it wasn't my fault, Barry."

"I want to see her body."

"This is getting too fuckin' morbid! Look, Barry, you just have to accept what happened."

"Not until I see her."

"We'll talk when you've calmed down."

Land hung up, and Barry ripped the phone out of the wall. He was promptly jumped on by three Interpol men and ejected from the place.

Several days later, when he was still passed out from a throughly unsatisfactory drunken binge, airline tickets were slid under the door of his room.

Barry told himself that Anna was still alive. When he could no longer believe that, Barry promised himself he would find Alex Land and kill him.

Six months later, following his breakdown and recovery, Barry managed to contact Land in New York and to lure him with fake cheerfulness out to his parents' lake cottage in Connecticut, closed for the winter. There, he'd almost made good his promise.

And now, seventeen years later, he was going to see Anna again.

A sign announced the place, but even the sign appeared to be part of the landscape, carved from redwood, set next to a giant scarlet ginger plant in flower. Behind an elaborately branching red candle tree lay the parking lot; he pulled in and parked next to a lacquered black-and-chrome pickup that hadn't trucked anything dirtier than pets or a group of teenagers. The vehicles parked around it were all new, expensive, foreign-made sedans with a sprinkling of sports models. He was glad he'd allowed the rental clerk at the San Francisco airport to talk him into taking the Firebird.

A series of stone slabs embedded in the ground rose in a curve around bushes and trees, most of them varieties he'd never seen before. The idyllic ascent ended at a spontaneous-looking cactus and rock garden, behind which a redwood and blue glass edifice soared in several directions at once.

Inside the shop, he felt he had somehow taken a wrong turn or stepped into a time machine. A bazaar, he thought at first, a *souk* in some North African casbah: heavy, color-drenched carpets hung over bamboo rods, brass pottery littered one corner, an ancient, much-scarred trestle table spilled a kaleidoscope of silks. Above were skylights, wherever structural roof beams intersected. Beneath his feet, parquet flooring. With every dozen steps, he moved into another time and place. Persia passed and he was in the American West; buckskin jackets, thonged suede jackets and trousers, a high old oak cabinet filled with antique rifles, a matching sideboard covered by saddles and harnesses of astoundingly detailed Amerindian tooling. Next was China: Aladdin vases as tall as he, embroideries, bronze cauldrons, dangling scrolls of brushwork calligraphy, tondos and octagons of waterpaint landscapes and formal portraits.

"May I help you?" said a tall, slender young man with a head full of long black ringlets. Barry was so disoriented by the place, he didn't answer at first. That's what made it so odd—in a marketplace, there would be voices, a hubbub; here it was Phillip Glass's insistent rhythms playing softly over a hidden sound system. This gangly youth with his spotted pony-hide vest and shiny black jeans was the first person Barry had seen since he'd entered.

"I know," the youth said, "you're just looking."

"I was looking for the owner."

The youth stared at Barry, the blank gaze that young Californians used to assess without threatening.

"One of them is over in the corner. I think I saw her with some customers before."

"Where, exactly?" Barry asked. "The floor plan here is . . ."

"A trip, isn't it? Over there, near the kimonos . . ." Then he vanished through the shelves.

Barry began to walk again, toward where the boy had gestured. He stopped when he heard voices—and picked out one voice from the others, saying, "Ah! Robert! Here are Carol and James. They want to see Katha's new jewelry." It was unmistakable, it had to be her voice.

Barry emerged into an area of the shop where stained glass hung from wires in sheets of every size and shape. Beyond stood the first recognizable shop counters he'd seen in the place, of heavily knotted wood, with sliding glass tops to display jewelry. Robert—the youth he'd just been talking to—and a young couple were here. But where was she?

He turned and walked again.

And came upon her. Anna was standing nearby at a huge,

carved mahogany armoire, changing the music on a CD player.

All he could see was her back, slim as ever, and her hair, blonder than he remembered. He couldn't believe he'd found her. The adagio of a Bach sonata surged forward, the violin rising to meet, then to entwine the filigree of harpsichord notes. He stood absolutely still, unsure of what he was doing here, afraid to move.

Anna turned into profile, slightly distracted, as though she were listening closely to the music. He could see that her features had softened somewhat, lost their youthful sharpness; she was tanned now, her hair high on her forehead, it shook and tumbled as she bent down to set some CDs in order. Within a second she would turn around completely and . . .

She faced him straight on, looked at him in puzzled recognition, changed her mind, decided she didn't know him, then her eyes seemed to glaze over. One of her hands groped out as though testing the reality of the air between them, as though by a wave of her hand she could make the apparition he was vanish, then it was abruptly drawn back to safety. Her eyes narrowed.

"Anna," he began.

She frowned and her unpainted lips came together, almost crushed together in a moue he so well recalled . . .

"It can't be . . ." Her voice wasn't merely disbelieving, it expressed horror.

"Anna! For seventeen years I was certain you were dead. I saw them shooting. He *told me* you were dead."

He took another step forward.

"Stay back!" She put out her hands as though to physically stop him and yelled out harshly, "Robert! Robert!"

"Anna? What's wrong?"

"What do you want? Why are you coming to me like this? Oh, my God, what's happening to me?" She turned around. *"Robert!"*

"I found out you were still alive. I wanted to see you again. To talk to you."

93

The young man in the pony-skin vest leaped out from between some shelving, followed by the two customers.

"What's wrong? This guy hassling you?" Robert asked. Without waiting for an answer, he started for Barry.

"Hold on! I just came to . . ."

Anna continued to stare at Barry.

By now, Robert had grabbed one of his arms, the other man his other arm. Barry shook them off. "Get your hands off!"

The two men again reached for Barry, who pulled back. "*Vamonos,* partner!"

Barry ignored him. Anna had fallen back against one of the counters. "I didn't expect this, Anna. You're making a big mistake!"

He turned and they followed him, guiding him through the aisles whenever he lost his way toward the front of the store. There, Robert reached forward and opened the door.

Barry stopped on the lintel, and yelled out, "I'll be back."

That comment earned him a shove from both men. Barry saw it coming soon enough to turn and make a jab at Robert, which connected weakly at the kid's shoulder. Before he could react, Barry left.

Expecting them to come after him, he cautiously walked back down to the parking lot. But neither man followed. He'd reached the final landing at the shop sign when he heard, "Barry! Wait!"

He stopped to watch Anna descend the steps. She was still upset, confused. She still moved agilely, and seeing her, his heart seemed to contract for an instant. She stopped a few feet away.

He wanted to touch her so badly; just a brush of her cheek, a minute caress of a finger.

"Barry?"

"I don't blame you for not wanting to see me again. I betrayed you. I know. But they told me that if I didn't help them get you away, the KGB would kill you. I had no choice. When I heard you were alive and here, I . . . I had to

94

know it was true, to see for myself. Now . . . if you want me to, I'll go away again. I will, Anna. Just say it."

She didn't. Instead, she came toward him and lightly touched his face. "In my mind, for seventeen years, you *were* dead! That was the only thing that helped ease my suffering, and at the same time made me suffer more."

He took her hand. "Anna . . ." He'd run out of words. "If it makes it any better, I've suffered, too . . ."

Before he could kiss her hand, she pulled it away, and looked at him sadly. "So. What do we do now?"

"Anna, I have a great deal to tell you. Something very important for the both of us. Can we? Now?"

"Yes. Yes. Of course. Give me a few minutes. We'll go somewhere."

She turned to ascend to the shop again, then turned to look at him.

"Just a few minutes," she repeated. "Then we'll go to Nepenthe. It's a restaurant, down the Coastal Highway."

"I'll wait right here."

They were sitting on the huge deck of the restaurant. Two martinis apiece already downed, a bowl of *crudités* and shelled nuts half-eaten, they gazed at the mile-high view of the Pacific. Eagles wheeled in the air, then suddenly plummeted to snatch a meal from the brush at the surf line. A peacock strutting on the side wall of the deck suddenly shrieked—sounding like several children being mutilated—and opened its enormous tail. It strode closer, turned, and fluttered the entire panoply of feathered colors at them, clucked a few times, then slowly folded its wings and strutted back along the wall and onto the restaurant's roof.

"That's Henry," she said. "He always displays for me. It drives the owner's daughter mad. He never does it for her."

"I'm glad you came," he said.

"It's very . . . strange, almost a miracle."

"There's more," he warned. He sipped his martini.

"Your hair looks very distinguished," Anna said. "A little gray at the temples like that."

"You're not gray at all," Barry said. "You look wonderful."

"Cosmetics," she said ruefully.

"No. It's you. You were a beautiful girl, now you're a beautiful woman."

"Were you sad, when you thought I'd died?"

"When I found out, I tried to kill Alex."

"Ingenious! But what could we expect? It was the Cold War. It was the CIA, the KGB. We were young. We were patriotic. We were ignorant. We didn't deserve any better."

"That's not true! We deserved *far* better!"

"How did you find me?" she asked.

Barry calculated what he was going to say. There was no way to soft-pedal it.

"A week ago, a teenage girl came into my shop in Boston. We became sort of friendly, had lunch once. She was a little odd, but appealing. I special-ordered some books for her. She told me something of her life. Most of it lies. But some of it—the weirdest parts—were the truth. She had a special gift."

"What kind of gift?"

"She's a psychic. She could tell me all sorts of things about my past and my future. With great accuracy. Things I'd forgotten years ago. Things I didn't even know."

Anna had reacted. But whatever she wanted to say, she restrained it.

"I sort of pumped her, and she blurted out all sorts of things. She told me she was part of a group of young psychics. Then she ran away. Strange, no?"

"Go on," Anna prodded.

"A few days later, the woman in whose house she was staying called and said Kyra had left me a letter. Kyra had gone away. This is the letter." He pulled it out and handed it to Anna, who pulled the table candle closer to read it. It took her ten minutes of close and astonished concentration. Then she looked up at him.

"I've lived with women in the past seventeen years," Barry said. "Only once was there a conception, and she decided to abort. But you see, while I was shocked by what Kyra wrote, I wasn't really surprised. She'd been so familiar somehow, right from the first time I met her. At any rate, I knew instantly who her mother is."

"Who?"

"You, Anna. Kyra is our daughter. Yours and mine. She's exactly the right age."

"It's not possible, Barry."

"I couldn't figure it out at first, because her eyes were dark and of course she's a bit younger than you were when . . ."

"It's not possible, Barry."

"The last time we were together, you told me you were worried about not having your period. You were already pregnant, Anna. You were!"

"Yes, I was pregnant. But I lost the child in the eighth month. A miscarriage. Because of the trauma I went through!"

"I'm telling you, you didn't lose the child. She's alive. Alex must have made sure she lived. Her name is Kyra Anthony, and I've met her, Anna. She sat this close to me. She took my hand. She looked into my eyes. She's our child, Anna. And, as you read, she has your gift, only it's much stronger."

"My baby died," she said quietly. "All those weeks of drugs and mental torture. I wasn't surprised when I miscarried."

Barry wouldn't argue. "Listen, Anna, for years I'd be with friends, and they would say things like 'If it weren't for the kids . . .' and 'What kind of world are we making for our children?,' and I would secretly smile because I didn't have that awful responsibility. Not me, not Barry Brescia! Before I met Kyra," he went on with his previous thought, "I believed that. I believed that without anyone to carry on, I would go out like a light bulb, just like that, only it would happen in a spot where no one ever looked and no one would think to replace it."

Anna crushed her lips together again.

"Kyra's lovely," he said. "Lovely, bright. I liked her before I knew. You will, too."

"But how can this be, Barry?"

"I just told you how. Land must have taken her, told you she was dead. As he told you I was killed. As he told me you were killed. He said it again yesterday."

"You saw him?" She'd asked quietly; even so, he felt the dread in her voice.

"He said you were dead. But his stepson told me you were still alive. He hates Land."

"So do I, God forgive me. I hate him more than anyone or anything in the world! He broke me apart. What they called 'deprogramming.' Broke me apart and killed my baby."

"No, Anna. Kyra is alive. And we've got to find her."

"But why would he do such a thing? Just to torture me more?" she asked.

"I don't know," Barry admitted. "But I do know we have to find Kyra."

They were silent a minute.

"What was . . . Kyra? . . . What was she like?"

"She was like you, Anna. Except for her eyes. That's what threw me off at first. Until I realized they were my eyes."

"She was unhappy? Frightened?"

"No. She was uncannily in control. Until she told me about herself and her friends. Then she panicked completely. I don't know why. Nor why she found me. Or how. And why didn't she know about you, Anna? And why did she disappear again? There are so many unanswered questions."

"Is it possible my baby lived?" Anna mused.

"You'll know it's true the minute you meet Kyra."

"All these years . . . I've been so afraid to . . . I thought they had destroyed my ability to be a mother. . . ." She put a hand up to her eyes.

"We can find her, Anna. I have leads. I have the names of two of those boys she was with. She said that one was written up in the newspapers a few years ago."

She put her hand down. "There's so much to think about! What if it isn't true? I don't know if I'm strong enough to handle disappointment, Barry."

"I promise you won't be disappointed," he said.

She hesitated, then said, "Maybe it is a time for miracles. If yesterday someone said you were still alive . . ."

"Think of it, Anna, our daughter! The child we conceived that summer when we loved each other so very much!"

Anna looked at him, sadness and hope mixed in her expression. "What do we have to do to find her?"

CHAPTER FIVE

Around four in the morning, Barry suddenly woke up. He lay in the dark for a few seconds, listening for sounds. Outside the shaded windows, a tree rustled in the wind, a barn owl hooted, then it was quiet again. He snapped on the bedside lamp and sat up. There was a reason he was awake. He got up and put on a sweater and slacks against the mountain-night air, sat in the comfortable-looking chair, lit a cigarette.

Once settled, all he could think of was how odd it was. Here he was in the Ventana Inn in Big Sur, California, three thousand miles from Boston, from the Ephemeris, from Elaine and Marty Kalb, from everything that had accumulated in the past half-decade of his life. Inn as in way station. He'd set something in motion and he'd persuaded Anna to join him, and now they were on their way.

Years before, when he'd come home from Europe and Operation Little Broom, Barry had been at another way station just like this. No. That had been different: far more desperate, for he'd discovered himself as a failure then. Discovered his own weakness, his capacity for betrayal. Discovered death. They had been hard lessons. The first day of classes at Columbia had arrived quickly enough. Still in shock really, Barry had stepped into the classroom and looked around. Everyone, even the teacher, had seemed so young, so naive. What could he possibly learn from them?

Nothing, he was certain. He walked back to his dorm, packed and left. He hitchhiked across the country, staying in communes and youth hostels for a day or two, then moving on. He lived in a motel room in a town outside of South Bend, worked a week for travel money in a town in southern Minnesota, worked another brief span in the Texas Panhandle.

Eventually he wound up in California, in fact not far from this inn, but inland, in a town named Tres Piños in the San Benito Valley. He'd found work as a lettuce picker; then, when his education was discovered, they made him a clerk in the office, and then at the local welfare office. Though he'd kept to himself for months trying desperately to sort things out, there had been times when he needed the company of a barroom. That's where he met Angela. She, too, was young and badly bruised by life. Unlike Barry, who hid the past behind silence and solitude, Angela wore the scars of her abused life proudly as though they were the Distinguished Medal of Honor. But deep in the night, she would leap out of bed and stare straight ahead, as though the headlights from the passing semis outside the windows were coming straight at her.

Angela had been married at sixteen and already had three children when Barry met her. One weekend, they went to Coalinga to see the kids. Angela stood outside the flat-roofed little school and waited until they all came out. She introduced Barry and told the kids they were going for pizza. The oldest child was a girl of ten, with Angela's eyes, green as new dollar bills. He tried not to stare too much at these children so as not to embarrass them with his pity.

Driving them back to their father's house after dinner, they'd stopped at a shopping center, where Angela and the kids had gotten out to buy toys. The oldest girl came back fast and looked so strangely at Barry that nervously he'd asked if she wanted an ice-cream cone. Yes, please, she'd said, so he bought her one. They returned to the car and she got into the front seat. He'd just lighted a cigarette and thrown the match out the window when he felt her hand on his crotch. He looked down. Sure enough, her soft little hand was caressing him through his soiled Levis. He looked at the girl—she was staring ahead, busily eating her ice-cream cone, oblivious to him, to her own hand in his lap. He had a moment of pure consternation. Then he realized. Somehow this was the only way she knew. He did not know how or why this had happened to her. She didn't seem tormented, abused, yet already at ten she'd decided this was how life had to be: A man bought you something, and you gave him something back. Her seeming indifference made it worse.

Angela and the other kids finally returned to the car, and the little hand casually folded back into her pinafore lap as though it had been there all the time. In the middle of that same night, Barry had thought about the girl and her acceptance of her role as a victim. He began to weep for the unalterable shambles of that child's life. "And there she was," he told himself, "licking away at that damn cone, making certain she didn't miss a bit of it or let any of it fall on her cheap school dress."

Angela hadn't asked why he was crying: In her world, even the strongest, most taciturn men were unable to fight off storms of inexplicable grief. But two days later, Barry had left, gone away without a word, a note, any explanation at all.

Why had Kyra gone away? Had she merely seen a middle-aged man wasting his days in a silly business, and thought the way idealistic young people always thought, My God! *This* is my father! *This* is what I've been searching for?

He had to find Kyra now and ask her, tell her, no, show her, he was more, could be more.

The reference branch of the Monterey Public Library had all major newspapers on file. Only, instead of the microfilm-viewing machines he remembered from his high-school and college days, there were now computer screens. Barry didn't recall the date Kyra had said that Lost and Found Jefferson had first come to public attention for locating the missing football team, so he accessed the file for the year before the current one, then checked the boy's name—and received a date. The reference-room clerk showed him how to "hold" the index entry, delete the rest of the file, and call up the appropriate file. He wondered if it wasn't merely a follow-up article to the original one. The date listed was mid-May. Barry didn't think there were blizzards that late, even in the Rockies. Or were there? He decided to try it anyway, and called up the May file for viewing.

And received a shock:

PSYCHIC BOY DEAD IN RESCUE MISSION the headline read on page one. The dateline was Denver, May 12, of the previous year. Barry read on.

A spokesman for the Colorado State Police and National Ranger Service said that George Washington Carver Jefferson was killed along with two members of the National Forest Service Rescue Team in a helicopter crash near Leadville yesterday night. The three had been on a search and rescue mission on the western slope of Mt. Elbert for the past two days, trying to locate a group of climbers feared lost in a spring avalanche reported by observers and members of the party who'd remained behind.

Jefferson, a nine-year-old Down's syndrome child, came to prominence two years ago, when his psychic abilities led local authorities to locate and rescue a bus containing the entire football team of North Denver High. Since then, according to sources within the Colorado State Police, the shy young boy has helped locate missing children, climbers, spelunkers and miners. Dubbed "Lost and Found" by the media, Jefferson was considered a rare example of ESP powers that were extremely reliable, although because of the family's religious beliefs, the boy was never available for testing by scientists or experts in the field of psychic research.

Following the boy's first success, Jefferson's parents chose to avoid the limelight, and all of his subsequent work for the state police and park service was done within a shroud of secrecy. After "Lost and Found" 's first spate of publicity, no further interviews have been allowed, and the boy's family moved to an unknown address. For this reason reporters at the *Post* have been unable to provide comments from members of the family concerning the tragedy.

None of the lost climbers reported to be upon Mt. Elbert have been located.

Stunned, Barry read on, discovering the names of the downed helicopter pilot and co-pilot on board in the crash; then, on a later page, he found a continuation of the story with diagrams of the mountain and the path of the avalanche, and the location (marked with a Maltese cross) where the helicopter crashed and was later discovered by a backup team. None of it provided any further elucidation of the main story, and "burial services for Jefferson will not be open to the public."

He found the reference clerk and asked if the article could be reprinted. It could be, for a dollar fee.

That done, he called Anna at her shop and told her the news.

"Is there a byline?" she asked.

There was. The reporter's name was Linda Hendricks. He assumed from the Denver newspaper.

"He can't be dead, otherwise Kyra would have said something," Barry argued.

"Perhaps the reporter could tell you more."

"I'm coming back to Big Sur. Can you meet me at my room? I have a portable computer there. We could use that to link up to Hendricks."

Anna agreed, and an hour later, he was keyboarding questions to Linda Hendricks of the *Denver Post*.

"All I know," her words appeared on the small liquid-crystal screen of his laptop, "is what's there. I'll send you the five previous articles I and my predecessor at the city desk here did on Lost and Found. That's it. Except . . ."

"Except what?" Barry flashed back at her.

"There weren't any reporters when the crashed helicopter and bodies were recovered. None of us ever got to see Lost and Found's body. And what we were shown of the pilot and rescue team could have belonged to anyone. There were no . . . In fact, except for the boy, no one else aboard was from anywhere near this area. The bodies were flown out a day later to D.C."

"Conclusion?" Barry typed back.

"We didn't really think about it at the time, even though we're trained to be suspicious. I guess because we focused so much on the local angle—Lost and Found. Maybe we should have dug some more. It's too late now."

"Could he have belonged to a group?" Anna asked. Barry keyboarded in the question.

"What kind of group?" the reporter queried.

"A group of young psychics. I met a sixteen-year-old girl a few weeks ago who said that she and Lost and Found were part of a group. She definitely spoke of him as living. The other name she gave me was Kevin Vosburg or Vosberg. From Los Angeles."

"If you want, I'll access that name into the files," Hendricks replied, "see what comes up. But I've never heard of any group. Jefferson worked alone until he joined up with the state police and rangers for special jobs. Can't help you."

"Dead end!" Barry said, gloomily.

"What about other child psychics?" he keyboarded. "Usually when something so unusual shows up, articles mention other ones."

"I'll look in our information files."

The cursor kept blinking on the screen. Barry looked away at Anna and the little table in front of her with a carafe of coffee and rinds from a Crenshaw melon. She wore a light-colored headband and a stylish sweater-dress. He hoped she'd put it on for him.

"I'm not giving up this easy," he said. "If this doesn't work, I'm going to L.A. and look up this Kevin."

"When?"

"This afternoon. Tomorrow."

"I'll go with you," Anna said.

"But what about your shop? You can't just leave your business?"

She smiled. "Robert and Alan will take care of it. Alan's my partner. He lives in Marin. He'll complain, of course. But he'll come."

"Great."

The screen stopped blinking. Hendricks was keyboarding something.

"You were right. About two months after Jefferson was killed, there was an article about psychic children in the Sunday edition written by a colleague of mine. But he used all my articles and whatever notes of mine my editor had on Lost and Found. He dismissed most psychics as fakes, but he did mention another child who seemed to be the real thing, although quite different from Jefferson. At least this one managed to kick up enough of a ruckus to get into the local papers."

"In Denver?" Barry asked. "Can I see it?"

"I'm sending the appropriate paragraph right now."

Barry read:

> Such stories about rocks falling on the houses of sexually repressed young girls are rife and usually unsupported by hard evidence. But whenever recent psychic events are spoken of by those in the know, the case of little Matty Stolzing from Santa Barbara, California, is mentioned. His powers are attested to by a half-dozen people, including

neighbors, the child's parents, and two local police officers.

A few months ago, a baby-sitter, hired by the Stolzings for the night, ran out of their apartment, screaming in terror, claiming the child had "made monsters appear from out of nowhere." A week later, the police were called in, and they, too, reported extremely realistic hallucinations, which appeared to have their source in the family's television set.

What makes the case of Matty Stolzing even more interesting is that the child had been tested at various psychiatric facilities and found to be severely autistic. Even odder, after his parents separated and Mr. Stolzing moved out of the Juanita Avenue apartment, there were no recurrences of the terrifying illusions.

"Well?" Hendricks asked. "What do you think?"

"I think you've been a great help. I'll check it out and get back to you."

"You can say you're working for me," she offered generously. "I can provide some sort of bogus press authorization. Just let me have an exclusive on the story if there is one."

"You bet. Thanks."

Barry pressed the "save" button to retain the entire conversation on his computer, then signed off.

"Looks like we're headed for Santa Barbara," he told Anna.

"Let me phone Alan. We'll leave early in the morning."

"You're really coming along?"

"Barry. I *must* know if Kyra is my child."

Barry found Carol Stolzing's address on Juanita Avenue without too much trouble: an apartment complex, two stories high, constructed around a pool and succulent garden, with railings on four sides, a dozen blank-looking doors, and curtained windows looking in on each other. Barry couldn't help but think it looked more like a motel than an apartment building—and typically Californian. The carpark beneath three sides was about as charming as the rest of the place.

He and Anna had called Carol from Big Sur as soon as they'd gotten off the phone with the reporter from the *Denver Post*. Naturally they had to be vague about why they wanted to see her, although they did say it concerned the boy. Carol Stolzing had been oddly complaisant. Barry used the two and a half hours of driving along the Pacific Coast Highway down to Santa Barbara to tell Anna something about his own life over the past seventeen years and to try to find out about her own past. Instead, Anna seemed more interested in how to approach Carol Stolzing. Who should they tell her they were? How much could they talk about Kyra? How far could they press Carol? And what about the child, Matty? What would he be like? It was work for a diplomat, for a psychologist, they would have to be delicate.

Carol Stolzing answered the door. She was a petite woman with a good tan, long blond hair, and surprisingly young. She seemed to have forgotten they were coming, and had to be reminded who they were.

The long, almost bare living room was dominated by a desk and computer, and she quickly explained that she was a "word processor—free lance. I work for the university, mostly. Typing up term papers for the students and occasional longer papers for the professors." She sat them down in the bright little kitchen with its Formica table and folding chairs and poured them instant coffee. All the while, she seemed distracted, as though she was expecting an important phone call, and in fact no sooner had Barry taken a sip from his cup than she announced that her car was being repaired and she was expecting to hear from the shop when she could go pick it up.

"You know Mr. Maxwell?" Carol asked.

She saw they looked surprised.

"From the newspaper in Denver?"

"We know Linda Hendricks," Barry said.

"You're here to talk about Matty, right?" Carol asked, fooling with her long hair. Before either could reply, she went on, "You know it's been almost a year since I've seen Matty. Hilton has him. Not that I wanted to give him up. But what could I do? I was only eighteen when he was born. Hell! I was only sixteen when I married Hill, and I didn't have a job or any money, so when we broke up, I went back home to live with my folks. *They* wanted to keep Matty, and my mom was sickly and couldn't have a baby in the house. So it made no sense . . . and anyway, *they* wanted him, Hill and . . ." She trailed off.

Her chatter allowed them to conceal their surprise, and their signals to each other. Anna was sympathetic and tactful: She said she understood how difficult it must have been for Carol. But, surely, as Matty's mother, she must still be interested in him, visit him and all.

"Well, of course I'm interested in him!" Carol said. "But you know, he was never an *easy* baby. Not that he cried too much or anything like that. I mean, not compared to other children. But when he was, oh, I guess close to two years old and not talking and not walking and . . . well, I knew something was wrong with him. We couldn't afford doctors, since Hill didn't have much of a job himself then. So we took Matty to the clinic here. They tested him for weeks, it seemed. Nothing wrong. He was in fine physical health, he was just a slow learner, they said. Lots of boy infants are slower, they told us. They catch up later," she added, defending herself.

"Well, it was one of our neighbors, this woman Eileen, who'd worked at a hospital in L.A., who told us what was wrong with Matty. I'd never even heard the word *autistic* before she said it. By then Matty must have been what, maybe twenty-eight months old. He still wasn't talking. He wasn't much moving around, and he didn't seem to notice much of anything going on around him. Hill would come home from work and try and play with Matty—you know, show him things, tickle him, throw him up in the air and catch him, the way daddies like to do. . . ." Carol bit her lip. "But Matty didn't react at all. Not to any of it. It was like he was a big doll or something. He didn't laugh. He didn't cry. He just looked at you. Well, not even *at* you, so much as at something near you. Although some people said he looked *through* you. Which I thought was just mean."

They waited for her to collect herself.

"Hill and I were having our own problems by then. Even so, we pulled together and read up on autism and tried to do all the things we had to. But nothing happened. Well, *one* thing happened. Matty began to watch television. *That* interested him."

Barry looked around. No TV anywhere in sight.

"I would turn it on for him. I was just learning word-processing at home at the time, and I liked to hear people's voices while I worked. It made me feel less lonely. So I would put it on during the day while I keyboarded. And Matty liked it. He looked at it all the time. You see, that was a good sign. *Anything* he might pay attention to was good for him. So I left on the TV even after my typing was done."

Carol glanced outside, at the little empty courtyard and the neatly tended cactus garden. Barry wondered if anyone ever used that flagstone terrace down there, or those chaise longues, or that pool.

"I became involved in learning some complicated new macrosystems at the time, so I guess I didn't really pay all that much attention to the fact that Matty was switching channels. But I'd come in to check up on him periodically, give him his bottle or something to chew on, and he'd have different programs on, different channels each time I came in. Of course, I assumed he'd gotten up and done it. You know, by hand, though he was always in the same exact position whenever I saw him."

She took a deep breath.

"One Saturday afternoon, it's raining. Hill's home from

work. He puts on a ball game. The Padres, his team, and he's watching the game when suddenly the channel is switched to a cartoon show. Hill gets up and switches it back. Before he gets to the sofa again, it's switched back to the cartoons. Hill calls me in and asks what's wrong with the damn TV. It's the only thing that works, and it's not even paid for. Well, I don't know. But no matter what channel Hill turns to, it always ends up back at the station with the cartoon show. So Hill calls up a friend and goes to watch the Padres game at his place.

"The next day, he brings the TV to be fixed. Thirty dollars for an adjustment. No problem . . . except that one day as I'm sitting here feeding Matty his lunch, the same thing happens to me. I'm watching *As the World Turns* and suddenly *Gobots* is on. I get this strange idea and ask Matty, 'You want to see the Gobots, honey?' No answer, of course, he didn't even look at me. But it was clear that we were going to be watching *Gobots*. I knew then it was Matty doing it."

She paused and looked at Anna. "Yours a boy, too?"

Anna hesitated, then said, "A girl." Her eyes avoided Barry's.

"Well, we'd always counted it lucky that Matty wasn't, you know, violent. What we read about all the time in those books and all was what they called 'unreasonable violence, toward themselves and others.' You know, some of those poor children just smash their heads against a wall till they knock themselves out cold. It's pitiful. But not Matty. So I'm thinking, Okay. I'll live with this. Of course, Hill is beginning to get some ideas, too, even though he doesn't actually *say* them to me. Just asks me all the time, 'How's Matty?'

"One night we leave Matty with a baby-sitter so we can go out to dinner to celebrate our wedding anniversary. Hill took me to that restaurant at the end of the Santa Barbara Pier. You ever been there? It's so nice. Well, we're having a good time for the first time in a long while, when suddenly a phone is brought to our table. The baby-sitter. Something's wrong, she's crying and all. So we rush home. The baby-sitter is standing outside the door, won't set foot inside the apartment. She's there bawling and saying she'll never sit for us again, our baby is a monster. So Hill pays her off and we go inside and there's Matty, just sitting there in his crib watching TV. We never did find out what— You want more coffee? I know it's awful. But if I use instant, I don't drink so much. It makes me so nervous!

"He was my *baby*," Carol suddenly burst out. "No matter what happens! Do you think I was wrong to let his father and her take him?"

Carol addressed Anna, who'd been intent on following what Carol was saying. "No. Of course not."

She looked at them as though not certain to believe them, then she took a sip of the by-now-cold coffee and went on.

"I can remember exactly how it happened. We'd gone to sleep and left the TV on. It was a small apartment, smaller than this one even, and Matty slept in the living room. Sometime during the night, I felt Hill get out of bed to go to the john, and I remembered the TV is still on. 'Shut it off, Hill,' I say. 'I don't want the baby to lose his sleep.'

"Hill's gone a few minutes, then all hell breaks loose. I'm not sure what I'm hearing, but it sounds like the furniture is being knocked all around. It's not an earthquake, because I grew up here and know what those sound like. I think maybe it's a burglar, and I jump out of bed and grab the stick we use to prop open the bedroom window.

"When I get to the living room, I see Matty's awake, sitting up in his crib, looking at the TV, which is all wavy lines. And there's Hill, banging into walls and furniture and all, as though he's trying to get away from something after him. I call out his name, but Hill yells, 'Watch out! It's behind you!' Well, there wasn't anything behind me. 'They're coming out of the TV!' he yells, and I'm yelling back, 'What's coming out of the TV?' But he's behind the sofa yelling, and I think, Lord, he's gone berserk. I don't know what to do. I go and shut off the TV and grab Matty and bring him out of the apartment. I was so angry and I didn't know what in hell was wrong with Hill. After a while, the night air got too cool, and I brought Matty back inside and put him to sleep in his crib. Then I crept into the bedroom. Hill's there, in bed, and he's still sort of wild-eyed, drinking Tequila in big gulps straight out of the bottle, and he won't talk to me, so I grab one blanket from him and go sleep on the living-room sofa, next to the baby.

"The next morning, Hill tells me that when he went to shut off the TV, things suddenly came out of the screen at him—Grizzly bears and sharks and he didn't know what else. Real things. Or at least they seemed real enough to him. He's certain Matty made them. That's the words he used, 'made them.' Hill's also sure that's what happened to the baby-sitter."

"*Made* them?" Barry asked.

"That's the word he used," Carol confirmed. "But after that, Hill won't even touch Matty, which, you know, isn't helpful for an autistic child. I try to make up for that, and I take him for more tests and things. But it happens again when I leave a friend here for a few hours and she completely panics."

Barry had to ask, "You never saw anything?"

"Of course I did. But I was his mommy. Matty made pretty things for me. Flowers and hearts and lots of little Mattys. And anyway, none of them were *real*. I could tell that."

Barry didn't know how to ask the question, and so was relieved when Anna did so. "How is it that your husband changed his mind so completely about Matty, and took him in?"

"Matty was cured," she said. And when they looked surprised: "Not of his autism, of course. That takes years. But the other stuff. Mr. Talmadge had read about Matty in the papers, and he cured him."

"Talmadge? Was he a doctor?"

"I don't know. He never said he was. But he wasn't afraid of Matty. He walked right in the room, lifted him up, put him on his lap, and began talking to Matty real quietly, like they were old friends. I could tell Matty liked him right off. 'Let's play together,' he told Matty, and I could tell they were making things—hallucinations I suppose you'd call them, right? They had a good time, and he asked if he could come again, and I said sure. He kept talking about a special program he ran with other boys and girls who were 'specially gifted' like Matty was, and how much my baby would enjoy it. I could tell Matty liked Mr. Talmadge, because he made cartoon versions of him when he wasn't there and they were always sweet, like the ones he made of me."

Without knowing it, Carol had set off alarms in both Barry and Anna.

"About this program?" Barry began. "Did Talmadge say where it was located or who the other children were?"

"Not really. Wait, I think they were down in L.A. somewhere. Some college campus. I'm afraid I don't remember. Naturally he wanted to have Matty join up with them. He even offered to fly us down there. I said I'd think about it. Then my mom had her cancer discovered and my dad wanted me at home to care for her and Hill wasn't here at all anymore and I knew he was off with that Tiffany at the launderette and everything just went from bad to worse in a few weeks. I held on a month, even though Hill never came home anymore, till I ran out of money, then I went back home to care for Mamma. By then I'd sold the TV, and so Matty wasn't any kind of problem. So I had to leave him with Hill. I thought it would only be for a few days."

They waited while she calmed down, then Barry asked Carol for her husband's phone number and address.

"They never let me see him," Carol said. "It's *her* doing, of course! But maybe they'd let strangers . . . You'll tell me if he's okay, won't you?"

Barry had to try one more time. "Was this Mr. Talmadge alone when he came to visit Matty?"

"Usually he was. Wait, the last time he was here, he came with a boy who played with Matty, too. A teenage boy. Prettiest boy I'd ever seen in my life. Like an angel come to earth. I remember thinking that when he said he'd been living in St. Joseph's, Arizona. I guess that's a town."

"Was he one of the psychic children Mr. Talmadge talked about?"

"Well, now that you ask, maybe he was. What was his name? Tim. Timmy. Timmo! That's right. It was Timmo. He said it was a Finnish name and that his people had come from Finland. He looked Scandinavian, too. Blond hair and blue eyes! Well, they were so blue! But if he was psychic, I never saw him do anything."

"No last name?" Barry had to know.

"Oh, God. I'll never remember it. It was Scandinavian."

Barry had notated "Talmadge, Timmo, St. Joseph's, Arizona," along with Hilton's phone number and address. He looked at the top of the page and the name Kyra Nilsson. Then he showed it to Carol.

"That's it! She his sister?"

"We're not sure."

Carol suddenly grabbed Anna's hand. "I had no choice. I didn't abandon my baby. I had no choice!"

"It's all right," Anna assured her.

"I know Matty's happy. I do. Really, I do! Sometimes I'll be sleeping and wake up and I'll see mountains. High, cold, brown mountains with snow on them. And I know Matty's sending me those pictures. They're lovely mountains, not angry or upset, just calm and majestic and serene. Big mountains. Not like the ones we have here in California. More like the Rockies."

Anna kissed Carol Stolzing and remained with her for a few minutes more while Barry returned to lean against the rented car. "That poor girl!" Anna said. "What she's gone through."

"The way she talked about him, I don't think we should call Hilton," Barry said. "We'd probably have a better chance of seeing them if we just arrived."

"If Matty is like she described him, we're not going to find out much about Kyra from him."

"True. But we do have two other leads now: this Talmadge fellow and the other boy. Even so, Matty's father might know something—a name, a place—that might be of help. What do you think, Anna?"

"It will be dark soon. We should go there now." She looked at the address. "I think I know where this is. A friend of mine lives nearby."

Barry let Anna have the wheel, and she drove through the center of Santa Barbara—Spanish mission style with red brick sidewalks, flowers in giant planters, palms lining every street, past the downtown shopping area, past a park with enormous palm trees, before slipping into what seemed to be a major artery until they were leaving Santa Barbara, headed north again. The city seemed to be behind them now, wide fields on their left, low brown mountains on the right side of the road, with a school or industrial complex just in view off a side road. Anna suddenly turned right, and the road seemed to narrow as it fronted miles of steel-mesh fence. They were nearing the Pacific, he could smell the ocean.

Anna drove along the fence for a while, then turned sharply again, and the road became even rougher. They were on a sort of ridge past whatever that installation had been. It seemed to Barry that if Santa Barbara had its Tobacco Road, this was the place—odd that even outside the city limits it should be so close to the ocean, where property values couldn't be cheap. On either side, a profusion of ragged broad-leaf banana trees and huge purple rhododenron bushes in flower partly hid houses, some of them looking as though they had once been hippie communes, others merely old houses in decay—yet all curiously picturesque and pleasant.

A final turn onto a dirt road led through enormous spreading bushes of candleflower onto a spacious untended lawn and another rickety house. Anna got out, and Barry watched her greet an old gentleman—no other word would do, he was so courtly. He wore unbuckled farm overalls with a too small T-shirt that exposed his white belly and navel. They hugged. Anna pointed to the south. The old gent said something. They hugged again. He was trying to persuade her to do something. She shook her head, kissed his cheek, then came to the car's front window.

"You don't mind, that I didn't introduce you?" she asked. "He doesn't like to be bothered by people. He's a stained-glass artist. A very nice man. I sell his work in my store. He told me the exact directions."

They traveled along the road another five minutes until Anna found what seemed to be a thick plantation of banana trees and parked at their base. This time Barry got out, too, and walked with her through the little copse. More lawn and several more houses: pastel-painted structures that looked as though they'd been prefabs built as housing for World War II officers.

Anna strode up to one door and knocked. Barry noticed a tricycle with one wheel missing athwart a well-weeded herb garden.

"They're gone!" The voice sounded like sheet metal rasping against itself in the wind. The voice belonged to a woman sitting in a wooden wheelbarrow outside the next shack, a huge Mexican sombrero over her face. The brim was lifted in a broad vee to reveal dark glasses and overrouged lips. Barry understood at once that the entire area must be some sort of "art colony."

"Hill and Tiffany?" Anna asked as though they were old friends.

"Gone camping!" the woman repeated. "They left yesterday morning."

Anna went closer to the woman.

"They just packed up and left."

"Do you know where they went?" Anna asked.

"Didn't care, didn't ask." She looked past Anna at Barry. "Did they take the little boy with them?"

"What little boy?"

"Matty," Barry said.

"Matty?" The woman was suddenly interested.

"Yes."

"No. He didn't go with them. You from the clinic downtown?"

"No," Anna said. "We're from Denver."

"Want to leave your name?"

"I guess we'll have to visit another day. Bye," Anna said. They began to walk toward the car.

"If you're looking for that weird child, you came to the wrong place," the woman shouted.

They stopped, turned around.

"Carol Stolzing said he'd be here," Barry said.

"Well, Carol Stolzing was wrong. He hasn't been here in ten, eleven months."

"You mean he's not living with Hilton and Tiffany?"

"Hell, no! They gave him away to some professor or other from L.A. He arrived in a big foreign car. Had a chauffeur and all, don't you know."

"Was anyone else with him? A blond teenage boy?"

"No. I would have noticed him. There was someone in the backseat of the car. A woman or girl, I'm certain, but try as I did, I couldn't make her out. The windows were tinted, and when he opened and closed the door, she seemed to be wearing heavy veils or something, as though she were in mourning. All I could see were her feet, and that she had long, dark hair."

"Could it have been Kyra?" Anna whispered to Barry.

Inside the car again, Anna said, "No wonder they won't let Carol see him. He's not here! Should we tell her?" Then she answered her own question. "She'll find out sooner or later, I suppose."

"It seems the more we look into all this, the odder it becomes."

"Maybe we should contact Linda Hendricks again?" Anna said. "Perhaps she'll know something."

"Fine," he said casually, hiding his pleasure at her determination. "We'd better find a motel for the night."

"No, tonight we'll sleep at Barenreiter's house. My sculptor of stained glass," she explained. "We'll eat dinner there, too. He already invited us."

It took them almost an hour to reach the Denver reporter via the computer, and she was as surprised as they'd been by Matty's disappearance. She'd never heard of Talmadge or Timmo, but she was pretty sure there wasn't any town in Arizona named St. Joseph's. She'd worked for the *Phoenix Star* two years before going to Denver. But she'd check on it. She agreed with them that it all sounded "very fishy indeed," and had already begun harassing the Denver coroner's office for a report on Lost and Found. She did have one interesting piece of information:

"I told you I would put through that name you gave me, Kevin Vosburg?"

"Did you find anything?" Barry keyboarded.

"Not exactly. I did find a Vosburgh, with an *h* at the end of the name. An Elly Vosburgh. A year and a half ago, she was arrested in the San Bernadino area for involvement in some sort of computer-bank scam. A few months later, she was arrested again, for arson. She tried to blame it on her younger brother, who was a complete paraplegic or something. Then she went bonkers and was put into Patton State Hospital. Guess what the brother's name was? You guessed it, Kevin."

"Where is he?" Barry typed.

"Not a clue. But you can find her. It's a minimum-security place, but Elly Vosburgh can't leave."

Toward morning, Barry was awakened.

He lay on the wicker sofa on the screened-in porch of Barenreiter's house. The cushions on the sofa were lumpy,

119

the pillow mostly air with a hint of feathers. Barry would never get back to sleep, and if he did, he wondered what condition he'd wake up in.

He heard a noise, it sounded like footsteps on the rickety staircase up to the attic room where Barenreiter had put Anna for the night. He listened more closely. She was coming downstairs.

She halted, a shadow in the porch doorway.

"Anna?" he whispered. "Are you sleepwalking?"

"Shh!" She sat down on the rickety wicker chair next to the rickety wicker sofa on the closed-in back porch of Barenreiter's house. "You'll wake up Klaus."

Their host was in a bedroom on the first floor, not far away, snoring. He sounded as though he wouldn't wake up if they invited half the state in.

"Did I wake you?" she asked.

"Not really. I've been lying here thinking."

"I haven't been able to sleep too well, either," she admitted.

He sat up, so that he faced her. In the moonlight Anna's profile was silver-blue, her slip a deeper blue, her limbs almost cobalt.

"You having second thoughts about this?" he asked quietly.

"No. Every step we take seems to make it all the more likely . . ." She didn't finish her thought. "But it is more and more disturbing, too."

"I know." He put a hand out and found hers.

"Anna?"

She stood up and he did, too, catching up with her at the doorway.

"I see some things haven't changed," she said. "You still sleep nude."

"Anna. My feelings for you haven't changed, either."

He began to kiss her. She turned her lips away so that he kissed her cheek, her neck.

"We'll wake up Klaus!" she whispered urgently.

He'd taken her around the waist and was nuzzling her nape.

"No, Barry." She pulled away, freed herself.

He let her go reluctantly. "Look I can understand . . . after such a long time . . . But I can't help myself, you know. With you, I mean."

She'd stepped into shadow. She put a hand out and caressed his cheek. "I just don't know, Barry. It's all been such a shock."

She moved away. He fumbled for a cigarette, lit it, flaring the porch into instantaneous soft, warm colors, her flesh, her pink slip, her bright eyes. Then into darkness. "Want one?"

"Barry?"

"Yes?"

"At the Nepenthe restaurant you told me a little bit about your life during these past years. You said something about the women you'd been with. But you never asked about me. About the men I'd been with . . ."

"Well? You want to tell me about all your men now?" he asked, slightly annoyed.

"I think I should. So it's all clear once and for all. You understand that when I was released after two years in their prison, all I wanted to do was to get as far away from those people as I could. I came here to California. I changed my name to Tanya Gregory."

"As in Gregorievna."

"That's right. And I found little jobs in Carmel boutiques. I became the manager of one shop. Then I met my partner, Alan. He'd inherited the land on which the shop is built, and he offered me a partnership in it. We were never lovers, Barry. Alan had a lover, a man. For a long time, many years, I never thought about being with a man. Then I met Peter. He was younger than I was and a little shy, and so we became friendly. We lived together about two years. He left when I said I wouldn't marry him. After Peter, there was another, even younger, man, Nikos, and again that ended

121

when he wasn't content with our living together. And last, there was Robert."

Barry remembered the slim young man in the pony-skin vest at the Big Sur shop.

"Are you laughing yet?" she asked.

"Why should I be?"

"Because I was getting older and older, yet I was looking for a twenty-year-old friend and lover. I found them easily enough, but they all wanted to be my husband, to settle down and have children, which was the last thing I wanted—the last thing I thought possible."

"What are you saying, Anna?"

"Do you know, I realized it about a month ago, I went to pick up Robert at some friends' house. He was on the lawn playing touch football, wearing only shorts, holding the football, and running the 'nickel pass.' Do you remember when you showed me that?"

"Yes."

"I had such a *déjà vu*!" she said. "I was horrified. Then I began to laugh at myself. My life has degenerated into nostalgia."

He took her hand in a way that said he understood.

"Try to sleep," she said. "We have a long day tomorrow."

"Where's Elaine?" Barry typed into the laptop computer.

"The john. She'll be out in a minute," Albert typed back. "You planning to return soon?"

"When you least expect it," Barry answered.

It was a clear morning, he could smell the tang of salt air through the open window. Anna was sitting across the breakfast table from him, having coffee. Despite the fact that she'd been unable to sleep last night, she looked fresh and lovely. Barry was sore all over from his stint on the wicker sofa. Barenreiter was up already—he seemed to have been up for hours—and could be heard soldering in the dilapidated shed on the other side of the house—his studio.

"The only reason I ask is that it's a little surprising for a boss to be away so soon after hiring someone new."

"Couldn't be helped," Barry replied.

"Of course, Elaine is a real help, and I can see why you feel so easy about leaving, as she's so serious and committed to the business."

Barry had almost typed back, "She is?"

Then Elaine was out and took over the computer's phone connection.

"Marty Kalb came by yesterday. And she *didn't* ask for you. I sort of thought you might be together."

"Forget about Marty."

"Are you spying on us?" Elaine asked.

Just then, a flashing sidebar on the laptop's screen went on:

TELEPHONE CALL FROM LINDA HENDRICKS, DENVER AREA CODE

"That's for me," Barry typed. "We'll talk later."

"It's like 'call waiting,' " Barry explained to Anna. "I didn't even remember it was a feature included."

The Denver reporter had no new information for them. But her digging into the Lost and Found Jefferson case had borne some fruit. She'd gone to the Coroner's Office herself, called in a favor from a clerk there and had gotten a look at the inquest folder.

"There was nothing in it," she keyboarded. "And when I had the clerk ask his boss why not, he was told the file was Code 23. Which means it's in the files of the NSA, in Washington, D.C. What do you think of that?"

"I think you should try to get into the NSA's files and see if there's a Talmadge listed."

"I'm a step ahead of you. I did that, and *all* I found was his name: Burr Talmadge. The file was locked up. For Eyes Only and all that bullshit. I'm going to keep on it."

"Burr was the name of the man in Kyra's letter," Anna said.

The next step was a call to the institute where Kevin

Vosburgh's sister resided. An appointment was set for them to visit later that afternoon.

Barry finally shut off the laptop and detached the modem from the telephone.

Anna smiled a little wanly. "I think I said too much last night."

"No, you didn't," he assured her.

It was a long drive from where they'd spent the night to the Patton State Hospital for the Emotionally Disturbed in San Bernardino. Although it was late morning, the freeways were crowded until they passed out of the L.A. city limits, where traffic loosened up. Once they'd skirted the city, it was close to two hours of driving past a monotonous landscape of nearly identical towns and hamlets, most of them with names of Spanish origin—El Monte, Covina, Alta Loma, Cucamonga.

"To think, this place used to be so beautiful," Anna suddenly said, as though she knew exactly what he was thinking. "Do you know what the Chinese call California? *Guei Mei*. The Beautiful Country. That's true of some of it, isn't it?"

"What we saw this morning, driving down from Big Sur."

She looked in the back mirror twice in a minute, and Barry wondered what she was looking at.

"The car behind us needs a new muffler and exhaust pipe," she commented, and rolled up her window.

She swung into the fast lane, and the speedometer went up to 80 mph as she sped away from the Plymouth's smoke and racket.

"You haven't asked me anything about Alex Land yet."

"What should I ask you?"

"He's retired. He and his wife own a horse farm in Virginia."

"No one ever retires from intelligence work," she said.

"I did. You did."

"You, maybe. But then you only worked for a few

months. 'What I did on my summer vacation.' As for me, well, Barry, I was retired by others."

"Want me to drive?" he asked.

"We turn here," Anna said.

"Are you sure? There's no sign!"

There was a sign, a small one, she pointed out, and made the turn. Citrus trees lined the road on both sides as she drove into what appeared to be the gates of a rather contemporary high school or small college. No electric-field fence, no high walls, only a toy gate house with a lackadaisical clerk on duty, reading the Santa Anita racing forms.

Parking wasn't difficult in the huge lot. At the main reception desk they were told that Ms. Vosburgh would join them in the cafeteria. The woman pointed it out to them on the map of the institute.

They found the cafeteria with no problem. The few people who were lunching were out on an adjacent lawn, which had been set up with picnic tables and colorful umbrellas.

Barry and Anna got coffee and went out there to wait. They'd been sipping in silence for a few minutes, when Barry heard behind him:

"Are you the people looking for me? I'm Elly."

A short, heavyset young woman in a pale green jogging suit. Her eyes were large, pale blue, and vaguely moon-struck, her mouth a tiny bow of lips, her nose a button in her huge, fleshy globe of a face.

She sat down and seemed calm enough.

"This is a lovely spot," said Anna, smiling.

"It is, isn't it?" Elly responded with a minimum of enthusiasm. "I just love it. I've been here at Patton, well, it must be a while now. I have my own room, and there's big pool area to swim and sun in"—her complexion was refined-flour white—"and gardens. Lovely. I'm just so pleased to be here!"

Barry and Anna exchanged looks that asked each other, "Is she sedated, tranquilized, brainwashed?"

Aloud, Anna said, "I hope you don't mind our visiting you here. You see, our daughter has disappeared. We're trying to locate her. We thought you might be able to help."

"I read about runaways all the time. It's a shame. What's her name?"

"Kyra Anthony. But I don't think you know her."

"Afraid not."

"But she did know your brother, Kevin. Perhaps if you could tell us . . . ?"

"Well, if she knows Kevin, then God help your daughter!"

That stopped Anna. Barry asked what Elly meant.

"Kevin Vosburgh is Satan on earth."

"Our daughter and your brother used to be in a group together . . ."

"EDGE you mean?"

"You know of it?"

"Oh sure, I know all about it. It was a group of kids with special talents. Only Lord help them, if they included him. He mayn't have had hands and legs, or at any rate, only itty-bitty legs, but that didn't stop him. I pity her."

Barry and Anna once more exchanged glances.

"They were friends," Anna began again. "Kyra liked Kevin."

"Of course she liked him. That's how the devil works. He wouldn't get anywhere if people didn't like him, now would he?"

Barry butted in: "Did you ever meet any of the others in EDGE?"

"Only Mr. Talmadge."

"You met Burr Talmadge?"

"Naturally. He came here to Patton to have me sign papers giving him guardianship over Kevin. You see, our mamma and daddy both died."

"I'm so sorry," Anna said. "So, this Mr. Talmadge . . . ?"

"Who'd want guardianship of a monster like Kevin? *I*

126

didn't! Not after all I'd gone through with him. Sure you don't want anything? I'm a little hungry."

Elly stood up and went inside.

"What do you think?" Barry whispered.

"She seems to want to talk. We listen, no?"

Elly returned with a wedge of coconut custard pie that was so good, she said, Barry simply *had* to taste it (he did), and she began to talk about Burr Talmadge and EDGE.

"Kevin found them, not the other way around. I mean, who would think of coming out to Fontana—that's where we used to live—to find him? He found them on his computer. I don't know how exactly. But he did. At first, all his dealings with Mr. Talmadge were through the computer. But then, someone came to look Kevin over, and he began to join their meetings and then . . . well . . ."

Anna asked if Elly knew where her brother was.

"Well, he wrote to me for a while. Not 'write' write. He'd use the computer, then just print it out. He has no hands, you see. Then, when I wouldn't answer his letters, he finally stopped writing."

"Where did he write from?"

"Colorado. It was some post-office box. Number one-two-three. I remembered that, it was so easy. He said they lived pretty far from any town, but that if I wrote, I should write to that box number."

"What town in Colorado?"

"Leadtown? Leadmont? Something with lead in it."

"In the mountains? The Rocky Mountains?" Barry tried.

"Uh-huh. In fact, he wrote that he was living right on the Continental Divide. That's where rainfall goes eventually either east to the Mississippi or west to the Pacific Ocean."

"Leadville?" Barry asked. He'd been looking through the road atlas, earlier.

"That's it! Leadville! Nasty name, but then I guess that's where he belongs. Up in the mountains far away from doing any harm. Not that distance will stop him. So long as he has a computer nearby, he'll always make trouble of some sort."

"How long ago did you last get a letter from him?"

"Little more than a year ago. I *know* I probably should have answered, but you don't know Kevin. And I do. . . ."

"I'm sure you have your reasons . . ." Barry began.

"When Kevin was born, our daddy took it as a judgment on him, you know: to have a deformed little creature like that! I was about fourteen or so, and I had to care for him, what with Mamma sick and all. I stopped going to school regularly. Daddy said girls didn't need too much education, anyway. Kevin was such a bright and happy baby, always laughing and smiling—and that angered our daddy. If Kevin had been sickly and poor . . . He blamed that little baby for our mamma's illness, though he knew as well as I did that wasn't so." Elly paused. "Sometimes people know things without knowing how they know them. You know what I mean?"

They said they did, and Elly went on.

"There was this sort of brick shack on the property, used to be a lemon-oil press back there at one time. Our daddy said that's where he wanted Kevin kept. So I cleaned it out and put his crib there, and that's where Kevin grew up. I promised Mamma I'd care for him, and I did. Even though he didn't have hands, he could use his little stumps of feet, and he began early to use objects in his mouth to do things, to play with things and to build things with. Pretty soon I could see how smart he was. And I began to teach him how to read and count, using whatever school books were left around in the house. Well, by the time he was four years old, Kevin had gone through all those, and he wanted more books. So whenever I'd go into Fontana to food shop, I'd stop in the public library there and take out books. Oh, he read everything!

"By the time Kevin was eight, he was reading at college level, and I had to get the books he needed. All kinds of things on electronics and science and all that. Then he wanted electronics equipment. He saw them pictured and advertised in the magazines. I asked him how we could afford it. And he told me he *had* to have them. I'd have to pay for them however I could figure out.

"That's when I began to steal. First it was shoplifting for meat and stuff, occasionally clothing. That helped a little. But even by mail order, electronics weren't cheap, and Kevin would put together all the pieces from a kit in one afternoon even without hands, and he would beg me for more. So I began to steal money out of our daddy's pockets when he came home drunk, which was almost always, by this time. That helped a bit more. I would go to electronics stores with his list for small items, and I would buy a little and steal a lot more. That was more dangerous, except that no one suspected a dumb old girl like me who couldn't even pronounce the names of things. After a while, Kevin had me driving around Fontana looking for castoffs, thrown-away radios, typewriters, stereos, televisions. I used to bring home whatever I found, and he would make them all work and reconnect them. He made us an intercom so Mamma could call us in the shack. Then he hooked up all the phones. But he wanted to make computers, and he needed more money for that.

"His first computer was made up out of all sorts of things—typewriters, radios, and old TV sets. But it worked well enough. And now he had a plan to get more money. He had me go open up bank accounts in two or three nearby towns, and he began to fool with the computer, and soon enough he'd managed to move money from other people's cash accounts into mine—corporations' petty cash, he said. I was scared of it all, of course, but he said it was so small they wouldn't miss a few hundred dollars a month.

"Now he had money to buy better computers, and he did. Soon the entire shack looked like the inside of a space ship, with dials, and lights blinking and machines whirring day and night. It was around that time that our daddy's drinking killed him. I always wondered how he drove home at night so drunk, and he always told me, the car knew the way.

129

Well, I guess that one night, it forgot, 'cause he ran off the road.

"After the funeral, Kevin moved into the house and took over most of the downstairs with all his computers and electronics. I'd become scared with the bank accounts, so he said okay, because now there were the lemon groves to sell off. Which is what we did. Piece by piece we sold them off to live on, and to pay for Mamma's medicines and doctor bills, and for Kevin to buy new equipment. Those were the best times for us, I suppose. Kevin had a carpenter in Covina build a chair to his design so he could move around to all the computers fast and comfortably—because that had become his world, you see. Everything outside came to him that way. He'd take classes at technical institutions through the TV and his computers, he'd play chess with people across the country, he joined scientists' clubs all over. He just loved it. He was in contact with all sorts of whiz kids like he was. He was involved in all sorts of special programs. With all that, he became greedy and began to talk more and more about money, and then he began to use the bank accounts again whenever we ran low on money.

"I was right at the bank when I was arrested. I tried to explain that I wasn't working for any company or gang. I tried not to, but finally I had to bring Kevin into it. Well, they took me home, and there Kevin was, in bed, acting like he could hardly talk, never mind operate a computer. I was so angry with him! But because of him and Mamma being in the shape they were, I was put on parole and so it wasn't that much of a problem.

"Then the bad times started. No money. Mamma getting worse. And Kevin began to taunt and mock me. He said all sorts of terrible things to me. I could see our daddy's bad side coming out in Kevin, and that was pretty bad. I don't recall exactly what incident finally did it, but one night I got so angry with him and fed up with my life as it had become, I set the house on fire, figuring he'd

130

burn up while he slept. After setting that fire, I just drove away and didn't look back. Of course, in my anger I'd clear forgotten about our Mamma, who couldn't even get out of bed. And I hadn't counted on Kevin's resourcefulness. He managed to crawl out of the house to safety. But not before calling every single fire department in the county. Well, the fire didn't spread as far in the house as I thought it would. But the smoke poured upstairs and asphyxiated Mamma. She died of her heart, poor thing. And, of course, Kevin told anyone who would listen that I set the fire, and I couldn't deny it, could I? Could I?

"So, I'm here, and I suppose that's right and as it should be, even though I'm a trusty now, and everyone will tell you I've never been a speck of trouble. But I guess that's okay, because now Kevin is way up in the Rocky Mountains away from anyone. But I'll tell you something else: As long as that boy is near a computer, he's a menace. A true menace."

"Well, what do you think?" Barry asked.

"It's an institute for the emotionally disturbed, no?"

"But not for pathological liars." And when she didn't respond, he asked, "Do you believe what Elly Vosburgh said?"

"Some, yes. Details, perhaps."

"Do you think that Kyra's deluded in her friend?" Barry asked.

"I wish I knew what to think."

Barry stopped the car at the first public telephone booth, a roadside phone set on a pylon. He connected up the modem to the computer and dialed Denver. Linda Hendricks greeted them with a question:

"Did you see Elly?"

"Yes. She told us the name of Burr Talmadge's group. EDGE, or possibly E.D.G.E., if it's a government operation, as you suspect."

"Got it," she replied. "I've interested one of my colleagues in all this. He's into computers, and he's been trying to hack into the various government files, including the NSA. No luck, so far. Perhaps with your information . . . Can you hold on a sec? . . . His name is Gunther."

She was away from the computer a minute, Barry guessed, while she went over to Gunther's desk or called him over to hers.

"Hello? Gunther here. I've gotten a key into the file, and now I'm putting in your acronym to see what happens."

Barry waited again.

"What else did Elly Vosburgh say?" Linda asked.

"Gave me a complete story on Kevin growing up. Seems he was born without hands or legs. Father disowned him. Kid's an electronic genius."

"Sounds fascinating. Listen, I checked into the Timmo connection. I was right, St. Joseph's isn't a town in Arizona. It's a juvenile correction home located outside of Winslow, and not far from the meteor crater."

"Another lead!" Barry said out loud to Anna. "We've found out where Timmo is."

She came to the telephone and began to read the computer screen, one hand casually on Barry's shoulder as she leaned over to see better.

Barry typed, "We think we may know where the group is."

"Where?"

"The Rockies somewhere."

"That would make sense if the government was involved," she typed back. "God only knows what the government has hidden in the Rockies!"

Gunther interrupted: "Listen, folks, I've used your code, and it popped open something."

"What is it?"

"EDGE is an acronym, as we thought. It stands for Extrasensory Development for Geopolitical Exploitation."

"What the hell does that mean?" Barry queried, then turned to look at Anna. Her hand had tensed on his shoulder. "What?" he asked her. "Have you heard that before."

"No!" Anna dropped her hand, moved away from him. "It just sounds so . . . cold!"

Gunther had keyboarded back that he assumed Barry's question was rhetorical. Linda added, "He's going to try to push into the file a bit more."

"Shit!" Gunther typed. "Look at this!

NATIONAL SECURITY AGENCY
WARNING!
UNAUTHORIZED ENTRY INTO THIS FILE WILL BE
DEALT WITH WITH THE UTMOST
ELECTRONIC SEVERITY

"What do they plan to do? Take away my laptop?" Barry typed.

"It's a Trojan!" Gunther said. "I can't chance it. I'm backing out. Sorry!"

"What's a Trojan?" Barry asked.

"Computer jargon for 'Trojan horse,'" Gunther explained. "While you're hacking a file, it secretly undermines everything on your hard disc, erasing it. Some Trojans do it instantly, others take weeks and only announce the fact when you've been screwed. I can't risk it. Sorry!"

"Damn!" Barry said out loud. "He doesn't want to take the chance," he told Anna. "Isn't there a way *I* can get in myself?" Barry typed. "I've got nothing on this disc worth saving."

"I'll look for a way for you to obtain a direct transmission," Gunther said.

"And I'll try by more old-fashioned methods," Linda said.

"Us, too," Barry said. "Thanks again. You've been an ace."

"Don't thank me," she typed back. "I wouldn't bother unless I were interested. This business is getting weirder the deeper we get in."

"Can you navigate?" Barry asked, handing her the road map.

After examining it, Anna said she thought they wanted

Route 40, further north. She began to map out several alter-native routes, occasionally asking his advice.

"Why don't you try to rest up," he suggested. "It's a long ride. You'll have to spell me later."

Once they'd driven past the Colorado River into Arizona, traffic thinned out considerably. As the sun began to set, the huge, flat tableland of the Sonora Desert gave way to stria-tions of mountains in the distance, like vast strips of putty laid down in haste by some giant hand to be sculpted later on. Chips of less eroded minerals in the far-off range re-flected the fading sunlight with tiny points of fire that skit-tered like distant people running with torches. Saguaro cactus and giant yucca reddened into silhouette grotesqueries against the lavender eastern sky. A half minute later, it was dark.

He looked at Anna, her head turned toward the passenger window, wondering if she were asleep, until she sighed quietly.

"Mind if I try to get some music on the radio?" he asked, and when she didn't protest, he began to punch buttons. The highway turned north, flat and clear on the left side back to the river, he thought; that might explain why he was receiv-ing stations from Las Vegas. One programmed classical mu-sic, which seemed right for evening driving, and he left on a Mozart piano concerto.

Barry checked his speedometer—75 mph, perfect cruis-ing speed on an April night in the Arizona desert. He could be taking his girl home from a dance or . . . He had to clear up some things, even if it meant getting her angry to do so.

"You aren't in the least bit curious about Alex Land yet?"

"Let's not talk about him, okay?"

If she wouldn't rise to the bait that way, he'd try another route.

"Why do you think Elly Vosburgh didn't talk about her brother's psychic ability? I assume he has one, otherwise he wouldn't be part of the same group as Kyra."

"I thought you would ask her," Anna said.

"There was so much to ask, it got lost. Why didn't you?"

Anna didn't answer, so Barry tried another tack.

"What about your mind-reading abilities? Is that something you still do?"

"No, I've tried to put all that completely behind me—after Paris and the horrible mess it got me into. Still, sometimes I can't help myself."

"Anna, there's something I always wondered about. Did your ESP, or whatever you want to call it, have anything to do with your work for the KGB?"

"Yes. That's why the KGB sent me to Paris. They believed I could use the ability to discover Western agents."

She looked away at the night sky.

"It's all so stupid, thinking of it now. They would tell me, go to such-and-such address, a dinner party or a theater or whatever. And I would go, and sometimes I would meet or even just see someone there—a man or woman—and I would think, yes, this person is an agent. He must be. I would report back. With no proof. Just a feeling."

"Did you feel it with me, too?"

"Very strongly, Barry, yet I couldn't believe it. What kind of agent could you be? I asked myself every day. You read football magazines and you slept through your lectures in the Sorbonne. You were careless, and thoughtless, all you wanted to do was make love until I was sore and tired and crazy. It went haywire with you. And all the while it was true! You were an agent."

"Anna . . ."

"It's funny, don't you think?"

"It's not funny at all," he said. "You were exploited."

"Extrasensory Development for Geopolitical Exploitation!" she reminded him. "What does that mean, Barry? I keep on trying to figure it out."

"What it means, Anna, is that someone may be trying to exploit Kyra, too."

*   *   *

"Yes! Well, we weren't aware of the fact that Timmo had relatives in California," said the administrations officer at the St. Joseph Reformatory for Boys with more than a little snippiness. "Indeed! We weren't aware of *any* relatives the boy had, outside of his deceased mother."

Barry detected a hint of nervousness as well in Mrs. Danielson's voice. Not nervousness toward them, he thought, so much as a general, all-embracing anxiety. Whatever its cause, he decided to brass it out.

"I'm Thor Nilsson's half-brother," he lied glibly. "We've never been that close. But I was always fond of the boy. So when I knew we were going to be in the neighborhood, I thought we should stop by and see Timmo. He loves it when we visit."

Tight-lipped, Mrs. Danielson said, "Yes! I'm certain he does. But the fact is, Timmo left our facility about a year ago."

The woman had been leading them down a long, high-ceilinged corridor that bissected the large old cinnamon brick building. Neither Barry nor Anna had seen a single boy yet, and few adults either. Signs of the place's restrictive nature were apparent enough: thick, small panels of glass with shatterproof wire patterns embedded high in double-thick metal-braced doors; wire-mesh screens with locks lacing every cabinet, window, or shelf.

"We at St. Joseph's Home like to think," Mrs. Danielson said, "that every boy has potential good in him, no matter what his past history may have been."

She had turned into a room, which she had to unlock to enter. As they followed her into the office, Barry noticed that behind the gray-streaked extra-tight bun of the woman's hair a single white thread from her blouse collar meandered delicately down the military drabness of her severely cut jacket. He longed to pull it to see if all of her would unravel with it.

"I don't understand," Anna was saying. "We heard nothing of Timmo being released."

Mrs. Danielson turned smartly, to face them with a dour expression.

"Yes! Well, he wasn't released so much as transferred to another program—on a temporary basis, of course."

"To another institution?"

"Not precisely."

"Well, then," Barry asked, "what kind of program?"

"Despite Timmo's antisocial tendencies, he had managed to show some other, outstanding talents."

"What kind of program?" Barry asked.

"Very small. Very select," Mrs. Danielson went on. She stood at a desk, near a tall, freestanding file cabinet of teak with brass fittings. The light in this room was softer than the oppressive high fluorescence of the corridors, but it did little to soften her features. "They were looking for boys with certain leadership qualities. Timmo has always been able to exert peculiar power over his peers, especially those with low self-esteem. Unfortunately, that wasn't always a positive factor in his relations here at St. Joseph's. I assume you know why he was placed here with us?"

"All I know is that he got into some kind of trouble."

"Well, it's more complicated than that, I'm afraid. Timmo's form of sociopathy manifests itself in a total disregard for others." She smiled, and it was like a skull smiling in a Halloween decoration, empty and mocking. "Timmo knifed two people before he came to St. Joseph's. In each case, he seemed to find it difficult to accept that what he'd done was wrong." That smile again, and this time, allied to what she'd just told them about the boy, it seemed even more mocking than before. "You look surprised, Mrs. Brescia."

"I . . . I wasn't aware of . . . why Timmo was here," Anna managed to stutter. Barry could tell she was as shocked as he was.

"But he changed while he was here?" Barry tried. "That's why he was taken into the new program?"

"Yes, well, I suppose *someone* thought he'd changed, or at

137

least didn't think that Timmo's sociopathy was as dangerous as before. Or perhaps they decided that in the long run it wasn't as important as his ability to mobilize other boys into a cohesive group—gang, whatever you might want to call it."

"That sounds something like the Eagle Scouts," Barry said.

"Yes! Well, not really." Mrs. Danielson said, automatically, it seemed. "At any rate, they were pleased with him in the program. And they planned to have Timmo return to St. Joseph's once the program was done, but . . . but he seems to have become somewhat disturbed by the change in circumstances, and more than a bit confused. From what I was led to undestand, Timmo thought he had failed rather than excelled in the special program. He'd evidently counted on the program in some indefinable manner, and he thought he would not be coming back to St. Joseph's, when in fact . . . " She let those last words hang in the air. "Whatever he thought, the day before he was to be returned to us, he disappeared, and it was later discovered that—I'm sorry to have to tell you this—he'd hidden and taken his own life."

"When did that happen?" Barry asked.

"A little more than a year ago."

"That can't be true!" cried Anna.

The administrator took the outburst for the incredulity that often accompanies shocking news and usually precedes appropriate grief.

"Yes! Well, I'm afraid so. Naturally you're upset."

Barry helped Anna sit on the small, hard, leather-covered sofa, while Mrs. Danielson turned to the files, opened a top drawer, and began to check through the index tabs. She pulled out a file, began to rummage through it, and came up with three sheets of official-looking paper, which she handed to Barry. One was a physician's report and certification of death, the second some sort of interoffice memo containing a fuller explanation of how the boy had been found, attached to a note to the institute's proctor about the "regrettable incident," co-signed by Burr Talmadge. This last was on NSA stationary and noted that copies had been sent to a half-dozen others in the agency. The third set of initials was A.J.L. In his surprise, Barry almost dropped the documents. It could be mere coincidence, couldn't it? Someone other than Alex James Land? Alex had said he was retired. Had made a point of it! Yes, but why bother to make a point of it? Unless he wasn't retired at all, yet wanted everyone to believe he was.

"May we have these?" Barry asked. He didn't want to alert Anna to what he was thinking. Not yet. Not until he'd checked into it further.

"Yes. Naturally we weren't aware of your existence at the time of the event, so we didn't know whom to notify."

"And Timmo?" Anna asked in a quiet voice. "Where is he. . . ?"

"Under circumstances such as these, he was interred by the agency that last had custody over him. I believe the body was cremated. All the information is provided for you." She pointed to the paper with the NSA stamp on it.

"Can we leave now?" Anna asked Barry. She had gotten control of herself and was doing a fine acting job. Even the staunch Mrs. Danielson was affected.

"I'm afraid I can't let you have the originals. Those are for our records. I'll have to make copies. We have a machine. It will only take a minute."

"We'd appreciate it, ma'am," Barry said.

Once the administrations officer was out of the room, Anna stood up. "It's terrible!" Anna said. "All of it."

"I'll say," Barry agreed. "This is the boy Carol Stolzing said looked like an angel?"

"And because he's an orphan, they think they can just say that he's dead, that he committed suicide, and no one will ask for him again."

Barry got up and went to the door to make certain no one was listening. When he was satisfied no one was, he said, "I agree that something's up, and it's not looking good, but I want those papers. I want proof. I want Talmadge's signature on that letter."

Barry was beginning to wonder why the woman was gone so long. He hoped to hell she wasn't in some inner office, at some other file, checking up on Timmo's relatives—or worse, calling the NSA to say they'd come by looking for Timmo. That would be . . .

"Yes! Here we are! Sorry it took so long." She handed Barry the papers, and he looked through them quickly, checking that all were there.

"I'm afraid we're rather upset about Timmo. We'd better go."

He folded the papers and stuffed them into the breast pocket of his jacket, then firmly took Anna's arm to help her out of the office and down the corridor—Mrs. Danielson's flats slapping the linoleum behind them all the way to the doors and out into the warm Arizona late afternoon.

It was sunset when they returned to the motor inn at Winslow where they'd checked in just before driving over to St. Joseph's. Anna seemed exhausted.

"Why don't you take a nap?" he suggested. "We'll go out and get a bite later."

Anna agreed. She took off her shoes while he set up the laptop to the phone. By the time he was finished, she was asleep. Anna looked as if she might be out for another hour or so. He'd see if Linda Hendricks was still in her office.

She was. "Well? What did you find out?" she began straightforwardly.

"According to them, Timmo Nilsson committed suicide over a year ago. He'd been part of some group funded by the feds. The body was allegedly cremated by them. It was never returned to St. Joseph's. All they got were papers. I managed to get copies of all the relevant documents."

"Wow!" she typed. "Fax them to me."

140

He keyboarded, "The administrator at St. Joseph's didn't say anything about Timmo having psychic abilities, but she did say he showed unusual talents in leading younger boys. Perhaps that has something to do with it? I don't know. She also said he was a sociopath. Had knifed two people. Sounds like a nice kid, huh?"

"None of them sounds very nice except our local hero," Linda replied.

"Any ideas from Gunther on how to get around NSA's Trojan?" he asked.

"Not yet. Check back later."

Barry signed off, and hit the "save" button to retain their conversation on the disc. He felt a chill. If only he could figure out what it all meant, that might make more sense.

He cleared the laptop screen and keyboarded the names of the five children in a column, and next to that their special abilities. He ended up with:

"Lost and Found"	Can locate people (things?); "killed" in accident.
Kevin Vosburgh	Computer genius (and psychic?); guardianship papers transferred by sister to Talmadge.
Matty Stolzing	Can do realistic hallucinations; taken by Talmadge nine months ago.
Timmo Nilsson	Can persuade others to do what he wants (sociopath—murderer); committed suicide over a year ago, no body.
Kyra Anthony (Brescia)	Can predict past/future events.
Burr Talmadge	Administrator? Organizer?

There it was, all laid out! But what did these six names add up to? Extrasensory Development for Geopolitical Exploitation, of course! But what exactly did *that* mean?

Overtired as he was from driving with only little catnaps in the passenger seat, Barry found he couldn't concentrate clearly, yet he knew he probably wouldn't be able to sleep. He turned on the TV so it was barely audible, then hunted through the channels looking for diversion.

"Barry," Anna murmured.

"I thought you were asleep."

He shut off the television and went to the bed.

"Feel better?" he asked.

"I slept a little. I'm hungry."

Anna sat up, lifted away locks of hair that had fallen in front of her face.

"It's been a very long time since I've been privileged to see you wake up."

She looked carefully to see if he were joking, then she smiled.

"This time, I don't have any help from the KGB," he said.

They both laughed.

Anna sensed that something was wrong the minute they got back to the motel.

The evening had been pleasant. Over dinner Barry had begun to tell Anna more about the time "in between," as he called it, the seventeen years, the different places he'd lived in, the different jobs he'd worked at, the different women he'd lived with. It all seemed to spill out of him effortlessly with Anna listening.

After dinner they had gone to a movie, and in the middle of it they had turned to each other and said, "Let's leave." Driving out of Flagstaff, they'd passed a sort of roadhouse, the Dance Right-In, and stopped. They'd taken a table against the wall and sipped weak cocktails and watched for an hour. Both had been approached to join in, and both refused. But when the "caller" had taken a break and slow

142

music had come onto the jukebox, their waitress, "Florence, from Florence Junction, downstate on Route Sixty," had told them in no uncertain terms that she wanted to see them "being a little romantic."

So Barry had asked, and Anna had accepted, and they'd danced close together to "I Only Have Eyes for You," under the fake pin-stars of the darkened ceiling, among the other couples, and they'd felt not a bit embarrassed or uncomfortable, then or afterward. Barry had held her hand, stepping off the little dance floor and out of the place. They were silent the twenty miles or so back to the motor inn, and he hardly dared think what might happen once they were back in that small motel room.

He was still thinking about it as they approached the gravel drive in front of the place.

"Wait!" she said to Barry before they turned in.

"What's wrong?"

"I'm not sure," she admitted. "Something isn't right."

There were five other cars parked in front of the single-story building. One hadn't been there when they left. But what did that mean?

"Look!" Anna said. "We didn't leave a light on in our room. Someone's inside."

Barry took the service driveway that went around behind the office. As they'd passed the wide office window, the elderly manager was clearly visible in the flickering blue light of a television.

"Stay here," Barry said, and got out of the car. He went around the rear of the motel. He counted off windows until he figured he was behind theirs. No lights on inside. Could Anna have been wrong? He moved cautiously to the end of the rooms, then around to the front.

A car was pulling out of the gravel lot onto the tarmac single lane that led out to the highway. He could see two men inside, then it was gone. A second later, he was at the door to their room—dark again. Anna was talking through the window to the hotel manager. He waited until she joined him.

"Did you see them?" she asked.

"I couldn't make them out. What did he say?"

"He didn't notice anything," she said.

"Let me go first."

"Don't you think it's safe?"

He unlocked the door, opened it quietly, and froze. He couldn't hear anyone. He'd have to chance it. He flipped on the light switch. The room looked like a tornado had torn through. Their clothing tossed everywhere, every hanger in the closet pulled down, every bureau drawer pulled out, rummaged through, dumped. But no one was there.

"Oh, Barry!" she cried, her voice dropped to its lowest register.

"That bitch at St. Joseph's must have contacted Talmadge or the NSA as soon as we left."

Anna had assessed the situation and reached the same conclusion. "The papers she gave you?"

"I still have them." He patted the breast pocket of his lined denim jacket.

"And your computer."

"In the car. But they did a very thorough job," he said. "We can't stay here tonight. They might be back. Let's clean this mess and pack up. We're getting out."

When they were packed, he said, "We'll go back to Flagstaff, find a place for the night. Tomorrow you'll fly back to Big Sur."

She looked up at him. He couldn't figure out what she was thinking. He'd felt so close to her only a short while ago. And now . . .

"We can't stop now, Barry. We'll drive to Colorado tonight. To Leadville."

He bent down and took her hands. "You don't *have* to. Why not go back to Big Sur. I'll stay in touch with you, let you know what I find out. I promise!"

Determined, she pulled her hands away. "We'll go together, Barry."

"They're onto us. This could get dangerous!"

She stood up. "I'll figure out the route. Finish in the bathroom." She found the road atlas and threw it onto the bed. "See! On page thirty-one and thirty-two. We stay off the highway, take the smaller roads. Look! Seventy-seven to two-fifty-four to sixty-three to one-sixty. We'll drive all night. Take turns."

"I don't understand, Anna."

"This is important for me," she insisted.

Three hours later, deep in the Navajo Indian Reservation area, just approaching the road that she assured him would take them around a tiny town called Many Farms, he pulled the car to the side of the road, walked a dozen yards, and urinated, trying to see in the cloud-filled night something besides darkness, then he returned to the passenger seat. Anna was behind the wheel. She put the car into gear and drove on.

After only a few minutes, in which it was obvious to both of them that he wasn't falling asleep as he was supposed to, Anna asked:

"When you saw him a few days ago, what did Land say about me?" She'd asked so quietly he wasn't certain he'd heard correctly. Finally, he thought.

"I told you before. He said you were dead. Why?"

"I can't help but feel he's connected in some way to all this."

"I know you hate him as much as I do, Anna. I just can't see where that connects to Kyra. To EDGE."

"I'm not sure, either. Let me tell you in detail what happened to me, Barry."

"Anna, I know this is painful for you."

"Even so. In Virginia I underwent a year of torture. Not physical torture. They're far too subtle for that. I knew what the situation was. I knew they could send me back to Europe, and in one week the KGB would find me and kill me, no matter how well I hid myself. Even in America, the KGB

145

might find me. By then I was prepared for death. Not that I thought it would be patriotic dying for the USSR, you understand."

"Anna, when I came back from . . . well, it changed *my* life, too. I dropped out of school. I separated from my family for good."

She looked at him, then back to the road. For a minute or so, she was silent. Then, as though choosing her words very carefully, she began to talk again, in a steady, measured tone of voice.

"I had to do what Land said. Naturally I revealed all of the KBG operations in Europe I knew of. But all I knew was some names, a few codes, a few telephone numbers, a few addresses. Mostly of Russian emigrés in Paris. Still, I was a big catch! I did a great deal of damage. All my friends, all the people I knew in Paris, were under suspicion. This saddened me, but I accepted it. I'd lost the game for my side.

"Two things I could *not* accept. One was that you, Barry, *were* an agent. My downfall. For years I couldn't understand or accept that. When they told me I was with child, I knew you had to be the father. Next, they went after my psychic abilities. Endless tests, hypnosis, drugs. I tried to pretend my ESP didn't exist.

"Little by little, I came to realize that after each session less and less of me returned to the rooms where I was locked in. 'Tell me, Anna G., tell me, the first time a boy touched you there.' 'Tell me, Anna G., the shape of your mother's breasts?' 'Tell me, Anna G., when was the first time you had one of your "feelings" about the future?' He had to know everything! Throughout the hypnosis and truth serum, I was awake, fully conscious. I answered all his questions, even when I wanted to curse them, spit in their faces!

"All the while, a baby was growing inside me, and I didn't know what to do. One day I wanted to abort—this was your child, Barry. I didn't think you should have the right to make a new life after what you had done to me. The next day I thought, What if from now on I'm locked in this room?

Never again would there be a chance for a child. I'm a woman, and to have a child is important. I thought, Yes, I'll have the baby, then what? It will be with its mother, naturally. Or will they take it, and give my baby away? Three, four times a day I changed my mind, but finally I decided having the baby was good, perhaps the only good from a bad situation. The father and mother are good-looking, intelligent, healthy. I know it was naive. But I was desperate!

"Anyway, one day they weren't injecting me. The next day no more hypnosis. The doctors said I'm six months pregnant, they don't want me to have any more drugs, any more stress. Land was gone. I didn't ask where. For the next two months I was treated very well. Land arrived again when my contractions began. Some doctor put a mask full of ether over my mouth. When I woke up, I felt terrible. I was in a hospital. When I asked for my baby, they told me it was born dead. My only hope gone!

"Land came back a week later to the usual room. He didn't ask questions. He didn't hypnotize me, didn't inject me. He brought out a violin case. My violin case, which the CIA must have taken from my flat in the rue du Champignon. He brought it to me, and was very sweet. He said, 'Anna G., you've been very good, very helpful, very cooperative. Here's your violin. Go on, take it.'

"I opened the case. 'Play for me, Anna G.,' Land told me. The violin fit right into my shoulder. The bow fit right into my hand. It felt wonderful. I was so happy, there were tears in my eyes for joy. My violin! This much remained, this part of me he could not touch, could not change. I began to play a Bach partita, one of my favorites. . . . Do you know what happened next, Barry? What came out of that violin when I played wasn't Bach, it wasn't me, it wasn't even music! I remembered notes, I remembered fingering. But I couldn't remember what music sounded like. 'What's wrong?' Land asked. 'Why have you stopped?'

"At that moment I realized what Alex Land had done.

Music no longer existed for me, like the baby that had grown inside me for eight months."

"Oh, my God, Anna, I'm so sorry."

"Don't be sorry, Barry. Because I had the last laugh."

"What are you talking about?"

"Land never learned what he so desperately wanted to know: why I had psychic abilities. Despite everything he did, he never found out, I'm sure."

CHAPTER SIX

Down on the plains, it might have been a warm early spring, but once they drove into the Rockies, the wind suddenly rose and the temperature plummeted.

Anna turned the car heater on. The double-lane road twisted higher with every turn around gigantic escarpments onto shelves of brown rock face streaked with glinting icy cliffs of snow, which in another ten minutes and five miles of spiraling ascent proved to be mere foothills. The road rose even higher, aspiring, it seemed, to the unsullied, frozen baby blue of the sky.

They were astonished by the weight and massiveness of mountains around them, behind them, looming ahead and on all sides of them. A sign listed a pass at 11,992 feet above sea level, which meant the mountains on either side of this sheer defile must be several thousand feet higher. And, when it seemed they could no longer ascend, there was a mass of ice-striated rock dead ahead and through it a tunnel, sinister in its dark emptiness and its length, then another pass after that. Finally their way broke from the highway to a smaller road, which seemed little more than a mountain goat path with a layer of gray concrete splashed over it. Barry didn't even want to wonder where, among all this, Burr Talmadge had established his headquarters for EDGE. Every rift and canyon in the surrounding area seemed large enough, deep enough, to hide an entire army base, never mind a few buildings and a half-dozen children. Just before Leadville, they crossed over a sharp ridge, and Anna, looking over the side, could make out a sheer drop several thousand feet deep, and within it, a tiny ice-blue rivulet.

Given the magnificent setting, the town of Leadville itself was a disappointment. It didn't possess the quaintness of Central City, which Barry had been to years before, with its nineteenth-century gingerbread houses. Leadville obviously had been, and probably still was, a mining town, set in a bit of a valley. Each building evidently had been erected in haste and rebuilt or expanded carelessly whenever necessary. They passed right through Leadville and had to circle back before they located a largish general store with a tiny lunch counter and a minuscule hand-carved sign with the U.S. postal logo.

It was late afternoon. After the lengthy mountain drive, both of them needed warmth and coffee, so they sat quietly, sipping and steadying themselves as Barry peered through a screen of hanging snowshoes to the little dowel-windowed booth with a post-office sign above it.

"Is the P.O. open today?" he asked the nearly chinless young waitress wearing a housedress and a puffy, down-filled vest.

"It's open anytime I'm here and want it open," she said, with a flat twang in her voice. "You want to mail a letter? We've got a rack of picture postcards over there," she said, pointing into an agglomeration of "Indian" blankets and accessories for wood stoves.

"Actually, I'm looking for some information. I've got a pen pal who lives up near here somewhere," Barry said. "I figured maybe while we were nearby, we could visit her. Only problem is, I don't know where she lives. All I have is a post-office box number. She's a kid, lives with some people."

Barry wrote the box number on the back of the napkin, then covered it with a twenty-dollar bill.

"Can't help you, mister," she said. "I'll get your change."

"Keep it," he said, but she returned with the change in a half minute, and couldn't help but notice how disappointed he and Anna looked.

"Let me tell you something, mister. A lot of people live up here in the mountains because they want to. You understand? And because they don't want to bother with anyone else. I don't know *where* most of them live. Every half-assed cleft in the hills is large enough for someone to have plunked down some kind of shack. More'n a few of them are on the run from someone or from something: the bank, the IRS, their wives, their husbands . . ."

"You must know *some* of them?" he tried.

"You're right, mister. But I don't know *most* of them. And I don't *want* to, either."

"You must know who comes to pick up the mail for this box?"

"That I do. Three separate people. Two men and a woman. Never saw any kid with them. They come at different times, on different days of the week. And I never said more than 'Here's your mail' to them. And they never said more than 'Thanks' back. They could be anywhere in a hundred square miles of here. You want to go look, go ahead. You want to park your fanny here and wait till one of 'em shows up, you're welcome."

"Let's go," Anna said quietly.

"Take your change," the woman said. "Nothing I told you is worth seventeen dollars and thirteen cents."

"Sorry I was so pushy," he apologized. "But it's actually my daughter we're looking for. I was led to believe she might be with these people."

"I wish I could help you, mister."

Out on the street, they looked up the bleak single road, then down it again. The same cars and trucks were parked as when they'd gone into the store. It was getting colder.

"Everything is a dead end," Barry said, and kicked the left front tire.

Anna looked at the sun beginning to set, and shivered.

"Maybe we should go back and buy one of those blankets," she said. "They look warm, and we can use one in the car."

"Sure, why not."

He followed her back into the store, where Anna began to browse through aisles crowded with camping gear. Aimlessly, he followed her, trying to think of what to do next. They were so close to Denver, they probably ought to drive there. Maybe he should find a telephone and call Linda Hendricks. It had been almost a day since they'd spoken. Maybe her friend Gunther had broken through the NSA file, or found a way for Barry to do so.

Barry spotted a public phone booth hidden in the elaborately "western" woodwork of the shop's decor, went out to the car for the laptop, returned, plugged the modem into the phone, and called. Linda wasn't in, and the co-worker who'd answered his call couldn't locate Gunther, either. Barry left a message for Linda saying he'd be in town later on, he'd call again. He was about to unplug the computer when he remembered that he hadn't talked to the Ephemeris shop in a while. He still might reach them: It would be seven-thirty in Boston.

"What's going on, Barry? Where are you?"

"I'm out of town, Elaine. And nothing is going on."

"If you say so." Elaine seemed hesitant.

"You fuck Albert yet?" Barry typed. It looked so aggressive, written out like that without the humorous inflection he would have given it if it were spoken, but it would distract her.

A pause while she decided how to respond, then the screen read, "Last night."

"How was it?"

"Okay. Barry, are you *ever* coming back?"

"When you least expect it. How else can I keep you on your toes?"

"Is that why you called so late? To make sure I was staying open?"

"For all I know," Barry replied, "you two could have

152

locked up hours ago and spent the time rolling around on the pyramids-and-obelisks display table."

"Bye!" she keyboarded.

Barry detached the equipment.

He looked around the store for Anna, then spotted her outside in the car. He headed out, walking through the housewares section leading to the door, when a towheaded little boy appeared.

"My mamma said *that's* who you're looking for."

The boy pointed outside to a tall, dark-haired man, who was just stepping into a Dodge shortbed.

"He picked up the mail?" Barry asked.

The boy nodded and vanished into another aisle. Barry turned to look straight through the store directly to the little post-office booth, where the chinless woman stood behind the doweled window, making an "okay" sign with her fingers.

"Let's go," Barry said, tossing the computer attaché in the backseat.

"What? What is it?" Anna asked.

"Someone picked up the mail."

By the time Anna had started up the car, the pickup was already out of town, but still in view. It continued south, and Anna kept a good distance behind so that it didn't look overly suspicious. When the Dodge turned left suddenly, she was able to follow more leisurely. This road was a single lane and rose along a sharp arrete adjacent to and above Route 24 for some time before crossing a small bridge over the chasm of the narrow Arkansas River. It veered west, where it began to drop in overlapping, long hairpin curves. The Dodge zig-zagged in and out of sight around the bends. Barry tried to look over the area through which they drove, checking for buildings that might prove to be the EDGE headquarters. All he could see were mountains—one peak higher than all the others.

At the bottom of the series of hairpins, a small sign noted MT. ELBERT, ELEV. 14,433 ft., the highest point in Colorado, dead ahead twenty miles. Where had he heard of Mount Elbert before? He seemed to recall the name.

They'd temporarily lost the pickup. Now he noticed it far ahead, and urged Anna to speed to catch up. After a rise of ten minutes' duration, the road coasted down, then dropped suddenly at a sharp bend opening out into a mountain glen filled with wildflowers in bloom. Alongside was the sheer face of a large mountain that must be Mount Elbert. Within the little dale lay scattered a few buildings in what Barry thought of as "Rocky Mountain Sun and Ski" architecture—great thrusts of huge cedar beams at improbable angles roofing enormous walls of glass alternating with gray stone.

He asked Anna to stop before the bend that gave them the best view of the place. Below, the pickup completed the loop down into the glen and pulled to a stop between two buildings. Barry and Anna stepped out of the car and walked another five yards to a sign that announced that this was the Independence Pass Ski Lodge, with all sorts of other relevant information.

From this vantage point, they could see the entire resort area: the main building and its extensions—probably lounges and restaurants; other buildings that might be dormitories. A few outbuildings. The ski lifts in the distance. The side slopes of Mount Elbert, now bare of snow.

Could this be EDGE headquarters? What better disguise than one of a hundred ski resorts in the area? But it seemed too public, too close to "Colorado's highest point," which had to attract gawkers. The buildings certainly seemed large enough to hold the children and a large staff.

They were startled when a voice shouted from nearby.

"It's closed for the season."

The girl was in hiking gear. She seemed to have appeared out of nowhere. With ruddy cheeks, a woolen hat over her hair and ears, a stuffed backpack, sturdy boots with high yellow calf flaps, she was not four feet away.

"Lousy spring for snow," she added. "We had one decent

pack on the slopes since early March, and that melted in two days."

"You work here?" Barry asked, wondering who she was.

"I did. It's been closed for three weeks now. Virtually every lodge here has been, if you follow the weather."

"We're from out of state." Which should be apparent if she noticed his California plates. "It was pretty bad there, too. We thought maybe . . ." he began. The place did seem deserted. "Was it a good winter?"

"Had to chase them away. I'm glad it's over."

"How come you're still here?"

"My old man does general maintenance." She pointed down, and Barry saw the pickup's driver come out of the largest building and cross over to another, smaller one. "We'll be here for another week, then close up till September. Idaho!"

"You're from Idaho?"

"No!" She laughed. "If you still want to ski, you should go to Idaho. Or even better, Montana."

If the resort had been crowded all winter, it would hardly be EDGE headquarters. Still, the man *had* picked up the mail.

"This is magnificent country," Anna said, making it sound sincere. "You wouldn't happen to know if there's any real estate available around here?"

The girl said they should try in Leadville. Barry tried a new tack. How could they make reservations for the resort to make sure they got in at the beginning of the new season?

"Write to us, care of the Leadville P.O."

"That's it? With that address, you'll still get it?" he insisted.

"Sure. Hell, we get the mail for everyone in the area. They come by our office and pick it up."

"You mean other people live around here?" Anna asked. "I don't see any houses."

"They're there. Not many," she admitted.

"Hidden between mountains?"

155

She shrugged, already bored. "I guess."

"I suppose you could hide a pretty big spread among some of these mountains," Barry said.

She looked him up and down, then said, "See you!" suddenly, and crossed in front of the car and began to descend the ridge.

The girl had settled the question of the mail pickup, but she was now clearly suspicious of them.

"Montana, you said?" he called after her.

"Near Glacier Park," she shouted back, already fifty feet below the road.

"Thanks for the tip!" he called back, and joined Anna in the car.

The girl had stopped, waiting to see what they would do, which suggested she was hiding something. Anna got into the driver's seat, and Barry directed her to back up slowly until he thought they were out of sight, then to stop. He'd noticed two rough-looking roads that led beyond the group of buildings, and wondered where they led to. Nowhere. One led to a slope area twisting to meet a ski lift, then dawdled off as a pony track. The other turned into a dirt track even sooner, and ended at what seemed to be a garage. Damn!

The girl was dropping down the rocks as skillfully as a mountain goat. A second later, the man who'd been in the pickup stepped out of the building. She must have shouted something to him. Shading his eyes with one hand, he looked up at the car. She also turned and looked up.

"If it's a front, it's a convincing one," Barry said.

"Something about it isn't quite right," Anna said. "I can't say what exactly."

"What about Mount Elbert? That ring any bells?" he asked.

"Maybe I should turn around, Barry. They're still looking."

She backed up until the car was out of sight from below, then reached a spot where she could make a U-turn.

"I sure as hell would like to investigate this place more closely." The thought of coming back alone, late at night, crossed his mind. Maybe.

"Let's go," Anna said.

She moved onto the single lane road and began driving back to Leadville. "What now?" Anna asked. "To Denver and Linda Hendricks?"

"I guess that's all we can do," he admitted. "We'll check into a motel outside of town. Call Linda Hendricks and . . . play it from there."

"You sound exhausted, Barry," Anna said, not unkindly. "Take a nap. Put on the blanket."

"You're right, I'm beat," he admitted.

He put the car seat back. The wind coming in through the side vent seemed icier than before, so he placed the blanket over both of their laps. The clock on the dashboard read 6:50, and as they descended past the outskirts of the town, he could see the sunset sharply delineating every rift and cleft and ridge into daylight and night.

As the car continued to descend toward Interstate 70, it darkened more uniformly around them. Barry finally began to doze.

He woke up suddenly, totally. It was dark inside the car. The pale green tints of the dashboard dials gave a little light, just enough to outline Anna's face and figure at the wheel in dim silhouette. Outside, the road was pitch-black.

Barry had been having a dream, and in the dream he'd been frightened. No, worse—terrified. Now, he couldn't remember why. He pulled himself up in his seat, looked out the passenger-seat window for some sign of where they were. Nothing but the dusky outlines of the passing rock face. It was 7:41.

"Sleep well?"

"All right."

Anna continued to look straight ahead. Now Barry noticed the high green-and-white signs that read ARVADA—5

157

MILES. They'd already begun the descent out of the Rockies toward Denver.

"Want to pull over and let me take over?"

"I'm used to driving on roads like this. You saw the highway from Monterey down to Big Sur."

He contented himself with lighting a cigarette and staring ahead.

"Just before you woke up, you were talking in your sleep. Mumbling. I couldn't make out words."

"Dreaming," he admitted.

Barry relaxed and inhaled the menthol and tobacco.

"I don't remember you smoking," she said.

"I guess I didn't. You're not going to lecture me about it?"

"No." She paused, then said, "Remember when I said that something about that resort bothered me, but that I didn't know what it was?"

"Do you know now?"

"Not exactly. But remember what Elly Vosburgh said about her brother writing her that he was on the Continental Divide?"

"Yes, so?"

"Check the road atlas. Is Mount Elbert on the Continental Divide?"

Barry reached under the seat for the maps, turned on the dashboard light, found the right page, and looked.

"Mount Elbert is slightly to the west of the Divide."

"West of it?"

"That's right. Why?"

"When we stopped the car and were looking down at the valley, we were facing north," Anna said. "The sun was to our left, true?"

"True."

"And if what Kevin said is true about how the water runs off, it would run east, toward the Mississippi, opposite the sun, true?"

"Yes. I don't follow you."

"While following the pickup, we had to half circle the mountain from the north, remember?"

He did.

"So we saw Mount Elbert from the north, or at least the northwest, and once we stopped, from the southeast, right?"

"I guess so."

"Where do clouds in this area come from? The rain clouds? The snow clouds?"

"They move west to east. And I suppose some snow comes from the north. Northwest."

"That's what I thought, Barry. Which means that more likely than not, the most amount of snow that fell would be on the northern and western flanks of Mount Elbert."

"I don't understand . . ." Then he did understand. "Yet the resort had ski lifts on the southeastern flanks!"

"Where there would be far less snow, possibly not enough for skiing!"

"Which means they were fake. Which means it probably is EDGE headquarters! Very clever of you!" He reached over and bussed her cheek. As he was pulling away, his glance included the windshield's rearview mirror. Two sets of headlights were directly behind them.

"If you don't move away, we'll have an accident," Anna said in a playful tone of voice.

"Hold on a second," Barry said, holding his position. "Have those two cars been behind us for long?"

Anna glanced into the mirror. "A while."

"Did they arrive together?"

She craned to check them in the sideview mirror. "I don't remember. Yes, I think so. What are you thinking, Barry?"

Behind them, the two cars kept steadily distant and at an equal distance from each other.

"Anna, we're going to change seats," Barry said.

"Is there a place ahead to stop?"

"We're not going to stop."

Anna glanced at him. "You're joking."

"If those cars are following us as I think they are, they'll pull something soon, before we get into Denver."

She looked up, to the side, resisting the impulse to turn around. "You're scaring me, Barry."

"I know you're a good driver. But if I'm right, it will take more than skill," he said. "Well?"

Anna was silent, then she said, cooly enough, "They are following us. You're sure about this?"

"Ninety-nine percent."

"All right. What do we do?"

He climbed into the backseat and checked the rearview mirror. No change in the cars behind them. Ahead, the road began to spiral wide and deceptively easy.

"Move right as far as possible."

She did as he said.

"More!"

"I won't be able to reach the brake!"

"We'll have to take that chance." He checked the rearview mirror, then climbed over the front seat, trying not to bump into her and not succeeding very well. Ahead the spiral turned and turned. He twisted past the steering wheel, tried to flatten himself against the left door and to check the sideview mirror, all at the same time. Behind him, the two cars were flashing their directional lights. Aware that something was going on?

He managed to get into place. Poor Anna was halfway in the seat, half over the transmission hump, trying to steer, one foot on the gas, the other still on the brake.

"Barry!"

"Move your foot off the brake! Quick!"

She did.

"Now the other one."

She did, and he slipped his onto the gas pedal. She'd steered them through one arc of the curve; the following turns got tighter and steeper. The cars behind had sped up, and now were only a few feet away.

"Anna! Let go of the wheel."

She did, and in the same instant the car behind bumped them. The steering wheel began to spin loose. Both he and Anna grabbed for it. Barry got it, and knocked her wrist off.

"Sorry! Sit back. Buckle up."

The car bumped them again, harder, but he had a grip on the wheel now. A sheer drop on his left.

Anna turned to look behind them.

"Stay down in your seat!"

The road dropped more steeply, and Barry decided it was now or never. He pushed down on the accelerator and let the engine and gravity do their work. The car shot forward. In the rearview mirror he could see one car drop behind, then speed up, the second car at its side, separated by only a few feet. The drivers seemed to be shouting at each other through open windows. Then they were lost in the turn. He hoped they didn't have guns.

"We're going eighty!" Anna said quietly.

There they were right behind, also speeding up.

He kept steering into the curve. "We may have to go even faster."

The blaring horn of an approaching truck coming up at them and its wildly blinking high beams filled the car to tell him his driving was erratic. *No kidding, buster! You try this sometime!*

Then he moved back into the other lane for the descending curve of the road, hearing the truck horn blare as it passed the two cars behind him. They'd been forced to go single file again. Not for long. Once more they moved side by side, and this time they bore down fast.

He sped to eighty-five mph. Handling the car at this speed on this kind of curve was now a matter of holding on and hoping.

"They're coming again," Anna said.

He passed into the opposite lane to negotiate the next ess, and saw a small stretch of cliff-bound straight road ahead.

"Barry!"

He felt the bump from the left rear suddenly, much harder

than before, and though he was prepared, he almost lost the wheel. There was another bump, again no longer mere warning, from the right, then one from the left again.

"Get down!" he shouted, and despite the fact that he could hardly control the car as it was, he accelerated to ninety, getting away from them again. Adrenaline was filling his chest, throat, head. Would this damn spiral never end? They were right behind him again.

Another blaring horn and set of blinking lights told him exactly how perilous his situation was. And now he was getting a stitch in his side!

He swerved in, then out again into the opposite lane. What he could see of the road ahead was an even tighter, steeper curve. The two cars were bearing down on him, one in each lane. Their passenger windows were open, and he could see hands with guns. He heard a soft pop outside the roof trim, then a sharp ping as the sideview mirror was grazed and shattered.

"They're shooting!" he said, as calmly as possibly. "Stay down."

Another shot knocked the mirror right off.

His side was killing him now, and the adrenaline was gagging him. That long final downhill hairpin was still ahead.

Anna began murmuring something in Russian.

"You okay?" he asked.

"Fine!" she said, boldly.

The straightaway, finally! Now he had a real choice. One final choice. At the end of the straight, the road slung down steeply into a dangerous tail, with a sheer drop over a thousand feet on his side.

"Anna, listen, I've got to try something! If it doesn't work, well, remember I love you. I always loved you. Trust me?" He took his right hand off the wheel and reached for her hand. Got it, pressed it, returned to the wheel.

"Bar-ry! They're right behind!"

"Hold on for dear life, and pray that no one comes at us

from the front," he said as he sped into the sharp U-turn of the hairpin, then hit the brakes as hard as he could, while turning the steering wheel sharply right.

"We'll crash!" she cried. The car slithered and shook, the wheels screeched burning rubber, but the car spun around completely to face uphill and then stalled. The two approaching drivers had only seconds to swerve to avoid crashing into them. The one on the left glanced off the front fender, obtaining just enough force to send Barry and Anna into the second car approaching on the right, which slashed their front fender and then spun around and smashed into a steep cliff wall. Its crash was followed a half minute later by the much louder and more resonant crash of the second car falling and exploding. It had gone through the guard rail.

Meanwhile, Barry was sliding downhill out of control in reverse. He tried the ignition once, twice. Nothing. They were rolling backward straight down into headlights coming up at them.

"Come on, dammit!" Barry yelled at the car, slapping the dashboard in frustration.

It caught finally, sputtering to life. He hit the brakes. Then forward into a U-turn just in time to avoid a car coming up at them. It went past with the driver all but sitting on the horn.

"Let's get out of here!" Barry said, and completed the turn into the straightaway.

She seemed afraid to move at first, afraid even to speak, then she sat up.

As soon as they were out of the mountains, he stopped the car on the nearest open shoulder of road, stepped out, stretched, massaged his side, and helped Anna out of the passenger seat.

She was unsteady and leaned close against the side and roof of the car. It was very cold now. Passing them already were the flashing lights and sirens of state-police cars, and a tow truck.

They held each other tight. Below them was the immense bright gridwork of Denver and its suburbs.

When Barry tried to kiss her, she pulled back and looked into his eyes.

"You know that Land sent them. And he'll try again, Barry."

"I know."

Because of the lateness of the hour, Barry was sure he wouldn't reach Linda Hendricks at her office. But not only was she in, she'd been waiting for his call.

"Where've you been?" she asked. They'd actually spoken to each other only a couple of times, so he couldn't be certain she was as excited as she sounded.

"Why? Do you have news?" he asked.

"Do I!"

"Should I hook the computer up to the phone?"

"Hold on a minute," she said.

He decided to hook it up while he waited. Passing the bathroom, he tapped the door and heard Anna say something. He peeked in. She was in the bathtub, covered with suds, washing her hair.

"I got her. She's got some sort of news," he said. "Save some hot water for my shower."

She laughed, spraying shampoo bubbles at him.

Barry sat down at the bedside table and began connecting the modem into the phone receiver, the modem into a port of the laptop, turning on the computer, accessing an open file, and putting it on "receive." He lit a cigarette and looked around the little motel room, listening to Anna humming in the bath, and waited.

It was deceptively peaceful. They might be any ordinary couple who'd been driving all day and stopped off at this nondescript "motor inn" a few miles south of Denver for the night. Barry was pretty sure that's exactly how they'd looked to the desk clerk when they'd signed in an hour ago.

"I'm back. Sorry, I had to take that call. It was about another piece I'm doing. Where are you?"

"A motel in Littleton. Along the Interstate."

"Better give me your phone number," she said. And when he had keyboarded it, she typed back, "What are you doing there?"

"We thought this would be safer than checking into a hotel in Denver." Before she could ask the obvious next question, he typed, "On the way down from Leadville we ran into trouble."

He could almost hear her thinking: Should I ask? He decided she might as well know. This might end up affecting her, too. "Two cars tried to run us off a cliff going down the long hairpin outside of Arvada."

"You're kidding?"

He tried to type out what had happened to them as succinctly as he could.

"Jesus! Who sent them after you?"

"We think it's the CIA."

"Wow!"

"We're sure they're connected to the kids. We don't know how. We also think they're really dangerous. Even to you. Take care there."

"I can handle myself," she replied.

"Well, you've been warned," he keyboarded. "Now . . . Did Gunther find a way into the NSA file on EDGE?"

" 'Fraid not. Nor has he come up with a way to patch you in, although he is working on it. But my D.C. contact came through with info on Burr Talmadge."

"Let's have it," Barry typed.

"A really mixed history. Talmadge began as a Senate page in the fifties. Got tight with one senator who was becoming senile. Insiders said that Talmadge ran the show for about six years."

"That doesn't have much to do with psychic kids," Barry interrupted.

"It gets better. Talmadge kept a low profile, married a

wealthy socialite who happened to be the daughter of a former governor. When the lady died seven years later, he inherited a bundle."

"Suspicious death?"

"Not at all. Leukemia. At any rate, Talmadge popped up in D.C. again in the late sixties, lobbying for federal funding for an expanded program for J. R. Rhine's group at Duke University. Purpose of the group—to study ESP in all of its aspects. The funding went through. Some people thought Talmadge was part of the CIA in some hush-hush group studying psychic discoveries. Are you with me?"

"I'm right here." Barry could hear Anna showering off.

"Evidently they helped some kid from Irkutsk defect. Supposedly he had psychic powers. They brought him to a safe house in Iran, and tested the hell out of him. The KGB re-kidnapped the kid back to the Soviet Union. But he'd tested really poorly, didn't have enough psychic juice to turn on a light bulb. A few years after that fiasco, Talmadge showed up at McGill University in Montreal. Involved in tests with some looney doctor who subjected volunteers to massive doses of LSD-25, lights, noise, psychic driving, vitamin overdosing, shock, all kinds of sensory deprivation. That was in the mid-seventies."

"That it?" Barry typed.

"After that, we can't trace him at all. But it seems awfully suggestive, no?"

Barry agreed. It linked up! Talmadge, Land, the CIA, going back to the sixties. But there was one crucial piece missing out of the jigsaw.

Anna was almost done in the bathroom. Barry wondered whether or not he should tell the reporter what they suspected about the resort at Mount Elbert. Would she be foolish enough to interfere at exactly the wrong time?

Before he could decide, he saw her type out, "Were you folks following a lead up in Leadville?"

"I don't know about Talmadge," Barry typed, "but I've had dealings with another CIA operative named Alex Land.

He's deceptive and ruthless. Stay away from Leadville, and *don't* get near him, okay, Linda?"

"Check."

"I'll call back tomorrow when I know more. Meanwhile, let's see if Gunther can break through that file or patch in a line for me."

"Be careful," she signed off.

Barry hit the "save" button, and when it was done, shut off the machine, disconnected it, locked up the laptop's attaché, and slid it under the bed.

"Think I can shower now?" he asked Anna. She was standing at the sink, toweling off her hair.

"Don't let me stop you," she said.

He felt refreshed when he stepped out of the bathroom a few minutes later, a towel wrapped around his waist. Anna was sitting cross-legged on the motel bed, a pale blue towel wrapped like a turban around her head, another around her torso. She was using the remote control to change channels on the TV. She looked lovely. Barry straddled the bed in front of her and began to nibble one of her knees.

"Stop, that tickles."

"It's not supposed to tickle. It's supposed to excite. In Paris the towels were pink."

He undid her turban, pulling it away so Anna's hair tumbled loose. He kissed her nape, her ears, her neck. "Your hair was very long then, so long you could braid it and it still went halfway down your back."

"You remember that?" she asked.

"I remember everything in Paris. Every moment." He moved in front and slowly pushed the towel off her breasts. "I've been remembering it for seventeen years." He kissed her breasts, unwrapping the towel from her waist. "How we ate raspberries and *crème fraîche* in the Bois." He licked at her navel as though to pop a berry out of it, and looked up at her. "Everything!"

She ran a hand through his hair, staring at him in the oddest way.

"I'm not that emigré girl anymore, you know, Barry."

"And I'm not that naive student, Anna."

"Then why . . . ?"

He stroked her upper thighs, ran his hands along her flanks. "Because no one is making us do it. . . . Because we are in complete possession of our senses and faculties. . . . Because we want to. . . . Do you need any other reasons?" he asked.

"Come here, Barry," she said, "where I can see who you really are."

He slid up the sheets, discarding towels as he went, and she lay back. They were naked now, face to face, inches away from each other. He reached for her, but she held his arms off with a gentleness that said it was temporary.

"Well?" he asked, eye to eye now. "Can you see who I really am, with all illusions—youth, Paris, everything—stripped away?"

"Yes. And do you see me truly, me today, not seventeen years ago?"

"I see a woman who has gone through hell and come back to tell of it, lost a great deal, and gained even more. I like you far better now. What do you see?"

"I see the father of my child," she said, letting his hands loose.

"Look at me, Anna, listen to my voice: I'm shaking with excitement and anticipation, just like a kid."

"Yes, isn't it wonderful?" she said, and folded herself into him.

Rain. Steady rain. Cold rain, Barry was certain, given the sudden draft from the window. He lay, swaddled in blankets, intertwined with Anna's body. He wrapped the blanket tighter around himself, tried to bury his head even deeper into her body. The room was dark, and outside the rain was loud, hissing under the tires of speeding autos on the highway. He heard the fogged horns of two semi drivers communicating. Another draft now found its way through the covers. He knew he wouldn't sleep again until he'd gotten up and shut the window. He was so unwilling to leave the touch of her body, even with the cold draft, that it would take a terrific effort to throw off the blankets.

Gently he pulled himself away from her.

In that moment, he wondered what the window was doing open.

He heard breathing that wasn't his, wasn't Anna's. It seemed to be coming from the area of the room directly in front of the bed. Someone in the room!

Now Anna was stirring in her sleep. Or . . . no, something else was happening, someone else in the room, near Anna. Two of them!

Barry sat up, turned to the lamp.

The burst of light came from above and was accompanied by a soft pop. Something hit the blankets at his right side. There was another burst of light and that same soft popping sound, this time much closer, then a sharp intake of breath, which he realized was his own. It took a second for the flash of lightning-heat to spread over his chest, paralyzing his arms, legs, as he fell back. Even with the intense pain, he tried to move, to protect Anna. He thought he heard her somewhere in the room, struggling. And he could do nothing to stop them, to help her.

A second of dull light as though a door was being opened to the corridor. Help. It had to be help. Darkness again. They'd taken Anna. Shot him and taken Anna. And he was helpless, wounded or dying, here in the dark, with another sound, a sort of gurgling rising from his throat, like bones being rubbed together. He thought, My God!, it does sound like a rattle!, and even though he knew he'd hit the bed solidly, he began falling, diving backward, plummeting.

BOOK TWO

ANNA

CHAPTER SEVEN

Anna awakened slowly as the vehicle began to bounce over rough terrain. Given her awkward position across the backseat with her hands and feet tied up, at first she thought she wouldn't be able to sit up. She still felt dizzy.

"You'll be all right." A man half turned from the front passenger seat. "We had to chloroform you. It'll pass in a moment." His voice sounded young, even gentle.

He looked forward again, just as the driver hit another series of deep ruts. Despite the darkness all around, Anna could make out two triangles of overlapping brightness from the headlamps in front of them, illuminating rock-strewn ground. They were in a four-wheel-drive station wagon.

"Sorry about having to tie you up," the young man said again, over the whine of the motor as it went into a lower gear. "We used silk. So there wouldn't be any marks."

The vehicle seemed to be slowing down as it entered a high-walled canyon. Anna decided she wouldn't talk to them, no matter how polite they were, no matter how many questions she had.

Now that her head was clearing, she remembered those last moments in the motel outside Denver. She'd been half pulled, half lifted off the bed, and had been dragged through the door. The motel hallway was dimly lit, but compared to the room it was glaringly bright. Enough for her to see Barry sit up, his head and chest in profile to the window.

She'd seen him put out a hand, then she'd heard two soft pops, one a few seconds after the other.

Barry! They'd shot Barry in the chest from a few feet away. In all likelihood killed him. And now they were taking her somewhere. How long had she been out, tied up in this backseat? Where were they going? Barry!

"We'll be there in a few minutes," the gentle-voiced man said, as though he knew what she'd ask. "We'll untie your legs so you can walk. It wouldn't make any sense to try to get away. We're in the middle of nowhere."

The vehicle passed out of the ravine and crossed a larger, open space. Ahead she could make out a flashing red signal. The driver stopped and flashed his own lights on and off. After a few seconds, he started up the engine again and crept forward. They drove uphill a bit, then over some rockfall, and finally bounced down onto a level surface. This area seemed to be enclosed. Anna could make out rock walls, separated by old wooden supports. Some sort of mine.

They stopped again, at a cyclone fence. The younger man got out and did something to a series of locks, and opened the gate. The four-wheel's driver crept forward, almost immediately turned left, and stopped. Behind them, the man closed the gate, locked it again, and rejoined them inside the idling vehicle. After a few minutes more slow driving, the driver stopped again. This time both men stepped out and opened the back door for Anna.

Anna knew she must remain alert, look around for her opportunity. She fought off hysteria by breathing deeply.

It worked. She was calm, almost serene, as one young man grabbed her legs out of the station wagon's door and undid the cords around her ankles, massaging them to get the blood flowing so she could walk. The other man was out of sight now, behind an outcropping, although she could hear him speaking to someone. Two, possibly three to one. Even so, she knew the way out. She waited until she was steady on her feet and the man who'd untied her had turned aside, then she acted.

Using her still-bound hands as a bludgeon, she hammered her fist into the back of his head, then turned and ran the way they'd driven. Her bare feet were sensitive, but that made her race even faster on the rock surface underfoot. She'd made it out of the corridor tunnel, had turned into the larger cavern, and was at the cyclone fence when she heard shouting behind her.

Nowhere to hide! And the gate went from floor to ceiling, attached to thick steel poles embedded in the rock. But she was desperate: She tried pulling up the fence from the bottom, attempting to open a hole big enough to get under. She heard their shouts closing in on her, and the unmistakable sound of boot soles approaching. She was tearing her fingers on the fence, breaking her nails, but she'd managed to rip up the thick meshwork only a few inches when she was grabbed from behind. She kicked and screamed. But there were two men, then three, and Anna saw the chamois cloth coming at her, descending over her face again.

Her first thought on reawakening was that she was still asleep, dreaming. It had been years since she'd had this particular, terrible dream, more a memory of her months as Land's prisoner than a dream—and all the more apalling for it.

"She's coming to," a woman's voice stated, flatly.

"I'm almost done," a man's voice replied.

Impossible to make out who was who. Both wore pale blue medical gowns, operating caps, surgical masks. As did another figure in the far corner of the gleaming room.

Anna was strapped down, her body tilted down from her head at a 45-degree angle. She was naked beneath a sheet partly covering her midsection. She couldn't feel anything at all.

"Should I administer more anesthesia?" the woman asked.

"I said I'm done."

He stepped away. No clamps, no forceps, no terrible glittering knives in his rubber gloved hands. Only a tiny opaque test tube.

"Okay!" he said. "That's it."

The woman removed blood-pressure straps from around Anna's arm, and began to tilt the table back to level.

The man pushed the sheet over Anna's legs, placed a tiny flashlight next to her eyes, peering into each.

"All appears normal here," he reported. "You're in excellent health," he said in a voice that now seemed nasal, midwestern. "We wanted to be certain."

"Why?" Anna found her voice.

He shrugged, almost laughed. "Sometimes a trauma can elicit all sorts of . . ."

"What have you done to me?" Anna asked, hearing the harshness in her voice, her throat made sore by chloroform.

"Nothing. Nothing at all! Standard physical exam. Heart, blood pressure, cervical. We've taken some blood. That's all."

She didn't believe him. She was certain he'd done something awful to her. Why else had she been brought here, knocked out, strapped down?

"Okay!" he said, as the other figure gestured. "We're out of here."

The silent figure stepped out of the room, leaving the door open. The table Anna was on had wheels. She was moved through the door, through a vacant corridor, then into a steel elevator, up to another corridor with high glass windows, through which she could see the glow of sunlight (How? Hadn't they taken her underground?), and finally she was wheeled into a room and left there.

Anna heard the door click. Locked. She looked down at herself. The pale blue sheet still covered her body, but the straps had been loosened around her hands and feet. Her fingers were covered with small Band-Aids where she'd torn herself on the cyclone fence. She tried raising herself, and succeeded with some difficulty in getting up into a sitting position and swinging her feet down. She still felt odd, unsure of her reflexes. Doubtless from all the chloroform.

She had to pull herself together.

Two deep breaths. Three. Better. Her head was clear. She dropped to the floor, stood swaying a moment, then felt the ground solid beneath her feet. She wrapped the sheet around herself like a Roman matron's stola, then looked around more carefully, telling herself that she didn't believe what she'd seen happen to Barry. It had been a distortion of light, of shadows. And anyway, she'd been half-asleep.

Where was she now?

A room, twelve feet square. A bed and a writing table built into opposite walls. A folding chair. A single door, through which they'd entered. Artificial lighting behind flush ceiling fixtures. The ceiling too high to reach even if she stood on the chair. What were those panels built flush into the walls next to the door? She slid them open—drawers containing clothing. One held the underpants she'd been wearing when she'd been dragged out of the motel bed. No bra. The slender closet contained a few smocks—no designer labels, but serviceable.

Another door contained a vanity—small sink, pull-out mirror, and a compartment with toiletries. No scissors, naturally, though there was a blunt-nosed nail clipper. Anna dropped the sheet and began to dress. She knew that she'd feel more in control once she had cleaned up and dressed. Aside from her underwear, there was nothing else to suggest she'd been prepared for, expected. This could be a room for any woman—a lab or medical technician, say—who'd quickly vacated it.

The room seemed honeycombed with various-sized compartments behind flush doors. One held a scant library: a few recent bestsellers, and magazines a woman might be interested in—*Elle, House and Garden, Ms.* A drawer in the table contained silverware and napkins (evidently she'd eat here, too) as well as writing paper and felt-tip pens, a deck of playing cards, a notebook. Wall sockets showed that a telephone had been removed, and probably a computer, as well.

Anna found a flat push button that provided light over the table, then she noticed such buttons near the bed and at the wall near the door. Above the desk, a compartment containing a small cassette deck and radio and a television. She tried both and they worked—but the stations that could be reached locally were few and snowy on the screen, equally few and static-filled on the radio. Another door slid open to reveal a toilet. Another, a stall shower, complete with towels, soap, shampoo, hair conditioners. The shower heads were built into the wall—as was a hair dryer. Whoever had designed the place had thought of everything.

She was certain she was being watched, though she'd not seen anything as obvious as a camera lens anywhere around the ceiling boards.

She moved to the bed, plumped up the pillows, and began to read one of the books. Probably because of how much anesthesia she'd been given earlier, she felt quite tired. She kicked off the flat slippers she'd found, and relaxed.

She wouldn't provide them with anything to use against her. Not a thing.

Anna believed she knew who "they" were.

Once again I am in the hands of my enemy! Anna thought, drowsing. And once again Barry is dead.

Afraid the food was drugged, she picked at her meals, eating only salad, without any dressing, and fruit. By the second morning, though, she was quite hungry, and she wolfed down the toast and a banana that she inspected carefully, if uselessly, for signs of needle marks. Later on that morning, she found a local radio station that didn't drift too much, and she kept it tuned low for company. Even though the station played mostly country-and-western music—never her favorite—occasionally an announcer would provide the time and weather and a smattering of world and local news.

Anna was reading a novel and half listening to the radio station at about nine o'clock that second night when she suddenly heard a soft-spoken voice in the room. She listened intently but couldn't make out words: It seemed like people having a conversation in a room next to hers, which she was somehow overhearing.

Quietly, casually, she put the book down, got out of bed, and put her ear to the wall. Nothing. Then she went over to the radio and turned up the volume. A whiny-voiced woman was wailing about how her man had gone to the package store and never come back, no more, no more. But above—or somehow *through*—her singing, Anna could hear another soft female voice almost dreamily intoning words. She retuned the radio, slipped off the station into static, then heard the voice with startling clarity:

"Who are you? I know you're there. What's your name? Will you talk with me?"

Anna stepped back from the radio speaker. Her hand had gone to her heart in surprise.

"Please talk to me. I want to be your friend."

Who could it possibly be? Anna reached forward and re-tuned the radio back into static, then directly onto the country-music station, then past it into static again. Once more she heard the voice clearly:

"I know you're lonely. I'm lonely, too. Won't you talk with me? Won't you be my friend?"

Something about the girl—for now Anna was sure it was a girl's, not a woman's, voice—seemed so sad, Anna was about to reply when she remembered where she was—and in whose hands. She couldn't be sure what this voice really was. It might be some new electronic-interrogation method, or a tape being played over and over to subliminally exert mental control. It might even be some new kind of hypnosis. They'd probably counted on her keeping the radio on for company, had allowed this one channel only to remain open, receivable, then . . .

"My name is Sancha. What's your name?" the girl plaintively asked.

Anna quickly reached forward and turned off the set.

For the next ten minutes, she trembled thinking how

easily she'd allowed herself, how close she'd been, to falling into their trap. She must never let down her guard. Never.

But as Anna went back to her reading, she kept thinking about that girl's voice, and her words.

On the third morning, Anna came out of the shower smelling fresh flowers in the room. A bouquet of speckled red carnations had been stuffed into a small beige vase.

Her first instinct was to go smell them. Instead, she held back, wrapped the bath towel around herself, and slowly brushed out her hair. They'd be on the lookout for signs of any sort of eagerness—any enthusiasm at all. Once you began accepting any kindness from your jailors, you were doomed to accepting your jailors altogether. Passive resistance had to be accomplished completely, thoroughly, minutely.

Even so, the flowers' brash sweetness filled the room, as she methodically brushed her hair and got dressed. On the foldout table next to the door was the usual covered metal tray containing her breakfast—another series of small tests. She didn't want to appear too eager for that, either.

Finally, almost casually, and only after she was certain she looked as she wanted to today, Anna went for the tray and returned it to the table where she ate. Passing the flowers, she accepted their aroma more fully, enjoying the burst of odor but making certain that it would appear she was indifferent.

When she took off the metal lid of the food tray, she had another surprise. A local newspaper had been rolled up between the larger plate and the carafe of coffee. Again, fighting instinct, she ignored it, removed it, put it under the tray—let them figure that out!—and looked at what she'd been served.

An omelet today. If it was mushroom or spinach, she immediately decided, she wouldn't eat it. Let them figure out the reason behind her whim. She poked open one edge:

Gruyère. Two pieces of lightly buttered toast. An orange half.

Anna ate slowly, having all the time in the world. The eggs were fresh, she noted. A step up from what she'd been fed in Virginia. So was the cheese. And the herbs seemed to have been freshly ground.

Only after she was done eating and had poured herself a second cup of coffee did she casually take up the *Denver Post*. It was an afternoon edition from two days before, she noted.

As she took up the paper, Anna glanced at the bold-print headline. It dealt with the tensions between the United States and Soviet Union, which had continued to build over the past few weeks.

Opening the paper, Anna glanced at the smaller, more local headlines, and spotted the one she knew she was supposed to see: MYSTERIOUS MURDER IN LITTLETON MOTEL. Anna immediately went to the top of the front page, found the index, and turned to page 45. The crossword puzzle was also there, wedged between a column of gardening advice and the bridge column.

She was controlling her breathing as she opened a felt-tip pen, flattened out the paper, and began the puzzle in the upper left hand corner: "musical term—light, jesting." Seven letters down. Across, the clue was "window part." Barry was dead—it was there in print, and so she had to believe it. *Scherzo,* she wrote down, *sash* across. A good beginning.

Slowly, deliberately, she finished the puzzle, leaving one blank—who knew whether an African fox was an *aase* or *aose* or *aise*?: It was one of those cheating words crossword makers and no one else used, except perhaps in Namibia.

She read the article about the motel murder twice. She wasn't mentioned in it, even though she and Barry had checked in together as Mr. and Mrs., even though she'd been seen and spoken to by the motel owner on duty that night. That was what they wanted her to know: not merely that Barry was DOA at a Denver hospital emergency room, but that as far as everyone was concerned, she hadn't been there with him and thus could not have been kidnapped from the room. She was to know that no one would be looking for her, because she no longer existed. Or if she did, not anywhere in Colorado. Damn them!

Anna dawdled on inside pages awhile, then rolled up the newspaper and put it back on the tray between the larger plate and the coffee carafe. Aloud, and in a voice controlled more by her anger than by desperation, Anna said:

"You used to be a great deal more subtle."

She replaced the cover over the food tray and stood up to go brush her teeth.

By midafternoon of the fourth day, Anna decided that her need to hear another human voice, even if it was only a radio announcer, was more important than whatever her captors might make of it.

She went to the radio again, turned it on, tuned it to the station—now playing Loretta Lynn—then slowly undressed until she was only in her underwear. Anna spread out a bath towel upon the floor and began to do her yoga exercises, starting with the Greeting to the Sun.

She had moved onto the towel for her back-bending asanas when she heard that same conversationlike series of voices through the harmonizing of a country group named Alabama.

Anna remained very still, listening intently but again unable to clearly make out words. Alabama finished its song, and she released her ankles, flattened out, then sat up in a full-lotus position and swung her body around so she faced the speakers. The announcer was talking—she ignored him. Then she heard the soft voice again quite clearly.

"I know you're there. I've felt you stronger every day. What's your name? Will you talk with me?"

Anna remained in her posture, stable, unmovable.

"Please talk to me. I want to be your friend. Why won't you talk with me? I know you're alone."

"How do you know?" Anna asked, calmly. "Can you see me?"

"Oh, no! But I can feel you."

That was interesting. "Really. How?"

"This may sound weird, but everybody has a specific density, off which radio waves bounce. It's like a signature. And since I'm a strong radio–telepath, I sense each person. Especially when they're as close as you are."

"Am I close to you?" Anna asked as blandly as possible; she'd sort out the rest of what the girl said later.

"Yes. What's your name?" the girl plaintively asked.

"Does it make a difference, since you already know my signature?" Anna asked back.

"I guess not. My name is Sancha. That's a Spanish name. I'm half Indian—Mojave."

"Are there so few people here that you were able to sense me?" Anna asked. The girl might also be a prisoner. But then how did she get to a radio transmitter, and how—with no apparent transmitter on Anna's end—were they communicating?

"There are lots of people around, but this building is shielded in certain ways for EDGE," the girl went on.

"You're part of EDGE?" Anna asked. She guessed the girl would say yes, and then Anna would know she was lying, was one of them, testing Anna. After all, she and Barry would have heard of another girl in the group by now, and they hadn't. Only Matty, Lost and Found, and Timmo. And Kyra, of course.

"I'm EDGE Number Two," the girl said.

That was an odd thing to say. Now Anna felt less certain that the girl was one of them. She'd have to ask more questions. "How are we speaking?"

"I'm modulating the frequency in your radio."

"Who else is listening to our conversation?"

"No one. Unless someone's in your room."

"I'm alone. Can we be heard through a speaker in this room that is being listened to by someone else?"

183

"Not unless it's strongly amplified. I've set up a very weak electrostatic force. I'm using transistors in your little radio to boost it, but it's got a limited range, only a few feet. Look at your body hair. It should stand up straighter as you get closer to the radio."

Anna stood up, raised her arm to look at the light blond hair on her forearm. When she stepped closer to the radio, the hair stood up.

"How do I know that doesn't usually happen with this radio?"

"I'll tune out for sixty seconds. Watch!"

The hair dropped almost flat. After about a minute, it rose again. Even so, Anna had to admit she didn't know enough physics to be certain.

"Who else is in the building?" Anna asked.

"Bernie. And Kevin's doing something at the mainframe. Everyone else is out."

Confusing. Who was Bernie? And could it be the same Kevin? This required thinking out.

"I'd like to finish what I was doing before, Sancha. Perhaps we'll talk later."

"Okay!" the girl said. "If you turn on the radio and tune it to around ninety-five FM, that's my best reception field. Tune back and forth across that area—that should set up enough current to notify me."

Anna said she would, and reached forward to shut off the radio. Once again she sat on her folded towel in full lotus. Only this time, Anna waited until she'd totally relaxed and cleared her mind. Then she inserted one thought—Sancha.

Three A.M. The hour of the wolf, according to an old Russian proverb. But then, Anna, too, could be a hunter. For if this girl, this Sancha, was one of them, as Anna thought, she would be awake, ready to take Anna's contact, indeed expecting it. Whereas if she wasn't connected, more than likely she wouldn't be expecting contact: She'd be asleep.

Anna tuned the dial past 95 several times and waited in the

static areas. No voice greeted her. Anna tried again every five minutes, then every ten minutes, for what she figured to be at least an hour and a half—no Sancha. Then she became drowsy and turned off the radio.

Anna tried to keep calm about the result of her little experiment. She could be wrong about her assumptions, though she doubted it. The very idea that she might have an ally in her captivity was disturbing: It hinted at help, escape. That could be the worst illusion of all.

"I'm fourteen years old and I suffer from neurofibromatosis, 'Elephant Man' disease, which I've had since birth and which is progressively debilitating. I probably have a little more than ten years to live. I'm of mixed descent, Hispanic and southern California Indian, which you could tell from my long black hair and the olive color of that part of my skin not yet affected by the disease—if you could see me. Where my skin has been affected, most of the left side of my body, the skin is abnormally thick, mottled, folded in over itself, so that my lip is twisted up, one nostril is contorted, one of my eyes almost closed off. I'm really quite deformed, not at all easy to look at."

It was the following afternoon, and Anna sat listening, picturing what Sancha was saying.

"I'm sorry," Anna said, not knowing what else to say. "That must be terrible for a young girl."

"I don't exactly know when I developed my P-E ability, or even at first what it really was. That's what Burr and the rest of us call it. P-E stands for psycho-eidism, and it can be anything from visions to hearing voices to, well, radio reception, which is my specialty. I'm pretty sure that I discovered my reception and transmission powers around the age of four. That was when I had my first series of *grand mal* seizures."

This is too strange to be made up, Anna thought.

"After that, I guess my mental 'wiring' got all screwed up," Sancha said, as though amused by the idea. "I wasn't all that surprised to be an epileptic, I guess because it also provided me with the opportunity to become a MEC. That's what all of us in EDGE are, MECs—mutual eidetic controls—because we can control our eidisms."

"I understand." Anna suddenly remembered something that strange woman in Santa Barbara had said about a girl in the car with Burr when he'd taken the Stolzing child. The girl had been veiled, the woman said. Why would she be veiled, unless she were deformed?

"Sancha, you said you grew up in California. Were you ever in Santa Barbara?"

"No, my family came from the south. Encinitas."

That theory shot down.

"Oh, wait! I was in Santa Barbara once. With Burr. When he found Matty."

Ah!

"I was the first MEC Burr brought in, and so I'm EDGE Two. Of course, Burr is EDGE One, though he's not a real MEC. And despite the numbering, it's not a linear progression so much as a geometric one, Burr always tells us—when two of us get together, our abilities are doubled; when we're three, our talent is trebled; four of us and it's quadrupled, and so on."

"I see," Anna said. "A geometric progression." But she didn't really understand. As she didn't understand after repeated explanations how she and Sancha were speaking or what a P-E was.

"Burr happened to be in the rescue mission that found me. Our plane was wrecked in the San Gabriel Mountains. It wasn't that difficult to locate me or my parents' bodies. From the moment I regained consciousness after the plane crashed and realized what had happened, unconsciously I began transmitting my plight with such a strong signal that it overrode all regular radio transmissions within a five-mile area. Not only ham-radio operators and a local TV station, but also radios on aircraft flying overhead. It took less than a half hour for a helicopter to pinpoint the wreck. Only a few hours for them to recover me from the high, rocky terrain."

An orphan. That certainly fitted the pattern of EDGE children that Anna and Barry had discovered.

"I think that brought on my 'gift' at its fullest. You know, a sudden realization while waiting to be rescued, that with my parents' death I was utterly alone. More so than another child. Because of my physical condition, I'd been living within their minds for years; my parents' thoughts had become a total 'background' to me. Alone on that mountain, I was suddenly out of contact with another human mind for the first time in years. I was completely terrified. I guess in my panic to communicate, my gift blossomed."

"I 'talked to' Burr long before he arrived. While he was still in the air, I linked up with him—and you know what? He didn't try to push me out, the way people, even my parents, sometimes did. . . . We really haven't been out of link since."

"He sounds like a very nice man," Anna said, politely.

"Burr's great. And EDGE has been the best thing he's ever done. I didn't understand at first why he was forming it. I assumed my gift was the best and strongest, and why should Burr bother looking for any more MECs? But I discovered that my talent had drawbacks. I could tune in and link up with one person, two, even three, without too much trouble. After three, the input of thoughts and emotions became so overpowering it meshed into total chaos—overload. And then, of course, because of my increasingly debilitating disease, I'm quite dependent upon other people. I'm confined to a wheelchair and all."

"But surely the others in EDGE help you," Anna said, probing. "Timmo, Kevin, Lost and Found." Sancha had only mentioned Kevin. This should come as a surprise.

"Timmo doesn't help. And Kevin can't. He's more helpless than I am. Lost sometimes does. But I'm motorized and get around on my own. And, of course, Kyra always helps."

Bingo! That was what Anna wanted to hear from Sancha, totally unprompted.

187

"Kyra?" she asked, innocently.

"She's my friend. Kyra and I are the only girls in EDGE. I guess that's one reason why we're so close. And then, of course, she's wonderful. Exactly the way I would want to be if I weren't . . ."

"And she's EDGE what? What number?"

"Seven. She was one of the last to join us, although since we've been together, it seems like she's been with us from the beginning. That's how it is with all of us. We mesh together so well. Even Timmo."

"It must be lovely to have a close friend like Kyra."

"It is. But since she went away and came back, she's been with the others a great deal more. With Kevin. And of course with Timmo. I suppose that's only natural, since they're the same age and everything. But I do sometimes feel left out. Especially when Kyra puts up her mind-shield."

Another fact confirmed. Kyra had gone away—to Boston to see Barry, Anna knew—and come back.

"What's a mind-shield?" Anna asked.

"It's a little hard to explain. But you see, when you're so deeply in contact with another MEC's mind as we are all the time, sometimes you have to get away and be private. So, over the months, each of us has found a way to put up a shield in our minds. It's not very strong, more like a lightly electrified warning sign. But when it's up . . ."

"I see. And Kyra's mind-shield has been up a great deal more since she's come back to EDGE?"

"When we're together, it's . . . well, it's wonderful! Every shading of a thought or emotion is available. But you know Kyra has so many calls on her attention by the others that . . ." Her words trailed off.

"I'm certain she'll spend more time with you soon," Anna said.

"I'm certain, too. And in the meantime," Sancha said brightly, "I have you to talk to."

"You haven't told Kyra or the others about me, have you?"

188

"I wasn't sure whether I should or not."

"I see."

"I mean, I don't really know who you are, do I?"

Anna wondered what to do. What did she have to lose, really? "I'm a prisoner, Sancha."

"A prisoner?"

"I was taken by men I don't know and brought here for some reason I don't know, and I'm being kept against my will."

There! She'd said it. Now to see what happened.

"You're not a MEC?"

"No, Sancha. I'm not."

"I don't understand. Who would . . . ?"

"Maybe Burr can tell you."

"No. I searched Burr's mind, looking for information about you. He has no idea you're here," Sancha said. "And anyway, Burr would never hold anyone prisoner."

"I didn't mean to imply he would."

"No one in EDGE knows you're here. . . . A prisoner!" Sancha repeated, as though it were inconceivable to her.

"Well, don't worry about it," Anna said serenely. "I'm going now. We'll talk later, all right?"

"All right," Sancha said, but her voice sounded disturbed.

Good, Anna thought, turning off the radio. If she is to be an ally, she'll have to come to me slowly, by small steps.

After her conversation with Sancha, Anna had been slowly coming up with an idea. She'd been trying to remember her physics classes, so she could figure out exactly what Sancha was doing with the radio, and she'd had a tiny but significant breakthrough. She remembered that television utilized radio waves; a great many more radio waves and much more tightly focused, but radio waves nonetheless. If Sancha could control transistors in the TV, then Anna should be able to see her—they could see each other—and even better, Anna could see where she was. It might be risky to ask Sancha. Despite all she'd heard from the girl about herelf and her disastrous past, Anna still couldn't be certain of her, or certain that others weren't somehow or other aware of their contact, their conversations. Even so, she had to try.

Would tonight be too early? Sancha might still be thinking about Anna being a prisoner, might have reached the conclusion that Anna had done something bad to deserve her fate. Perhaps she should wait?

Anna couldn't wait. As soon as the food tray had been removed, she turned on the radio and the TV above it on the shelf, and dialed to contact Sancha. The girl's voice took a while to arrive on the radio, and she seemed a bit surprised when Anna made her request about communicating via TV.

"It might work. I never thought to try. But I'll need a video monitor, too. I have an idea. EDGE is meeting in the control room in about an hour. There are plenty of monitors there. If I went a little early, I'm sure Kevin would let me use one."

So Anna waited, the radio playing static. She assumed that whatever field it was that Sancha put up was so quiet as to be ignored by whoever was watching Anna. Either that, or they were hearing and watching everything. Now she'd see how far she could push them.

Finally she heard Sancha's voice, and slowly got up and went to tune the radio more exactly.

"Okay. I'm in the control room," Sancha reported in. "Kevin is busy at his computers. Try tuning your TV."

Anna changed the channels rapidly, checking to see if the snow on the screen turned into recognizable patterns. One time she was able to receive the channel she'd gotten before, otherwise nothing.

"Play with the antenna," Sancha suggested.

The antenna was built in.

"It must be attached to a general antenna for the headquarters. Try to wiggle the antenna wire on the back. Do you see it? It should be flat, a covered double wire."

Anna found it and did as Sancha suggested. After a few

minutes of dialing and manipulating the wire, she was about to give up.

"Kev," she heard Sancha ask, "how would I boost amplification in this monitor?"

Anna heard a boy's voice telling her something. She kept wiggling the wire and changing channels, and suddenly she had a picture.

"Oh!" Sancha said. "You're pretty!"

On the TV monitor Anna saw a body in a wheelchair wearing a long, dark skirt, pale blue sweater, and white sneakers. Sancha's legs and hands were visible as she played with the long yellow hair of a Barbie doll. And Anna could hear her voice as she hummed to the doll, but where her head should have been, Anna saw only a sort of mist. Yet she could see behind the girl: what looked to be rows of seats in a steep amphitheatre. Anna could also see on either side of Sancha: an arc of curved wall with various computer terminals, gauges, dials, and oscilloscopes.

"I hope you don't mind that I'm covering my face," Sancha said. "You might not be ready to look at me."

"You're in the control room?" Anna asked. She felt as though her visual world, limited to her cell for so long, had expanded astonishingly.

"We're not far away, which is why this is working, I suppose. But I don't think we can do it for long, because we're having a work session here in a few minutes. Unless . . ." Anna saw her hand reach out to what was probably a dial. "Can you still hear me?" Sancha asked.

"Clearer than before."

"But I won't be able to talk to you once I start working with the others."

"I see," Anna said. "Would it be possible for you to give me a wider view? To tilt away from the back of the room?" she asked.

"I'll try," Sancha said, and Anna saw her hand reach up to adjust the TV monitor.

The picture opened out to show a long, curved wall

banked with computers. Someone sat in a large, oddly shaped leather chair, partly turned away from Anna's view. He was encased in wires attached to the computers, like a spider within its own softly swinging web. That must be Kevin Vosburgh.

The big contoured chair turned suddenly to face the monitor, and inside it was an—enormous infant! At least that's what he looked like at first. A big baby, with tiny, bandy little legs and minuscule sneakers, and a big round stomach, not easily disguised in his orange sweatshirt and khaki shorts. A big child's head with thin blond hair, big ears, large brown eyes, pug nose, baby's lips. Then, of course, Anna noticed the two oddest things about him: He had no arms, not even undergrown ones, like his feet. And in his teeth he held a thin aluminum rod, which he used to operate the keyboards, and which he immediately and deftly replaced into a diagonal pocket sewn on the bias across the front of his sweatshirt. Anna vaguely remembered what his sister Elly had told them about Kevin—she was glad she wasn't right in the room with him, or she might not have been able to hide her initial repugnance.

"That's better, Sancha," Anna said. "Will you have to shut this off when the others come in?"

"Don't know," Sancha replied. Then: "Kev, are you using this monitor later? Or can I keep it open? I'm doing an experiment."

"I don't need it," Kevin said in a slightly irritated tone of voice. He glided on thin guide rails along the floor within the contoured chair from one computer screen or keyboard or series of dials to another, stopping suddenly, then moving on.

"I think I'd better fuzz up the picture from this side," Sancha suggested, "so no one sees you."

She did something with a knob, but in no way affected the picture Anna was receiving.

Two other children came into the room. A gangly chocolate-skinned boy in gray-denim coveralls, a brightly striped T-shirt, and tall lime-green sneakers. Could that be Lost and Found? Anna had expected . . . well, what exactly *had* she expected?

And that must be Matty holding onto Lost and Found's hand all the way down the aisle until they'd reached the platform of the amphitheatre. He let go and began to tumble about on the floor.

Matty was only a baby, Anna thought, her heart going out to him immediately. He had auburn hair, freckles, and large blue eyes. He didn't speak, and he didn't seem to look directly at anyone or anything. Was he blind? Anna asked herself, then she recalled Carol Stolzing talking about his autism. He wore a cherry-colored sweat suit, and began to play with a crystal erector set. As Anna watched, she realized the crystal wasn't preformed or manufactured, but emanated somehow from Matty's fingers, growing up and around him in a bizarre and wonderfully elaborate construction until it towered over him. The boy looked at it, appeared to change his mind, shook his head, and the crystal evanesced into air. A hallucination, Anna supposed.

Matty looked up then, straight ahead. His eyes seemed to make contact with Anna right through the video screen.

Could he see her? Did he know Anna was here?

Anna was so busy watching the child that she'd missed someone else coming into the room. Slouched now in the chair next to Matty was an extraordinarily handsome blond teenager reading a comic book, earphones over his ears, tapping his feet, oblivious to the scene: Timmo. He looked to be about fifteen or sixteen, with ice-blue eyes. He was dressed in a close-fitting silver-colored T-shirt that looked almost metallic, supple black leather pants, and heavy engineer boots. Timmo had a beautifully formed and proportioned body. Anna knew this most attractive package contained a dangerous sociopath. Looking at him, Anna sensed that like most other teenage boys, he was also a powerhouse of energy.

To his right, a few feet away, Lost and Found Jefferson

had opened a folding stool and was holding upon his lap the most elaborate abacus Anna had ever seen, flicking the mahogany beads of one line, the tan cedar ones of another, the pale yellow beads of a third row, and the pure white ones of a fourth row so quickly she couldn't follow. An adult voice was speaking to him. With each series of numbers he heard, the boy clicked off beads with a rapidity of motion Anna hadn't seen even in the offices of San Francisco's Chinatown import houses.

"Where's your friend Kyra?" Anna asked.

"Wait a min. Here she is," Sancha said, and reached up to do something to the dial.

The view on the screen opened about 45 degrees to an even wider arc, and Anna saw her. Kyra was standing at a computer bank between two video monitors on which the faces of two men—technicians, Anna supposed—could be seen. All three were talking back and forth. Kyra had pulled back her long, dark hair and swept it high. She wore pale green sweat pants and a royal-blue spandex halter. She was young and lovely, her lithe body reminded Anna of herself at the same age until Kyra turned out of profile into three-quarter's view displaying Barry's eyes and eyebrows. Anna knew in an instant that this was her daughter, their daughter. Seeing Kyra after thinking and doubting and wondering for days about her, Anna felt her heart suddenly hurt. For a moment, she couldn't catch her breath.

Kyra walked over to where Sancha sat in the wheelchair. She touched Sancha's face right through the whitish mist, and lightly patted the head of the Barbie doll. Then she went over to Kevin and bussed his forehead. He pretended to ignore her, saying out loud, "Right!" to Lost and Found, who looked up with his sweet, dense Down's syndrome face and softly said, "I was right!" then bent to his work again. "Can't let him be a dunce all his life!" Kevin said to Kyra, as though defending a position. "Functions of numbers may elude him, but he's pretty good on the beads."

Lost and Found came up with another answer.

"Right again!" Kevin cheered him.

When he put the abacus down, Kyra hugged Lost and Found, then they all moved toward the middle of the room, where Timmo was still sitting, listening to his Walkman and pointedly ignoring Matty, who was climbing all over him and the chair. Sancha had placed herself as far away as possible, and her face remained shrouded in mist.

"Where's Burr?" Kyra asked, speaking aloud for the first time. When the girl spoke, Anna was reminded of her mother's voice.

"In the control booth," Sancha said.

Anna now noticed a tall, gray-haired man descending the stairs from a booth built halfway up one sidewall of the amphitheatre. With him were two other men, both middle-aged, one of whom he introduced to the children as Ted Gielen. The other he didn't introduce at all. The two men looked official. They sat in the first of many rows of the auditorium. What was going on? Anna wondered. Why were they here? But she didn't ask Sancha, who for her own part seemed to have forgotten that Anna was tuned in, hearing and viewing all that was going on.

Speaking in a silken voice that seemed specifically developed for persuasion, Burr said, "I have a new project for EDGE."

The children, even Timmo and Matty, seemed to sit up mentally at that. Burr looked up at the booth he'd stepped down from and asked Bernie to darken the room.

"Bernie's in the control-room booth," Sancha now told Anna, using a "smaller" voice, which apparently the others couldn't hear. So the girl hadn't forgotten her. "Bernie's lowering a large curved video screen into the control room. Can you see it?"

Anna could. Photos of various sorts flitted over its surface, before one settled.

"Anybody know what it is?" Burr asked.

"Looks like stars," Timmo said noncommittally.

"Northern Hemisphere, spring constellations," Kevin explained. "That's Polaris. The tip of the Big Dipper. Ophiucus is nearby."

"Quadrant fourteen, North-northwest," Sancha detailed it even more.

"Pretty good," the unnamed observer said, trying not to sound impressed: After all, it could have been anywhere.

"Shooting stars!" Lost and Found chipped in.

"Kyra?" Burr asked.

"Is it a film? Or real?"

"You tell me," Burr said.

"Bernie is hooked up to somewhere outside," Kevin said. "I've just traced it through my mainframe. He's getting that by a feed. It's real."

"Approximately one hundred fifty-six degrees west, twenty degrees north," Lost and Found said.

"Must be coming from one of the seven big observatories on the big island of Hawaii" Kevin added.

"Time status?" Burr asked Kyra. He seemed to be showing off for the visitors."

"In light years? For which star?" Kyra asked, to a small gasp from Gielen.

"No, hon, the whole picture."

"It's happening now," Kyra said firmly.

"And that"—pointing—"isn't a shooting star!" Sancha said. "It's man-made."

"Correct. It's—"

Before Burr could say anything, Kevin had the object they were discussing in a close-up. He'd focused upon a battered-looking communications-and-weather satellite with a bad wobble.

"The old 1979 Toshiba/RCA job," Sancha said to the others. "I've used it before to skip/check some weird atmospheric transmissions."

Kyra said, "It's going to crash soon. Near the Obsk River in northern Siberia."

"That's pretty much what our Houston people figured," Gielen admitted.

"Why don't we give it a hand?" Burr said calmly.

Up in the control booth, Bernie switched from film to a schematic of the satellite.

The focus closed in again, and Anna now saw the satellite in 3-D in orange outline, meaning, she supposed, that another satellite camera's infrared was superimposed over the 3-D design to provide greater detail.

"As you kids can see, it's got a few whacks," Gielen said apologetically.

"Won't you mind losing its spy capability?" Kevin asked.

"They've got sixteen other spy satellites still up there," Sancha assured him.

Gielen sputtered.

"I've found the structural weaknesses responsible for the wobble," Timmo said.

"Good," Burr said. "Why don't you kids destroy it."

"You mean we can zap it?" Timmo asked. He seemed unable to believe his luck.

"The Japs are going to be pretty surprised," Kyra said.

"So are the Russians," Sancha put in. "They've been monitoring it closely."

"We had no indication of that," Gielen said.

"They were using microwave frequencies," she assured him.

"Well, kids, let's zap it!" Burr said. He went and sat down next to Gielen and the other man.

"Guys?" Kevin said. "Kyra, Sancha, Lost, do you have it?"

They said they did.

"Matty!" Kevin said. "Catch it!"

Anna watched with fascination as Matty produced in the center of the control-room platform a perfect hallucination of the satellite, so real that Timmo could walk over and inspect it. He did so half dancing (still wearing the Walkman), and with obvious delight. Then he put out one finger, and Anna swore she thought she saw a pale blue light shoot off his outstretched finger and instantly spread out into a

197

dozen probing, flickering beams of light, like electricity made visible, surrounding the entire satellite-hallucination.

"Right there!" Timmo pointed to a spot that didn't look any different to Anna from the rest of the battered metal casing. "Make a target, Matty!"

Instantly a perfect red circle within a circle target appeared where Timmo had pointed.

"Twelve million dollars! Bam!" Timmo said. "Let's get it!"

They all seemed to be focusing upon Timmo, who'd returned to a central built-in chair, and he appeared to Anna to be focusing on the hallucinated satellite's target. Suddenly the hallucination exploded.

Anna was so surprised, it took her a few seconds to register that the others were all looking up at the video screen, where pieces of the real satellite were hurtling off in a dozen directions at once.

"Strike!" Timmo shouted, jumping up as though in a bowling alley.

"How did they do that?" the other observer asked.

"This is fun! Let's do another one, Burr!" Timmo said.

"I'm afraid we don't have any other dead satellites," Gielen quickly said. He appeared both pleased and a little stunned.

"There are plenty of meteoroids," Kevin said. He moved Bernie's video scan around the upper atmosphere until a few irregularly shaped iron-rich chunks of space rock appeared on the screen. "Look, Burr!"

"Fine!" Burr said. "Try one of those."

The children did, exactly as before: Sancha explaining that she and Lost and Found would pin down the object's location and mass, Kyra would time its speed and any rotation, then set up a probable orbit, which Kevin's calculations would mathematically correct. That done, Matty would bring down a perfect double of it into the control room, where Timmo would find it's structural weakness. They'd all focus through Timmo and blow it up.

Anna couldn't comprehend how destroying what was,

after all, an image of an object actually worked, and understood even less when Sancha explained it for the observers.

After knocking apart two more meteoroids, Timmo miscalculated the stress points on one especially irregular long chunk of meteor, and they managed only to split it in half. Kevin yelled out "Spare!," and the children focused to knock out the two remaining meteoroids.

"This sky-bowling is really great!" Timmo said, and the others agreed.

Burr got up from the sofa and came over to tell them that their time slot with the Mauna Kea Observatory was up. He'd try to get more time tomorrow.

"You mean we have to depend on Lamrons?" Timmo expressed all of their disappointed feelings.

"Can't you try to arrange an outside hookup?" Kyra asked Kevin.

"Nothing illegal, Kevin," Burr warned.

"Don't worry," Kevin said. "It'll be such a gentle tap on their cables, they won't even notice it."

The lights went on fully, the video screen blanked and rose up out of Anna's view. The two government men conferred with Burr a few minutes; then he sent them out of the room, saying he'd talk to them later.

At the top of her screen Anna noticed a man stand up and a door opening. He'd been sitting in the top row of the auditorium, unnoticed by herself or anybody else. He remained still for an instant in the light from the outside corridor to gaze at the control-room platform. No doubt about it—it was Alex Land.

CHAPTER EIGHT

"**I**f you could keep the screen open, it would be a big help to me," Anna said.

"I guess I can. But the control room is empty most of the time."

"That's okay," Anna said. "It gives me something else to look at besides these four walls."

"Okay," Sancha said.

It was the following morning, and Anna had just finished her breakfast: two coddled eggs, two pieces of toast and coffee. She'd need the coffee today. After watching and listening to what had taken place in the control room, Anna had lain awake most of the night.

At first, her thoughts had been confused by all she'd witnessed. The display of extraordinary powers, what the children merely thought of as a game—"sky-bowling" they were all calling it before they left the control room last night—was in reality an insidious weapon far more perilous than Star Wars. When perfected and unleashed, it could unbalance world power.

Then, of course, there was seeing her daughter for the first time. How could Anna let Kyra know who she was? Once she did, she might be able to influence the girl. But would Kyra believe her? Trust her? Even accept her?

And the other children. What of them? Although Sancha had tried to explain to Anna how completely they meshed together through their minds, Anna didn't know what that really meant. Years ago she'd done months of ESP testing with Rhine cards and various electronic devices, and she'd proven to be an effective "transmitter" of thoughts and an even better "receiver." She thought of her abilities merely as "instincts." What she'd seen with these children was quite different, quite real. They were another species altogether.

And Land. Although she'd been shocked to see him, in her heart, Anna had known he would appear sooner or later. What she still didn't get was why he'd kidnapped her, instead of killing her along with Barry. Why did Land need her? What further role could she have in his scheme? Anna wasn't certain even where she was: EDGE headquarters, no doubt. Were they underground? How deep? And where, exactly?

Keeping the video and tuner open in the control room was a first, tentative step. Anna wasn't sure exactly where it would lead, but she was certain the more information she could gather, the better. She was pleased that Sancha had agreed to it.

"If you could somehow or other lock it open," Anna suggested, "so no one can fiddle with it."

"I'll ask Kevin how to do it."

They went on to talk about the other children and about Burr, whom Sancha clearly adored, and finally even about her Barbie dolls—Sancha possessed an enormous collection of Kens and Barbies and all their various accessories.

"By the way," Sancha said out of nowhere, "someone noticed you last night."

Matty. Anna didn't have to ask. "How do you know?"

"I just do."

"I see."

"It's a little difficult to explain. Matty's completely non-verbal. Kevin's done some checking into autism, and he said that no one knows why an infant is so traumatized he'll become utterly unable—or unwilling—to notice anything in the world around himself. We don't know if Matty is typical. While most autistic children seem totally closed off from life—not responding to sights, sounds, smells, or, most important, touch—Matty *does* respond. We in EDGE are able to get into Matty's mind and communicate with him."

Sancha explained that Matty's MEC began when he started "making" television, even when the TV set was turned off.

"Kevin thinks Matty did most of what is called 'parental-affect attachment' to various figures on television. Mighty Mouse and Big Bird, the Smurfs and Road Runner and the cartoon Mr. T.

"Matty forms a cartoon caricature of each of us. Kyra's tall and willowy with lots of hair and huge dark eyes, Kevin's sort of roly-poly with tiny roller-skate feet and his calculating rod is alive and has a nose and eyes—and that's how Matty recognizes us. He also has an image of Alma, the woman who feeds and bathes him—which Burr helped build inside Matty's mind. I look like the Pillsbury doughboy, all soft and warm."

Sancha said that while inside his mind Matty "hallucinated" about 90 percent of the time, he'd also developed the ability to produce hallucinations around him. At close range, these appeared intensely real.

"I never know, when I go into Matty's nursery, what will be there," Sancha said. "Sometimes it's a garden, at other times the inside of a huge cave, which stretches hundreds of yards in any direction, although I know his room is only a twenty-by-fourteen-foot rectangle."

Next to Timmo, Sancha said, Matty had the strongest energy of all, because his MEC was so untarnished by outside life.

"What did Matty make of me?" Anna asked.

"Because you were on TV, he liked you," Sancha said. "It was just an image of you, really. Quite pleasant."

"You mean he was able to see me past all the snow?"

"He sure was."

"Did anyone else?"

"I don't think so," Sancha said. "I was specifically checking with Matty. But . . ." She hesitated. "Lost gave off your coordinates a few times. He does that all the time, unconsciously. We call it 'leaking.' But since your coordinates are no different from ours, Kevin disregarded them."

"Then I guess I'll stay a secret between us and Matty," Anna said.

"That's fine with me," Sancha replied, as Anna thought she would: Lonely people seldom liked to share their few contacts. "If you want, I could open a link to Matty's room."

"I don't think so," Anna said, again knowing it would please Sancha. Anna had her own reason: She was uncertain of the wisdom of being in further contact with the uncanny little boy. "But do try to lock open my contact to the control room."

"I will."

Sancha had said the control room was seldom used, and that first afternoon proved her right. Anna saw a cleaning man wearing army fatigues come in. He casually swept and mopped up the platform area, then left. She also got a look at Bernie—a tall, slender young man who reminded her of Robert back at the shop in Big Sur (It seemed so far away. Would she ever return?) as he came and went from the booth set high in the auditorium wall.

Just before dinnertime, Kevin's automated chair slid down the center aisle onto the platform. He ignored her video monitor, went to another section of the wall, used his mouthstick to tap something into a keyboard, sat back looking at the result, frowned, then shut it off and began to leave. He'd spent a total of five minutes in the room, and Anna was starting to think that she'd never discover anything through the monitor when she saw Kyra come in the same door Kevin had entered and shut it behind her.

Almost at the top of the aisle, Kevin's chair stopped. Anna couldn't see Kevin's head from this angle, but Kyra had changed into looser clothing—a bulky sweater halfway down her thighs and black tights. She stood there, her arms folded over her chest, blocking his way.

"You've been avoiding me ever since I returned," Kyra said.

Kevin backed the chair down the aisle, and Kyra followed. When they'd reached the platform, he turned the chair toward a door that opened directly off the platform.

Kyra saw what he was doing and skipped over some seats to stand in front of him, once more blocking his way.

"Kevin, I *have* to talk to you!" Kyra said.

"What for? I'm busy!"

Kevin turned toward the control-room wall and moved to within a yard of Anna's video monitor. He withdrew his mouthstick from his pocket and began to keyboard with it.

Kyra snatched the calculating tool out of his mouth.

"Let's talk, Kev. And don't say we have nothing to talk about!"

He glared at her. "You know, Kyr, you've become a real Lamron!"

"*You're* the one who's become a real Lamron, even though I was the one away from EDGE."

He tried to turn away from her in the chair, but Kyra spun it around again so he had to face her.

"I'm back, Kev. Doesn't that mean anything to you?"

"Sure." said in a blasé tone of voice. "Welcome back. Rah-rah!"

"Everyone else missed me. I thought you would."

"Maybe."

"Well, you know better than anyone else why I had to go."

"So?" He continued to sulk.

"Well, I'm back now, and nothing has changed."

"Really!" Said with sarcasm.

"We're *all* equals, all friends in EDGE, Kevin!"

"Yeah, but some of us now are more equal than others. That's from Orwell's *Animal Farm*. You should read it sometime, Kyra."

"What I did doesn't change anything."

"That's not what I'm talking about," he said, resisting.

"It's so difficult talking with you. I wish you'd open your mind to me again. Speech is so awkward. So hit and miss."

"My shield's up, and it'll stay up."

"*You're* the one who hacked into the EDGE files," she argued. "*You're* the one who made it possible, Kev. Until then, I had no idea who my natural father was."

"You didn't leave EDGE just to go take a look at your father," he said in an accusing voice.

"You haven't even asked me about him."

"Answer my question, Kyra."

"Then you tell me why I left."

"To make sure that you could live outside EDGE. That was the real reason. That business about finding Barry Brescia was just an excuse."

"Would you open your shield long enough for me to 'share' something with you?" she asked.

"What?" Suspiciously.

"For a minute," she pleaded. "One minute."

"Any attempt to manipulate my emotions . . . !" he warned.

"Sixty seconds," she insisted.

"But that's all. Go on."

They were quiet, facing each other. Anna supposed that Kevin had let down his mind-shield and they were communing mentally.

"That's all I wanted to show you," Kyra said aloud. "You can close up again, if you want."

"I know you suffered when your MEC came on, Kyr. And I know you suffered while you were in Boston, but . . . the truth is that you *could* make it outside if you had to, Kyr. None of the rest of us can."

"If that were true, I wouldn't have come back," she argued.

"If it weren't true, you would have been back in a few days, a week, instead of a few months. Admit it, Kyra."

"Okay, I admit it. Hard as it is, I could make it outside. But I don't want to! I want to be *here,* with you, with all of you! Can't you accept that?"

"Fine, I accept it," he said.

"I do love you, Kevin, you know that."

"I know."

"Then we're friends again, despite our differences?"

"I guess so."

Kyra seemed relieved. She kissed his forehead. "Now I *really* feel I'm back," she said. "Now what's all this nonsense about you shielding yourself?"

"Timmo doesn't sleep with you anymore," Kevin said matter-of-factly.

"So."

"He spent the night with that new Lamron."

"Land? You're kidding!"

"Not that it makes any difference to you," Kevin commented.

"It doesn't really, as you know, Kev. Our relationship was only physical . . . You know, Sancha did say something about how when she first met Land he had the vibes of teenage boys on him. I thought at the time she simply meant that he was old enough to have adolescent sons."

"What's important," Kevin said, "is that Timmo's been closed to us for eighty-five percent of the time in the last week. And he's been with that Lamron most of that time. While you were away, they went off together somewhere, too. I don't like it one bit! It's bound to unbalance EDGE."

"Especially given all the influence Timmo has over Matty and Lost," Kyra agreed. "Is that what you're hiding with your mind-shield up?"

"That . . . and some other things."

"Well, what should we do? Do you want me to play Mata Hari and get Timmo back in my clutches?" Kyra joked, clearly enjoying the idea.

"Obviously Land has something that you don't and that Timmo needs."

"I'll find out what it is," Kyra said. She began to push Kevin's chair off the platform.

"Meanwhile," he was saying as they ascended the aisle, "I'm trying to find out exactly who this Lamron is. I've already begun hacking into all sorts of government files. But Land's file is sealed more tightly than any I've ever encountered."

Too bad, Anna thought. She could tell them. She could tell them all about Alex Land.

"What's a Lamron?"

"Where did you hear that?" Sancha asked.

"I just heard it," Anna said.

"It's an EDGE term for non-MECs. It's 'normal' spelled backward."

That meant Land wasn't a MEC. Not that Anna ever really thought he was.

It was the following morning, and Sancha was in her own room, one not much larger or different from Anna's save for the shelves filled with dolls. Sancha had arranged a hookup from the video monitor to her own room, "for more privacy," earlier that day.

"Then I'm a Lamron, too," Anna said.

"Yes. But a very nice Lamron," Sancha said, and slid her wheelchair back from the monitor to fetch a particular Ken doll she wanted to show Anna.

In her excitement, Sancha didn't see what Anna could very clearly make out: Kyra standing in the doorway opposite the monitor, watching them. At least Sancha didn't immediately realize Kyra was there. After a moment, she seemed to pick up on her presence.

"Who are you talking to?" Anna heard Kyra say as she closed the door behind her.

The screen went blank on Anna's side, and so, she assumed, on Sancha's monitor, too. While the tuner remained open—Anna could hear the sounds of the wheelchair and Kyra's footsteps on the wood floor—she couldn't hear a word. They must be telepathing.

What happened next in Sancha's room would be critical to her future, Anna believed, as well as to that of EDGE. Once again she wondered how she could tell Kyra who she was: It wouldn't be easy, and the girl might have all sorts of reactions—a negative one would ruin any chance for Anna to escape.

So Anna was both disappointed and almost equally relieved when she heard the girls' voices again, Kyra reminding Sancha that there was a meeting in the control room later that afternoon.

The screen went on again. Kyra was gone.

"That was close," Sancha said, back on-screen again. "Now where was I? Oh, right. With this Ken. It's a very special one. Only a hundred were made. . . ."

Anna spent the hours between the incident in Sancha's room and the meeting in the control room trying to come to a decision. She decided she would have to confront Kyra sometime, no matter the outcome. She'd missed a good opportunity before, or at least allowed Sancha to let her miss it. It wouldn't happen again. She'd have to do it soon. It was a risk, Anna knew; but what other choice did she have?

The children had just gotten settled into their places in the control room, the video screen had been lowered, and the room partly darkened when Burr came into the auditorium with Gielen and Alex Land. They took the same front-row seats that Gielen had taken with the other government man the previous day.

Burr settled himself and gave a general greeting to the children.

Matty had spread out a half-dozen comic books on the floor and was sitting in front of Timmo's central chair, staring at the pictures. Anna doubted that he could read—she was surprised even to see him paying such close attention to the comics.

"Matty, honey, you'll have to concentrate!" Kyra said sweetly, and he put the comics away. Kevin was doing some calculations at a keyboard. Lost and Found was already using his abacus.

Like the day before, the children worked together on their "sky-bowling," having a good time for maybe an hour altogether. Everything seemed ordinary to Anna—or at least as ordinary as these extraordinary children could be.

Then, after about the tenth "hit," Timmo suddenly put down his copy of *Guns and Ammunition* magazine and said, "When are we going to start doing something serious here? Screwing around with skyrocks is fun. But how about another satellite or something?"

"Settle down, Timmo," Burr warned.

"He's right," Kevin spoke up—to Anna's surprise. "You've all seen what we can do. Why waste our time? Don't you have something meaningful up there for us to work with?"

"Like what?" Gielen asked.

"Like a Commie satellite," Timmo said, eagerly.

"And cause an international incident? No, thanks," Burr said.

"What about your early-warning-system satellite?" Kevin said.

"What about it?" Gielen clearly didn't like the turn the conversation had taken.

"It was modified by the last space-shuttle team," Kevin said, matter-of-factly, "to have the capability of reflecting laser beams. How about letting us play with that?"

"How do you know that?" Gielen had stood up in surprise and was shaking off Alex Land's restraining arm.

"Come on, Lamron," Timmo said. "We know just about everything you guys are doing up there."

Gielen turned to Burr and Land. "That project was coded 'No Outside Eyes'!"

"Talmadge? What do you know about this?" Land asked.

"Burr had nothing to do with it," Kevin said.

"I'm going to have to call D.C. and notify them of this serious breach of security," Gielen said, beginning to leave the control room.

"Wait a sec, Ted. Well, Talmadge?" Alex Land said. "You still haven't said anything to defend yourself."

"Don't be foolish," Burr said. "You know as well as I that Kevin's telling the truth."

"Am I to understand by that, Talmadge," Alex Land said, really casually, "that you're unaware of what your own group is doing on a day-by-day basis?"

Before Burr could respond to Land's accusation or Gielen's obvious frown of disapproval, Land went on, "Are you telling us, Talmadge, that you've lost control of EDGE?"

Burr appeared irritated, but willing to storm it out.

"Or maybe it's merely that EDGE has become so varied in its abilities and potentials that one man isn't enough to oversee its activities?" Land asked, in a seemingly more conciliatory tone of voice.

Gielen stopped frowning. It was clear that he was absorbing all this and that the person in D.C. he was about to telephone would soon hear it, too.

"It should come as no surprise," Burr finally said. "For months now, you people have been stiffing us financially, holding back on EDGE on all levels. I've tried telling you of our progress, and all I've gotten in return has been excuses."

"What you're saying, Talmadge, is that EDGE requires a larger administration. I think he's got a point, Ted," Land went on. "Obviously the NSA has underestimated the real potential of EDGE. You can't expect a staff this small to be able to deal with all sorts of problematic details and still develop operations.

"What's needed here, Ted," Land concluded, "is someone to help oversee things. So that Talmadge will be free to work with the kids more closely. If, for example, I were to move in full time . . ."

Burr was speechless. Worse, as Land was saying it, both Talmadge and Anna, watching through the monitor, realized it had all been set up earlier, with Timmo as the front man; and that Land's offer was about to become a fact, through Gielen.

Land turned to Gielen. "So, Ted, when you're on the phone to the home office, mention that I'll be staying on." He smiled at the children. "Once you have less to do, Talmadge, you'll realize how overworked you've been."

Burr was looking down at the floor. Poor Sancha's hands were shaking. The younger children didn't seem to understand what had just occurred. If Kevin and Kyra had a reaction to the power play just accomplished, they were keeping it to themselves.

"I'll go call D.C. and set it up," Gielen said. "And I'll ask how EDGE can be used alongside the infrastructure we already have in place."

He left, and Timmo and Alex Land followed. Kevin appeared to be busy shutting down the computer. By the time he was done, Lost and Kyra and Matty had left the control room by the platform side door. Kevin turned in the doorway to ask if Sancha was coming.

She looked at Talmadge, who'd remained sitting on the sofa, lost in thought, and said, "Burr?"

"You go on, honey," he said, waving her out. She slowly followed Kevin in her wheelchair.

Anna watched Burr Talmadge as, alone now, he slumped forward in his seat and put his hands over his face. He stayed that way for almost an hour.

The full effect of what had occurred in the control room earlier didn't strike Anna until dinnertime. There, on her metal food tray, along with a rather ordinary chef's salad, was an unopened split of champagne. Dom Perignon. Looking at the slender little bottle, Anna knew Land was celebrating his coup over Burr Talmadge and the government bureaucracy. If she hadn't witnessed Burr's downfall this afternoon, the arrival of the lovely bottle might have been merely a puzzlement. But she had witnessed it—and Anna was frightened by its implications.

After eating, she flipped on the television and radio, tuned to the FM area that would signal Sancha.

The girl took time to respond, but Anna read on, keeping cool.

"Isn't it late for us to be talking?" Sancha finally answered. "I was getting ready to go to bed."

Pajamas were laid out on a chair, the bed turned down, a few favorite dolls placed upon the blankets to keep the girl company.

"It's an emergency," Anna said.

"What kind of emergency? Are they taking you away?"

"The emergency concerns you. You and all the others in EDGE."

"I don't understand," the girl all but whined. She was evidently tired, and wanted to go to sleep. Anna wished she could actually see the girl's face. At least she'd have a better sense of where they stood—even with a deformed face, there would be some expression to read there.

Anna promised herself she'd remain patient. "You seem to have forgotten. I saw and heard everything that went on in the control room today."

"What do you mean? Nothing went on! We sky-bowled, then left."

"Don't play games with me," Anna said. Then she had an awful thought: What if Sancha hadn't understood anything of what occurred?

"Burr, your good friend Burr, was very upset, wasn't he?" Anna said.

"Those men were being mean to him again. I don't know why we need them around all the time. Kevin says it's because we're funded by the government, and that's why we always have to be polite to them."

"Sancha, listen carefully. I think those men are trying to separate Burr from you children."

"That's not true! Burr specifically told me before dinner, 'Don't worry, angel. No one will take you away from me.' "

Anna saw this was going to be difficult.

"From what I saw and heard today, Sancha, I'm not certain Burr will be able to guarantee that in the future."

"You're *wrong*!" Said with desperation.

"Perhaps I am. But I think this might be a good time to let some of the others know I'm here. Kyra, for example."

"No!" Said firmly. "No! That's a bad idea."

"But, listen, Sancha. I'm not sure you understand everything that's going on."

"And you do, Miss Lady Prisoner!"

The sassy brat!

"I'm not saying that," Anna said carefully. "But two sets of eyes and ears are better than— What's happening?" Anna all but cried out. The video picture was skewing, turning into horizontal lines, those lines fluttering on a diagonal.

"I'm losing the picture," Sancha said.

"I can still hear you," Anna said.

"So can I," Sancha said, but her words erupted into static, noise.

Helpless, Anna watched as the video monitor turned to snow, the tuner emitted nothing but static. Oh, God. Land had discovered the connection and interrupted it. That meant . . .

The monitor cleared and she was looking into another room, one lined with computers and terminals, dials and gauges and . . . Kevin's face staring into Anna's. Next to him, Kyra.

"How did I get here?" she asked.

"I intercepted the frequency," Kevin said.

"Does Sancha know?"

"Not yet."

"But why . . . ?"

"We'll ask the questions, here," Kevin said.

"Who else is on this channel?"

"I said we'll ask—"

"It's crucial that no one else is," Anna explained.

"Crucial to what?" Kyra spoke for the first time.

"To everything. To EDGE."

"Look," Kevin broke in, "exactly who in hell are you? And what are you doing here?"

"If you don't tell me who else is on this line, I'll turn off my side," Anna threatened. "Then you'll know nothing."

A brief silence. A telepathic conference?

"No one else is on this channel. No one else even noticed it," Kevin said. "Satisfied?"

"You're certain?"

"Of course," he answered irritably. "It was a clean cut, and I set up warning Trojans to cut us off if anyone else breaks in."

"Then Land doesn't know we're talking," Anna said.

This time the two children looked at each other.

"Are you working for Land?" Kyra said.

"You must be joking."

"Look, we've done a voice-pattern check on you and a facial scan," Kevin said.

"What for?"

"You don't check out," he answered.

"What do you mean, I don't check out?"

"Neither your voice print nor face match any personnnel in headquarters' security file," Kyra said.

"Which means you don't belong here," Kevin clarified. "You're an intruder."

"How many people are here, anyway?" Anna asked.

"Several hundred. Are you going to tell us who you are?" Kyra asked. "Or do we cut Land in on this conversation?"

"Don't bother. I'll tell you. But I'm not an intruder. How did you know about me? Sancha said—"

"We've known about you for days," Kyra said.

"All of you?"

"Not all of us. And not to the same extent," Kyra said.

"Does Timmo know? Because if he does, he'll tell Land in an instant. That mustn't happen."

"Why not?" Kyra asked. "What are you afraid of?"

"Who are you?" Kevin repeated. "Just tell us that."

"I'm a prisoner," Anna said. "Land's men kidnapped me out of a motel in Littleton about a week ago. They chloroformed me and tied me up and brought me here."

"What's your name?" Kevin asked.

"Tanya Gregory," she said, using the name she'd lived with since leaving her CIA captors, years ago.

"An alias," Kevin said. "Given your accent, I'd say you're Eastern European. Probably Slavic."

"Yes, it's an alias. My former name was Anna Kuragin. Anna Grigorievna Kuragin."

"Russian?" Kyra asked. Kevin had his mouthstick in and was keyboarding something. "Are you a spy?" Kyra tried.

"No. Listen, I told you, I'm a prisoner! I was kidnapped and I'm being held against my will. In between the times I was knocked out, they took me into a large cavern. There was a huge lift that went down. Are we underground?" Anna asked.

"Maybe," Kyra said.

Why were they being so difficult?

Kevin hit the keyboard one more time, then dropped the mouthstick into the pocket sewn diagonally across his shirt. "Where are you being held?"

"I don't know. I haven't been out of the room."

"Let me see the room. Can you move the TV around?"

"I never tried to."

"Try to now."

Anna pulled the TV forward, making certain that cables and wires remained attached. It came half out of the cabinet.

"Move aside," Kevin commanded, "and shift it slowly left to right in as full an arc as you can."

Anna did as told.

"Now push it back in."

Again she did what he said.

"I videotaped that," Kevin said. "I'll run a schematic against the headquarters blueprints and know in a—"

He stopped, looked at Kyra, who seemed to be frowning, and said to her, "How else can we know exactly where on the base she is?" He stopped again. "We have to, Kyr! I'll explain later." To Anna, he said, "Hold on a minute." Then to Kyra, pointing to what must be a computer screen directly beneath the monitor: "There! Her room must be in that wing. Four rooms identical to each other and to no others on base."

"Have you located me?" Anna asked.

"You're in an auxiliary medical wing. To my knowledge, it's not used."

"Am I near you?"

"Not too far away," Kevin said, stopped again, and said to Kyra, "I *told* you I'll explain later." To Anna, he said, "Kyra and Sancha and I know about you. Lost hasn't a clue, though he leaked your location a dozen times."

"Matty saw me—I don't know how."

"We know. But he doesn't have a name for you, so you're just another cartoon. Do you know why Land had you kidnapped?"

"Not really, no."

"There!" Kevin said, and took out his mouthstick to tap the keyboard again. He mumbled something else Anna couldn't make out, then dropped the mouthstick back into his pocket and mused, "I thought I'd come across the name before."

"In Land's file?" Anna asked.

"No, I haven't been able to get very far into that—yet!"

"In Barry's Brescia's file, then," Anna declared, watching Kyra's face as the girl read something on the computer screen below the monitor.

"Kyra," Kevin said, "meet one of the KGB's most effective operators of two decades ago—code name, Rapunzel."

Kyra looked up at the video monitor at Anna and slowly shook her head.

"It says that you're my . . ." she couldn't complete the sentence.

Anna did it for her, sadly but triumphantly: "Your mother, Kyra."

For the first time since Anna had seen her, the girl's maturity and sangfroid had vanished. Two red spots appeared on her cheeks. She was clearly confused, unhappy, out of control, and not liking it one bit.

She turned on Kevin, angrily. "You knew all the while?"

"No, I didn't. Given all the factors, I thought it probable that . . ."

"Don't lie, Kev! You knew! That's why you've been sealed off from me! All that stuff about Timmo was just a lot of—"

"Wait a minute, Kyr! I didn't know anything for sure. How could I?"

Kyra had moved away from Kevin, away from the video monitor, too. Her posture, her stance, were defiant, angry.

Still on the defensive, Kevin said, "Look, Kyr, I read about Anna and how she and Barry lived together in Paris. The same summer you must have been conceived. Once I'd found out that Barry was your father . . . I put two and two together. That's all. I couldn't be sure. I couldn't very well go and ask someone in the CIA, could I? What would I say? 'Hey, I've got a question about some secret file I broke into'?"

"You could have asked Alex Land," Anna said. "He knew all about it."

Kyra glared at her.

"How? How could you just . . . abandon me!"

"I *didn't* abandon you."

"Why?"

"Kyra, darling, listen. I was in an American jail cell. All during my pregnancy I was subjected to months of interrogation, to all sorts of drugs, to hypnosis, who knows what else? And then I was told my baby was born dead. If you want to call that abandonment . . . well, then, I have no excuse . . ."

She wanted to believe; Anna could see Kyra half step

217

forward, begin to say something. Then she stopped and asked in an unforgiving tone of voice, "Why are you here now?"

"I told you, Land kidnapped me."

"I mean, how did you find out after all these years that I wasn't dead?"

"Barry came to me."

"Barry!"

"He found me, I don't know how. Barry's a very clever man. I didn't believe him at first. But he convinced me to help him find you. And because I wanted to believe him, and because I wanted to finally settle the past we'd shared together, I went with him. And even though I'm once again Land's captive, I'm not sorry I did." Seeing no response, Anna went on, "We followed a trail of names you'd once mentioned to him. We were very persevering, and we got some help. Eventually the trail led to the Denver area and—"

"If that's true, why isn't Barry with you?" Kyra demanded.

Anna hesitated. What she said next might be exactly what would tip Kyra either on her side or against her.

"The men who dragged me from the motel in Littleton," Anna began. "I saw them shoot Barry. From close range. In the chest. He fell back against the bed."

Kyra looked too shocked to ask anything.

"A few days ago, a newspaper with a story about a man being murdered in that motel was put on my breakfast tray. The report didn't mention that I or any woman was with him. Earlier that day, when Barry and I were in the Rockies, someone tried to run us off the road, off a cliff." Anna began to speak very quickly now.

Kyra felt around for a chair and sat down. She continued to stare up at Anna, but it was clear she didn't know what to think.

"Barry is still alive," Kyra said firmly.

"What do you mean? I saw them shoot him," Anna said, bewildered.

"I know my father is still alive," Kyra said.

"If he's still alive, he'd need medical care," Kevin said, as much to Kyra as to Anna. "He'd have to be in a hospital. I can do a computer search of all admissions to Denver area hospitals."

"Look for John Doe admissions, too. They never mentioned his name in the newspaper," Anna said. "Look for anyone of his description admitted eight nights ago, no matter the reason for admittance."

"But why haven't Land's men found him by now?" Kevin asked. "Just to follow what you're saying."

"I don't think they've looked. They must believe they killed him."

"Why do they want you?" Kevin asked.

"That's just it, Kevin. I don't know!"

"Okay," Kevin said, gearing up for work. "That's something else I can find out. I'll break into headquarters' files and see what they're up to. And I'll use the computer to check hospitals."

"Kyra?" Anna tried. "I know there's nothing else to say, but I want you to know that—"

She was interrupted by a tap on the door outside Kevin's room.

"Sancha," Kyra said morosely. "She's figured out we cut her line."

"Kyra, try to understand." Anna didn't know what else to say.

Kyra stood up and opened the door. Sancha wheeled into the room, looked up at the video monitor, then around at the other children. She hadn't put up the mist around her head, and Anna saw the girl's face for the first time. Half of it a pretty, chubby-cheeked, dark-eyed, olive-skinned girl. The other half a horror of growths and lizardlike skin crushing her eye and lips beyond recognition.

"Kyra?" Anna tried again.

Her daughter used the distraction to run out of the room.

"What's going on here, anyway?" Sancha asked.

CHAPTER NINE

"I've found six possibilities," Kevin reported the following afternoon. "Four John Does and two men with names were admitted to hospitals more or less in a forty-eight-hour period a week ago. Three are listed as having gunshot wounds. Two of those are in intensive care. One's still comatose."

"Great work." Kevin was a whiz! "What are their names?" Anna asked.

"At Denver General, they have a Thos. Jannke and a G. Straw."

"Not even close," she commented. "Were either of them shot?"

"Both! Guess Saturday nights can be dangerous around there. Both are now listed as being in serious condition, and both have chest wounds."

"What do you think?"

"Could be either, or neither," Kevin said, logically.

As usual. He'd been logical last night; he was logical today. Not to mention helpful. A great deal more helpful than Anna might have expected given what his sister Elly had said about Kevin. But then, Anna suspected that Kevin had done a lot of growing up for a thirteen-year-old since he'd been in EDGE. It wasn't just that he'd finally been given all the computers and equipment he'd ever desired, not merely that at last he'd been handed responsibility and power and the respect that accompanied them. No, it was something else, perhaps something to do with Kyra, Anna thought. She'd not forgotten that conversation in the control room she'd overheard between the two of them. What had really happened there? Thinking over it, Anna concluded that Kevin had acted like a jealous lover. And he'd been brought around by Kyra just as she would have brought around a jealous lover. Did Kyra know how Kevin felt about her? Anna didn't think so. But if Kevin believed he had to hide his passion with Kyra, he could still spread it around on those close to her—her parents. That, Anna concluded, was the only reason he was helping her.

He'd done more. He'd patched her video/tuner line back into Sancha's room as well as back into the control room, while keeping it open in his "office." He'd attached a soft, low-pitched buzzer on his end to alert Anna in case any of the three of them needed to speak to her. It wasn't escape, it wasn't freedom, but it was communication, contact—and right now that was a great deal to her.

"Have you spoken to Kyra yet today?" Anna now asked.

Kevin shook his head. "She's still pretty conflicted."

"Maybe she'll confide in Sancha."

"Everything's gotten way beyond Sancha."

Which was why Kevin hadn't let the girl into their full knowledge of Anna, but merely insisted she "share her friend" with them—which, to Anna's surprise, Sancha had accepted, displaying even more docility than Anna had expected.

"Do you think Kyra will come around?" Anna asked.

"Maybe. Listen, I hacked into those EDGE files you asked about. Unless they're bullshitting the records, I don't see that they want anything out of the ordinary with you. So far, they've just done a routine physical on you. Full battery of blood tests, pulse, blood pressure, urine analysis, the usual stuff they do for general physicals for all of the staff. You're in good health, by the way."

An hour later, as she was standing on her head—an asana

of her Yoga session—something snapped into place in Anna's mind. "G. Straw," Kevin had said. Golden Straw! Of course! It was so simple, it had almost slipped past her. Barry had told her in the car on the way here that in Operation Little Broom her code name had been Rapunzel, Land's code name Rumpelstiltskin, and Barry's had been—Golden Straw! G. Straw was the name he'd registered under at the motel.

She dropped to her feet and got on the tuner/video. Sancha answered from her room. No, she didn't know where Kevin was. She telepathed him in his room, but he didn't respond, so she assumed he had his mind-shield up. So must Kyra, who sometimes answered Sancha's summonses to Kevin. Anna asked Sancha to shut off her monitor so she might look for Kevin visually. Sancha reluctantly agreed.

The monitor in Kevin's room wasn't turned on, either. Where was he?

Anna got the control room, scanned it, and concluded Kevin wasn't there, either. Well, she'd just have to wait.

Anna was about to tune out again when she noticed two people seated in the auditorium. Kyra and Timmo! What was going on?

They were in end seats across the aisle from each other, about three-quarters of the way up the auditorium. Both had their legs thrown over the seats in front, and were resting casually, talking. Timmo's earphones were around his neck. Anna couldn't hear what they were saying, but she could see their lips moving.

"You looking for me?" Kevin on the tuner.

"I was," Anna said. "But I switched into the control room and . . . Kyra and Timmo are there. You don't think she's telling him about me?"

"I can amplify the pickup," Kevin said.

"I hate to invade her privacy," Anna said.

"But you're uncertain what she's up to," Kevin finished Anna's thought aloud. "I understand." Suddenly Anna heard voices. "How's that?" Kevin asked.

It was rough, obviously artificially boosted, but better than nothing.

"What's *your* complaint?" Timmo was saying. "*You* close off all the time!"

"It's different, Timmo," Kyra responded.

"Anyway, it's *your* fault! Not just yours! *All* of yours that I learned how to do it."

"We couldn't handle you otherwise. You were 'leaking' violent shit all the time."

"You liked *some* of it, Kyra. You all did."

"Matty and Lost are just children. And poor Sancha!"

"You don't think they don't have sex and violence fantasies?"

"That's not what we're talking about."

"Yeah, well, who *is* this Burr, anyway? What right has he to . . . ?"

"He found us. He brought us together. He *conceived* of us."

"Yeah? I've heard otherwise. And we've grown beyond him. His thinking is small, limited. Burr's got to get over the idea he controls us."

"Burr presents our front to the world, without which we can't exist."

"Anyone can do that. Alex could, too."

"You're right. But the others are used to Burr," she said.

"I know. I know. Listen, you're not burned, are you? About . . . you and me? We couldn't last. Know what I mean?"

"Anyone who gets too close to you gets hurt," she said blandly.

"I dont *want* it that way. It's the energy. I've got more of it in me every day. That fingertip beam keeps coming stronger and stronger. That mind-shield I threw up? I could block forever! And the energy just keeps on building up inside me."

"It's probably hormonal."

"That's what Alex thinks. It's too much for me to use up, Kyra."

"Give more energy *to us*."

223

Timmo dropped his legs off the seat and leaned forward across the aisle to make his point. "You don't understand! Energy comes *back* to me from everything! The radio headphones don't just make music, they fill me like a battery! Whenever I'm riding on the three-wheeler, it vibrates energy into my nerve endings. Comic books send waves of energy. Even you emit it. Your pulse, your heartbeat, your breath. It fills me up so much sometimes, I feel like I've got to release, release, release . . ."

"Timmo?"

". . . release!" Timmo concluded, looked around himself, then leaned back against the seat's arm.

After thirty seconds, Kyra asked, "What kind of energy does Land give off?"

"None."

"None?" she asked.

"Alex absorbs! You understand, Kyra? Alex is a really hungry guy. He's a gaping pit. He can't get enough."

They were silent a few seconds.

"That must be seductive, Timmo."

"You know it!"

They were silent a few seconds longer.

"I'm afraid for you, Timmo. For you and Land."

"It's not that I *want* to feel this way, Kyra."

"I understand, Timmo."

"Don't hate me."

"How can I hate you? You're part of me. We're part of each other."

"The weirdest thing is, I really *like* you."

"I know, Timmo."

Kyra stood up and hugged Timmo. He was taken aback, and Kyra quickly released him, then ran up the aisle and out the door. Timmo remained where he was a little while longer, then he walked down to the control-room platform, climbed into the fixed chair Anna had seen him in before, put on his headphones, turned on his Walkman, and began to snap his fingers.

"Had enough?" Kevin asked. The video picture changed to his work room. "She did exactly what I asked her to do."

"Now I really feel like a snoop," Anna said.

"You had to know," he concluded, matter-of-factly. "Now. What was it you wanted to talk to me about?"

"G. Straw is Barry."

The mouthstick came out of his pocket, and Kevin began to keyboard something—calling up the hacked file to check what she'd said, Anna supposed. After he spent a minute scanning the computer's screen, the stick fell out of his mouth, and he looked up at her.

"Hey! You're not bad! But if he's in bad shape we're not going to be able to just pick up a phone and call his hospital room."

Anna hadn't thought that far. Of course Kevin was right. But what kind of help would Barry have in Denver?

"That reporter for the *Denver Post*!" she said aloud. "Linda . . . what was her name? Hendricks!"

"Someone at the *Post* tried hacking into the EDGE file at NSA a while ago. But my Trojan stopped them," Kevin said.

"That was her!"

"I don't know," Kevin said, unconvinced.

"It was! Or rather a friend of hers named Gunther. It was!" Anna argued.

"Let's slow down a sec," he said. "We've got to move really carefully here. If Barry is Straw and he is alive, we don't want *anyone* but his friends to know that we know. A wrong contact . . . and whammo!"

Kevin was right, of course.

"Let's think this out, okay?"

Anna agreed, disappointed as she was, and they signed off. She realized why she'd been so eager. She was alone again. And still a captive, no matter whom she might overhear and see on the video monitor.

*   *   *

The rest of that day was a distinct letdown. After Kyra's talk with Timmo, Anna had expected her daughter to come to her—if only via the TV monitor—to talk with her, to ask questions (she must have scores of them), to open herself up. But Kyra didn't try to contact her. Sancha did, wanting to talk about her one, seemingly endless topic of conversation—her Ken and Barbie dolls. And toward dinner, Kevin did.

"I hacked into Denver General's financial files to see if I could come up with anything on G. Straw," he announced. "And I made what might be an interesting discovery."

"Shoot!" Anna said, intrigued with his inventiveness.

"Straw entered the hospital's emergency ward at three-fifteen A.M. via a local police-liaison ambulance service. Which suggests that someone in the motel was alerted or awakened by the incident, found him shot, and called an ambulance."

"The time seems right," Anna said.

"Neither the emergency room nor intensive care at Denver General demand payment for the first twenty-four hours. After one day, the hospital's financial office prepares an account, making inquiries about how the patient will pay the bill."

That didn't seem out of the ordinary to Anna.

"Okay, get this. Regarding G. Straw. When he was moved into intensive care and upgraded from "critical" to "serious" condition, he gave out this health-insurance number: 058-23-7890 V4. Are you with me so far?"

"I'm with you."

"That's a company health plan. I tried poking into the Social Security Administration terminal for proof, but I got a half-dozen Trojans warning me off. Evidently they've been hacked before."

"Can you find out . . . ?" Anna began.

"I already did," Kevin said. "Health-insurance files are much easier to crack than those at the SSA. The number belongs to the *Denver Post*. What do you think of that? This Linda person must be helping him already."

"You're a genius, Kevin!"

"Well-known fact. I still say we move cautiously. It still could be a trap."

"I understand," Anna said, admiring the boy's maturity. "By the way, have you talked to Kyra today?"

Sudden Kevin turned his chair around to face the far corner of his room. Anna saw a window opened perhaps six inches, and on the ledge, a tortoiseshell cat.

Kevin moved his chair toward the window ledge, and as he approached, the cat leaped up to a shelf filled with thickly bound loose-leafs, which looked like manuals and computer documentation.

"Do you see it?" she heard Kevin ask.

"The cat? Yes, of course," Anna replied.

"Pssst," Kevin said, moving the chair nearer to the shelf. But the cat was too high for him to reach it. After a minute it settled itself down and began to wash its face. Kevin scooted his chair over to the window and closed it, then turned around to face Anna. He looked uncharacteristically puzzled.

"Don't you recognize the cat?" she asked.

"We don't have any animals down here," Kevin said. "None are allowed."

"Maybe this one crawled in somehow."

"I don't think so. I'm going to do something. Now watch very carefully, because I may ask for an exact description from you."

Using his mouth, Kevin picked up a pentel and flung it in the direction of the cat. To Anna's surprise, the pentel was thrown directly at the cat's rear end and . . .

She gasped. "It went right through!"

"You saw that?" he asked.

The cat had jumped up. Now it sat down again on the shelf and was sniffing the pentel where it had landed.

"I *saw* it, but I don't *believe* it."

A timid knock on Kevin's door was repeated.

"I was expecting this," Kevin said, a smile forming on his lips. "Come in!"

"What's going on?" Anna said.

Lost and Found opened the door. He was holding Matty by the hand.

"Puss!" Matty said, instantly spotting the cat. As he toddled toward the shelves, the cat got up and casually leaped down to where Matty stood. The little boy petted it for a second, then began to laugh. Instantly the cat zoomed out the door, followed by Matty and Lost and Found.

"Hallucination," Kevin said. "By the way, I've rearranged your video capability, so different rooms are on different channels. Just turn the TV dial. And," he added with another one of those smiles, "I've cut a fourth channel out of headquarters' own security system, so you'll have something else to look at." With that, he signed off.

Anna woke up in a cold sweat. She'd been dreaming, she knew, but aside from the fact that it had been frightening, she didn't recall what the nightmare had been about.

Anna knew she wouldn't sleep again for hours. She got out of bed and turned on the lamps, put on her bathrobe, paced a bit, sat down, stood up again, looked through the magazines she'd read every inch of already, looked at the books again.

Anna put the books back on the shelf and turned on the radio. She wasn't able to find the country-and-western station. She'd been certain it was on twenty-four hours, no? She moved the dial on and around it.

To Anna's surprise, she heard Timmo's voice, quite clearly.

"Want to see something interesting?"

"What?"

That was Alex Land. Where were they, what was going on?

Anna turned on the video monitor, turned the channel past Sancha's room, past Kevin's, past the control room, and landed—where had she landed? It was dimly lit. Outside? Kevin had said something about connecting her to the headquarters' security system. There must be cameras outside the compound, and that's what she was seeing now.

"Something I've been working on," Timmo said.

Anna made out a concrete pathway curving away, and upon it two figures moving toward her, arms around each other.

"What?"

She made them out more clearly.

"You saw a little bit of it a few days ago, in the control room," Timmo said.

"That blue light? What is it? Electricity?"

"More like electromagnetism. I've learned how to make it. Watch!"

Timmo separated himself from Land and half turned around. He seemed to be concentrating on something—that hunk of rock the size of a man's head that lay some ten feet away? Timmo put out his left hand, and Anna noticed the boy was wearing that same metal fingertip guard on his index finger he'd worn in the control room when they'd exploded the communications satellite. Sort of like a guitar pick. She supposed it was to channel the force.

The blue light shot out through the metal guard, hit the rock, surrounded it, and began to strike off sparks like flint.

"I'm hitting any metal particles in the stone that respond to the magnetism in my beam," Timmo explained to Land. At the same time, Anna saw the rock become smaller, denser, hotter.

The rock exploded.

"Jesus!" Alex couldn't help himself.

"Neat, huh? Right now, I can only do it with objects containing metal particles or with their own magnetic basis. But I'm still working on it."

"It's great!" Alex admitted. He looked impressed.

"And the best thing is, it's all mine. I don't need the other kids to use it!"

"Who else knows about this, Tim?"

"Don't worry! I'm not letting Burr know how far I've gotten with it. No one but me's ever going to know that."

"Not even me?" Alex coaxed, placing an arm over the boy's shoulder and pulling him close.

"Maybe," Timmo said.

"Maybe I can do something nice to persuade you," Alex cooed.

Anna watched the two approach the security camera and pass under it out of view. She continued to look at the outdoors, at the half-revealed shapes of buildings and walls, and the barest edge of what appeared to be a domed roof—the control room? Tomorrow she'd see it all in daylight.

"They're going to take you up to the executive offices at noon," Kevin said. "I don't know why."

"Why?" Anna shuddered at the possibility that at last she would be taken to see Land.

"Couldn't you cancel it through the computer?" she asked, hoping panic wasn't too evident in her voice.

"They aren't using the computer. We've got about ten minutes. Listen, I've been thinking about this, and I've come up with something. The wing your room is in is guarded at both ends. But not the individual rooms. I can unlock your door automatically from here. Once the door is unlocked, you split and go into another room, the one closest to the left exit, and once there you hide as well as you can until you see your chance to get out of the wing."

Escape. He was talking about escape!

"When they come to get you," Kevin continued, "you won't be in your room, and they'll go nuts. I'll try to add to the confusion. And you'll get out."

"Won't they look for me in the other rooms?" she asked.

"Not right away, they won't. They'll concentrate on your room, call the security guards. That's when I want you to get out of the wing altogether."

"Where will I go? I don't know my way."

"Someone will be there to meet you."

Anna thought about it. If she were caught, what would they do to her? Nothing, she suspected, but bring her back. She really had nothing to lose by it.

"They'll see that I'm not here the minute I leave the room. I'm sure I'm being watched, although I haven't been able to spot the cameras."

"No sweat! You and I are going to set up a static field in your room that will knock out any cameras or radios. Do you have a nail file?"

"A small one."

"That'll have to do. Get it," Kevin said. And when she had: "Now pull the TV out of the cabinet, like you did before." When she'd done that: "Turn it around so that you can see the back panel."

"I've got it."

"Use the tip of the file part like a screwdriver, and undo the two screws closest to you."

That took a bit of doing, since Anna was afraid the fragile file would break, but she persevered and finally got them off and lifted the panel.

Kevin began giving quite explicit directions about the jumble of wires and transistors and chips underneath the TV tube within the set. Anna did exactly what he said, loosening several wires and retying them.

"You're going to lose the picture, but that's not important," Kevin said.

Anna checked the front. As he'd said, the screen was just lines.

"Fine! Now . . ."

She went back into the set with the nail file and pried out the two transistors he specified, tying them together with a wire he made her rip out from somewhere else.

"Do you have anything metal on you?" he asked. "A locket? A watch?"

"Two rings. One gold. One silver."

"Forget the gold. It's a lousy conductor. Is the silver plated or an alloy?"

231

"It's a Navajo ring. A copper and tin alloy. I'm not sure in what proportions."

"It's fine! Now be careful! Separate the two strands of the wire and wrap the copper-colored one around your ring. See anything?"

"No."

"Hit it lightly with the other wire."

A spark shot off. Anna almost dropped the TV jumping back.

"Do it again!" Kevin said. "It's not enough voltage to hurt you."

Anna prayed as she touched the wire to the Navajo ring again. This time it sparked and went on sparking, settling into a continuous tiny, visible, open electrical current. She explained what was happening to Kevin, who was pleased.

"Okay, now tie it all up with the other wires, and slowly, very gently, push the TV back into the cabinet. Very gently."

When she'd done that, he asked, "Do you feel anything odd?"

The hair on her arms and the back of her neck was standing on end, and she could hear a buzzing in the air.

"Great! That means the open electrical field is still going. It has a cumulative effect. Now move away from the TV. It will get a lot stronger. Are you ready to split on my say-so? You may have to move fast. What we've set up will reach a point where it will cause a short in the TV, the fuse, and any other fuse even near it. That should blank all the electricity in your wing, including any door locks, including any cameras watching you. But the tuner will go, too, so that we won't be able to talk anymore."

"I'm ready," she said. The buzzing was now clearly coming from within the TV. Anna could see the hair on her head now begin to rise away from her scalp. "It's getting very strong now, very loud."

"Can you see anything else?"

The front of the TV. Starting from the top, a black mass

seemed to be moving down the front of the screen, like ink poured over it.

"That means it's working. Won't be very long now. Ready?"

Anna was expecting an explosion. Not a loud one, but an explosion nonetheless. Instead, she heard a soft pop from within the TV, and that was all. The electrical buildup in the air seemed to be gone. And there was less light in the room because the overhead ceiling fixtures had gone out. It had worked.

"Kevin?" she asked.

No response.

Anna was afraid to touch either the radio or TV. So she went to the door and turned the knob. It opened.

She was inside a darkened corridor perhaps thirty feet long. At one end she saw the bouncing glimmer of a tiny penlight through what must be a glass door and she heard a man's voice—the security guard at that end, doubtless—probably on a telephone-intercom, speaking in that demanding, complaining voice that meant he didn't know what the hell was going on and didn't like it.

Anna closed her door, waited long enough to let her eyes adjust to the darkness, then felt her way along the corridor wall toward the tiny bouncing glow of the penlight. She prayed they didn't have an emergency generator ready to immediately take over. She reached a slight depression in the wall, another door, tried its handle—also unlocked—and moved on. She was about ten feet from the guard now. There had to be another room here. There was. She felt the slight depression, the door panel, the knob. It turned, it opened. Then she cracked the door open, enough to see it was a room similar to the one she'd been in, and like hers, with a single small clerestory window letting in a bit of light.

What if she went in and they got the electricity working somehow? Wouldn't she be locked in again? The nail file still in the pocket of her smock might be wedged in so that the door didn't lock. Maybe that would work.

On the opposite side of the glass door, there were more voices now, and another, much larger, far brighter flashlight. Anna no longer had a choice—she entered the room, shoved the file point into the space between the lock and its opposite part just enough so it wouldn't show from the corridor, and shut the door. No click. She flattened herself against the wall behind where the door would open, and listened to silence punctuated by her own beating heart.

Now what? Kevin had said she should wait until they came looking for her. But what about the guard? Kevin said he would help them look, leaving the way clear for her to exit. Would he really? And wouldn't they be suspicious enough to have another guard there?

So many "what if"s.

Anna tried the wall switch. No light. The electrical current was still off. Good. She resisted the urge to open the door an inch, a half inch, just to see what was going on. Instead, she moved to where the door panel met the wall, so she could hear better. Still nothing at all.

This was insane! How had she let Kevin talk her into it? Yes, it had worked so far. The electrical part of it. That he knew about. But all the rest? Insane!

Voices in the corridor. Two men and a woman. Anna once more resisted the urge to open the door, then she couldn't resist any longer. She opened the door as little as possible, just enough to see flashlights wavering in the darkness and three figures scurrying past the door, hurrying toward her room.

It seemed an infinity before she heard the man's voice shouting as he ran back down the corridor past her door: They'd gotten to her room and found it empty. Another infinity before two men's voices passed by again.

She heard the guard saying, "No one could have left. I was at the door all the time. Did you look in the lav? She might have been frightened when the lights went out."

She waited until she could no longer see or hear them. Then Anna opened the door further, slipped out, and headed down the darkened corridor toward the glass doors at the end of the wing.

The handle was an exit break-bar. She pushed it down, holding her breath. And—Kevin was right!—it opened. She turned around to make sure no one saw her. No, they were all still in her room. She could see an occasional beam off a flashlight as they checked everywhere.

Anna groped along the wall, wondering where to go next, what to do if someone approached her. Pretend she belonged there?

Another corridor, then there was a staircase down which she almost fell. Anna heard the voices behind her again, louder, with a greater sense of urgency. They were looking for her outside the wing now! She stumbled her way down the steps and reached another corridor. Now where?

The sudden glare of a flashlight almost blinded her, but was instantly gone. In its wake, halos filled her sight. But through them she was able to make out the fact that they'd come from a different corridor. She must be on an adjacent branch. Safer, if not safe. She continued to grope her way forward, feeling door panels on either side of the corridor, hoping none would suddenly open on her. How long was this damn corridor? Behind her she heard more shouting, people running. They'd come this way in a minute, a second, a . . .

She groped forward for a doorknob. Anywhere else would be better than this dark, unknown hallway. Wall, wall, more wall.

Anna froze. Her hand was touching something strange, rounded. Oh my God! Could it be—*hair?*

She pulled back, stifling a scream.

"Hi!" a voice softly said.

A tiny penlight went on, and Anna saw a small, mahogany face, its childish Down's syndrome features distorted by the sharp-edged beam.

"Kevin said to come with me."

Anna reached out and touched the boy's shoulder, trying to bring her heartbeat down to merely hysterical.

"Kevin said . . ." the boy repeated.

"I'll come with you."

"Hold on," he said, and switched off the light. It took Anna a few paces to keep up with him. Then they were in step.

They seemed to wander down darkened hallway after darkened hallway.

"Be careful," she once said.

"I don't need a light," he replied proudly, and she remembered Lost and Found's preeminent skill at locating anything, anyone, anywhere.

After another series of turns, he asked her to wait, while he stepped forward and opened a door. It gave onto a glowing curved corridor of windowed light from without.

"Go fast now," Lost and Found said, and he ran around the corridor. Anna tried to keep up with him, and at the same time to find out where she was. Below the windows she saw neatly clipped lawns, curving rampways like those she'd seen through the monitor last night, a few low buildings.

"Come on!" Lost and Found urged her. Anna looked away from the windows and saw him disappear into another hallway. She followed. At the end of it, the boy stopped at a door, then went in.

A minute later, Anna was inside the room.

"You!" Kyra stood up. "What are *you* doing here?"

Before Kyra had stood up and drawn the blinds, Anna had gotten a look out the sliding glass doors that gave onto an enclosed lawn—a chaise longue opened for sunbathing, a magazine and soft-drink container nearby. Lost and Found explained that he'd only done what Kevin told him to and left the room. Kyra tried to telepathically "raise" Kevin and failed, so she decided that for the moment she was stuck with Anna.

"You have every right to feel abandoned," Anna said. Once she'd gotten over the girl's surprise and decided that her daughter wouldn't give her away to Land's men, she'd sat back and tried to relax. God knew when she'd have to be on the move again. "On the other hand, when you heard that Barry was your father, you went looking for him, didn't you?"

"That was different. I didn't expect to meet him. I just wanted to look him over."

"Well, you looked him over. What did you see?" Anna asked.

"I don't know. Not what I expected."

"You mean he wasn't the handsome young hero you expected from reading the CIA files?"

Kyra looked up at Anna—just the way Barry did whenever something Anna said had struck home.

"Maybe you think my life has been a little strange, Kyra. But it happened. It's a fact. Don't you think your life isn't just a little strange?"

Kyra cracked a tiny smile—Anna's mother's smile, precisely.

"Maybe so," she admitted. "But it's mine."

"And the other was mine."

"The Barry I saw was a middle-aged man with a vulgar, rich girlfriend. He ran this . . . dumb little shop! He had coffee stains on his shirt! He . . ." She couldn't go on, she gave up.

"You're saying that heroes should die young. Even so, you didn't run away from him. You were attracted to him."

"I wanted to hear him explain how that could have happened to him."

"Why didn't you just ask him?" Anna suggested, and answered herself. "Ah! Because then you'd have to tell him who you were. And you were too busy playing the mystery lady to give yourself away."

"What's the difference now. I'll probably never see him again."

"Not so. Kevin's found Barry."

Kyra's expression changed at that. Then changed back.

"There! I'm right!" Anna declared. "You did like Barry. He thought so. Barry was never wrong about women."

"He was certainly wrong about you."

Anna ignored the comment. "Kyra, let me tell you something. He's a wonderful man, Barry. I love him and I realize that I've never loved anyone else. No matter what you think or do about me, I wish someday you'll come to love him, too."

No smart remark from Kyra. Just a glimmer between them of something: understanding? Then Kyra said, "What's all this crap about Alex Land?"

"I can't begin to tell you how dangerous he is."

"To you."

"You have no idea how manipulative and scheming and ruthless he is. His bond with Timmo . . . I don't know what to think of that. It endangers all of you."

"You don't understand how EDGE operates, Anna. We're like one person with six bodies. No one can come inside who isn't one of us. Not Burr, not Land, not you, not anyone!"

"Maybe that's how you *were*," Anna said. "Not anymore. Don't think I haven't seen and heard plenty in the last few days. Wedges have been driven into your one mind with six bodies. Your group is in a state of flux, and you are ripe for unscrupulous people to take advantage of you. Beware, Kyra."

"You'd say that whether it was true or not. Because of some dim idea that you and Barry have concocted about coming here and taking me away again."

"That's not so."

"Then why did you come, if not to take me away?"

"At first, we merely came looking for you. And only because you'd gone to see Barry. Then, as we made discoveries about Land's role in EDGE, it became more imperative that we find and warn you. We've both had dealings with this man, Kyra. . . . At any rate, we were motivated by fear for you. And as we got closer, it became more obvious that he wanted us away. First our motel room was trashed, then those two cars tried to drive us off the cliff. That was when we became certain you were in danger."

"But I'm *not* in danger. How can I explain? EDGE is me. I fit in here. I don't fit anywhere else. I know things that have happened in the past. I 'see' them in visions. I know where and when and how they happened with great accuracy. I also have visions about the future. Sometimes not as clearly. But I do. It's very difficult to live like that."

"Why? It could be useful."

"A few years ago, I was just an ordinary thirteen-year-old girl, interested in boys and clothing. Then I began getting these visions. My parents—my adoptive parents, that is—took me to an optometrist, to a psychiatrist. They had me tested for brain tumors, you name it. I went through months of doctors, hospitals, CAT scans, all sorts of tests."

"That must have been very upsetting."

"I learned to control my MEC, except maybe in dreams, and we in EDGE all discovered that our individual abilities meshed perfectly together. And we meshed perfectly together, and we were incredibly strong together, whereas separately we were strange, deformed, freaks!"

"Kyra, no!"

"Yes, freaks!" the girl repeated. "Myself just as much as Sancha. That's why we're together and why we have to remain together. That's why I can't go with you and Barry. I can't ever go back."

"You realize what that means, Kyra?" Anna said. "It means that you are saying no to a great deal else that life has to offer—romance, the loving companionship of another person, children . . ."

"Matty and Lost are my children. As for the rest . . ."

Kyra didn't complete her sentence, but quietly, firmly declared, "My life is with EDGE. It can't exist without me."

CHAPTER TEN

"You won't be too surprised to hear that they're looking for you," Kevin said.

"They can't be looking very well," Anna said. A few minutes before, she'd walked down the corridor from Kyra's rooms to Kevin's and hadn't been stopped; in fact, she hadn't seen another soul.

"You're safe as long as you're here," Kevin said.

"No one's allowed in our wing," Kyra confirmed.

"And most of them wouldn't dare come here if they were invited," Kevin said. "But they are busy looking," he repeated, with a slight smile. "The entire base is on alert."

"Is that what you have on the screen?" Anna asked, pointing to one of the computer terminals.

"Nope! That's a conversation I've been having with your friend at the *Denver Post*."

"Linda? Can I read it? What did she say about Barry? Is he G. Straw, as I thought?"

"Take a seat. Have a look for yourself." Kevin gestured to a wheeled keyboarder's chair. Anna moved it to the computer screen and began to read the conversation.

"Hit that red button to make it unravel," Kevin instructed.

Although it was clearly in English, the dialogue Anna read off the terminal was so guarded and wary on both sides that it sounded like a quite close but totally different language, one devised not for communication but rather for the greatest possible persiflage.

"I don't understand." She turned to Kevin. "There isn't a single mention of Barry here."

Kevin and Kyra had been communicating telepathically, their faces slightly tilted toward each other. Kevin broke away first.

"Neither of us could afford to give away any important information. But look there!" He slid his chair next to Anna, quickly slipped his mouthstick out of his shirt pocket into his lips, and hit a button that underlined two lines, then, lower down, another few lines. The mouthstick dropped back into his pocket.

"See?" Kevin said. "That's where I told her I would be willing to talk *only* if she put me in direct contact with Barry. See her response suggesting that she'd have to get an okay from him?"

"I guess," Anna said. "Now that you've pointed it out."

"Note later on, where she more or less admits that we can't get through to him, except through her. At any rate, it's good news."

"But we still have to decide what to do about Anna," Kyra said. Evidently that had been one of the things they'd been "discussing" a few minutes earlier.

"Who else knows I'm here?"

"Everyone in EDGE."

"Except Timmo!" Kevin said. "He's been out at the pond all morning, with his shield up."

"And once he returns?" Anna asked.

"Who knows?" Kyra said. "We can't really stop him from getting inside the younger kids' head, but maybe . . ."

"I wouldn't want to be Alex Land if he crosses us," Kevin said.

"You can stay with me tonight," Kyra finally said. "I have a spare bed."

"Sancha has also offered to put you up," Kevin said.

"Thank you! All of you," Anna said, "for making me feel

welcome. I know I can't stay here. The sooner we can talk to Barry, the sooner I'll get out of your way."

"That's all right," Kyra said. "We've never had a guest here before. It'll be interesting to see—"

She stopped in midsentence, both she and Kevin alerted to something Anna didn't hear at all.

"What is it?"

"Matty!" Kevin said.

"What's going on?"

"He's having a fit or something," Kevin replied.

"I'd better go!" Kyra said, and headed out the door.

"Wait for me," Kevin called after her. Anna helped him slide on the bulky chair into and down the hallway of the children's wing. Amazingly, she could hear Matty's voice yelling, "No! Go away!" Amazingly, because Sancha had told her and Kyra confirmed that no one had ever heard Matty yell anything to anyone. He'd always communicated before in pictures, or through other nonverbal means, although Anna herself had distinctly heard him call his hallucinated cat.

Sancha had also come out of her room to see what was going on, as had Lost and Found, who stood in the hallway looking on. Kyra, with Kevin and Anna right behind her, arrived just as Matty's nurse, Alma, backed out of the door and slammed it shut.

"What the hell is going on?" Kevin asked.

"Burr isn't here!" Sancha said, unasked.

Alma was goggle-eyed, shaking like a leaf. "Don't go in!" she shouted when Kyra touched the doorknob. She turned to Anna, grabbing her arm. "I've had plenty of experience with Matty's hallucinations, but I've never seen anything like this!"

"What started him up?" Kyra asked.

"I don't know, miss. I really don't know. The alarm in his room went off, and I came running to see what it was."

"I'd better go in," Kyra said. "Matty could hurt himself."

"Don't!" Alma insisted.

"Let's try 'calling' first," Sancha suggested.

The four of them went into the telepathic mode Anna had seen them in before. Evidently there was no response, but some sort of force charged through the door at them. Although it wasn't in the least bit physical, everyone felt it and everyone stepped back. Alma cried, "He's after me," and scuttled away down the hall, shouting, "Don't go in! You'll be sorry!"

"We've got to," Kyra said.

She opened the door. Anna didn't know what to expect. What she saw was fog. Or rather, dark thunderclouds filling the room, with long, sharp, dangerous bolts of lightning shooting out in all directions.

The minute Kyra moved toward it, she was repulsed. She stumbled back. "It's some sort of super mind-shield he's put up," she explained to the others. "I can't seem to move past a certain point. It feels like a wall."

"I'll try," Kevin said, and sped his chair into the fog, only to come sailing back out. "Jeez! He's got some sort of power-house aimed at us."

"Perhaps," Anna suggested, "someone who isn't a MEC won't be quite so affected by it."

The children looked at each other, communicating.

"Are you sure you want to try it?" Kyra asked.

"I don't want to see him get hurt," Anna replied.

"We should send Matty a picture of Anna," Sancha said, "so he knows what to expect."

They did so. To no response whatever from within the fog. Then, as they stood there on the lintel, the dark cloud that had filled the room seemed to contract, to lift off the ground until it was a few feet off the floor—and Matty wasn't to be seen.

"He's inside the cloud," Kevin said.

"How?"

Anna could see the little boy's clothing and toys and the room's small furniture scattered all about as though there'd been an explosion.

Seeing that, Anna became so afraid for Matty's safety, so convinced that something had happened to the child, that

243

panic took over in her. She charged into the thundercloud, feeling the hallucinated lightning flicker like gnats suddenly attacking her arms and face and legs.

All was quiet. She was inside—a vast space! Anna didn't know how else to describe it. She was on a mountain peak, miles high, surrounded by clouds, with other mountains in the distance, entire ranges of them, and deep valleys with rivers winding through them. She had somehow or other stepped right, and now stood on a rock outcropping. And there, a few feet away, a tiny black cloud floated above the mountain crest.

"Matty, darling? Where are you?"

The little black cloud churned and parted, and there was Matty, surprised to see her.

Not as surprised as Anna was to see him. He was sitting with his legs crossed as he usually did when he was on the floor playing. Only he was sitting about five feet off the ground. Floating.

"Mamma!" he said in a little boy's gleeful voice.

He'd spoken again.

"That's right, Matty. I'm Kyra's mamma."

Anna walked toward him, but stopped before reaching him. All sense of perspective was gone: She had no idea where she was.

"Look what *I* can do!" Matty smiled at her. Matty actually looked and spoke directly to her!

"That's wonderful!" Anna said. Gingerly she put out a hand to pat his head, unsure if he, too, were a hallucination. No, Anna touched his smooth, fine hair, his tiny ear. "Wonderful, Matty! How did you ever learn how to do that?"

"Why are you crying, Kyra's mamma?"

"Oh, Matty! I'm just so relieved—I thought you were hurt!"

He reached out and took her hand and stood up—stood up in the air!—and reached over and gave her a big kiss. Then he sat down again, in midair.

Anna remained with him a few minutes, as he explained how he'd "seen" levitation (he even called it by the right name) in one of Timmo's comic books and talked about it with Lost and Found, who thought it was "neat," and so Matty had decided to try it. When his nana had come into the room to tuck him in, he hadn't wanted to lose his concentration, so he'd put up a "shield" like Timmo had done and . . . Of course Anna understood. He was just trying out his abilities like any other four-year-old, saying, "Look, I can ride a tricycle! Look, I can fly a kite! Look, I can levitate!"

"Nana's gone. You can put down your shield, Matty!" Anna said.

"Yes?"

"Absolutely true, cross my heart and hope to die if it isn't."

"Okay!"

Kyra came into the cloud then, and joined Anna in admiring Matty as he walked around the room in midair, dispersing the hallucination-cloud so all the other children could also see him and admire him. Of course, Matty wanted to try it outdoors right away, and Kyra said she'd take him for a walk, shrugging her shoulders at Anna as if to say, What else can I do?

"You're very brave," Sancha told Anna.

"Just trying to earn my keep," Anna replied. "But I don't understand. Matty spoke to me! He understood me and answered me back!"

"Are you sure it wasn't hallucinated?" Kevin asked.

"What I saw was. But he was verbal," Anna insisted. "And we all heard him yelling at Alma before."

"She's right," Sancha said. "Matty's learned how to talk."

"Or has known how all the while and just now decided to talk," Kevin commented.

"He talks to me," Lost said, nonplussed.

Which seemed to settle that. Kyra and Lost and Found left the room with Matty, who was still walking in midair.

When she and Sancha were alone again, Anna bent down to pick up some of the strewn clothing. "Look at this mess! Do you think Alma could be persuaded to come back and help clean up?"

"Someone will take care of that!" a new voice said behind her.

Alex Land. With him, two security guards.

"You've certainly led us on a merry chase, Anna G.," he said in his most honeyed tone of voice. Then, rougher, to the guards: "Get her!"

Anna steeled herself against the future with contempt and memories of the past—forces no torturer could strip away. She was prepared, less than an hour after she'd been dragged and thrust into a makeshift cell, to hear its bolts shoot back, to see two figures coming for her.

She didn't resist, didn't ask where they were going. They didn't touch her, but stood one in front, one in back, as she walked. They got into an elevator, ascended, stepped out, and Anna recognized the curved, windowed hallway she'd run through with Lost and Found earlier that day. They were going in the opposite direction now.

Down a short staircase, through a tall steel door and . . . they had brought her to EDGE's control room! She stepped onto the platform she'd seen on the video monitor over the past few days and immediately thought how spacious the auditorium was, how deeply half-moon the curve of the wall of computers and electronic equipment, how high the dome above, now opened in a pie-shaped wedge, through which shafts of light fell, illuminating the central chair upon which lolled Timmo, his head a helmet of pale, sunstruck hair. Behind him stood the figure of Alex Land.

Anna barely had time to notice them, to glance at Kevin facing her in his chair, Sancha nearby in her wheelchair, and Kyra standing between them, her arms akimbo in defiance, when someone was at her side, tugging at her skirt. Matty, looking up at her, smiling. Instantly joined at her other side by Lost and Found. What . . . ?

She was going to reach down to pick up the smaller boy when she heard:

"Who's going to tell me what this is all about?"

Burr Talmadge had pushed his way through the same doorway Anna had entered, past the soldiers who'd escorted her. He was wearing a sports jacket and carrying a soft attaché case. He looked as if he'd been traveling, and had just arrived back. He spoke with authority.

"We all just quit!" Kevin said.

"Quit?" Burr asked in irritation, taking off his jacket and tossing it and the attaché onto a front-row seat of the auditorium area. "What do you mean quit? Quit what?"

"EDGE," Kyra said.

"What? Why?"

"Ask him." Kevin indicated Land. "He broke the cardinal rule. He invaded our privacy."

"Is that true, Land?" In turning from Kevin toward the man, naturally Burr had to notice Anna. "Who are you?" he asked. "Who's she?" he asked Land.

"A Russian spy," Timmo declared.

"What?" Burr was thoroughly confused.

"She is," Land said.

"Used to be," Kyra said. "Seventeen years ago."

"Someone had better tell me what this is all about. Who are you?" Burr asked Anna outright.

"I'm Kyra's mother."

That stopped him.

"That's right. She was taken away from me at birth. By him!"

"Land is holding her prisoner," Kyra said. "But Sancha made contact with her, and we helped her escape. She was with us, in our rooms, and he came in and took her away."

"Which broke the cardinal rule of invading our privacy under which EDGE operates with NSA," Kevin explained. "That being so, our contract is null and void. You'd better phone D.C., Burr, because as of right now, we're out of here."

"I don't believe this," Burr said. "I'm gone less than a day . . . Sancha?"

"It's all true."

247

"What's true?"

"What Kyra and Kevin told you."

"Fuck it!" Timmo said. He'd moved to the edge of his seat now. "They're conspiring against me and Alex! They're all in it together!"

"How would you know what happened, Timmo?" Kyra asked. "You weren't even here!"

"I know! She broke in here to learn our secrets and tell the Commies," Timmo said. "She's nobody's mother!"

"Just because you never had a mother," Kevin jibed. "Or at least one who'd admit to it!"

"You'll be sorry for that, worm!" Timmo jumped off the seat.

"That's enough, Timmo," Burr said.

Timmo wasn't to be stopped so easily. Burr had to put out an arm to hold him back.

"They've been plotting against us," shouted Timmo.

"How can that be possible?" Burr reasoned.

"It is! They all put up mind-shields so I wouldn't know. But they couldn't fool me."

"Come on, Timmo," Burr said. "You know as well as I, that's a lot of nonsense. Where did you get these crazy ideas?"

"From comic books," Kevin said.

"You worm! You slug!" Timmo fumed, trying to get past Burr.

"Timmo, stay back, I said! What's gotten into you?" Burr pushed the boy away. "Go! Sit down. Now!" Turning to Anna: "I don't know who you are or what's really happening here, but we've all got to calm down and reason this out. Land, why aren't you saying anything?" And when he still didn't respond but merely put a hand on the shoulder of the obviously still-steaming adolescent, who'd reluctantly sat down: "You should know that I didn't go to Denver as I said, but to D.C. to meet with the NSA."

"Did you?" The ironical tone couldn't hide Land's surprise.

"We had a long talk about EDGE and its future. As well as any future connection to the various agencies represented here at the base."

"Did you?"

"Yes, we did. Ted Gielen and, well . . . some other people," Burr went on, not heeding what Anna clearly thought was a warning tone in Land's voice.

"And?"

"And . . . Ted's changed his mind about the setup here, as we'd discussed it previously, a few days ago."

"In what way?"

"Well, as you displayed so effectively a few days go, I really do need help with the group and all the administrative duties involved. But Ted has since come around to my way of thinking on the matter."

"Which is?"

"That I choose who will be working with me and EDGE. Ideally, it would be someone who's had a great deal more experience with MECs and P-E phenomena. I believe I managed to get everyone to share my thinking on that."

"Did you?"

"Naturally you still have a role in all this. Perhaps not as decisive as you'd earlier suggested."

"That was agreed?"

"It didn't take much for everyone to see the wisdom involved in such a reorganization."

"I'll bet."

"And I'm certain you'll eventually come to see the wisdom in it."

Land didn't answer. His hand seemed to have dug quite painfully deep into Timmo's shoulder. The two remained as still as a tableau vivant, dour father standing hand on shoulder of stiffly erect son.

"Alex?"

Land suddenly released his grip on the teen. As though he were a coiled spring, Timmo snapped off the chair so quickly that he was a blur of hurtling body. Anna thought for a moment that she saw an object glint in his outstretched hand. Timmo's suddenness and the force of his thrust knocked Burr flat on his back.

Timmo was back on his feet, staring down almost in

surprise at the glittering steel knife he had just driven into Burr Talmadge's heart. Before anyone could register shock, he spun away, up the aisle, and out of the auditorium.

Completely ignoring Burr, Alex Land had run after Timmo. Kyra had pushed the smaller children out of the room, ordering Lost and Found to take Matty away. She'd turned to the two soldiers who'd brought Anna and yelled at them to get medical help immediately, come on, get moving!

Not that speed made a difference now. Anna dropped to her knees, searching Talmadge's carotid artery for a pulse, trying not to look at his open eyes with their look of astonishment, his agape mouth and blood-soaked teeth, the single thin line of blood that had burst his lips and trickled down his chin.

Anna covered Burr's face with his handkerchief. She had been vaguely aware of Sancha moaning in a low voice in the background. The second it was confirmed that Burr truly was dead, Sancha began to convulse in her wheelchair as though an electric current were being sent through her body. Horrible to watch as her arms and legs and head jerked spasmodically with such energy. It would be a wonder if she emerged without at least a few fractures. One medic checked Burr's corpse, then joined his colleague, who was attempting to subdue Sancha.

"There's medicine to stop this, or at least control it," he said.

"We've got to get her to the clinic!" the other medic said.

"Hurry!" Kyra had urged.

She remained with Sancha on and off throughout the rest of the afternoon and evening, returning back to her rooms only at night, falling into an exhausted sleep.

Oddly, given what had happened to her earlier, Anna had been free to go wherever she wanted. At least within the building. After leaving Kyra at the clinic, she checked back with Kevin, who'd returned to his rooms and seemed best able to cope with the shocking incident by immersing himself in his computer. He was too busy even to remove his mouthstick and speak to her.

Anna looked for and found Matty and Lost and Found, neither of whom appeared to have really understood what had occurred with Burr. She stayed with the children, accompanying them through dinner, and finally watching TV with them another hour before tucking them into bed. All the while, she'd felt uneasy, like a kindergarten teacher pretending that some unspecified catastrophe wasn't about to fall on all their heads.

The following morning, Kyra was already awake and getting dressed when Anna raised herself up from the spare bed that had been made up in her daughter's room.

"Timmo's back," Kyra said, tonelessly.

"I'm sorry, Kyra."

"Land's agreed that you're EDGE's guest. He won't touch you. You can go out, move around freely. But you won't be allowed off-base. I understand from Bernie that you were with Matty and Lost. It might be a good idea to try to stay with them today. I'm going back to the clinic."

"How's Sancha?"

"She stabilized with the shots they gave her. But . . . she may be out of whack for a while. She and Burr were . . ."

"I know. Sancha told me how close they were."

Kyra was ready to leave. Anna was waiting for her daughter to turn on her, to blame her for making it all happen. If so, Anna wouldn't defend herself, how could she?

Instead, Kyra said, "You were right about those two. We should have listened to you." And when Anna didn't say anything: "You saw, didn't you, exactly what happened? Land built up the anger, and Timmo acted it out. He was like a guided missile."

"I saw."

"I don't know what's going to happen next. But it's not safe here for you."

Before Anna could suggest that it was no longer safe for Kyra, either, for any of them, her daughter had left.

After seeing the smaller boys at breakfast and promising to

go outside with them in an hour, Anna knocked on Kevin's door.

He refused to discuss Burr's death, was, in fact, in a curiously upbeat mood.

"I've talked to Barry," he announced.

"When?"

"This morning at the hospital. He seems to be making a pretty good recovery. Up and walking about."

"I wish I could have talked to him."

"It was only through my mainframe and his laptop and the *Denver Post's* connecting line. I was afraid that once we were in contact, you-know-who might find out and try to hack into the line. I couldn't take any chances by alerting you."

"Did he try?" Anna asked.

"No. I'd attached all sorts of Trojans, which would have broken contact immediately. I've hard-copied our conversation for you to look over. Don't let *anyone* else see it, and destroy it as soon as you've read it, understand?"

He gestured toward a few pages of dot-matrix printed matter, which Anna stuffed into her skirt.

"I'm also trying to figure out a way to get you out of here. It's not easy. The lifts are guarded at both ends."

"Then we are underground!" Anna said. "But it's like daylight."

"Go outside and see exactly where you are," Kevin said. "I think you'll be pretty amazed by the place. Even I'm impressed by the technology. What a bit of skill and planning and a pile of American taxpayer money won't do! You realize, of course, that this is an SDI base? The Star Wars program," he explained.

"I thought that program wasn't fully funded yet."

"Yeah, well . . . you'll see."

"I'm supposed to take Matty and Lost to the pond later on," she said. "What about Kyra? What will she do when Barry gets here?"

"No idea. Nothing until she's certain Sancha's okay."

"She's very loyal. I know how fond you've become of Kyra," Anna began, and stopped. "How fond of each other

252

you've become. And I also know that you're aware that Kyra may not belong in EDGE . . . at least not entirely, or not as much as some of you. . . ."

"Not belong?"

"What I mean is, that Kyra has choices in life the rest of you may not have, choices she's going to have to face soon."

Kevin turned away from Anna. He didn't want to hear this.

"I know. I won't interfere in Kyra's decision," he said quietly. "Whatever that turns out to be."

"I hoped you wouldn't. Thanks, Kevin."

"Although what Kyra decides or how I react to it might turn out to be a moot point," he added.

"What do you mean?"

"I'm real close to cracking a pretty tight file. But I've already said too much," he concluded. And picked up the mouthstick and began to do some keyboarding. The conversation was at an end.

Anna and the children got back to EDGE's wing in the main building of the base just before lunchtime. It had been a curious morning, not only because of where they'd been, what Anna had seen, being "outside" for the first time.

True, the base was huge, maybe a mile across, a gigantic cavern carved out of rock by water or some other natural erosion many thousands of years before. And it had been wonderfully built and equipped by the men who'd descended into it: brick walkways past other buildings, gardens, and finally, close to one enormous looming wall of the space, a natural pond, which had been formed by underground springs. Small fish of a kind Anna had never seen before swam in its shallow waters. A score of palm trees had been added for shade—they seemed huge, fast-growing—and there was a small beach, which was where she and the children encamped. What Anna had taken for sunlight was instead a series of enormous lights, like those she'd seen in sports stadiums, built at various levels up the cavern wall.

Back in their rooms, Matty and Lost and Found had been

given lunch and put to bed for a nap. Anna sat in Matty's room watching him sleep. Somewhere within her, Anna sensed an ache mixed of longing and hope, which she remembered feeling only once before, years ago, when she'd been carrying the baby that would turn out to be Kyra. She had to admit she couldn't keep her eyes off Matty. She was bowled over by how he walked and the little gestures he made, his smiles and his frowns and the soft, high pitch of his voice whenever he chose to speak. She coveted the little boy, she knew, wanted him for her own.

The door opened. Kyra looked in and gestured for Anna to step out.

"I've been looking all over for you!"

Anna shut the door so they wouldn't wake the children.

"Is it Sancha?" Anna asked, picking up the sense of emergency in her daughter's voice.

"No. She's fine. Better than expected. She's awake and alert and she's already begun demanding her Ken and Barbies. It's Kevin. He found something."

"This morning he said he was trying to crack open a certain file."

"You'd better come with me," Kyra said.

Uncharacteristically, Kyra checked around the corridor as though making certain no one was watching them.

"Come on!" she insisted.

Anna followed her into Kevin's rooms. He seemed in no way panicked by whatever he'd discovered; instead, he gestured for Anna and Kyra to take seats at each of two computer screens, finished something at his terminal, then dropped his mouthstick into his shirt pocket.

"You know," he began, "that in the past week or so, I've been delving into files I had no business seeing."

"The files on Alex Land," Kyra said.

"I told you you needn't bother," Anna said. "I can tell you more than you want to know about that one."

"So you said, Anna. And you were partly right. I did manage to get into Land's files, and they were certainly interesting in their variety of activities over the past two decades and in the sheer nefariousness with which Land carried out some of his operations. I already knew most of that when you arrived here, which was why I bought your story so willingly."

"Thank God!"

"However, you should also know, that Land, whatever one might think of his methods, has pulled off a series of intelligence coups that would be hard to match. He's managed the near-impossible, cutting through bureaucracies to get whatever he wanted, and managing to use them all—CIA, FBI, NSA—without alienating any of their leaders, or any of the last three administrations in this country. You'll admit that's quite a feat."

"Barry insisted he wasn't in the CIA anymore," Anna said.

"What's the point of all this?" Kyra asked.

"We should know how powerful the man is if we're planning to move against him," Anna said.

"Exactly!" Kevin concurred.

He got hold of his mouthstick and hit the keyboard. On all three screens now something showed up:

EDGE—AUTHORIZED EYES ONLY

"Among all the cross-indexed files, this one intrigued me. I've been hacking files since I was six years old," he told Anna. "I know every way possible to get into them. There are few that can't eventually be broken into—given perseverance and caution. I've devised all sorts of warning devices against detection, against being detected. So believe me when I tell you this EDGE file was a tough one to break into."

"But you did!" Anna said.

"What did you find?" Kyra asked.

"Look for yourself!" Proud of his accomplishment, Kevin used his mouthstick to release the file, pages of it unscrolled slowly, a stately march up each of the computer screens.

"Why are some sentences backlighted like that?" Anna asked.

"Those, friends, were closed to me even after I'd gotten into this file. Obviously the most secret agenda of the EDGE project. No one, not the people funding him, not the NSA, no one but Land himself, ever saw those. Until right now!

"The material was massive, years of it," Kevin continued. "It took a while to go through it all. Maybe I should just outline those parts of it that are relevant."

"Shoot!" Kyra said.

"The function of this group was obvious from the very beginning," Kevin went on. "Land wrote that it was 'to act as a covert arm of the United States Armed Forces—' the group would be responsible for disruptive actions on mental and physical levels.

"That's pretty chilling. There are in-depth files and profiles of each of us in every possible area of physical, psychic, and psychological development. We all had nicknames. I was 'Flippers,' Matty 'the Movies,' Lost and Found 'Black Radar,' Timmo 'Time Bomb,' Sancha 'Radio-Head,' and you, Kyra, were 'Snatch.' Those names were referred to again and again in various files and reports."

Anna and Kyra looked away from the computer screens where they'd been following Kevin's words, and their glances crossed.

"Remember, these are his private files," Kevin said. "Not what he showed to other people. Land first got interested in psychic powers and their strategic possibilities when he learned about the Russian program. Anna, that was the program you were part of."

"But I had very weak powers," protested Anna.

"Nevertheless, you were a MEC. After Land grabbed you, he subjected you to extensive testing . . ."

"Torture, you mean. He 'deprogrammed' me to find out everything I knew about the KGB."

"Yes," Kevin said, "but what he really wanted to investigate were your psychic powers—that was the real purpose of all those drugs and the hypnosis. And, of course, it was an undreamed-of bonus when he discovered you were pregnant. He decided to take the child to see if MECs were genetically determined."

There was a little gasp from Kyra.

Kevin continued, "He placed Kyra in an environment where she could be carefully monitored. At the first sign of her talents, he had her isolated and tested. He trained her to develop her MEC to its fullest potential. So, Anna, *you* were the real beginning of EDGE."

"I may have been," said Anna, "but I have no part in the group now. Why has Land brought me here instead of just killing me?"

"In scanning some of the more recent files, I've figured out where Land is heading lately," Kevin said. "Recently he's decided that Matty and Timmo are the most valuable for his purposes."

"Because their MEC powers keep on growing?" Kyra said.

"Right. And because they're so unsocialized, so amoral, they have no constraints on the directions in which their powers will grow. He'd love to get rid of the rest of us, but he can't yet."

"And Land can guide Matty and Timmo in whatever direction he chooses."

"We saw a most unfortunate example of that yesterday in the control room," Kevin said. "On his own, Timmo wouldn't have hurt Burr. But some sort of fusion has taken place between Land's purpose and Timmo's action."

"Does he know about Matty's levitation?" Anna asked.

"I'm sure he does. I suspect once Land feels that he's got Timmo fully in control, he'll start in on Matty."

"He can't!" Anna cried. "That lovely little boy!"

"Yeah, not when Land gets through with him," said Kevin.

"But Kyra is the one member of EDGE that Land can't control. She's the one person who doesn't really need EDGE, who could live in the Lamron world."

"That's not true, Kevin," insisted Kyra. "I could never leave EDGE."

"Yeah, well that's not what Land thinks," said Kevin.

"He got really scared when you left to go find your father. And that's why he brought Anna here instead of killing her."

"Why?" asked Anna incredulously.

"You're his trump card. He can use you to manipulate Kyra if he needs to."

"What about Barry? Was he going to use him, too, at some point?" asked Anna.

"He doesn't care about Barry," explained Kevin. "He thought they'd killed him. They *will* kill him if he tries to interfere anymore. Still, he's our only hope. We're at a stalemate with Alex Land."

Anna felt Kyra's arm around her shoulder, looked up into her daughter's large, dark Mediterranean eyes—Barry's eyes—and tried to be brave. Her love, hers and Barry's, had lasted through years and the pain of betrayal and loss; it had lasted through the mutual belief that the other was dead.

"Wait a second. I've made contact with the *Denver Post*," Kevin said suddenly, looking at his computer screen. "They're looking for Linda Hendricks now."

"It'll work out okay," Kyra said while they waited, trying to alleviate the somber mood.

"I've got her!" Kevin exulted. They saw him in a frantic mouthstick keyboard conversation.

"What's going on?" Kyra finally detached herself from Anna to stand up and look at Kevin's keyboard. "Oh, no!"

"What?" Anna asked. She, too, stood up, and began to walk toward them.

Kevin turned around and dropped the mouthstick back in his shirt pocket.

"Barry got out of the hospital this morning. He rented a car and left Denver three hours ago."

"You haven't told him how to get here, have you?" Anna said in an agonized voice. "This time they'll kill him for sure."

Kevin looked ruefully down at his lap.

"Oh, Christ, Kevin," said Kyra angrily. "What could you possibly have been thinking of?"

"I'm telling you," Kevin said softly, "it's our only hope."

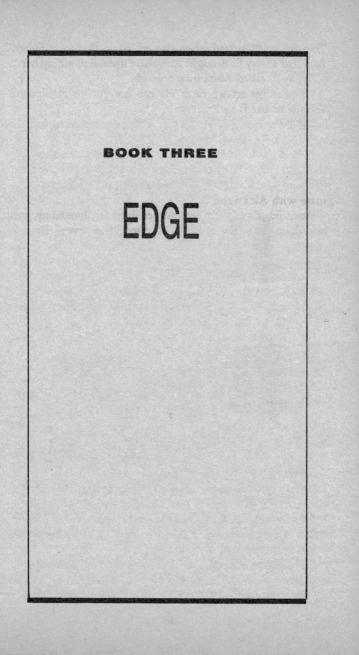

BOOK THREE

EDGE

CHAPTER ELEVEN

Barry had passed a town called Malta fifteen minutes ago, and was driving along a two-lane state road when he looked up and saw what looked like a large army helicopter moving ahead, then skittering across the mountains out of sight.

Coming? Or going? A good sign either way. There were no military bases shown on the road atlas for this part of Colorado. Or at least none that anyone would admit to. EDGE headquarters had to be nearby.

There was a hot stab of pain in his ribs. Pain had become a familiar companion, ever since he'd awakened in the intensive-care unit with a bouquet of tubes sticking out of his wrist.

Even after ten days, and even with the codeine-laced Darvon, it was still a solid presence, dulled now, yet with occasional sharp little reminders whenever he turned too suddenly or in the wrong direction.

At the hospital they'd changed his bandages several times daily, and had managed to completely drain the two "clean" wounds, continuing to marvel at his luck—"Shot from close range and not a single major vein or organ touched!" the young intern repeated talismanically every day—and Barry had been told, and now knew, that whatever pain he felt was from the healing process, burst tissues and rib bones drawing together inexorably.

His rented car had just topped a ridge, and the double-lane

road dropped into a long, narrow valley. Scrub pine and gorse grew up the sharply angled sides of what seemed to be slabs of yellow-and-brown rock. He could see Mount Elbert's southeastern side, the only side unapproachable by dirt roads from this narrow highway. At one point straight ahead, a deep, infolded ravine met the valley. At the conjunction, Barry noticed, the highway went over a small metal bridge with hip-high corrugated sides, just as Kevin had said it would.

He slowed down so he could read the small sign that announced the meeting of the two rivers.

Barry parked, got out of the car, and looked around. Nothing much to see. No cars, no buildings at all. Hardly any vegetation. Not a point of interest or landmark anywhere—aside from the mountain and the small, fast-running rivers.

The sun had passed its meridian. He calculated where north must be, then south. He still didn't see anything. Kevin had said a thousand yards. Perhaps he ought to look around a little?

He parked and loped along the road onto the rounded rock shelf that formed the tip of the triangle where the rivers met. There he began walking south, counting his wide steps. At two hundred yards, he was in the midst of a jumble of rock, the highway hidden from view, the sound of the rivers suprisingly distant. At four hundred, he was already in another flat area, sere, rock-strewn, uninviting. Around him, the uptilted sides of mountains seemed to come together. He kept walking until he'd reached six hundred yards and was stopped by a rock face that extended in all directions. He followed it around one side, and when that ended in a coulisse, he backed up and went around the other way, finding a gulch that continued on. Eight hundred yards and it still went on, seemingly leading nowhere. Rock litter underfoot. What if Kevin had given him completely bogus directions?

After Barry had counted off about 950 steps, the narrow cleft opened up onto a sudden, enormous oblong space, which went off in two directions. Straight ahead was another rock ridge, but he could already see a large cavern opening, hidden only a minute ago. And while it appeared to be closed in by fallen rock, there was something inhabited about the entire spot—he couldn't say what, exactly.

Barry skirted the cavern—then began to climb its outside. When he reached a point nearly a hundred feet off the ground, he had a good view of the surrounding area. Straight ahead was the gorge he'd come through. To his left, a wide-open space that seemed to have been purposefully flattened—they would need a flat place for the helicopter to land. Yet there was no runway here, nothing to show a chopper had either risen or landed recently. He climbed higher, and ended up facing in a more westerly direction than before. He saw an old railroad track, the rails completely pulled up, the remaining iron ties buried amid weeds.

Facing north, he found the ribbon of highway, the bridge, and—what was going on?—next to his rented Mustang, a state-police car. Two highway policemen were peering inside the car, trying the door handle, speaking to each other, looking around for him. They would stay for another five minutes, he figured, before shaking their heads, giving up, finally driving off.

Barry clambered down the rocks. He was on the ground now, at a different angle to the cavern opening, when he saw it: a slat of wood so wind-carved and sandpitted its white lettering was merely a ghost of script, declaring this to be the Cantry Bauxite Company, Thurlow Valley, Colo., Excavation #9, 1879. Below that, a smaller sign read: NO ENTRY FOR NONCOMPANY MULES. SEE MANAGER FOR ALL CART-HAULING.

A powerful, almost industrial stink came from whatever lay inside the mouth of the cave. Bauxite was a metal ore, wasn't it? He recalled seeing some in a high-school chemistry class years ago, remembered the teacher calling the clayey substance an early version of aluminum in an oxide base. He hadn't particularly remembered any odor—or toxicity. Was he smelling bauxite now?

"Let's see where you go to!" Barry said, and began to pick his way through the fallen rocks at the mouth of the cave. He recognized the odor as sulfurous—more bark than bite—held his handkerchief to his nose and mouth hoping that would protect him, and half stepped, half tripped down several large boulders at the cave opening.

At the bottom of the rockfall he arrived at a flattened floor. It was obvious now that rocks had been placed to hide the spot and could be taken away for entry and egress. The cave floor was gouged by double tracks that might have been made either by wagon wheels a century ago or truck tires a week before. He walked on, passing rough-hewn Ponderosa pine beams on either side, crisscrossed above to support the high rock roof. After walking five minutes, he still had enough light to see, although he didn't know how—he couldn't make out any obvious source of illumination.

That's when he saw the floor-to-ceiling fence of chain mesh about a hundred feet ahead, and the huge gate panel. Unlike the signs outside, this was shiny and new. The sulfurous odor and rockfall had been engineered to deter the curious. Behind the fence somewhere lay EDGE headquarters, as safe from prying eyes as Alex Land could make it.

Barry couldn't see much beyond the fence, except what appeared to be the natural back wall of the main cave. How to get through the fence? The gate was posted solid into the cave floor by steel rods, chained closed with a huge combination lock. Wasn't Kevin expecting him?

Then he heard a noise—an engine. Barry got out of the way, behind a ledge. An All-Terrain Vehicle carrying two soldiers drove out of the hidden cavern corridor and up to the gate. Barry was close enough to hear the passenger report into his pocket radio, saying all was okay; he was entering, and Corporal Turrel was going on patrol.

The soldier who'd spoken got off the ATV, walked up to fence, reached in through the mesh, turned the combination until it opened, slid open the gate. The driver went forward, past where Barry had scrunched himself as deeply into shadow as he could. When Barry looked forward again, the first soldier had closed the fence behind him and relocked it, checking to see that the big lock was tight.

"Hey, Don? Don't get lost out there," he shouted, before he went off back through the corridor. The driver waved without looking back.

Barry waited till both were gone before he opened up the laptop computer, attached the cellular phone he'd had the reporter purchase the day before, and dialed the number that Kevin had given him.

All connected, turned on, accessed, waiting. It rang and rang. It was ten minutes to one. Kevin should be expecting him? But the screen remained blank. Was he supposed to do something else? He didn't remember any other signal agreed on between them.

Finally the ringing stopped, as though it had been picked up. Yet nothing appeared on the screen.

He waited. This was insane. How did he expect to get past a locked fence and what might be scores of security men to . . .

"B. B?" appeared on the screen.

"Yes," he typed back. "There's a combination lock on the fence. And there are soldiers here."

"There's been a change of plans."

"What are you talking about?" Barry keyboarded back.

"We've decided that it's too dangerous for you to come here."

"Who's 'we'?"

"Anna, Kyra, myself."

"You've got to be kidding. I got out of a hospital bed and drove a hundred miles to get here. I'm not about to stop now."

"Barry! This is Kyra. Kev's right. The *worst* thing you could do is come down here."

How did he know that was Kyra? No voice: only gray letters upon a liquid crystal computer screen. It could be anyone.

"How will Anna get out?" he keyboarded.

No answer to that.

"Great!" he said, keyboarding. "Put Anna on."

After a few seconds, the screen began to print out.

"They're right, Barry. You mustn't come here. That's exactly what he wants."

"Are you okay?" he keyboarded. "They haven't hurt you, have they?"

"I'm fine. I'm not hurt."

"How are you going to get out of there?"

"I don't know yet. We'll think of something."

Not good enough. "How do I know they're not making you say that?"

"You don't. You have to take it on trust."

Sure, he thought.

"Why don't you rest for today until Kevin figures out some other way. You must still be in terrible pain."

"It's not that bad."

"Go back, Barry. Kevin will contact you soon. Please, Barry. Find a motel or . . ."

"I have to know why you don't want me to come down there," he insisted.

"I forgot how thick-headed you can be."

So now, on top of everything, they were going to argue!

"Look, guys!" It was Kevin. "I don't know how long I can keep others from interfering with this line. It's not very well protected."

That was the first piece of information that made sense so far today.

"Don't come here, Barry!" was Anna's final message.

"I'm not going back!" was Barry's.

The screen went blank, the phone signal was a continuous buzz.

He closed up the laptop and stuffed it and its attachments under a shelf of rock, pushing a rock in front so it wouldn't be found.

Now what?

He'd been counting on Kevin's help to get in. He'd have to do it on his own. If only he had a uniform, he could try to pass for one of them. But where would he get a uniform? Off a serviceman, of course. Unfortunately, the soldier was on the other side of the fence.

Wait! One soldier was behind the fence. The other had driven out and must still be around here somewhere on patrol.

Should Barry go to look for him or just wait?

He went back to the boulders at the lip of the cave and saw a rock he liked better than the one in his hand. He bent to pick it up, half turned in his effort, and there, almost hidden by shadows in a cul-de-sac sat the ATV. Asleep across its front seat, was Corporal Don Turrel, his cap pulled over his eyes against the light.

Clearly a dereliction of duty. With serious consequences.

A few minutes later, Barry sat in the ATV outside the barrier and honked. The other soldier came sauntering out.

"I thought you were supposed to take an hour?" he began, then stopped when he saw Barry. "Who are you?"

"Lieutenant Kresge. Don Turrel was called back to base. Some kind of family emergency. I was dropped off on the same chopper that took him back. Didn't you hear it?"

"I guess I was too deep in." He made no move to unlock the gate.

"What's the deal here?"

"Sentry patrol. Nothing special."

"That's what they said."

Still no move to let Barry in.

"Listen, before I begin patroling, that chopper ride really twisted my guts. You got a john anywhere around here? My stomach's feeling really weird."

"Inside."

Finally he reached through the fence mesh for the lock, began to turn the combination.

Then the gate was open, and Barry edged the ATV through.

"That way." The soldier pointed in a different direction from where he'd come. "There's a toilet at the end."

Beyond the gate, the cave extended crosswise to its entrance. Barry managed to turn the unwieldy vehicle and heard the gate close behind him. He drove slowly through the narrow corridor, lighted by a series of argon lamps embedded in the rock ceiling.

He stopped the ATV at two huge open elevators, each large enough to carry a hundred men or several vehicles. Before he could do more than peer at the lifts, the other soldier was coming toward him, one hand a bit too close to his revolver hip, the other pointing.

"Down there. First wooden door. It's not much."

"The way I feel"—Barry pretended a sudden cramp—"almost anything'll do." He dropped off the other side of the ATV, making sure the vehicle was between them, in case soldier boy got nervous.

The rock corridor narrowed until no vehicle would fit through except perhaps a cart attached to a single mule. No other soldiers. In fact, nothing but two ancient-looking wooden doors. The first the john, the other must lead to the stairway down that Kevin had mentioned when they'd planned this via computer yesterday.

Barry opened the first door and left it ajar as he went in, angling it to maintain enough space between the door and molding so he could watch the soldier. He'd wait until the guy was looking the other way, then make a dash for the other door.

The soldier kept looking in his direction. Then he picked up his pocket radio and began to speak into it.

Damn! Barry had to move fast. He slid out and along the rock wall to the second door. At first it didn't open, and he had to give it a good shove. It opened and he was facing a wooden stairway. Here goes, Barry thought, stepping forward. He closed the door behind him, found a half-broken piece of wood beam, and wedged it into the door. Let soldier boy try to get past that! He began to descend.

After what seemed to be about a hundred feet, the stairway stopped at a rock landing and zigzagged the other way. The walls were striated rock, poorly lighted by a few ancient, widely spaced incandescent bulbs. He almost had to feel his way forward—obviously this way wasn't regularly used.

Barry calculated that he'd dropped about ten landings when he first began to hear the sound. Initially it was only an irregular vibration through the tips of his fingers upon the walls, then a full humming. The levels had been marked in red paint long ago, though the light was so poor he hadn't been able to read them very well. He heard water trickling and the soft clatter of pebble slides. If he were to be trapped here by a rock slide, no one would come to dig him out.

Clearly level eleven was mined out long ago. So were the next five levels down, each series of tunnels separated by three, sometimes four, landings of stairway. Just before he reached level seventeen, Barry stopped, looked up, realizing there was almost no light above him and virtually none below.

Barry closed his eyes and began to slow-breathe for calmness as he'd been taught years ago: Open hand closes one nostril with a thumb, inhale deeply through other nostril to the count of five, then close the other nostril with another finger, release thumb, exhale to the count of five, breathe in again to the count of six, reverse, and repeat to the count of six, then seven, then nine, then eleven, ah, better! He was calm again. He opened his eyes, and continued to descend.

A landing later, the humming he'd heard above returned. There was also a sudden glow of light from the end of one tunnel that fanned out from the landing foyer.

Through the ragged-edge gaping hole in the rock floor, it had to be at least a thousand feet to the ground below. At least a thousand feet down to what looked from here like a small glass-and-metal village surrounded by gardens, a wood at one end with a small pond, possibly fed by underground streams down the walls; at another end what appeared to be a pumping station, an electrical generating plant, probably also heating and air-conditioning units. The buildings appeared to be scattered about a semicircular paved piazza, connected by ramps and paved paths. Next to the piazza, a building with a tinted blue-glass dome. That would be some sort of control center, he supposed. All of the subterranean village was lighted by gigantic banks of arc lights erected at various levels down the sheer surrounding walls.

Only when he knelt down, then fell onto his hands and stomach so that his head was through a ragged opening in the rock floor, did Barry see that this level of the bauxite mine formed the roof of an immense open chamber. From this angle, too, he could make out the two reinforced steel towers of the open elevator shafts emerging out of rock and dropping to the ground.

The stairway ended after another few landings without opening into any more tunnels. At the very bottom of the stairs hung a sort of wooden basket or cage, evidently constructed by the bauxite miners when they'd cut this far down and discovered the enormous cavern below. They must have built this crow's nest with its planked seats to get fresh air, possibly just to get away from the bauxite dust in the tunnels.

Barry sat there, too, looking for a way to get over to the elevator shafts. He also needed a minute to catch his breath and rest in light and clean air. Once, years ago, he'd stood at the top of the World Trade Tower in Manhattan seeing the earth curve away in every direction, buses the size of pinpricks below. He felt that high now. So high that unless someone had a telescope pointed in his exact direction from below, he'd go unnoticed.

No question about it, he'd have to use the lifts to get down.

He climbed back up into the tunnel, and began to walk in the direction of the elevators. Once or twice he had to stop and retrace his steps where the floor beneath him was broken through or seemed shaky. After switching back several times, he arrived at the shaft of the first elevator, which he knew had a lift at the surface.

Would the guard up at the surface hear it move? Probably. Would he think anything of it? Only that it was being called for from below. That couldn't be too unusual. Barry hit the call button, then hid where he would be able to see the elevator arrive without himself being seen, just in case.

It took about five minutes to descend to his level, and from where he was hidden, Barry saw it was empty. He got in and descended.

Would anyone on the ground notice its descent?

Apparently no one did, or at least not while the elevator was a hundred feet off the ground. Even so, Barry kept as close to the back of the giant open lift as possible, at the same time trying to see if anyone on the ground might be looking up. After a while, passing bank after bank of those baseball-field-type arc lights, he began to form a plan.

Barry stopped the lift manually forty feet above the ground. He could make out six men on desultory guard duty at the bottom of the two elevator shafts. Was this usual, or had they been put on the alert? No way Barry was going to find out.

Near where he was stopped, small ledges and a sort of steel-cable handrail were constructed for workmen to reach the banks of arc lights for maintenance and repair. After what it had taken him to get this far, it was simple enough for Barry to step off the lift and leap onto the narrow ledge, to move carefully along it to the first installation. Once he was behind one of the huge fixtures, he had to contend with its bright glare—even from behind—and its strong heat, and to look down for a safe place to drop to the ground.

Not at the center. As Barry scanned the wide, curving cavern, he spotted the only fairly protected way down. Three light banks away, the installation seemed half shut off. Palm trees grew quite nearby. They would provide exactly the cover he needed.

When he reached the arc light among the trees, he slid off

the ledge, holding the bottom support of the light bank, clawing his way down the cavern wall—sandstone embroidered with veins of schist.

He half slid, half inched his way down, until he was within foliage.

In the midst of the coolness of ferns and palm trunks, still catching his breath, Barry looked up. He couldn't see the hole in the ceiling through which he'd peered down before, nor the wooden cage hung from the end of the stairway. Where to now? What he needed was a map.

Eventually he had to leave the cover of the garden. He seemed to be on the outskirts of the little village. He passed around a huge glass-covered vegetable garden and a pumping station. The few workers in the garden didn't seem to notice him—thanks to his uniform. Then he was inside the village, uncertain which of the almost identical low, flat buildings was where he'd find Anna and Kyra.

Barry selected one of the curving-pathed ramps that led directly into the central plaza. He was nervous at first, then he saw that while there were soldiers around, including a pair of burly MPs, they didn't pay attention to him. He relaxed a bit and walked as though he knew where he was going, and finally stopped at a glass, louvered doorway.

Here goes, Barry told himself, and entered.

A foyer branched into what seemed to be offices, and there was a flight of steps up.

At the top of the stairs he found himself in a long, curving corridor, with windows along one side. He glanced into what appeared to be a brightly painted, good-sized playroom with a breakfast table and a kitchen hidden from his view, from which Barry could hear a woman's voice humming. Other rooms seemed to be bedroom suites—one with shelves of dolls, another with comic books scattered all over the floor surrounding a low padded-leather chair. His intuition had hit right: These were the kids' rooms, the kids in EDGE—unless he was totally off. But where were the kids?

He opened a door onto what seemed to be an electronics

lab. A half-dozen computer screens, three or four video monitors, all sorts of equipment that he didn't even know the names of ranged around two walls. Kevin's room?

"Anybody here?" he asked aloud.

He shut the lab door—at least he was in a relatively safe place for the moment—and thought. The various computer screens made him wonder if he dared use them to try to contact Kevin. Or would that alert someone else to his presence—Alex Land? He couldn't take the chance.

As he sat and looked around himself, Barry thought he noticed ghosts of figures flickering upon one video monitor. He slid a swivel chair over, fiddled with the dials to brighten it to full color, and succeeded in sharpening the picture.

There, at a curved wall of computers, was a boy ensconced in a large, oddly shaped chair and physically attached to the machines by scores of wires leading from a metal gridwork on his shirtfront: Kevin Vosburgh! And that had to be Matty Stolzing on the floor playing with a crystal erector set that appeared to emanate somehow from the little boy's fingers. It grew up and around him in a bizarre and wonderfully elaborate construction. There was Lost and Found Jefferson, working an elaborate abacus he held. Where was Kyra?

There! Walking past Lost and Found toward someone in a wheelchair. Barry couldn't see who it was. Then he made out the repulsive face, one half normal, the other contorted beyond recognition. Clearly a girl, from her brightly colored skirt and embroidered Navajo vest, and from the delicacy of her hands as she combed out the long yellow hair of a Barbie doll. Who was she? Evidently a member of EDGE Kyra had never mentioned.

And there, at last, was Kyra. She was wearing her hair loose and had on sky-blue sweat pants and a burgundy halter made of some metallic-looking material. Seeing her now—after thinking he'd never lay eyes on her again, Barry felt immensely relieved.

Then he saw the boy, half sitting upon, half lying across, a built-in chair not three feet from where Kyra perched. He was reading a comic book and oblivious to the others. Barry recognized the boy as one of the two he'd met at Alex Land's horse farm. Alex had told Barry he was one of his stepsons.

No doubt about it. Barry remembered the boy riding up to them on the roan stallion and shouting that he'd seen rats in the barn. Barry had never spoken to him, all of his attention given to the other lad, what was his name? Dean. The one he'd sympathized with. But this had to be Timmo! The sociopath! He had to be. And to think, Alex Land had all but flaunted him at Barry while denying any knowledge of Kyra.

On the video screen, Barry saw beyond the children to a few rows of auditorium seats. There was Anna, looking down and sewing.

Barry stood up in surprise. She was safe, with Kyra and the children, just as she'd said. Safe and looking totally unconcerned. That was odd. Barry wished he could contact them, let Anna know he was here, find out exactly where they were, discover why she seemed so blasé about everything.

Barry fiddled with the dials and succeeded in getting sound: Kyra saying, "What, Kev?"

And Kevin's surprisingly mature voice responding, "I'm not sure. Maybe a fuse burnout or a loose wire." The boy's head dropped, and lifted again with a curious thin metal rod between his teeth as he advanced toward the monitor.

Barry quickly fooled with the dials and arrived at a much wider view of the room, which included all of the children on the platform, Anna in her front-row seat—he could now see that she was repairing the shoulder stitching of a tiny shirt—and beyond her, too, up the rows of seats to the back wall.

The double door at the centermost of the three aisles that cut through the auditorium opened, and Alex Land appeared, attended by a man in the type of suit and with the sort of bearing that Barry had come to associate with the government: He must be from NSA.

Alex loped down to the platform and didn't even glance at where Anna was sitting. The other man hurried to catch up.

It happened so quickly Barry almost missed what Land's entry revealed, if only for a second. Before the double doors closed again, Barry had seen beyond them to a wall of curved windows exactly like those he'd passed through to get to this room. He'd been right outside not ten minutes ago!

"Sorry to keep you all waiting. It was unavoidable. I'm sure you're all curious about why I asked you to gather here."

Kyra looked bored and half turned away, attempting to appear intrigued by a particularly uneventful oscilloscope. No one else said a word to reveal their curiosity.

"The reason is, we've had a security alert on the base," Land went on, as though they'd actually expressed interest. "There's been an incident at the surface that . . . well, we're not completely certain if . . . But you kids know all about it, don't you?"

"Meaning what, exactly?" Kyra asked indifferently.

"Meaning," Land went on in that same unofficial-unctuous tone of voice, "that you kids have such special abilities that doubtless you know what's going on without us having to tell you. Sancha?" He turned to the deformed girl in the wheelchair.

"There was an incident," Sancha said. "On the surface. I 'overheard' the guards' radio conversations. It's difficult not to, they're on such broad beams."

"Lost, can you give us the location of the intruder?" Land said.

"Assuming there is an intruder," Kyra commented dryly.

"Yes, of course," Land stood corrected.

"Sure, he can, but it won't do you any good," Kevin interrupted. "It's too close to where we are. You'd need a three-dimensional-coordinates chart that broke down the entire base. You don't have anything minutely detailed enough to help you."

"And what about you?" Land asked Kevin.

"If you mean have I monitored your so-called 'alerts,' sure."

"Well?" the other man prompted.

"Well, nothing!" Kevin responded. "It's none of my business."

"Perhaps Kyra knows a bit more than she's letting on." Land turned to her.

"No!"

"I see. We're not going to be very useful, are we?"

"Maybe this little fella will help," the NSA man said, moving toward Matty.

But by the time he'd taken a few steps to reach the boy, Matty had raised a palisade of sharply pointed crystal around himself.

The man stopped in his tracks.

"Don't worry, Ted," Land said. "It's an illusion. Go on! You'll see."

Ted looked unsure, then moved forward and reached out to touch one needle-sharp spire. He pulled back his hand, revealing a tiny red wound.

"Illusion, my ass!"

Both men were surprised.

"Matty's learned something new," Anna said, almost smugly, Barry thought.

"I see," Land commented.

"How long do we have to hang around here?" Timmo asked, obviously irritated. "I want to go for a swim."

"I don't know how long. Just until we're sure no one managed to get in."

"The lifts are guarded on both ends," Kevin said. "How else can someone get down here?"

"They can't!" Alex stated. "And they would have been stopped. So, just be patient until we get the all-clear."

"I'm not waiting much longer," Timmo warned.

"We'll be in my office if you need me," Land said. Then he added, "Timmo?"

Timmo waved without looking in their direction, as Land

and the NSA man left the control room. Anna had gone back to her sewing.

Suddenly something new was going on in the control room.

The children had turned to each other in silence. Even Timmo, the central figure because of his location among them, sat up straighter. They were completely still.

They must be conferring telepathically.

Suddenly Timmo spun around in his chair and said aloud, "No fucking way!"

The others also moved. Sancha, Matty, and Lost back to what they were doing. Only Kyra and Kevin continued to look at each other briefly. The conference was over. With what result?

Kyra spoke first. "Timmo refuses to stay open. So, difficult as it is, we're going to have to talk it out." Matty looked up from his crystal construction and let it collapse to nothingness again. Timmo adjusted the volume on his Walkman. "We *have to* Timmo! The future of EDGE depends upon this."

"Why?" Timmo demanded. "Because you say so?"

"Because we're no longer unanimous," Kevin said. And looked around to make sure the others understood. "And if we're no longer *one,* then we're . . ."

"Not EDGE," Kyra said, flatly.

"I don't see any problem," Timmo declared.

"You wouldn't," Kevin commented dryly. "Put simply," he said, "do we allow ourselves to do what Alex Land and other people want us to do, or not?"

"Why not?" Timmo said. "Alex is okay."

"It's more than that," Kyra said. "We have to define ourselves once and for all. Burr is dead. . . ."

"Rub it in," Timmo said.

"She's stating a fact," Sancha spoke up.

"We're on our own. Alex Land can never take Burr's place. No one can. But it was probably time for us to be on our own anyway."

"Continue," Kevin said.

"Timmo, Sancha, Kevin, Lost, Matty?" Kyra addressed them. "Have you ever wondered why you're a MEC? Why MECs exist anyway? What special purpose we have in life? Why we're so different? What meaning we have for the world and what meaning the world has for us? Have you?"

Barry wondered whether Anna and Kyra had talked this over, or whether these were all Kyra's ideas. Why didn't Anna say anything? This was her opportunity to influence them for good.

After a silence, Sancha spoke up shyly. "I have . . . recently."

"Me, too," Timmo said.

"Tell us, Timmo," Sancha prompted him sweetly.

"I thought it was something special . . ." Timmo obviously felt uncomfortable. "Something extra I was given," he went on, having difficulty expressing himself. "You know, to make up for how badly I was treated as a kid."

"Okay," Kyra said. "But since it *is* something special, doesn't it carry responsibility with it?"

"Maybe," he said reluctantly. Then, with more force: "But you know I've gone out of my way for you guys."

"We know."

"You understood that sometimes I can't control it."

"I understand, Timmo." Said with compassion.

"We *don't* have to be spineless wimps!"

"Which we will be," Kevin quickly said, "if we go along with someone who tries to manipulate us to his own ends. Alex Land or anyone else."

"How's he manipulating . . . ?" Timmo began.

"He kidnapped Anna and brought her here. Why else, except to force me to do what he wants?" Kyra argued.

"Didn't you want to see her?" Timmo asked.

"That's not the point!" Kevin said, losing patience. "Land brought Anna here to make sure Kyra will stay with EDGE."

"If the ends justify the means," Timmo hesitantly said.

Then, with more force: *"I think they do, if it was to keep Kyra from going away again."*

"Anna isn't *your* mother!" Kyra said. *"You're* not under pressure."

"My mother never cared for me," Timmo said, then glared at Kevin as though daring him to comment.

"He's hopeless!" Kevin turned back to his computers.

"Can't you understand?" Kyra argued. "We've got to be careful. We're too powerful not to be. Once we've agreed to one wrong, there will be another and another, until . . ."

"What wrong? We have a job to do, and we should do it," Timmo declared.

Kyra tried another way: "What if Alex wanted you to do something you didn't want to do?"

"What?"

"Anything. I don't know. . . ."

"Commit suicide," Kevin said. "For the good of the U.S. of A."

"Why should he want that?"

"Suppose it made the difference," Kyra said, "between a free America and a Russian invasion."

"Alex wouldn't ask me to do that," Timmo said, but he sounded uncertain.

"What if he did, Timmo? What would you do?"

Timmo almost jumped out of the big chair as he passionately declared, "I'm not interested in dying, you guys. But if I have to, I will. And I'll take every MEC and every fucking Lamron in the place with me!"

"Calm down, Timmo, it was only an example," Kyra insisted.

"I knew this would happen with Burr . . . gone," Sancha said, sadly.

"We always have another contingency plan," Kyra said grimly.

They were silent again. But in Barry's mind, the understanding began to grow that if the children were somehow forced to do what they didn't want to, they might . . .

279

"Group suicide: I agree," Sancha said.

He waited for Anna to speak up—this was the perfect chance.

She sat there sewing, every once in a while glancing up at Matty.

The hell with this! Barry thought. Anna may not want to interfere, but I do.

He shut off the video monitor and started down the hallway. Where it met the other corridor, he could hear voices. No sense being stopped now. He'd have to go around.

In the other direction he came upon a ramp and steps identical to those he'd taken coming up. The voices were coming closer. He had to go down now, no matter where it led.

The steps ended in a windowed doorway, and just outside were a woman sergeant and three men in uniform: MPs, from their insignia.

Barry slowed down, stopped, calmed himself. He opened the door, walked out, and said "Sergeant, I need an escort. Yourself and"—looking at the other men—"you three better come, too!" They joined him without a question or comment.

"Did Mr. Land tell you why I'm here?" he asked the sergeant.

"Not really," she said hesitantly.

"Because of the security alert. He wants me to take the older girl and the woman to where he'll be certain they're safe."

His statement contained just the right amount of fact in it to be plausible, and she seemed to buy it. But what if Land had posted guards outside the control room?

"No one else knows about this," Barry said, "and I can't have interference from anyone who may be unaware of my mission. Can you take me in a back way?"

The sergeant looked flustered, but one of the MPs said, "I can, sir."

"Let's go," Barry said. "I don't expect we'll encounter resistance, but when we arrive, I want weapons drawn, just in case. Once there, you will escort us in a lift up to the surface. Is that understood?"

Understood. He'd used exactly the correct mixture of crisis and authority in what he'd said to be obeyed. Looking at the three large young men, Barry was now glad he'd stumbled onto MPs. Besides their strength, their own sense of authority would help his plan.

They entered what appeared to be a rather classy-looking mess for enlisted men—it resembled a Palm Springs restaurant—through double doors, into a side kitchen, then through a large food-storage area, past huge walk-in refrigerators and freezers, and into an all-glass corridor. A short stairway up, and they were inside the arc of a hallway. If Land had posted guards, they were no longer here.

"There." The sergeant pointed to one double door in which a small tinted-glass oval window was embedded.

Barry looked in. He was about fifty feet from the computer area, far above and to the left of the children. He'd move slowly through the darkened auditorium so as not to startle anyone into resistance.

He repeated his instructions to the sergeant and the MPs, who had already taken out their revolvers. As the door swung shut behind Barry, the atmosphere seemed to thicken.

He took three steps down the aisle toward them and stopped, backed up into the shadows to make certain they were alone. Yes.

Kyra saw him first. So surprised, she didn't speak. Barry went over to Anna. "We're leaving. C'mon."

"Barry!" Anna dropped her sewing. "What are you . . . ?"

He embraced her, but didn't get the response he expected. "What's wrong?" he asked.

"I *told* you not to come! You're so stubborn!" Anna said.

"Well, I'm here now!" He stated the fact.

Anna was touching his shirtfront. "I saw them shoot you, and I saw blood all over your chest. . . ." She seemed upset just remembering it.

That was better.

"I guess in the dark they missed my vital organs," he explained, opening his shirt a few buttons to show the bandages. "It looks worse than it is."

"One day they showed me a newspaper with an article about it."

"We concocted that. The woman from the *Post* wrote it up so they would think I was a goner and not come after me again."

"That was very clever, Barry. And so was using your code name. But coming here wasn't at all clever."

"I know what you said, and I understand why. But I'm here now, and we're all going to be together from now on. You, Kyra, me."

"How do you plan to get us out?" Anna asked.

"I have soldiers outside that door. They'll help us."

"And you don't think anyone will try to stop us?" Anna asked. "It's half a mile to the elevators."

"I know, Anna. But we have to try. The soldiers are armed."

"You're certain they'll protect us?"

"C'mon, Anna, we're getting out."

"As you say, Barry," she hesitantly agreed, but she still appeared worried, and looked around the back of the auditorium as though expecting someone any second.

Barry found himself thinking they'd really done a job on her, but Kyra had come to the edge of the platform, and he turned his attention to her.

"Anna said you'd probably ignore our warning. She knows you pretty well," Krya said.

"After coming all the way to see you again, doesn't your old man at least get a hug?" was Barry's response.

"Sure."

By the time he and Kyra separated, Anna had put her sewing into the pocket of the shift she wore and had taken Matty's hand.

"Matty's coming, too," Anna said. Then, to the little boy, who looked up at her as fondly as she looked at him: "Aren't you, darling?" He shook his head in assent.

"I still don't understand," Kyra was saying, "how you managed to get in."

"Obviously I'm the security alert everyone's looking for. We'd better go."

Kyra tried to break free of Barry's grip. "I . . . can't . . . just leave Kev . . . and the others. Kev?"

Kevin was facing away from her, paying attention to a computer screen. "Just go with them, will you?"

"But what about EDGE? What will become of you?" Kyra protested.

Barry immediately saw what was happening. "Look, since that's the problem, we'll *all* go!" He went over to where the deformed girl was still combing her doll's hair. "C'mon, honey. Kyra, you take Lost and Found."

"*I'm* not going anywhere," Timmo declared, pulling off his earphones. He'd been watching Barry's arrival and subsequent greetings as though it meant nothing to him. Now he mobilized for action.

"Stay if you want," Barry said. "Kevin? We've got to hurry!"

"I can't leave my . . ." Kevin looked fondly at his computers, "for those Lamrons to screw up."

"They'll hurt you, Kev," Kyra tried. "You, too, Tim!"

Timmo climbed onto the built-in chair. He leaned back against the seat to declare, "*No one's* going to hurt *me!*"

Anna had Matty in her arms, Kyra had Lost and Found by the hand. Barry began to push Sancha's wheelchair down the ramp off the stage. "We don't have time to argue," he said. "Let's go. Kevin? Aren't you coming?"

"I can't."

"Forget about the damn computer. We'll get you another one."

"You don't understand," Kevin said, his voice bleak. "Kyr, you know why."

Kyra leaned over and whispered to Barry, "He wants to protect us. He can, through the computers."

"Forget all that!" Barry said. "Anna! Go out that doorway," pointing to where he'd entered before. He gave San-

283

cha over to Kyra, and headed back toward the stage for Kevin.

Timmo shouted, "*Nobody's* leaving, unless *I* say so!"

Kevin spoke up. "Don't be a Lamron, Timmo! You heard what we said before. If we're forced to work for others, we're as good as dead."

"*I'm not going to die. Not now. Not ever!*"

He pointed a finger toward a wall, and a narrow blue-white beam shot out. Alarms began to clamor.

Kevin slid over to a keyboard and hit a button. The alarms were shut off.

Timmo tried again. But the alarm system had been rendered inoperable.

Kevin had lifted off a keyboard and set it into his lap. He was using a mouthstick to program something. He dropped the stick into his pocket, and yelled, "You guys get out of here! I'll cover your retreat."

"Kevin!" Sancha called.

"Go!" he called back. "Get them out of here, Barry!"

Reluctantly, Barry dropped off the stage into the aisle. The others were slowly moving up the aisle.

Timmo gave up trying to sound the alarm and ran to the control-room doors. Kevin used the mouthstick to do something else.

The doors loudly snapped locked. Anna stood at the back-aisle doors holding Matty.

Timmo began to pound on them with his fists. From the other side, Barry could hear someone pounding back.

"Open these locks, worm!"

"Forget it, tinman! I'm closing down everything in this base!" Kevin said.

In an instant, the lights went off in the auditorium. Only the glow of computer lights and monitors still illuminated the huge room.

The omnipresent sound of the air-conditioners suddenly ceased.

"What are you doing?" Timmo shouted.

Kevin seemed to gloat. "The water. Air. Lights. Now the phones."

"The lifts!" Kyra shouted. "You have to keep the lifts turned on, Kev."

"You can't do this!" Timmo was beside himself. "Alex needs it. *We* need it."

"Too late," Kevin said, backing away in his chair so smoothly that Timmo was caught in a tangle of wires.

"No, you *don't*!" Timmo shouted. He reached around and pulled a cable line out of the mainframe. Holding it in both hands, he appeared to concentrate upon it. The auditorium lights flickered a moment and came on again.

Next the hum of the air-conditioners started up again.

"Ha!" Timmo shouted. "See? I've got enough energy to do it. Enough to run the whole damn base if I want to!"

The locked doors snapped open, but the lights had begun to flicker again. Although Timmo was still holding the cable, he'd put one hand up to his left temple and was shaking his head back and forth, as though trying to clear his mind.

"I'm trying to seal all of the various connections, so he won't be able to feed them power anymore!" Kevin called out.

The doors snapped shut and locked again, the lights flickered again and once again died down. The back auditorium doors opened, the female sergeant and one MP helped Anna and Matty into the darkened corridor.

Timmo was concentrating on the big cable again. He began to take on a blue-white aura.

"I'm going to confuse him with transmissions," Sancha said.

Timmo's aura was glowing in waves all around his body.

In seconds, glass dials all over the control wall began to shatter with the high-frequency pitch Sancha emitted. Barry couldn't hear it, but even standing behind her, he could feel a strong tingling in every nerve ending rising, rising. As the frequency continued to rise ever higher and began to course through the metal handles, he had to let go of the wheelchair. Now light fixtures all over the auditorium and even the bulletproof glass windows in the booth above the stage began to shudder and smash. Timmo fell to his knees. He plugged his fingers into his ears, and his face was contorted in agony.

But Timmo somehow managed to control the transmission and was now beginning to absorb it—and worse, to send it back. Once again, his face relaxed as he stood up and smiled. He darted out a hand at Sancha, and a bolt of sinister blue-white light hit her and the wheelchair, coursing through chair and girl like electricity run amok.

"I get a charge out of you, radio-head!" Timmo yelled.

Before Timmo could do anything further, Barry ran in front of the wheelchair and heaved it up the aisle as hard as he could through the double doors. In the moment before he could get Sancha out of the room, he saw the blue-white light diffuse as her body began to violently convulse.

"Ha!" Timmo was jumping around on stage. "Ha! HA! HA!"

Anna and the rest headed for the doors. But Kyra didn't move. She looked pale and frightened.

"Get out of here!" Barry tried to hustle her out.

"No, this is our only chance," she said to Barry. "You'd better step back." To the little boy, she said quietly, "Matty, you have to play! I'll help!"

The little boy squirmed in Kyra's arms as giant networks of crystals, like those Barry had seen him playing with before, suddenly rose up from beneath the child's tiny sneakered feet and shot out toward the stage, directly at Timmo.

"Make it real, Matty," Kyra said. "Like before!"

The crystal flew around Timmo like curved spears, meshing into latticework.

Barry took advantage of Timmo's surprise to sidle through a row of seats and head toward the last aisle where he might get around the platform and reach Kevin.

"Bind him, Matty!" Barry could hear Kyra shouting.

Timmo was reaching up with spears of blue fire and

punching holes in the fine crystalline lacework rising on all sides around him.

"Make it stronger than *that*, Matty!" Kyra urged.

As Timmo continued to hack the crystal away, it began to double in thickness, then triple, and quadruple, until in seconds Barry could no longer clearly make out Timmo's figure, he was so encased, distorted, and refracted by the surrounding crystal.

"*Thicker!*" Kyra yelled. "He's breaking through!"

The crystal structure now seemed to sweep around and around Timmo, as though a giant hand were wrapping it.

From within his crystal cage, Timmo could be heard raging. But the crystal continued to thicken and rise around him with astonishing speed. Timmo continued to push it out in sharp spikes, deflecting it out from himself on all sides with the same force and speed that it came to him. Now, all Barry could see was a blue-white figure within the crystal. In seconds, the crystal cage had become a porcupine of jagged spikes.

The crystal was now a gigantic hundred-spiked mace.

Kevin gasped and began to move his chair as far away as possible along the guide rail from Timmo. He was stopped: The rail ended. He couldn't retreat any further.

Kevin's computer wires began to snap free from their connections and crystallize. Then they began to writhe around the computer board like hundreds of glass snakes.

As quickly as he tried to free himself from the computer attachments, they sprang loose and turned to attack him.

Barry moved out of the row of seats, trying to get to Kevin. But he was stopped by a phalanx of crystal spears.

Helpless, Barry watched as the wires danced around Kevin's face and body, transformed into writhing crystal needles, and then turned to strike the boy. Simultaneously piercing Kevin's head and body, their crystalline glitter darkened scarlet with blood. Kevin let out a series of high-pitched screams, and twitching in pain, he knocked over his chair. But a hundred more needles stabbed into him as he frantically waved his flippers. The wires completely covered him, and their twisting center—Kevin's head and body—was finally stilled. All Barry could make out amid the icy pincushion was a blood-red core.

"Who's next?" Barry heard, and a dozen crystal needles jabbed toward him.

Barry ducked low and began to sidle under the seats, hoping their metal bottoms would protect him as he crawled back toward the center aisle. He looked up once, only to see the upholstery punctured, ripped open by crystal spikes, only inches from his eyes. At the end of the row of seats, Matty had gotten away from Kyra and now stood boldly in the open aisle.

"Matty! Get back," Barry yelled.

It was enough to distract Timmo. Barry pulled free of the area of needle-pierced seats, and scooped Matty into his arms.

"Stop now, Matty!" Barry yelled into the boy's ear, until the boy put his hands down. Then Barry ran like hell up the aisle and into the corridor.

When they'd gotten through the door, Barry dropped the child, and turned to look back through the window. Apparently Timmo wasn't following them.

All Barry could see was a mass of crystal. Strangely, it was now almost transparent, and Timmo was completely visible: The earphones were back on the teenager's head as he stood on the seat of the built-in chair. Eyes shut, he twirled and gyrated to the music. A blue-white glow emanated from his body serenely, almost beautifully.

Kyra took Barry's arm. "Sancha didn't shut down fast enough."

He pulled himself away from the fascinating spectacle through the window. The girl was on her back on the corridor floor, twitching spasmodically. One outstretched hand still clutched her Barbie doll, rhythmically smashing its beautifully combed head against the tile floor.

The three MPs stood watching, horrified.

Anna took Matty and kissed his forehead.

"We've got to get out of here," Barry said to the sergeant. He looked through the window again. The crystal spikes were up the aisle almost at the door, as though growing organically. Timmo continued to spin and gyrate, now so astonishingly fast he seemed to rotate and turn in midair, a blur within his own blue-white light.

"He looks like he's . . ." Barry didn't know how to explain what his eyes were seeing.

"He's dancing." Kyra was looking, too. "Like Shiva. And like Shiva, he'll destroy us. He's too strong, Barry. He absorbed each of our MEC powers like a sponge. We can't do a thing against him."

"Don't worry. We'll be okay," Barry said.

"Poor Kevin!" Kyra suddenly began to tremble. Barry held her.

To the others, he said, "He's growing stronger. We have to move fast!"

As though to support his fear, the building suddenly began to vibrate.

Sancha was reduced to head-to-toes shuddering as though suffering from advanced Parkinson's disease. No one could look at her face, but Kyra managed to get Sancha into her chair and grab her hand and begin talking to her. In that moment, the floor beneath them shook suddenly, as though from a small earthquake.

"Sergeant!" Barry commanded. "Get us out of here!"

She snapped to attention, and with the other MPs formed an escort. Anna handed Matty to Barry, and kissed the child, then she and Kyra took hold of the wheelchair with Sancha in it. Barry took Lost and Found's hand, leading them around the corridor and back to the stairway down to the lower floor. Two more shocks struck, and Matty began to whimper, holding on extra tight, and Barry realized the amazing little creature he'd witnessed a few minutes ago was still a frightened child. He talked to Matty, trying to calm and comfort him as they hurried outside. Windows were popping out of frames and shattering both inside and out.

Kyra looked at Sancha in the wheelchair, reached over to cover the left side of her face with the girl's own long hair. "I've got to get her to the clinic. They have some medicine there to control her convulsions," Kyra said.

"You have to stay with us." Barry said firmly.

He grabbed one of the MPs and told him to get the girl in the wheelchair to the medic. The young soldier hefted Sancha over his shoulder and took off running.

"She'll be okay once she's there," Barry tried to comfort Kyra.

"We've done a terrible thing," Kyra said, "giving Timmo that crystal! He's able to use it somehow to consolidate his energy."

"You mustn't blame yourself," Anna insisted, just as they all heard a strong, sharp report, like a redwood tree snapping in half.

Barry looked up and saw the giant radio antenna in the building across from the dome. Blue-white electricity was flashing all over its structure. Bolts of lightning began to shoot out of its tip in a series of sharp explosions.

The shuddering vibrations they'd felt inside the control center now began to thud along the ground outside. As Barry's group cleared the area of low buildings heading toward the lifts, men began running past them in the opposite direction.

It was a ten-minute walk. Barry could already see the guards standing around the lift area, hesitating whether or not to go back to the center or remain where they were. The second huge elevator had begun to descend.

"He said—" Lost began, and was interrupted by an enormous rumbling around them. The ground itself seemed to hum and vibrate, though they were far from the plaza and dome. The little group could barely keep on its feet until the temblor passed. "He said that he'd kill everyone."

"He's located a structural fault in the cavern," Kyra made herself heard. "He's going to bring it all down!"

A second later, they heard a sound like tearing metal high above.

"Look!" Anna cried, as a portion of the tunnels of the bauxite mine, which Barry knew formed a ceiling over the vast open space, began to break loose and fall. Giant slabs of rock knocked out two banks of arc lights as they crashed down.

Suddenly panic broke out near the lift. People hesitating before now began to clamor to get on.

Arc lights from the two fallen banks began to explode in the distance as they struck the wall or cavern floor, which only served to increase everyone's hysteria. Barry heard someone thank God the arc lights and lifts were connected to an emergency generator at the surface.

The MPs had opened up a space on the elevator for the group. Anna held Matty in her arms, drawing Lost and Found close to herself. All of them safe in a corner of the huge lift, quickly filling up with hysterical people.

Barry and the MPs went forward to close the elevator to other boarders. They finally managed to get the waist-high wooden door up, and Barry saw soldiers and people in lab coats from all over the area streaming toward the lifts.

"Can't we get moving?" someone behind Barry shouted.

The lift began to slowly jerk up—an inch, two inches, a foot off the ground—with excruciating slowness.

"Can't we go *faster*?" someone else shouted.

"It's overweighted."

"*You* get off!"

Kyra suddenly grabbed Barry's arm. "Sancha! She'll . . ."

Before he could stop her, Kyra squeezed past people and was over the side of the lift.

Anna turned to Barry. "Barry! Bring her back!"

He was torn between going after his daughter and staying. "What about you and the kids?"

"We're going up. We'll be all right!"

Of course she would be.

"Go, Barry! Before Kyra is hurt!" she insisted. "Be careful."

As though to speed his way, she lightly brushed his lips.

Barry worked a path through the rising, overcrowded lift and jumped. He began to run back to the center of the village.

The vibrations along the ground were almost constant now, accompanied by sharp, irregular cracks of what seemed like thunder, as another weakened section of roof collapsed and another half-dozen arc lights exploded and went out. One or two people were helping colleagues injured by the falling debris, but everyone else was headed toward the lifts. No one thought to stop him. What had been artificial daylight was now a chiaroscuro of stormy twilight.

When he reached the central plaza, Barry was shocked by how rifted the cement and tile was. He looked at what had been the dome. Its walls were split apart from within, but instead of being dark inside, it emitted a glowing blue-white light. Gigantic crystal stalactites grew out in every direction. Another tremor, and he was knocked to his hands and feet. In a few minutes, the plaza would be completely impassable.

As more of the rock ceiling fell and more arc lights exploded, Barry found the clinic after trying a half-dozen doors. Inside was a mess, racks of medicines, lab tables, machinery strewn everywhere as though by the hand of a reckless child. At the end of the corridor he found an unconscious but still breathing man in a lab coat. A doctor, probably knocked out when the ceiling had fallen in. Barry managed to get him conscious enough for the man to begin babbling something about "the girl! Help the girl!"

"The deformed one in the wheelchair?"

"The girl! She was . . ." The man pointed to where the ceiling had caved in completely.

Barry half dragged, half carried him outside the ruined clinic and managed to find a man and woman in lab coats who more or less agreed to get the doctor to the lifts. His burden gone, Barry went back into the room.

"Kyra! Sancha! It's Barry! Are you there? Either of you?"

He shouted their names again, then started over the debris. It was still rather loose. He was stopped almost immediately by freshly falling rubble. He began to dig in several directions, using his hands like shovels.

"If you can hear me, make a noise. Any kind of noise!"

He almost didn't register when he spotted the very tips of a lock of long black hair between two broken sheets of wallboard.

Kyra! He frantically began to dig, moving piece by piece the broken ceiling tile as gently as an archaeologist. Now he found a finger, another, an entire hand, a wrist.

He felt for a pulse, didn't find it.

He dug further, quietly cursing, baring the arm right up to her armpit. Her head must have been thrown backward with the force of the collapse. If he could only move that square-yard chunk of ceiling board in front of her! Done! He used it to prop up other boards threatening to fall, reached through the debris, and brushed her torso.

Now he had a few inches of her vest in his hand. Wait! Kyra had been wearing a halter, metallic burgundy. Not a Navajo vest!

He continued to open up the space, careful of the loose stuff all around them, until he'd cleared most of her chest, enough to see where the smooth, flan-colored skin became thick and reptilian, folding in and over itself. One shoulder was a mixture of soft and rough, fair and ghastly flesh. It was Sancha.

He still had to find and check her carotid artery, so he continued to dig until he'd uncovered the thick folds and dewlaps around her chin and was able to get a hand around her neck. No pulse. None at all.

He stopped, pulled back, looking at his own filthy, torn hands. Where among all this would he find Kyra? And in what condition?

Barry pulled back and released the slab of mortarboard he'd been holding up to get closer to the girl. The rubble cascaded down to cover her awful skin and flesh, her lovely hair, until only one hand remained sticking out, poised with its fingers spread, and on one, a band of hammered silver with carbonized designs. Lovely hair and a beautifully shaped hand. The markings of a lady.

"We won't forget," he said, and he kissed her outstretched hand, slipped the ring off, and onto his pinky. "I promise."

Another rumble below ground shook him out of his thoughts. He still had to find Kyra.

"Barry? Is that you?"

Kyra's voice came from behind. He turned to see her stepping into the clinic doorway.

"You're all right!" He stood up. They were separated by rubble.

"I'm fine. Why aren't you with Anna?"

"Sancha . . ." He began to speak, instead half turned toward where her body lay.

"I know. I tried to stay with her until . . . When the ceiling crashed in, the doctor shoved me out."

He found it easy picking his way through the mess to get to her. "I was afraid you were in here, too!"

Outside the clinic door, new debris had fallen over the ramp. Long rifts now zigzagged the paved path.

Barry grabbed Kyra's hand and began to lead her through the rubble-strewn street.

"This way!" she insisted.

"The lifts are the other direction!" Barry argued.

"The second lift was comandeered. I saw Land and his people get on. I know another way, Barry. I've explored this entire place, remember? I once saw a small hidden elevator."

Barry didn't much care for the idea of meeting Land again. "Okay, your way, then. But let's hurry!"

Another section of ceiling fell, a huge one this time, and with it an entire series of tunnels from the bauxite mines. Then six more banks of arc lights exploded, causing a sudden blinding glare. When he opened his eyes again, Barry faced a crepuscular dimness. They stumbled through an herb garden and onto a stone path.

At the end of the path, through trees, was an old wooden shed.

"That it?" he asked.

"A small elevator built by the miners to first come down here. It's pretty old and rickety, but it's our only chance."

The door was locked. He found a chunk of rock and used it to knock off the rusted hinge.

"If everything's this rusted, we'll never make it up," he commented.

A giant temblor rippled over the ground.

They went inside, into darkness.

"Straight ahead, Barry! There's a trapdoor."

He felt for it with his arms straight out in front of him, finally located it, found a turn latch, opened it. The light coming in from above was only a smidgen better. He reached into his pockets for his cigarette lighter. Its flare allowed him to see a small elevator, barely big enough for him and Kyra, yet like the larger lifts with waist-high walls, one of which could be unlatched. He pulled first one, then the other of the two rusty-looking cables. They seemed taut enough. At least nothing fell down when he tugged at them.

"Find the control?"

A simple lever. "What there is!" he called back to her in the dark. "This looks like it hasn't been used in a hundred years!" he added, reaching out to grasp her hand.

The little building shook with the next shock. But he managed to get Kyra into the elevator, got in himself, lifted up and latched the side wall, and turned the lever crank.

"Better pray this works!"

It creaked and whined, the pulleys shrieked and sang, and the lift began to move.

After a half minute of ascent, they pulled out of the utter darkness and into whatever light remained inside the cavern. The lift rose more easily now on its ancient, wooden open framework, which had been craftily erected within a narrow slot of cavern wall. They were twenty or thirty feet above the ground already; the shack and garden directly below were growing small.

"Looks like we're in business," he said, and felt the adrenaline begin to ebb out of him. He leaned back against the elevator's wall trying to catch his breath, saying to himself, I'm too old for this kind of crap. Five, even, three years ago, I could have . . . Kyra held on to him, however, and that felt good, almost worth it all.

Below, giant fissures crisscrossed every paved path and road, bissected every building still upright, and had begun opening up cracks in the cavern walls themselves. Only two or three distant banks of arc lamps still gave light, here and there, in the vast space, so that what he could see was extremely spotty and distorted. As they continued to steadily climb, his eyes were drawn to the blue-white glow below, no longer recognizable as the dome, but merely a huge, pulsing crystal that seemed to push energy out of itself as it grew.

"You feeling better?" he asked. He wondered about the other lifts. He looked in their direction. The first one was still climbing, still in sight, at least five hundred feet above the second one.

The rattling little elevator kept rising. Through the darkness, he heard the sound of a muffled explosion. He pulled Kyra close to his body, hoping the elevator didn't stop.

When the sound had died down again, he looked toward the giant elevators. They were still moving, the one with Anna on it still ahead of the one with Land.

Kyra pulled away. Very calmly she said, "When Land saw us for the first time about six months ago, he chose Timmo, because he had so much pure energy and it was so undirected. And because Timmo would respond to authority, and who knows what else Land did to manipulate and control him."

"You mean they thought alike?" Barry asked, recalling the boy in the barn, stomping the burning rats.

"Exactly. Kevin and Sancha and I had already developed consciences."

Below them was a new sound. Barry looked over the side of the lift, and the crystal seemed to have spread throughout what was left of the village, and was throbbing madly.

"But Land made a mistake," Kyra went on talking, explaining, "because it wasn't Timmo but Matty who was the truly powerful one among us. Because of his autism, he was not aware of any limitations on his MEC. He could do anything he could imagine—levitate, make material out of nothing! You saw!"

"He helped us a lot," Barry said, recalling how gallant the child had been. "He protected us."

The first giant lift had reached the place where the bottommost mines had been. Anna and the kids would be safe now.

The walls around them were vibrating regularly now. Below, the muffled explosions were coming at spaced intervals. The whole place was going to blow!

"What if Timmo escapes?" Barry asked.

"He can't escape, Barry. Timmo *is* that energy. He's probably burst right through his skin by now."

Below them, the white light had gone slowly yellow, then orange.

"Poor Timmo," Kyra mused, sadly. "All his life has been restraint. Now that he's taken all the power he's ever wanted, he has to release it. Kev once speculated exactly that. Kev said it would be like the largest, longest orgasm ever. Kev understood."

"Kevin! What a fucking waste!" Barry said aloud, and felt it: the boy's keen intelligence, snuffed out!

Seconds later, to Barry's consternation, the elevator stopped.

"He's got all the power, Barry. He's absorbed all the electricity. We're stuck here!"

"The hell we are. There is a series of vertical rungs built

into the wall only a few feet away from us. You and I are climbing out!"

Kyra looked down, then quickly backed up.

"I can't, Barry. I'm already terrified."

"We have no choice." He edged in front of her, bent down, and ordered, "Grab around my shoulders, and when I lift you, get your feet around my waist. One, two, three!"

She was lighter than he'd expected. Even so, she was frightened and with good reason. He climbed over the lift's sidewall, grabbed onto a set of narrow metal rungs, and pulled them both up—they were more than a thousand feet above a cavern that could come down around them any minute.

Finally, he got one hand securely in place and managed to inch his entire body over to the rungs, so that his feet were on rungs, too.

"We're going up," he announced, and began to climb. Feeling like a fly crawling up a wall carrying another fly on its back, he pulled hand over hand, foot over foot, at each step, counting each one.

After a while, Kyra shouted, "Look up, Barry! We're getting close to a tunnel."

They were only a dozen feet away from a tunnel opening above. Yet each move he made up another rung required a stop, a rest. His back and shoulders, his legs and arms, all began to scream out in pain.

"Only nineteen more rungs to go! Eighteen now, Barry!"

With every six inches to the next rung, her weight seemed to increase by ten pounds, the strain in his arms doubled.

"Twelve more, Barry! Eleven! Ten!"

He was developing a charley horse in his left leg. The pain was unbearable. He had to stop. That was even worse.

"Kyra, kick the back of my left leg."

"Why?"

"Kick hard, now!"

She kicked him.

"Again! Harder! Oww!"

298

"Sorry! You asked . . ."

Her second kick direct-hit the cramp, the shock smashing the muscle knot. It ached dully now, but just about all of his body ached dully now. At least it wasn't incapacitating pain, like before. He began to climb again. Now his gunshot wounds and the bandages being pulled by her grip on his chest and back smarted.

"Nine. Eight. Seven more!"

The pain in his arms and shoulders increased tenfold. Her weight seemed to double with every six inches he moved up.

"A few more. Five! Four more!"

Below them, he felt and heard and then saw the light from an enormous explosion. Its force, along with all the strength remaining in his body, sprang together and shot him up the few remaining rungs through a gaping hole in the floor and onto a staircase, where he fell facedown, shouting, "Cover yourself," as the explosion roared below them.

When it was finally over, Kyra was still holding on.

"Barry?"

"I'm still here."

"Barry, try to crawl up to the top of the staircase. Go slowly. Don't ask questions. Don't look behind."

He tried his arms and legs—rubber. Then he raised himself up on his hands, on his knees—wobbly, but if he could lock them into place . . . Yes! He could do it. Then slowly unlock them, one at a time . . .

He began to crawl up the stairs, as he had done the rungs before. Exhausted as he was, this was easier, the angle better, but the staircase must have been knocked loose by the explosion; it wobbled badly whenever he moved, and, no, he didn't want to look back, not for anything.

At the top of the landing Kyra let go of his body, moved aside, and sat up. Barry rolled over into a sitting position and slowly looked down the stairway they'd just spent five minutes crawling up.

It hung in the middle of nothing, a wooden staircase shakily dangling, connected to this end but to nothing else, while thousands of feet below in the darkness, a gigantic blue-white crystal throbbed, although it was cracked in a thousand places.

It took several minutes for him to take it all in. When he was able to speak, Barry said, "That's not the end of it, is it? You said before that it was like sex. A kid like that can come two, three times in a row, can't he?"

"We'll move as soon as you feel ready again, Barry."

"Ready or not, I'm not sticking around." He rolled over onto his hands and knees again. "Climb on, we're going."

"I can walk. I'm not afraid anymore. Besides . . ."

Compared to the sheer verticality of the rungs, the climb up the staircase through the tunnels without her weight was almost a frolic. Barry tried to keep his fears and his hopes under control as they ascended the stairs, feeling more tremors below them and knowing now what those could mean. Kyra was very quiet, and he had to wonder if she was somehow able to share in the growth of the new cataclysm brewing below them. How telepathically involved was she with that monstrosity?

They'd gone up a dozen stairways, and now Kyra wanted to stop and rest, but Barry reminded her all too vividly of that staircase suspended over nothing. One more blast and if they were one level too low because they'd rested . . . They went on climbing the rickety staircases through the dark, and even that couldn't distract from the pain he felt all over.

"Barry, it's beginning again!"

"How close are we to the top?"

"Close. I'm afraid, Barry."

"Can't you shut him out?"

"He's too powerful. One more landing, I think. It's like he knows I'm here and he's reaching out for me. Determined to get me."

Barry could feel the strong vibrations under his feet, in his hands, too, wherever they touched the staircase or walls. He got up the landing, and ran right into a door. They'd made it to the surface! He found the bar he'd placed there, removed it, shoved the door open into the corridor at the very place he'd descended from before. No one in the tunnel that he could see—the old incandescent bulbs were out, but it was bright compared to where they'd come from.

"Let's go." He grabbed Kyra's hand.

He stumbled forward, trying to brace himself with his hands along the walls as he ran. There was the chain-mesh fence, the gate swung ajar and braced open, he supposed by the people escaping from the giant lifts. Great! And there, the main tunnel ahead of them. And light. There was light there, and fresh air . . .

As they ran, the vibrations thudded and rumbled so strongly Barry couldn't keep himself or Kyra from lurching from side to side, from wall to wooden support-beam.

Suddenly the tunnel shook as though slapped. The roar went on and on. The rock ceiling began to crack, and the old pine beams began to fall in front of him, and there was heat and light and a screeching like a million bats let loose out of hell all at once. Barry felt Kyra plucked out of his hand, and as he turned to grab at her, he was hurled forward into the darkness.

CHAPTER TWELVE

"**C**hrist Almighty! Get a look at you two!" a voice swore.

"Is anyone else still in there?" another voiced asked.

It was a while before Barry could see without squinting.

"Need help, young lady?"

"I'm all right. Just bruised," Kyra said.

"Sir, was anyone else with you?" The police officer repeated the question.

From the outside, the mouth of the cave didn't look very different from when Barry had first seen it. The entrance, even the old wooden signs, were intact. But hundreds of people were milling about, military personnel and people in lab coats and casual wear—scientists and technicians, Barry supposed, who'd been working on various projects in the base. They must have all come up on the two large lifts and gotten out in time to miss the second large blast. Not all of them had escaped the first explosion from below, however. Handkerchiefs were wrapped around arms and foreheads and shins to staunch wounds; shirts and blouses and trouser legs had been ripped. People were audibly moaning, a few wandering about calling out names, looking for friends. Others were huddled together, holding each other. A few were laid out flat on the ground, covered by jackets. Four Colorado State Police vehicles were parked in a shallow fan at the entrance, and highway cops were busily distributing bandages and blankets from first-aid kits. Where, amid all this, were Anna and the kids?

"Did everyone get out?" Barry asked a blond crew-cut policeman.

Just then a good-sized Army helicopter took off from behind the cavern entrance. Barry tried to peer through the sheets of dust it swirled into the air to see who was on board. Impossible.

"You folks are the last we know of. But there hasn't been an official count yet."

"The chopper?" Barry asked, as the young policeman concentrated on Kyra's bruises.

"That's the first one that's arrived. It took only the worst injured."

"Someone must have called from below to get it here before Kev managed to cut all the phones," Kyra said.

"A woman with two small children—did you see if they were on board the copter? A black child about nine. And a white one, about four years old."

"I helped carry the folks on, but I didn't see anyone like that," the cop said. Then, to Kyra: "I'm going to swab and bandage these cuts and bruises."

"Three didn't get out," Kyra said, nodding behind the cavern.

"You next, sir?" He began to treat various gashes and wounds on Barry's face, neck, and hands. "Three? You know that for certain?"

"I saw two die. The other . . ."

"I'll have to report that," the highway cop said.

"You said everyone else got out?" Barry asked.

"Two lifts full."

"They're all here?"

"A couple of ATVs took off just as we were arriving. Don't know where they were headed. Down the road, I guess."

"Did you notice a woman around my age, with the two little boys I mentioned before, inside the vehicles?"

"Can't say for certain, sir. We never even knew there was an entire underground base here!"

"Sorry to keep asking, but I've got to find them!"

"I understand your concern, sir. There! That should hold you." He'd finished the rough bandaging.

"I've got to find Anna and the kids," Barry told Kyra. "Stay here."

"I'm going with you," Kyra said.

She took his arm, and they moved through the crowd, searching.

"Barry!" Kyra stopped him. "Wasn't she with us before?"

It was the sergeant whom Barry had commandeered to get Anna and the children out of the dome. She and two of the same MPs.

"You made it!" the sergeant said, when Barry and Kyra approached. "How? You weren't on the second lift. We watched it fill up."

"We should thank you," one MP said, shaking Barry's bandaged hand. "We might have been killed down there if it weren't for you."

"Did you know that was going to happen?" the other MP asked. "Was that why . . . ?"

Barry stopped them. "The woman and children. Where are they?"

They looked at each other.

"They got out! We escorted them right out here," she insisted.

"They're not here now!" Barry said. "Could they have been on one of the ATVs that took off?"

"I think so, yes," the MP said. "But they're safe. Mr. Land was with them."

Safe? Christ!

"Which way did they go?" Barry had to know.

"Up to the highway. That's all we could see from here."

"We went back in to help the injured," the sergeant said.

"What the hell happened in there?" the MP asked. "What blew up?"

"You'll hear all about it. Don't you have any idea where they went?"

"How did you get here, Barry?" Kyra interrupted.

"By car." Of course. If it was still there.

He hurried off in the direction where he'd parked the car, Kyra struggling to catch up. They'd gotten away from the cavern when they heard someone shouting. Barry looked back. It was one of the MPs urging them to hold on a minute.

"Do you know how to use one of these?" he asked, unholstering a small service revolver and offering it and a clip to Barry. When Barry said he did, the MP insisted he take it, explaining, "If you guys are going to wander around here, you may need it."

It turned out they almost needed it a few minutes later.

Three civilians from below ground had found the Mustang and had broken the driver's side vent. They were inside the car, trying to jump the ignition, when Barry arrived. He dangled the car keys in one hand and pointed the gun at them with the other as he politely asked them to step out.

"We didn't know it belonged to anyone," one man whined.

Barry sent up sheets of dust as he roared through the loose-packed dirt onto the paved road.

"Where are we going?" he asked, after five minutes of speeding along the highway. "Do you have any idea?"

Kyra shrugged. "Keep going. But slow down, so I can see."

After another ten minutes, Kyra shouted, "Stop here!"

Barry screeched to a stop in the middle of the highway.

"I don't see anything!"

"There! Look, Barry!"

A small sign, barely visible, read PRIVATE AIRPORT. MEMBERS ONLY.

"Turn there," Kyra insisted.

"Yes, ma'am." He burnt rubber crossing the highway and up the road.

The airfield lay a half mile ahead and was a small one, only a few hangars, only a couple of runways, a handful of Cessnas and Piper Cubs, and as they drove closer, just visible on the side of a hangar attached to a single-story brick building, a small private jet.

Its motor was idling, ready to taxi out from this side runway.

Uncertain exactly what they'd find here, Barry didn't want to take any chances. He backed up the Mustang behind the hangar, out of sight of the runway. "Stay here," he told Kyra.

No one in sight. He got out of the car and ran up the landing stairs into the jet. A pilot was already seated, checking gauges and dials, but there were no passengers in any of the six seats.

Barry backtracked out of the plane and headed for the small building.

The office door opened up at that moment, letting out Alex Land, Anna, Lost and Found, and Matty.

Land and Anna spotted Barry at the same time. Anna called his name.

"Go back," Land ordered Anna. "Get back into the building." She didn't move.

Alex looked at Barry almost fondly. "You have more damn lives than a cat." He seemed amused. "We were certain you'd bought it downstairs."

Ignoring Land, Barry yelled, "Bring the boys here, Anna!"

"They're all coming with me," Land said.

"You've got to be kidding!"

"Not at all. We're regrouping," Land said. "EDGE must continue."

"Why must EDGE continue? So it can be exploited and manipulated by bastards like you?"

Alex's mouth set suddenly. "You've never understood, have you, Barry? EDGE can save humanity from itself. We really can."

That "we" wasn't lost on Barry.

"The world has blundered on without EDGE's help before," Barry answered.

"EDGE will soon become the most important force in world politics, Barry!"

"Keep saying that, Alex. Keep deceiving yourself and those jerks in Washington."

"You've gone through terrible experiences, Barry, and . . ." Alex soft-soaped him.

"What do you know of what I've gone through?"

"Do you want Kyra and Kevin and Sancha to have died in vain?" Land asked. "Only through the continuation of EDGE will their memories be kept alive, their sacrifices be made good."

Talking about those poor kids as though they were Green Berets! And he thought Kyra was dead. That was interesting.

"What is it about you, Barry," Land asked, amusement back on his face and in his voice, "that you have to constantly make these heroic and utterly futile gestures?"

Barry began to slowly back away from the building, his gun out and cocked where Alex could see it. "You're getting on that plane, Alex. Alone. Get moving."

Land walked past them and out of the building. Barry and the others followed.

At that moment, out of the corner of his eye, Barry saw someone—Kyra.

"Get back in the car!" Barry yelled.

"What's going on?" Kyra asked.

"Do what I say!"

Her moment of hesitation was just enough for Land to act. He grabbed Kyra and, using her as a shield, pulled her up the ramp into the jet. Barry saw Land push her inside, shouting to the pilot to take off. He spun half around and kicked the mobile stairs hard away from the plane door. His action caught Barry completely off guard. The stairs came shooting right at him, forcing him backward, stumbling. He lost the revolver. Anna went flying in another direction.

"Get the kids!" Barry yelled to her.

Land was still shouting at the pilot. He was trying to manually shut the jet hatch.

Barry watched as Anna gathered Matty and Lost and Found to her side, and, protecting them, backed up into the hangar office where they'd be safe. Barry found his balance, got up, and ran forward in what felt like slow motion as Land, continuing to tug at the door mechanism, looked up and saw him coming and began to say something, "No" or "Don't" or maybe even his name.

Barry was even closer as the jet began to move. Land lost his balance for a moment, just long enough for Kyra behind him to get up and pull Alex backward onto the floor. The plane had begun to taxi.

Barry managed to catch onto the back of the wing. He held on, shouting at the pilot, who evidently couldn't hear him over the noise of the engines. Barry sidled along the wing as close to the fuselage as he could, trying to keep from being knocked off as the plane completed its turn from the side tarmac onto the takeoff runway. Inside, at the half-open door, Land and Kyra were tumbling, wrestling. An uneven fight: He'd have her in a minute, and he still had the gun.

The jet veered again to straighten out, but it did so exactly in the right direction for Barry to swing and get one hand and a leg into the hatchway. Land was still distracted by Kyra as Barry begged his muscles to try just once more.

He let go of the wing, and aimed his body at the hatchway. A burst of pain erupted from him as his bandaged chest slammed against the fuselage. He'd been able to get both hands together on the hatchway latch, at the expense of almost blacking out from the shock. Beneath his dangling feet, the runway sections were getting smaller and smaller, the lines of demarcation sliding by faster and faster, until they were only a blur as the jet shot forward.

It took an enormous effort, but Barry managed to slowly pull himself up and to tumble inside the plane.

Land was standing, a revolver in his hand, facing him. Barry huddled inside the hatchway, holding on to whatever he could to absorb the shock. Land had less of a purchase. He was groping around with his free hand, trying to grab onto the ceiling. Using his back braced against the door, Barry kicked out hard at Land and sent him barreling into a seat. But he recovered almost instantly and had the gun on Barry.

"I should have done this years ago!" Land said. "After you tried to kill me. I don't know why I waited so long. Maybe because it was more fun thinking of you alive and being tortured by the past every day of your life." The revolver was only inches away, pointed directly between Barry's eyes. "But I've had all my fun. And now your life is over!"

The jet was suddenly buffeted from one side. Taking advantage of it, Barry rolled away behind a seat as the cabin bucked and rode out a gust. Land frantically tried to grab at something, anything. For a moment, as the jet continued to shudder, Alex appeared to dance in the air like a puppet with its strings cut. Then he was sucked out the open door. He flailed to hold on to a side rim of the hatchway for a few seconds, but the suction tore his fingers off, and he was gone.

Barry got up in time to see Alex's body slip under the back wheel of the plane.

The hatch door slammed shut long enough for Barry to get up and hold it, force it closed and locked. The noise and wind inside the cabin ceased. Barry yelled to the pilot to abort the flight.

Kyra, who was in the aisle, half sat up, shaking the dizziness off. She looked at Barry, bafflement on her face.

Barry went to her, lifted her onto a seat, and knelt there, holding her hands for a long time.

"Where . . . ?" Kyra began.

"Gone!" he answered.

"Anna? Matty? Lost?"

"All safe," he responded.

"You?"

"I'll live. You?"

She touched her jaw gingerly. "He socked me!" she said indignantly. "I saw stars. Red, green, blue."

"You put up a hell of a fight," Barry said. "There's no doubt whose kid you are."

Ahead, the pilot removed one side of his headphones and half turned around. "Is anyone going to tell me exactly what's going on?" he asked.

"Back to where you picked us up," Barry said.

The pilot looked around and evidently didn't see whom he'd expected as passengers.

"Where's the boss?"

"Had an accident with an open door!" Barry said.

"Oh, hell!" the pilot swore, and turned to his controls again. It was none of his damn business. He just flew 'em.

The jet began to turn in a wide arc. Its engines whined as it slowed down.

"How did you . . . ?" Kyra started to say. Get onto the plane, she meant.

"College-athletic-star heroics," Barry answered. "He was right on the money about that!"

Barry thought, Yes, Alex Land had been right on the money about all of it. He'd known Barry inside out. Barry had never met and probably would never again meet anyone who would ever know him so well. It was sad, in a way, losing that.

Five minutes later, he and Kyra were waiting for the ramp to be pushed alongside the open door. Anna and Matty and Lost and Found were together on the tarmac waiting for them. They would finally be together, this time for as long as they decided.

Barry had one more thing he had to say to his daughter while they still shared this last moment before a new life could begin.

"Tell me the truth," he said. "You knew all this—this crazy plane ride with Land and you and me—you knew it was going to happen, didn't you? Weeks ago? Or days ago?"

Kyra seemed surprised at his question. She smiled enigmatically, as though testing out an amazing new feeling upon herself, before she said with evident pleasure, "You know what, Barry? The truth is—I had no idea!"

Avon Books presents
your worst nightmares—

...haunted houses

ADDISON HOUSE   75587-4/$4.50 US/$5.95 Can
Clare McNally

THE ARCHITECTURE OF FEAR
                      70553-2/$3.95 US/$4.95 Can
edited by Kathryn Cramer & Peter D. Pautz

...unspeakable evil

HAUNTING WOMEN   89881-0/$3.95 US/$4.95 Can
edited by Alan Ryan

TROPICAL CHILLS   75500-9/$3.95 US/$4.95 Can
edited by Tim Sullivan

...blood lust

THE HUNGER   70441-2/$4.50 US/$5.95 Can
THE WOLFEN   70440-4/$4.50 US/$5.95 Can
Whitley Strieber

TOP-SPEED THRILLERS
WITH UNFORGETTABLE
IMPACT
FROM AVON BOOKS